Pamela Evans was born and brought up in Hanwell in the Borough of Ealing, London, the youngest of six children. She is married and has two sons and now lives in Wales. She has had seven novels published including *A Barrow in the Broadway* ('a long, warm-hearted London saga' *Bookseller*), *Lamplight on the Thames* ('a good story and excellent observation of social change over the past forty years' *Kingsbridge and South Hams Gazette*), *Maggie of Moss Street* (' a good traditional romance, and its author has a feeling for the atmosphere of postwar London' *Sunday Express*), *Star Quality* ('well peopled with warm personalities' *Liverpool Post*), *Diamonds in Danby Walk* ('a heart-warming family saga' *Newtownards Chronicle*) and *A Fashionable Address*.

Tea-Blender's Daughter

Pamela Evans

KNIGHT

First published in 1994
by HEADLINE BOOK PUBLISHING

First published in paperback in 1994
by HEADLINE BOOK PUBLISHING

This edition published 2002 by
Knight an imprint of The Caxton Publishing Group

10 9 8 7 6 5 4 3 2 1

ISBN 1 84067 404 0

Typeset by CBS, Felixstowe, Suffolk

Printed and bound in Great Britain by
Mackays of Chatham plc, Chatham, Kent

Caxton Publishing Group
20 Bloomsbury Street
London WC1B 3JH

Tea-Blender's Daughter

Pamela Evans

KNIGHT

First published in 1994
by HEADLINE BOOK PUBLISHING

First published in paperback in 1994
by HEADLINE BOOK PUBLISHING

This edition published 2002 by
Knight an imprint of The Caxton Publishing Group

10 9 8 7 6 5 4 3 2 1

ISBN 1 84067 404 0

Typeset by CBS, Felixstowe, Suffolk

Printed and bound in Great Britain by
Mackays of Chatham plc, Chatham, Kent

Caxton Publishing Group
20 Bloomsbury Street
London WC1B 3JH

To my sisters, Iris and Daphne,
with memories of a hilarious interlude
in Spain during work on this book.

Chapter One

Sunday luncheon came to a dramatic halt in the Slater home when the daughter of the house, Dolly, flew in the face of family tradition and challenged her father's authority.

'Frankly, Daddy, I think you're talking out of the back of your head,' were the words that silenced all other conversation in the dining room. 'There are two sides to every argument and the general strike is no exception.'

The echo of these rebellious words shredded the nerves of everyone present, including Dolly herself who didn't lightly stand up to someone who could unnerve hardened men, let alone a girl of eighteen who had been raised to accept his faults as virtues and revere him.

Henry Slater's fist thumped the table, rattling the crockery and slopping the water in the crystal jug on to the starched white table-cloth. Pale-faced Ken, a sensitive boy of seventeen, added to the brouhaha by nervously dropping his eating utensils on the solid oak floor with a reverberating clang.

Drained of colour, the lady of the house, Edie, threw her daughter a warning look, silently imploring her not to continue along this road which would serve only to infuriate her husband and make the rest of the day hellish for them all. Creating an unbearable family atmosphere was Henry's forte; he was a master at it.

'And who asked for your opinion?' he boomed, his gravel voice husky from years of chain smoking.

Dolly observed the man whose protruberant grey eyes held all the warmth of graveyard chippings. He was oddly proportioned with a face like an unfinished sculpture, square and craggy, with a squashed nose and bushy moustache. He had a tall frame and spindly limbs which, combined with his corpulent middle and stooping shoulders, meant his expensive clothes never hung properly and always looked as though they'd been slept in. His greying dark hair was too wiry to stay sleek, no matter how much grease he ladled on to it. A look of the poverty to which Henry Slater had been born had never quite left him somehow, and his appearance was more that of a barrow boy than a prosperous tea merchant with a blending and packing factory conveniently situated on the banks of the Thames.

'No one asked for it, Daddy, as you very well know,' said the indomitable Dolly, only a slight breathlessness betraying the fact that she was not as confident as she seemed.

'Know your place then, child, and speak when you're spoken to.'

'Oh, for heaven's sake, I'm not a child, and this is nineteen twenty-six and not the Victorian era,' she reminded him, brown eyes hot with indignation, plump cheeks brightly suffused. 'Surely I'm entitled to an opinion?'

'*You?* An opinion?' he growled derisively. 'What do you know about anything?'

'Not as much as you, obviously, because I've not been around as long,' she admitted frankly. 'But I've a good brain and I'm old enough now to make up my own mind about things.'

'You're just a girl,' he said. 'You know nothing.'

'If I'm so dim, how come I practically run your office?' she wanted to know.

He tutted loudly. 'God Almighty, you'll be claiming to run my factory next,' he said, hot with temper and mopping his brow with a handkerchief.

Ignoring his sarcasm, she pursued the point she was trying to make. 'All I'm saying is that the strikers aren't as bad as you're making them out to be. They're only trying to help their own kind after all. Even I can see that it isn't right for the miners to have to take a reduction in wages. Surely you can sympathise with them about that? I mean, it will be hard for them to manage . . .'

As Henry drew a ferocious breath, his phlegm-ridden chest rasped and bubbled. 'Are you suggesting that I should praise the buggers who are trying to bring the country to a standstill, and my business along with it?' he said, his face pink and blotchy and gleaming with perspiration.

'Of course not,' she replied in exasperation, 'but I don't think you should condemn people without even considering their side of the story.'

'The strikers and their supporters are just a bunch of hooligans,' he stated categorically.

'You're doing it again and it simply isn't fair . . .'

Henry Slater wasn't about to change the habits of a lifetime by actually hearing someone out. 'Let me tell you this, my girl,' he interrupted, his harsh vowels revealing his humble beginnings, 'it's people like me who are the backbone of this country. People who stand on their own two feet and don't expect something for nothing.'

'As I understand it, the strikers aren't asking for something for nothing.'

'This is what built the Slater Tea Company,' he continued as though she hadn't spoken, pointing to his own head. 'And these.' He spread his huge knobbly hands proudly. 'My brains and the labour of these two hands have made me what I am today. I didn't go whining to anyone for help.'

'But not everyone is like you, Daddy,' she said, thanking God for this.

'No one could have had less going for them than me when I first started,' he continued, completely absorbed in self-congratulation. 'And I built one of the finest tea companies in London, without any help from trade unions or the government or any of that precious education you set so much store by.'

'I know you did, but not many people are blessed with that sort of ability.'

''Course they're not,' he agreed, swelling with pride at what he mistakenly assumed to be his daughter's admiration, 'so they should be bloody grateful there are people like me to provide jobs for them, and they should stop making life so difficult.'

'All right, so perhaps a general strike isn't the answer,'

she conceded, 'but I suppose they can't find another way to make their point.'

'They're just a bunch of riff-raff.'

'That's a wicked thing to say.'

She was silenced by the thud of his fist on the table for the second time. 'You, of all people, should be on the side of management,' he roared, panting with fury, 'instead of spouting all this socialist rubbish. You work in my office, you've seen the havoc the strike is causing.'

Dolly couldn't argue with him about that. Although he didn't employ union labour, many of his workers had answered the call of their kind and not come into the factory. Slater's were also experiencing serious difficulties in getting the tea from the dockside warehouses into the factory for blending and packing, despite the efforts of troops and volunteers to keep transport moving, and the fact that their raw material came upriver from the docks into Slater's wharf.

'Anyway, support for the strike is fading fast so they're wasting their time.' He erupted into a fit of coughing which left him wheezing and sweating even more. 'People just won't stand for having their lives disrupted. Good job an' all. If it goes on for too long, I'll lose so much money I'll be forced to lay people off. And I'll tell you this much, lady, it'll be *me* the workers will blame even though they'll have brought it on themselves. I tell you, the lower classes want wet nursing.'

She gave a dry laugh. 'No fear of their getting that at Slater's, is there?' she said cuttingly.

'Don't you *dare* criticise me and take the strikers' side,' he bellowed. 'You, the daughter of a factory owner, should know better.'

'I'm not taking their side,' insisted Dolly, voice rising in frustration at his narrow viewpoint. 'I'm just trying to make you see that they are human beings who are entitled to a point of view. Just because it doesn't happen to be the same as yours doesn't mean they are wrong.'

'Human beings?' he snorted furiously. 'Don't make me laugh. They're more like wild animals, fighting with the poor buggers who are trying to keep the country going by driving public transport and food lorries.'

'From what I've heard, tempers are running high on both sides.'

'You'd be dancing to a different tune, my girl,' he said, ignoring her last comment, 'if you had to use the tram or bus instead of being driven about in a motor car.'

Dolly remained silent, realising that this argument wasn't about the strike at all. It was about her father: his lack of compassion, his need to exert his authority at every opportunity. Fair enough, she accepted what she had been brought up to think was right, that the father of the family should be respected as the head of the house. But she could not accept that this should mean total unquestioning submission for every other member of the household.

'Looks like the weather might be going to brighten up,' intervened Edie tremulously, taking advantage of the lull to try to calm the quarrelsome atmosphere. 'It's been so darned chilly lately, you'd never believe it was May.'

'Yes, I think perhaps you're right, Mother,' agreed Ken shakily, glancing towards the leaded-light windows through which rays of weak sunlight were catching the edge of the maroon velvet curtains and forming undulating patterns on the wood-panelled wall. 'The sun is trying to come out, look.'

Henry treated his wife and son to a withering stare. 'I couldn't care less about the weather,' he informed them sternly. 'I'm only concerned with finishing my meal in a proper civilised manner.' He glared at Dolly. 'I'll have no more arguments at my table, if you don't mind.'

'Quite right, dear,' agreed Edie in the fearful, staccato fashion which had become second nature to her. She was relieved that Dolly seemed to have quietened down. What was the matter with the girl? Why couldn't she be like everyone else and accept the fact that there was no point in arguing with Henry?

'If you'll excuse me?' said Dolly, pushing back her chair and rising.

'I certainly will not,' bellowed Henry. 'You just sit down and finish your meal.'

'I *have* finished.'

'So what's all that best quality roast beef doing on your plate then?'

'I've had sufficient, thank you.'

'You'll *not* let good food go to waste in my house,' he declared. 'I won't allow it.'

'Sit down, Dolly, for goodness' sake,' urged Edie, worn into feebleness by years of domination. 'And let's continue with luncheon in peace.'

Dolly did not comply but looked pityingly at her mother, who could only be described as expensively dowdy, her brown hair curled on top of her head in pre-war style, tailored blouse frilled at the throat. Physically she and Dolly were similar. Both were a little on the plump side with round cheeks, a deeply bowed mouth and saucer brown eyes. But whereas Edie's eyes were dull with resignation, Dolly's shone with spirit.

'I'm sorry, Mother, but someone has to stand up to him,' she said, painfully aware that she was going too far but driven on by the strength of her convictions. 'Or he'll trample the whole lot of us into the ground.'

Edie drew in a sharp breath. 'Oh, Dolly,' she begged wearily. '*Do* stop making a scene.'

'You heard what your mother said,' commanded Henry, brandishing his knife and fork threateningly. 'So for Gawd's sake, just sit down and let's have no more of your nonsense.'

Ken's grey eyes seemed to protrude even more than normal against the pallor of his skin; his dark hair was slightly damp from nervous perspiration. He was a thin, gentle boy with similar colouring to his father. He coughed to clear his constricted throat. 'I expect Dolly is feeling too upset to finish her lunch,' he suggested hopefully, his voice cracking nervously. 'So perhaps it might be best if she was allowed to leave the table?'

The whistling sound of Edie sucking in her breath grated into the silence like a knife scraping on china. Henry observed his only son with pleasurable malice for he welcomed the chance to have a pop at Ken.

'Well, well, so the snivelling cissy does have a voice after all,' he boomed. 'It's a pity you've chosen to take your sister's side against your father.' The sardonic smile turned to a scowl. 'I hope you're going to apologise to me for your lip. You'd damned well better be!'

''Course he is,' said Edie swiftly. 'Say sorry to your father at once, Kenneth.'

Dolly exchanged a look with her brother, a slight nuance in her expression assuring him she would forgive him for backing down. She and Ken were pals; they understood each other.

'Sorry, Father,' he said, bowing his head in shame at his own cowardice.

'I guessed you wouldn't have the backbone to stick to your guns,' said Henry, in a perverse criticism of the meeting of his own demands. 'You've always been a spineless young whelp.'

'Is it any wonder?' said Dolly courageously. 'The way you've demoralised him. Humiliating him at every opportunity . . .'

Another aching silence fell while they waited for Henry's explosion. But although his face turned red with temper he merely said in a strangled voice, 'Sit down at once, Dolly, and finish the meal Cook has prepared for you. Then perhaps the rest of us can do the same.'

The reply was the scrape of her chair on the highly polished floor as she pushed it out of her way and marched from the room, her shiny brown hair bouncing behind her.

Poor Ken feared he might be about to exacerbate the situation by having to leave the table to be sick. He tried to eat while the room fell ominously silent in the wake of Dolly's departure. How he hated the dining room with its

9

permanent smell of stale tobacco from Father's endless cigarette-smoking. The elegant interior was synonymous with misery for Ken who dreaded family meals where mortification from Father was so often on the menu.

'Dolly doesn't mean to be rude, Henry,' Edie was saying in a pitiful effort to appease her husband rather than to exonerate Dolly. 'She's just a bit headstrong, that's all.'

'Ungrateful, more like,' he grumbled. 'You should do something about her, Edie. You're her mother, you should be able to control her.'

'I do what I can, Henry.'

'Well, it's clearly not enough, is it?' he exclaimed. 'You let her get away with murder. Her bobbed hair, for example. She should never have been allowed to have it cut that way.'

'It's the fashion for young women these days, dear,' Edie said weakly. 'There's a bit of a craze . . .'

'That's as may be, but it isn't ladylike for a daughter of mine,' he interrupted, stabbing food on to his fork in a rough manner. 'That girl is completely wild.'

'Yes, Henry.'

'I shall have something to say to her later on, I can tell you,' he said, speaking with a mouth crammed with roast potato, his table manners having failed to improve along with his bank balance. 'I won't take that sort of cheek from a slip of a girl, daughter or no daughter.'

'Of course not.'

'But I'll finish my meal in peace first,' he mumbled through a full mouth. 'I'm damned if I'll let her upset my digestion.'

'Dolly has always had a mind of her own, even as a child,' said Edie, pouring herself a glass of water to soothe her dry throat.

'You don't have to tell me that,' he said, tutting and raising his eyes. 'After all I've done for her, you'd think she'd show some respect.'

''Course you would, dear.'

'Gawd knows what more a girl could want,' he complained. 'She has a lovely home, an interesting job, and she's never kept short of pocket money or nice clothes.'

'Mmm.'

'I've even gone to the trouble of arranging for a fellow to court her.'

'I know, dear. You're very good to all of us,' said Edie.

'She simply will not accept the fact that I, as her father, must be obeyed without question,' Henry continued, almost as if he was alone in the room. 'Look how she complained when I wouldn't let her stay on at school. Went about with a face like a drainpipe for days. I ask you, Edie, what use would book learning have done her?'

'Well, I . . .'

'Bugger all, that's what,' he said before his wife could reply further. 'She'd have ended up as a hatchet-faced school marm with no chance of getting a husband.'

'Mmm.'

'And it isn't as though I'm the sort of father to make her stay at home just because she's a girl, is it?' he went on. 'She has a thorough knowledge of the tea trade thanks to me, not to mention the evening classes in shorthand and typing that I've paid for. Many businessmen I know of won't let the women of the family near their place of work.'

You only do so because Dolly's useful to you and she comes cheap, thought Ken, listening to his father's hypocrisy with self-loathing because he was too frightened to do anything about it. He felt terrible for failing to support Dolly just now, especially when he recalled the times she had landed herself in trouble with Father on her brother's behalf.

Ken's compunction almost choked him. Boys were supposed to protect their sisters, *not the other way around*. How he longed to tell Father what he thought of him for all the years of misery he had inflicted on them all. But he never did. Father spoke and he stood to attention, it was as simple as that. On the odd occasion that he did manage to show some spirit, as he had just now, he never had the courage to follow it through. The terror that had been instilled into him as a beaten young boy was too deeply embedded.

It wasn't as though he still had the beatings to fear, for they had ceased when he had left school and gone into the business, presumably because Father had considered it undignified to assault someone who almost matched him in size. But there was still the constant mockery and the insinuations that Ken could never be a real man because he lacked his father's ruthlessness and indestructible self-confidence. Being humiliated in front of the workers, who were supposed to look up to him, was the worst part and Ken wouldn't blame them if they detested him for failing to stand up for himself.

He had not been sent away to boarding school like the sons of other businessmen of Henry's acquaintance, mostly because Father didn't see the necessity for anything beyond the most basic education, but also, Ken suspected, because he had been useful to have around, fetching and carrying at the factory from quite a young age.

Like Dolly he had left school and gone straight to work for his father full-time. Unlike Dolly however, who by the mere fact of her gender would never officially aspire beyond the rank of office dogsbody, he was learning the business ready to join in its management later on. But how he would ever command the respect of those he was supposed to manage unless he learned to stand up to his father, was quite beyond him.

'Will Miss Dolly be coming back to the table, Madam, or will she be wanting her dessert on a tray in her room?' asked the maid.

'Neither,' Henry answered abruptly, before his wife had a chance. 'She's finished her meal.'

'Right yer are, sir.'

While the maid served them with plum tart and custard, Henry mulled over recent events with displeasure. He didn't seem able to rule his daughter in the same way as he ruled everyone else. She was in awe of him up to a point, he could see that, but still managed to defy him. This was anathema to a man who firmly believed that failure to control meant being at someone else's mercy, as he himself had been with his own father.

Downright ingratitude, that was what it was. When he

remembered the misery of his own deprived childhood – one of seven living in a tenement in Stepney with a drunken father who had beaten his sons as a matter of course and a mother who'd given up caring and died in childbirth when Henry had been quite small.

Even now, he winced when he recalled the hidings he'd taken. But at least they had built his character, made a man of him, which was more than could be said for his own pansy son. Yes, his children had had it too easy, that was the trouble. They'd never wanted for anything. By the time they were born, Henry had left his relatives and the poverty of his childhood far behind. And all through his own efforts . . .

At twelve years old, he had gone to work for a tea merchant as a boy labourer, moving tea chests about the factory, sweeping the yard, loading and unloading the horse-vans. At that time he had had no particular liking for the tea trade as such, it just happened to be a tea merchant who had given him a job. But, desperate to escape from his poor home, he had put his all into the work, making sure his efforts did not go unnoticed by his employer.

Being naturally quick-witted, Henry had made it his business to ask questions about the trade and to impress his superiors with his increasing knowledge. His employer, an astute businessman, had seen profit in such a keen spirit of enterprise and had deemed it wise to teach him the trade properly with a view to the future, especially as the growing popularity of factory-blended and packed tea was making competition ever fiercer.

By the end of the century, when Henry was nineteen, he

was an experienced taster with a discerning eye as well as palate; he could judge the quality of a leaf at a glance. By then he was a valuable asset to the firm but Henry was keen to set up on his own, albeit in a very small way, with the little money he had managed to save.

Wishing to sever all connections with his family, he had moved to West London and rented a tiny shop near Hammersmith Broadway. With his limited capital he could only afford to buy a couple of chests of tea at a time which he then sold over the counter, some of it loose and some packed by hand. Soon he was able to afford a small blending drum in which he carefully mixed blends using the best of several teas, including a less expensive one to keep the price economical. This venture was so successful he made enough money to employ someone to run the shop while he himself went out in a horsedrawn van, selling bulk and packet tea to grocers.

It quickly became clear that the wholesale side of his business was far more lucrative than the retail trade so he went over to it entirely, closing the shop and moving to a factory on the Hammersmith waterfront. By the time he was twenty-five he was well established with a fleet of green-painted vans delivering tea to shops all over London and the surrounding areas.

By then he could well afford to set himself up in a house and take a wife to look after his domestic affairs. Since he didn't want a rich or clever woman who might challenge his authority he went calling on the seventeen-year-old shopgirl of one of his customers, a dull shy little thing called Edie. It was the perfect match. Her humble background had made her malleable, and his self-esteem was kept nourished by her gratitude to him for the comfortable life he was able to give her.

Dolly ought to be like that, he thought. She knew how hard he'd struggled to give them a good life. Damn it, he told the family about it often enough. The wretched girl was too clever by half and he was at a loss to know how to bring her to heel.

Perhaps he should get her married and off his hands as soon as possible? Yes, that was probably the solution. He would have a word with Frank Mitchell on the subject. Get him to speed things up. Now Frank was one person he really could control. Utterly.

Upstairs in her bedroom, Dolly stood by the window looking out across the large garden with its shrubs and trees and neatly trimmed lawns, verdant with the season and bordered by high, ivy-covered walls. She was feeling physically ill from the effects of the altercation with her father; sick and shaky with a churning stomach. What was it about the man that struck fear into the hearts of them all? He was only a human being. And at least he had never been violent towards her in the same way as he had poor Ken, presumably because he didn't consider that daughters needed the physical chastisement he believed essential for building the characters of sons.

Honour thy father and thy mother. That was all very well but it was a tall order when the father was a heartless bully and the mother his spiritless sidekick without a mind of her own. Dolly felt guilty for having such thoughts and feelings. These people were her parents. She wanted to love and revere them, to feel close to them, to look on them with pride. But they didn't make it easy. Surely part of the parental role was to encourage children to take an intelligent interest in the world about them, not to try to squash their spirit every step of the way.

She reproached herself for being unfair to Mother who had, after all, been brought up in a more submissive age. If only she tried occasionally to defend her offspring against Father, especially Ken. But she *never* had that Dolly could remember.

Running a trembling hand over her moist brow, she felt her head throbbing and her heart still pounding from the argument. She supposed it was a sign of weakness to allow anyone to have such an effect, though hardly surprising having grown up under a regime of tyranny thinly disguised as parental discipline.

It had to be said, though, that when it came to material things, her father was munificent towards his family. She turned and looked back into the room, running her eyes over the finely carved wardrobes that were filled with good quality clothes; the gilt-edged dressing table covered with silver-backed hair brushes and porcelain scent sprays. Oh, yes, as a provider Henry Slater couldn't be faulted. The Slaters enjoyed a comfortable lifestyle in a tree-lined avenue near Ravenscourt Park. And all because of her father's diligence and enterprising nature, as he was so fond of telling them.

But visible signs of affection had never been on offer to the children of this fine household. Father was above such things; Mother was too busy grovelling to him to show them any love.

To give Father his due, he worked very hard. Dolly was at the factory every day, and saw the heavy load of responsibility he carried. But she had a sneaking suspicion that he enjoyed playing the martyr because it kept them all in his debt. He was a lonely man for all his achievements. His only friend seemed to be Frank Mitchell, and one could hardly call that a true friendship since Frank was paid to provide it.

Outside, the breeze gusted through the trees and rattled at the sash windows. The sun was suddenly swallowed by a bank of racing clouds, darkening the room and making Dolly shiver. The unsettled weather felt more like March than May, with a chilly wind and heavy rain clouds about to do their worst at any moment. But none of this lessened Dolly's desire to escape into the fresh air and take a respite from the claustrophobic atmosphere of this house.

Slipping into her beige-coloured Burberry raincoat and matching hat, she hurried downstairs and out of the front door. Even before she passed through the double gates into Maybury Avenue, huge raindrops were already beating through the plane trees, pounding on to the grass verges and trickling down her neck off the brim of her hat.

She didn't turn back. In fact, in this mood of discontent, she wished she was leaving home for good. She felt ready to stand on her own feet, and hungry for freedom. But it wasn't done for girls of her background to flee the nest except to get married. Oh, well, all in good time, she thought. The current troubles will soon blow over. None of it will seem so bad after a brisk walk.

Making her way past a row of dignified houses with spacious gardens, all set well back from the pavement and shielded by privet hedges and trees, she lifted her face to the elements, invigorated by the wind and rain on her fevered skin. Already beginning to feel calmer, she strode on with no special destination in mind.

Bill Drake rubbed a patch of condensation from the steamy, rain-spattered window with his fingers and looked out into the narrow street, grey and dismal beneath the leaden skies. The heaviness of the rain indicated it wouldn't last, but it was certainly making a quagmire of Galton Road at the moment. The craters in the road had become lakes and the broken pavements were covered with puddles. The dilapidated terraced houses, which were mostly rented out as flats or rooms, looked shabby and forlorn with their peeling paintwork and dusty windows staring out into the wet Sunday afternoon.

A gloomy outlook indeed. But not nearly as dreary as the atmosphere inside this flat, Bill thought, turning to look into the room. On the oil cloth-covered table were the dirty dishes from Sunday dinner, which had been fatty mutton, overcooked cabbage and potatoes swimming in lumpy gravy. In an armchair by the hearth his mother, Maud, was sleeping, fat knees wide apart beneath her wrapover apron, mouth gaping and quivering as she snored, her dark curly hair falling on to her brow in a straggly mass.

In the chair opposite slept her husband, Bill's stepfather, Alf, his cap perched over his eyes. Both were sleeping off the effects of a lunchtime session in the pub, paid for in part with the money Bill gave his mother for his keep.

With a sigh of dull resignation, he cleared the table and took the greasy crockery into the scullery, a cheerless cupboard of a room with a cracked sink, a grubby gas-stove, a rickety wooden table and an ancient kitchen dresser painted dark brown and cream. Heating some water in the tin kettle on the stove, he washed and dried the dishes and put them away in the dresser with a kind of automatic diligence. Everything he touched felt damp and sticky and the air was sour with the smell of boiled greens.

For want of an alternative, he mooched aimlessly back into the living room and sat down on the brown leatherette sofa which also served as his bed, since Mother and Alf had the only bedroom. Bill had been raised in this flat and had slept on the sofa even when his father had been alive. But things had been different then. The place had been clean and cheerful and welcoming. Even if the meals had been cheap and basic, at least they had appeared at the appropriate times and had been properly cooked. Dad hadn't earned a fortune as a labourer at the docks, but his money had been adequate and regular.

His father had died of TB six years ago when Bill had been thirteen. Everything had changed then. Mum had seemed to stop caring. She'd let herself go; sat about the place weeping all day; didn't bother to clean up. Then she'd taken up with Alf who'd been a widower living in the same street. He'd taken her out to the pictures and the music hall to cheer her up. And cheer up she had. Since they'd been married all she seemed to care about was going out to the pub or the pictures. She certainly had no time for her son except on Fridays when he brought home his paypacket from the tea factory where he worked as a labourer.

Maud came to with a grunt and focused her eyes blearily on Bill before twitching and snorting and going back to sleep. Suddenly unable to look at this scene for a moment longer, Bill rose and went to the window, feeling unbearably trapped in his mean home. Where could he go for a bit of privacy? The only place a person could be alone around here was the lavatory, and that was outside in the yard and shared by the other tenants which usually meant someone else was beating on the door.

He was nineteen years old. It was time he seriously considered finding a place of his own. He'd been thinking about it on and off for ages but whenever he broached the subject to his mother she always managed to talk him out of it. He was under no illusions. It wasn't his company she would miss so much as his contribution to her household budget. He didn't hold this against her but she had her life. Now it was high time he had his.

But for the moment he needed a break from this place, to clear the stench of the hovel from his nostrils and soothe the frustration that knotted him up inside. Taking his shabby brown raincoat from the back of the door, he left the building and splashed along the street with no particular aim in mind. He didn't care where he ended up as long as he was out of those oppressive rooms for a few hours.

Chapter Two

Leaving Maybury Avenue and heading towards Hammersmith Broadway, Dolly felt the tranquil atmosphere of Sunday afternoon stir with unaccustomed activity and an undercurrent of danger. Throngs of people in King Street almost matched the Saturday shopping crowds but they were entirely male. Groups of men were noisily discussing the strike. They crammed into shop doorways and gathered outside pubs and the picture palace as rain gave way to sunshine, gleaming steamily on the wet pavements.

Dolly's nerves were taut as she fought her way through for tempers were running high here. Ugly sounds buffeted her as strike supporters quarrelled with those holding opposing views. Some were even coming to blows. Suddenly the air was clamorous with cheering and whistling from the direction of the Broadway. The ensuing stampede carried Dolly along with it, painfully aware of her vulnerability amongst this boisterous male gathering.

An immobilised tram in the Broadway was the cause of the jubilation. A vociferous crowd clustered around it, saluting and waving their caps in triumph. Managing to fight her way to the fringes of the mob, Dolly climbed on to the window ledge of a pub and peered over the sea of bobbing heads. From here she could see that the vehicle was overrun with strikers who were leaning out of the windows and shouting to their mates victoriously.

Police constables were attempting to push through to the volunteer tram-driver and his policeman bodyguard who were trapped on the tramcar platform. Scuffles were breaking out all around Dolly. Stones were being hurled recklessly as tempers got out of control.

She scrambled to the ground and jostled her way towards safety. But her attention was caught by a man clutching his cheek and writhing in agony. He'd obviously been struck by a missile and was staggering towards the doorway of a nearby barber's shop where he leaned against the window, holding his face.

'Here, let me help you,' she said, going up to him.

The man looked up and narrowed his eyes at her contemptuously. 'Clear off, yer silly cow,' he growled, his face screwed up with pain. 'This ain't no place for a toffee-nosed tart.'

Undeterred, she put a sympathetic hand on his arm, alarmed by the blood that was soaking through the grubby handkerchief he was pressing to the wound. 'Here you are,' she said, handing him her own spotless hanky. 'That might help a bit but you need a doctor to look at it. It might need stitching.'

'What I don't need is the likes of you interferin',' he told her, refusing to take the handkerchief. 'So just bugger off and leave me alone.'

'You 'eard him,' she was told gruffly by a man in a rain-soaked donkey jacket. Seeing her genuine concern, however, he added in a more conciliatory manner, 'I'll see he's all right, Miss. You'd better get away from 'ere before you get 'urt.'

'If you're sure I can't help, then?' said Dolly doubtfully.

'Just get orf home, ducks,' he said in a gentler manner.

Another man appearing on the scene was much more hostile. 'I know who you are,' he said, scowling fiercely at her from beneath a battered black hat. 'You're the daughter of Henry Slater, the tea merchant.'

'Yes, that's right.'

'Thought as much. I worked for 'im once,' he said with obvious dislike. 'I didn't stay there long, but long enough to know what a pig the man is.'

Her own feelings of animosity towards her father were forgotten in the filial instinct to defend him. 'Hey, that's my father you're talking about! You've no right to call him a pig . . .'

'Oh yes I 'ave, 'cos that's what he is, and everyone round here knows it,' the man interrupted. 'So why don't yer just sling yer hook back to yer posh 'ouse that he can afford through paying cheap for 'is labour? You ain't welcome round here.'

'Yeah, clear orf,' shouted the injured man. 'We don't want your sort contaminating us.'

'I was only trying to help,' she said, feeling peeved. 'But I'm going, don't you worry.'

'Good job an' all,' said the man who had insulted her father, and without further ado gave her a hefty shove to speed her on her way. His strength was such that she lost her balance and crashed to the ground, landing in a muddy puddle.

Bill Drake was so deeply preoccupied with his own thoughts as he approached the Broadway that he was in the thick of the disturbance before he realised anything serious was going on. There was complete chaos in the area of the stationary tram. People were cheering, others fighting. The police were trying to clear a path to the driver. This was what happened when people didn't get a fair deal, he thought. Their frustration got out of control.

There was no point in his staying around here, he decided, elbowing his way to the back of the crowd. This was developing into a real free-for-all, with some of them scrapping for the love of it rather than any genuine conviction.

Hello, what was this? *The boss's daughter at this sort of a shambles?* Blimey, her old man would have a fit if he knew. It couldn't be . . . but, yes, it was definitely Dolly Slater. He didn't know her to speak to but he'd seen her at the factory often enough to recognise that face. She was getting stuck in by the look of it too, he thought, seeing her talking to some men. Stupid bitch. Fancy tangling with this crowd of troublemakers who could tell by her clothes that she wasn't on the side of the workers; factory girls couldn't afford the sort of gear she was wearing. A classy-looking bird like that was bound to provoke resentment among this bunch of extremists.

He found himself unexpectedly concerned for her as

voices were raised in her direction. Bill couldn't hear what was being said but it certainly wasn't a declaration of friendship. Being a fair-minded man, he couldn't see how her being on the side of management gave them the right to be so rough with her. Oh, now they really were overstepping the mark, he thought furiously, as he saw one of them push her over.

By the time Bill managed to shove his way across to her, her assailant had disappeared into the crowd. 'Here,' he said, reaching out his hand to help her up. 'Grab hold of me and let's get away from here before you get into any more trouble.'

'You look a proper sight,' he told her.

'Thanks! You certainly know how to make a girl feel good.'

'You've got muddy marks all over your mac, and on your face.'

'It's that filthy puddle,' she said, wiping her hands and face with a handkerchief. 'It's all over me.'

'Are you all right though?'

'Yes,' she said, grinning, 'but I won't be able to sit down for a while.'

He laughed.

'It isn't funny.'

'I'll say it ain't,' he told her, his expression darkening. 'You could have been seriously hurt. And all through your own daft fault! I mean, fancy having a barney with that lot o' thugs.'

'All right, don't rub it in.'

'What possessed you to go to a strike demonstration anyway?'

'I didn't intend to,' she explained. 'I was out for a walk and just sort of ended up in the middle of it.'

'The same thing 'appened to me.'

'You've no call to criticise me then, have you?'

'I'm not out of place at a thing like this, though.'

'There is that,' she conceded.

They walked on in silence.

'Hadn't you better go home before it starts rainin' again?' he suggested.

She didn't reply but scrubbed absently at her face with her handkerchief.

'Will you be all right on your own or shall I go with you?'

'No thanks.'

'Suit yourself,' said Bill with noticeable asperity. 'I only offered because I thought you might be feeling a bit shaky after falling over.'

'And I only declined because I'm not going home.' She paused thoughtfully. 'Not for a while anyway.'

'Oh, well, that's up to you,' he said in an insouciant manner.

'Mmm.'

'If you're sure you're all right then, I'll leave you to it and be on me way.'

They had left the busy Broadway behind and were in a quieter part of King Street. Dolly had been too shaken by her fall to take much notice of her rescuer. Now she turned to him and observed a tall, broad-shouldered young man

28

with dark wavy hair and warm brown eyes.

'Thanks for helping me up,' she said.

''Sall right,' he said with a nonchalant shrug.

A closer look revealed his face to be vaguely familiar. 'Don't I know you from somewhere?' she asked.

'I work in your dad's factory,' he informed her.

'Yes, of course,' she said, smiling warmly.

'Bill Drake,' he said, offering his hand.

'Pleased to meet you, Bill,' she said and shook his hand. Why did touching his hand seem different from greeting any other person she knew?

'Your father would blow a fuse if he could see you now, mixing with the rabble.'

'That's not a very nice way to describe yourself,' she said.

'I'm a labourer in his factory which amounts to the same thing.'

It didn't say much for her father or society in general, she thought, but there was no point in denying that class barriers did exist. 'I'm sure my father doesn't regard his workers as rabble.'

'He certainly doesn't regard them as friends.'

'Well, no . . . but there is a middle course.'

'Still worlds apart, though.'

'Yes, I suppose so,' she was forced to admit. 'But his attitude isn't something I necessarily agree with.'

'Perhaps not, but it's the way things are.'

The factory and office staff were segregated at Slater's and, apart from with Frank, friendliness between family and employees was strongly discouraged by Henry. So

Dolly didn't have much to do with shop floor workers. She usually managed to defy her father by being pleasant when she did have cause to go into the factory, though.

'I must admit that Father would hit the roof if he knew I'd been anywhere near a strike demonstration,' she told Bill with a wry grin. 'So, I'd be very grateful if you wouldn't mention having seen me there to your mates at work. Father has a very good way of finding out about factory gossip. His name is Frank Mitchell.'

'Your father's right hand man?'

'Yes.'

'And your boyfriend too, by all accounts.'

She gave a casual shrug. 'Well . . . he's supposed to be, but Frank's more of a family friend really.'

'Oh, well, that's none o' my business,' he said casually.

'No, of course not.'

'Don't worry though, I won't say a word about what you've been up to.'

'Thanks a lot,' she said, with a melting smile.

Observing her more closely, he saw a young woman who could only be described as chubby, being short and rather plump. She wasn't bad-looking though. Her face was sort of sunny, cheerful and smiling, with pink cheeks and eyes that shone. Untidy bobbed brown hair blew about in the breeze, her rain-hat having been removed and stuffed into her pocket because it had fallen into the puddle and was wet.

He moved back in a valedictory manner. 'Well, so long then. See yer around.' He was smiling because she had taken his mind off his troubles and lightened his mood.

Dolly's spirits had perked up too. She met his eyes, deciding that she liked him and wanted to know him better. 'Are you going anywhere special now?' she asked.

'No, just mooching about.'

'Me too,' she said. 'So why don't we mooch about together?'

He maintained a doubtful silence.

'Go on, be a devil,' she teased gently. 'We could go to the park.'

'It's all very well for you to be so casual,' he said.

'I'm suggesting a walk in the park, not a weekend together in Brighton,' she laughed.

'Even so . . .'

'Oh, come on, where's the harm in it?' she said lightly.

'None at all for you, but if your old man finds out I've been hanging about with his daughter I'll lose me job,' he told her, frowning darkly. 'It might only be humping tea chests about all day, but it's better than nothing.'

'He won't find out,' she said, with an irresistible smile. 'And if the worst happened and he did, I'd tell him it was all my idea. I wouldn't let him sack you, I promise. So stop worrying!'

Her persuasive charm was finally too much for him. 'All right, you win,' he said, his eyes twinkling, and they walked towards the park together chatting companionably.

'It really is too bad of Dolly not to be here when she knows you're coming to tea, Frank,' said Edie, offering him some cucumber sandwiches from a tea trolley in the sitting room, a well-appointed area with fat sofas and chairs, plentiful pot plants and a piano with family photographs covering the top. 'I do hope nothing untoward has happened to her.'

'Where's she gone then, Mrs S?' asked Frank Mitchell whose heavy build and shovel-like hands seemed more suited to hunks of bread and dripping than these dainty sandwiches so prettily presented on lace doilies.

'I'm not really sure,' said Edie evasively.

'Stormed out in a huff,' put in Henry bluntly. 'That girl needs taking in hand, Frank. The sooner you two get married the better.'

'I'm game, you know that, boss,' he said in his slow drawl, 'but I don't think Dolly's ready to settle down yet awhile.'

'What's her being ready got to do with it?' asked Henry, who would have married Dolly off at birth if that had been possible. Whereas sons could indulge their natural impulses without fear of reprisals, an unmarried daughter was a hazard. Being so dominated by Henry, Frank Mitchell was the perfect choice of son-in-law because his loyalty to the Slater family was assured.

This state of affairs was not accidental. The sole purpose of Henry's taking on a dim-witted orphan boy all those years ago had been to mould him into obedience and groom him for a unique position within the Slater organisation under the official title of 'general assistant'. Henry had seen to it that Frank's rough edges had been refined just sufficiently for his conduct to be acceptable, but not enough so that he got above himself.

'She'll do what you tell her if you let her know who's boss.'

32

That'll be the day when Dolly takes orders from me, thought Frank, who had often wondered if teaching chickens to play poker might be easier than trying to court Dolly Slater. It wasn't that they didn't get on well enough in a casual kind of way; she'd grown up with him being around so was used to him. But as for this so-called courtship that her father was so keen on, well, she obviously had no intention of letting that develop. But it was what Henry wanted so Frank pursued the allotted course with his habitual compliance for all good things came from this source and Frank would walk through fire for Henry if necessary.

Frank Mitchell was twenty-eight years old, a great bruiser of a man with sandy-coloured hair and docile blue eyes which reflected his personality. He had never looked back since Henry had taken him into Slater's direct from a children's home. The tea trade was largely a gentlemanly sort of business but this didn't stop a hard man like Henry from making enemies. As well as serving as his minder, whilst carrying out menial management tasks at the factory under his direct supervision as a front, Frank was also required to be his friend, confidant, drinking partner and occasional chauffeur when the boss didn't feel like driving himself in his gleaming Armstrong Siddeley.

Servility was hardly anathema to Frank because his limited intelligence meant he needed guidance in thought as well as deed. He wasn't too slow to realise that he was on to a good thing, though, for Henry paid him well enough to keep a nice little flat and to run a motor car. That was a bloomin' sight more than he'd have had if he'd been left to find his own way in the world. If Henry now wanted him as a son-in-law, far be it from Frank to object. Personally he thought he had more chance of being invited on to The Brains Trust on the wireless than getting Dolly to agree. But if it were to happen, his income would be adjusted in accordance with his new obligations, and there would be no question of his being expected to take on more responsibility in the business because of his family status. Henry understood that Frank had no wish for that sort of burden.

For the moment, however, he concentrated on easing his employer's mind, albeit temporarily. 'She'll come round to the idea in the end, boss, you just leave it to me.' Since Frank never worried beyond the present moment, he was able to sound convincing.

'Perhaps I should go and look for her?' suggested Ken, eager for an excuse to escape from the misery of another family meal, albeit a less formal one. 'She might have had an accident, or something.'

'Huh, it'll be nothing like that,' opined Henry, who held nothing back in front of Frank. 'She'll be walking the streets just to make us worry, I bet.' He sighed wearily. 'I ask you, what sort of behaviour is that for a well-brought up girl?'

'It's very rude of her not to be here, Frank,' said Edie, who shared her husband's eagerness for an early marriage for Dolly, simply because there would be a lot less aggravation in the house without her around, forever talking out of turn and stirring up trouble. 'I'm really sorry. I must say, I feel most embarrassed.'

'There's no need for that, Mrs S,' said Frank amicably, for he never got rattled about anything, 'just so long as she hasn't got mixed up in any trouble.'

'Trouble?' said Henry, observing Frank quizzically over the rim of his tea-cup.

'There was quite a crowd in the Broadway when I came past on my way here,' he explained. 'I think there must have been some sort of strike demonstration or something. You know 'ow out of control they can get.'

'Bloody hooligans,' said Henry.

'I'm going to see if I can find her,' said Ken, genuinely concerned for his sister on hearing this news.

'I'll come with you, mate,' said Frank. 'We'll go in the car.'

'I can't think where the girl has got to,' fretted Edie.

The object of their speculation was happily ensconced on a park bench, far too engrossed in her new friend to notice the time passing. They hadn't stopped chattering all afternoon, except to attend to the ice cream cones Bill had bought from the vendor at the park gates. Dolly had never met anyone with whom she felt so much in tune. Bill seemed rather shy but was not dull as she'd been taught to believe the labouring classes were. In fact, he was very intelligent and shared her regret at not having been allowed to stay on at school past the age of fourteen.

As the rain had held off, the paths were beginning to dry in the weak sunshine, though moisture was still dripping off the trees on to the sodden grass. The air carried the scent of May blossoms mingled with the fresh smell of wet earth.

Sunday afternoon strollers were out in force now that the rain had stopped, though most were swathed in mackintoshes and carrying umbrellas.

'What's a girl like you doing wanderin' about the town on her own on a wet Sunday afternoon, anyway?' Bill asked.

'There was the most dreadful row at home,' she explained, frowning at the memory. 'I had the audacity to disagree with my father about something and all hell broke loose. I needed to get out to cool down.'

'I know the feeling.'

'You too?'

'There wasn't a row,' he explained, 'but I was feeling a bit cheesed off with the restrictions of home. I thought a walk might help.'

'The screaming ab-dabs, eh?'

'Yeah.'

'I get those quite often myself,' she said, looking at him earnestly. 'It must be something to do with growing up and needing more freedom.'

'Probably.'

She glanced at her watch. 'Oh lor', it's half-past four. I'll be late for tea and in even more trouble.'

'It isn't your day.'

'That's a fact,' she said with a half smile. 'What about you? What time do you have tea?'

'No set time,' he said, because it was easier than explaining that his mother's one weekly concession to a domestic routine was Sunday dinner. After that it was up to Bill to see to his own meals if he could find anything in the larder with which to do so. 'It doesn't matter when I get back.'

'Flexible parents, eh?' she said.

'Something like that.'

'You're lucky. Meal times are set in stone in our house,' she said ruefully. 'Being late is practically a hanging offence.'

'You'd better get back sharpish then.'

She turned and smiled right into his eyes. 'I don't want to go.'

'I don't want you to either but nor do I want you to get into trouble.'

'I've so enjoyed myself,' she said softly.

'Me too,' he said, turning pink and staring at his shoes, conscious of the fact that they were almost worn through at the toes.

'Perhaps we could meet again?' she suggested to his downward-looking profile.

He looked up quickly and turned to her. She noticed how alert his face was, his gentle brown eyes so bright and intelligent, even though he was frowning.

'You know that wouldn't be a good idea,' he said regretfully.

'If we're careful, no one will find out.'

His frown deepened, and she thought how fresh and youthful he looked, his skin clean shaven and smooth, his firm mouth a healthy red. There was a wholesomeness about him which she found irresistible.

'I'm not sure that I want to go out with a girl who would be worried about being seen with me,' he said.

She was quick to put him right. 'I wouldn't be worried because I would be ashamed or anything,' she explained earnestly. 'It's just that . . . well . . . you know how things are.'

'Exactly, which is why I said it wouldn't be a good idea.'

'Oh, Bill, do say you will,' she said impulsively. 'I'd really like that,'

'But you already have a boyfriend,' he reminded her.

'Frank isn't a boyfriend in the real sense of the word, I told you.'

'He looks real enough to me,' he said, 'and it's common knowledge at the factory that you're his girl. I've seen you together in his car.'

'He drives me to work and back, that's all,' she explained.

'Is that so?'

'Well . . . I'm not saying I'm not officially supposed to be going out with Frank,' she admitted, chewing her lip thoughtfully, 'but it isn't my doing . . . or Frank's either for that matter. It's all my father's idea.'

'You've a mind of your own, surely?' he said sharply.

'Oh, yes, I've one of those all right,' she said. 'But my father is a very dominant man. He has a way of making people do things. I don't dislike Frank, and he doesn't demand anything of me.'

'That's hard to believe.'

'I know it sounds odd but Frank and I don't actually do anything together, and we are almost never alone. Our so-called courting consists of his coming over to the house and chatting to my parents, mostly Daddy. Like I said, Frank's more of a family friend than a boyfriend to me.' She paused to clarify the situation in her own mind. 'Daddy is obviously hoping we'll get married eventually. There isn't a chance of that but it's easier for me to seem to go along with what he wants for the moment, rather than have him trying to marry me off to someone else. The devil you know and all that.'

'It sounds a very peculiar arrangement to me.'

'It is, but when you have an overbearing father like mine, you have to find ways of outwitting him while appearing to do what he wants.'

'Why are you trying to get me to go out with you when you know he won't approve?' he asked.

'Because I really like you,' she admitted guilelessly. 'And I want to know you better. Is that so terrible?'

'You don't care if I lose my job because of it then?' he said.

'Of course I care,' she said emphatically, 'but I won't let that happen.'

'How could you stop it?' he asked. 'I can't imagine your father taking orders from you.'

'Of course he doesn't. But I'd tell him, if Bill goes so do I, and he wouldn't like that because he needs me in his office.' She looked at him gravely. 'It's all academic anyway because he isn't going to find out.'

A smile lit up his face, putting the twinkle back in his eyes. 'You're a proper case, you are,' he told her. 'It's usually the man who does the asking.'

'Mmm, I know, but being Henry Slater's daughter does limit the possibilities in that direction,' she admitted frankly, 'because most of the men I meet are employed by him and therefore off limits.' She paused with a devilish look in her eye. 'Let's face it, if I wait for you to ask me out, I'll wait forever.'

'No doubt about it,' he said candidly. 'I don't look for trouble.'

'So, since I've broken with tradition by taking the initiative, how about meeting me outside the park gates tomorrow night at seven?' she suggested brightly. 'We could go to the pictures, if you like.'

Finally he surrendered. 'All right then, but if I lose my job I shall hold you personally responsible.'

'I'm willing to take the blame,' she said, slipping her arm into his. 'Come on, let's walk to the park gates together.'

'There's no sign of your sister round 'ere, is there, Ken?' said Frank, driving his Ford round the Broadway for the umpteenth time.

'No, I don't know what could have happened to her.'

'Whatever was going on 'ere seems to be over anyway,' remarked Frank chattily. The crowds had gone; the road was busy with private motorists but there were no public transport vehicles or indications of any trouble.

'Mmm.'

'Dolly's probably gone to visit a friend or somethin',' said Frank, without a trace of pique.

'Doesn't that annoy you?' asked Ken.

''Course not, why should it?'

'Well, you and Dolly are supposed to be going out together, aren't you?' said Ken, whose query stemmed

40

entirely from curiosity and not criticism of Dolly. He was at an age when such things were beginning to interest him. 'I should think a chap would be pretty peeved if his girlfriend wasn't at home when he called to see her.'

'Nah, son, there's none o' that business with me and Dolly,' said Frank, amicably. 'We've known each other too long for that sort o' caper. I'm part of the furniture in your 'ouse.'

'Yes, I know, but even so . . .'

'I feel at 'ome at your place whether Dolly's there or not.'

Ken didn't usually give much thought to his father's minder. He'd been coming to the house for so long he was taken for granted by everyone. But even Ken could see that the so-called 'going out together' of Frank and Dolly was a complete misnomer because they never went anywhere together. Still, like everything else in the Slater family, it was probably all Father's doing, and Dolly would only go along with it until it suited her to do otherwise.

'Oh, well, as long as it suits you and Dolly, I suppose that's all that matters,' he said.

'You know me, son, I ain't the sort to ruffle me feathers about anythin',' said Frank, proceeding along King Street.

'That's true.'

'Waste o' time getting het up about things,' Frank remarked chattily. 'Waste o' time drivin' round looking for your sister an' all, 'cos she just ain't here.'

'She certainly doesn't seem to be,' agreed Ken.

'I think we might as well go back to your place, mate,' said Frank. 'She's probably back by now.'

Oh no she isn't, thought Ken, his heart lurching as he spotted Dolly at the park gates. *She's with a chap!* Even worse, Ken recognised the fellow as one of the labourers from the factory. He and Dolly were gawping at each other like a pair of clowns, apparently oblivious of anything else. What was the matter with his sister? Did she have a death wish or something? Not content with causing havoc at lunch, and failing to turn up for tea, now she had completely gone off her chump and was hobnobbing with one of Father's underlings.

There'll be fireworks when Father gets to hear about this, thought Ken, as the car drew closer to the park entrance. Frank might take everything in his stride, but Father certainly didn't. Frank was sure to tell him about this. Ken's heart was in his mouth as the car cruised towards the park gates and the unsuspecting couple.

Chapter Three

'Looks like trouble ahead, Frank,' lied Ken in an attempt to divert the other man's attention from the park gates.

'Where's that then, son?' he asked, peering into the distance, 'I can't see anything.'

'Right up there near the bend in the road,' lied Ken. 'There seems to be a crowd on the pavement.'

'You must be seein' things, mate,' said Frank, squinting ahead.

'Probably something to do with the strike,' persisted Ken. 'Someone was telling me that a mob tried to overturn a private car the other day because the driver was giving lifts.'

'Mmm, I 'eard about that an' all,' said Frank, craning his neck to see beyond the cars in front. 'But I'm buggered if I can see any sign of bother now.'

'It must have cleared,' said Ken with a sigh of relief as soon as his sister and her boyfriend were safely out of sight. 'Or perhaps I was imagining things.'

'You ought to take more water with it,' chortled Frank.

Ken managed a dutiful laugh. His satisfaction at having averted an immediate crisis was diminished by fear for his sister's future happiness if she didn't mend her ways. What on earth had possessed her to take such a risk?

There was no room in Dolly's mind for caution or common sense as she walked home with a spring in her step. She was far too wrapped up in memories of Bill Drake's gentle smile and gorgeous brown eyes. As she turned into Maybury Avenue it started to rain again, huge drops blowing into her face and drenching her hair. Her clothes were still damp from her earlier soaking too, and felt clammy against her skin. But she didn't give a damn!

Having lived vicariously through the feverish crushes of various girlfriends, she assumed that this must be what had happened to her. Friends had rambled on endlessly about some sort of an inner glow mingled with acute physical awareness – 'indescribable' was a common adjective. Now she knew exactly what they had meant. It was a heady mixture of desire and emotion, quite different to the mateyness she shared with Frank who was her only comparison.

Thoughts of Frank were a sobering influence; they reminded her of home and Sunday tea for which she was very late. She didn't waste compunction on Frank whom she knew would not be bothered by her absence. She was in for a trouncing from Father, of course, but that hardly seemed to matter in the excitement of the moment. In her present mood, anything was bearable!

'Blimey, you come into money or something?' said Maud, shuffling sleepily into the kitchen to find her son whistling the tune of 'Bye Bye Blackbird' and setting out the tea things while waiting for the kettle to boil.

'Leave it out, Ma,' said Bill. ''Course I 'aven't.'

'All this whistling about the place of a Sunday afternoon ain't natural when people are trying to sleep,' she clowned. 'So what's goin' on?'

'I'm in a good mood, that's all,' he told her breezily, sawing at a loaf with the breadknife. A cracked basin of shrimps and another of winkles were set out on the kitchen table. They would all have helped themselves at varying intervals had Bill not decided to make a proper tea-time of it today as a celebration of his good fortune. Brimming over with a sense of well-being, he felt generous towards the whole of humankind, even the slovenly couple he lived with. 'So I thought I'd get the tea ready and lay the table, proper like . . . be nice for us all to eat together.'

'Who's coming?'

'No one.'

'Why bother then?'

'Because it's the proper way of doin' things,' said Bill.

'Oi, oi,' said Maud with a raucous laugh. 'When boys o' your age start talking about doin' things proper, there's usually a girl behind it. You met a nice young lady, have yer, Bill?'

''Course not,' he lied swiftly, because he knew his mother would spoil things for him with vulgarity if he told her the truth. What was there to tell, anyway? He'd spent the afternoon with the boss's daughter and was seeing her tomorrow night. It hardly amounted to a love affair. But the stirrings within him said otherwise. In fact, it was almost as

45

though his life had changed course. He felt chosen and special – not a labourer without prospects but a man with the world at his feet. Just the thought of Dolly made his pulse quicken.

It was lunacy, of course. He'd be out of a job if Henry Slater got wind of his being within a mile of his daughter. Even apart from that, it could never come to anything because Bill didn't have the money to court a girl like Dolly in the manner she would expect. A night out at the pictures or a variety show and a fish and chip supper once a week was about all he could afford after he'd paid his mother for his keep.

But for all that, he still felt like a changed man – as though meeting Dolly this afternoon was some sort of a turning point in his life.

'I know all about boys who are a bit too quick to deny 'aving a girl,' said Maud with a knowing smile.

'What do you know, Ma?' he asked.

'It usually means they've got a bit of stuff tucked away somewhere.'

'Wouldn't you like to know, Ma,' he said, grinning at her, for even her sluttishness couldn't upset the way he felt at this moment.

Dolly was busy at her typewriter when Ken came into the office they shared at the factory one hot summer afternoon. Over his ordinary clothes he wore a long white linen overall, his hair tucked out of sight into a draw-string mob cap, which for reasons of hygiene was compulsory dress for anyone with cause to go near the unpacked tea.

'Phew, it's steaming in the factory today,' he said, putting his clipboard down on his desk and peeling off his protective clothing. He slipped on the jacket of a dark business suit, that was draped across the back of his chair, over a stiff-collared white shirt, dark tie and waistcoat which was standard office dress for management at Slater's regardless of soaring temperatures. He mopped his moist brow with a handkerchief. 'Dear, oh dear, I don't know how the packers can stand working in such heat all day.'

'It can't be very pleasant for them in this weather,' she agreed. 'Even I'm hot and sticky and the offices are quite cool in comparison.' The sun was streaming through the windows and her hands felt slippery as she turned the heavy roller on her typewriter to remove a finished letter. Her official role at Slater's was secretary to her father but there was much more to the job than just typing his letters. Having a thorough knowledge of the business she was able to cope with diverse tasks. As well as dealing with tea brokers and chasing up deliveries from suppliers, she also dealt with customer queries and discussed deadlines with the printers who produced their packets, bags and display material. Sharing an office with her brother was Father's idea. He said that Ken didn't qualify for an office of his own just yet. Dolly didn't mind in the least because she enjoyed his company. 'Still, they know that the factory has to be kept warm and dry and accept it as an occupational hazard.'

'Oh, yes, they're fully aware that if the tea gets damp it can go mouldy and cost the firm a lot of money.' He glanced towards their father's office next door. 'Is he back from the printer's yet?'

She shook her head. 'No, he telephoned to say he won't be back in the office until later this afternoon. His meeting has gone on longer than he expected,' she explained. 'I think he's trying to negotiate better rates with them or something.'

'Probably trying to screw them into the ground,' said Ken. 'But at least it gives me a bit of time . . .'

'What's the matter – problems on the factory floor?'

Although Ken was still quite young, as a Slater son and junior member of the management team he was expected to take a certain amount of responsibility. This entailed his keeping an authoritative eye on things when his father wasn't around. Unfortunately, his sympathetic nature often brought him under fire from Henry for being too lenient with the workers.

'I'll say,' he admitted ruefully. 'There's a new girl in the packing department who's still a bit slow and causing bad feelings with the rest of her team for holding them up. They're giving her a really hard time because she's costing them money, being on piece work.'

'Oh dear,' Dolly tutted. 'Does she have potential to speed up or is she naturally clumsy?'

'She certainly isn't clumsy,' he said emphatically, 'but her training period on time work wasn't long enough. The other girls are making things worse by nagging her and making her nervous and even slower. She's only fourteen and fresh out of school.'

'So what she really needs is more experience on time work 'til she picks up speed?' suggested Dolly.

'That's right,' he agreed, 'but you know what Father's

like about that. He insists that everyone is put on to piece work at the earliest possible moment. His instructions are that if they aren't working at a good speed immediately after training, they're no use to us and must go.'

She frowned disapprovingly. 'That man is quite beyond the pale.'

'You're not kidding,' said Ken ruefully. 'If he finds out she's slow, he'll sack her on the spot.'

'Have you spoken to the supervisor about it?'

'Yes. She's on the side of the experienced packers which isn't surprising as her money depends on the output of the whole department,' explained Ken. 'The general view is that they can't afford to carry passengers, and frankly, Dolly, I can see their point. But it's so unjust to sack the girl.'

Leaning on her desk, Dolly mulled the problem over. 'I'll go down and have a few words with them if you like. See if I can get them to take it easy on her. They might take more notice of a female member of the family.'

'No, you'd better not, Dolly,' warned Ken with a cautionary shake of the head. 'You'll only get into trouble with Father. You know how he disapproves of your getting involved in anything on the factory floor.'

Dolly was grinning as she slipped into a freshly laundered overall and mob cap. 'So what's new about my being in trouble with Daddy?' She turned at the door to ask the girl's name.

Ken hesitated for a moment but finally succumbed, grateful for his sister's indomitable spirit and the fact that she was so very good at handling this sort of human problem. 'Mabel Trump,' he said. 'They call her Mabs.'

'Leave it to me,' she told him confidently.

'You're incorrigible, Doll,' he said, his expression changing as he remembered something. 'And on the subject of your taking risks . . .' He reached into his trouser pocket and took out an envelope which he handed to her. 'A certain person asked me to be postman again.'

Her face lit up as she took the precious envelope and slipped it into her overall pocket to read when she was alone. 'Thanks, Ken, you're a good sort. Bill and I really appreciate your helping us.'

'Do be careful, Dolly,' he said, frowning.

'You bet your sweet life I will,' she assured him.

'Not only for yourself but for Bill too,' he said gravely. 'He'll come off worse than you if Father finds out what the two of you are up to.'

'I can't stop seeing him, Ken,' she whispered, her expression becoming deadly serious. 'So please don't ask it of me.'

'But, Sis . . .'

'Sorry, Ken, but it's out of my control,' she said with a helpless shake of the head. 'I know it sounds dramatic . . . it's something I just can't explain.'

'Oh, well.' He sighed heavily. 'It's your life, but I really think you're pushing your luck.'

Closing the office door behind her, Dolly made her way along the corridor with its dismal green walls, past her father's office next to Frank's, and the general office where she could see clerks and typists hard at work through the glass partition. Then there was the accounts department, the sales office and the tasting room where a team of experienced tea-tasters, headed by a man called Bert Dixon, checked the quality of the tea samples, the accuracy of existing Slater blends and constantly experimented with new recipes for the blends of the future. Passing a number of other offices, she pushed through the swing doors into an area where stone stairs led down to the factory. Pausing on the landing, she looked round to make sure there was no one about before taking the letter from her pocket, her heart leaping at the sight of Bill's handwriting.

Darling Dolly,
I love you so much and want the world to know it.
Same place, same time tonight. I can hardly survive
till then.
Bill.

She put the paper to her lips before replacing it in the envelope and stuffing it back in her pocket, her fingers lingering on it lovingly.

It was three months since that first magical Sunday afternoon. What she'd at first thought was a crush had proved to be a love affair. It had been a time of emotional extremes and rapturous, clandestine meetings while her parents and Frank thought she was with her friends.

Trusting each other completely, she and Bill had exchanged their most intimate thoughts and feelings. They'd talked about families, friends and the agonies of growing up. They'd even touched on the sensitive issue of the class system which divided them. He'd been truthful with her about his poor home; she'd admitted that all was not sweetness and light in the Slater household.

Being first love for them both, they had become obsessed with each other, possessive and blind to reality. Dolly became moody, alternating between ecstasy and despair depending on how close she was to seeing Bill. Their differing backgrounds and financial status seemed unimportant to her. If he didn't have the price of two cinema seats where they could huddle together under cover of darkness, then she paid. It really didn't matter. Even the fact that their love affair could cost Bill his job did not diminish their mutual compulsion. He had become even more reckless than she was and said that she was more important to him than any job.

Deliberately closing their minds to the fact that there could be no future for them as a couple, they existed only for the present and their stolen moments together. They had almost perfected the art of pretending they were just like any other courting couple, albeit that they were forced to meet outside their area or in secluded corners of the park, often using a gap in the fence after the gates were closed in the evening.

Naturally Bill objected to her being labelled Frank Mitchell's girl, and repeatedly asked her to end her association with him. But she saw safety in the present arrangement. If she officially ended things with Frank, her father might make it his business to find out why.

But for the moment, she forced personal matters to the back of her mind and concentrated on the job in hand. Hurrying down the stairs she made her way through a maze of corridors and into the packing room, feeling its dry warmth and breathing in the overpowering scent of tea.

This department was peopled entirely by single females. No married women were employed at Slater's at all, and male hands only came in here to take away the heavy platforms of packed tea to the loading bay where it was put into vans for delivery. The huge room was kept spotlessly clean; sweepers worked continuously all day on the floors and tea dust was sucked from the air by vacuum ducts in the ceiling.

The packers were arranged in groups of seven around a work bench, three either side and one at the end. The first pair of girls, who were called funnellers, caught the tea into packets as it was automatically weighed and dropped through a funnel from a hopper in the room above. Each funneller then placed the filled packets in rows of four beside the wrapper next to her who wrapped the tea and passed it on to the labeller who stuck the label on. From here it was passed to the parceller at the foot of the table who parcelled the small packets into large packs and stacked them on to a platform to be taken away by the men.

Raised voices led Dolly to the table with the problem. She didn't need telling which one was Mabs Trump, or that she was not the sort of girl to be easily intimidated for all that she was tiny.

'Give a gel a chance, won't yer?' she was saying to her workmates, big blue eyes flashing in a sea of freckles beneath her mob cap.

'You're 'olding us all up, and it ain't right,' said someone. 'We're losing money while you're fumbling about. My dad's out o' work so I need every penny.'

'I can't help it if I ain't bin trained proper,' said Mabs, her small face flushed and shiny with perspiration. 'Give us a couple more days and I'll beat the lot of yer.'

Realising they had a visitor, the packers greeted her with a polite: 'Good afternoon, Miss Dolly.'

'Good afternoon, ladies. I understand you have a problem,' she said.

'Yeah, Mabs 'ere is all fingers and thumbs,' said Sadie Peters, a busty blonde with somnolent blue eyes. 'And our pay packets are gonna be thinner 'cos of 'er. We know she can't 'elp it but none of us can afford to be short.'

Mabs Trump fixed her eyes on Dolly with a determined gleam. 'Give us a chance, Miss Dolly. Jobs ain't easy to come by and I'll be good at this once I've got the 'ang of it. Me fingers might be small but they're ever so nimble.'

Dolly observed the tiny fingers holding the tea packet as Mabs shook the leaves to the bottom. Dolly's sense of fair play told her that the least the company could do was to give the girl a chance to prove herself. She decided to take matters into her own hands.

'I think we'd better put you back on to time work for a bit longer until you get quicker at it, Mabs,' she said kindly. 'I'll have a word with the supervisor about it right away.'

'Thank Gawd for that,' said the woman with the unemployed father.

'Yeah,' agreed Sadie. 'I'm savin' up for a marcel wave.'

Mabs beamed, two dimples appearing in her little round face. 'Thanks ever so much, Miss Dolly,' she said. 'You're a good sort, just like your brother. He said I oughta be given a chance too.'

'It's a pleasure, Mabs,' said Dolly, inwardly groaning at the thought of the almighty bust-up there would be with Father when he found out what she'd done.

As she turned to go, she was unnerved by the appearance of Bill.

'Wotcha,' said Sadie, giving him an inviting look. ''ow are you today, mate?'

'Not so dusty thanks, Sadie,' he said, looking very flushed.

'That's good,' she said, her glance lingering on him rather longer than Dolly thought necessary.

Bill seemed embarrassed by her, Dolly noticed, watching him turn his attention rather too quickly to the stacked tea platform.

'Is this one ready to go?' he mumbled, looking towards the packers.

'Yeah, all ready, my love,' said Sadie in a tone that Dolly, in her sensitised state, translated as affectionate.

Hypersensitive to what she imagined was some sort of eye contact between Bill and Sadie, Dolly flew into such a fit of jealousy she had to restrain feelings of violence towards the girl. The idea of Bill with someone else was physical torture to her. Feeling miserably like an outsider in their world, dread filled her heart. Had there once been something between these two? Was there still? Of course not, she admonished herself. Pull yourself together, woman!

Managing to calm her wild imagination, she moved away without looking at him as he began to wheel the loaded platform across the room. After a few words with the supervisor about Mabs's return to time work, Dolly left the department.

Outside in the empty corridor she waited, praying that he would not let this unexpected opportunity pass him by. She was not disappointed. He appeared almost at once and they fell into each other's arms, hugging and whispering.

'I mustn't stop more than a minute or I'll 'ave the chargehand after me,' he told her breathlessly.

'What was all that about with you and Sadie?' she asked.

'All what?'

'She seemed to make you uncomfortable,' she said. 'You turned scarlet.'

''Course I did. Having to face that crowd of women is enough to make a pigeon blush,' he said softly. ''Specially seeing you there when I wasn't expecting it.' He ran his fingers around the inside of his collar. 'Phew, I'm still sweating now.'

'I thought you fancied her and I wanted to scratch her eyes out!'

'You're the only girl I fancy, surely you know that by now?'

'Yes, I do really,' she said, reminding herself that his shyness was one of the things she loved about him.

'I think it was really nice what you did for little Mabs,' he said warmly. 'She's only a kid.'

'It was the only fair thing to do,' she said in a low voice. 'But Daddy will go through the roof when he finds out that I've put her back on time work.'

'Poor you.'

'You can say that again . . . I think I'll try to get Frank on my side,' she said thoughtfully. 'More for Ken's sake than mine, really. Daddy will jump at the chance to have a go at him for passing the problem on to me when he should have sorted it out himself, Daddy's way.'

'You talk about being jealous of Sadie,' he said with a sudden change of mood. 'Now you know how I feel about Frank. I want that man out of your life, Doll.'

'Yes, I know you do. I'll have to sort it out somehow,' she said. 'Let's talk about it tonight.'

'It can't come quick enough for me,' he said, his tone softening.

'Nor me.'

The sounds of movement echoed in the corridor. Springing apart, they went their separate ways.

'So can I count on your support, Frank?' said Dolly, having explained the Mabs Trump situation to him. 'She only needs a day or two back on time work. It won't cost the company much.'

'No,' said Frank.

'Why?'

'Because your father pays my wages and is entitled to my loyalty.'

'Surely you can disagree with him occasionally, especially when he's in the wrong?'

He shook his head, eyebrows meeting in a frown. 'I suppose I could do,' he said blandly, 'but I ain't going to.'

'Well . . . that's nice, I must say!' she retorted.

'Listen 'ere, Dolly,' he said in a neutral tone, 'you and me might be going out together but my first duty is still to your dad.'

'But what I did was right, Frank,' she said impatiently. 'You must admit that?'

'If it ain't what the boss wants, it ain't right in my book.'

'Oh, come on. I've used my own initiative and put a girl back on to time working for a day or two. I haven't taken it on myself to introduce some massive bonus scheme or something,' she said briskly. 'Hardly the crime of the century, is it?'

'Your father doesn't like you to interfere in problems on the factory floor, you know that,' he said with infuriating calm.

'But the company wasn't being fair to the girl in taking her off time work too soon,' she pointed out hotly. 'The amount of training needed varies from person to person and she hadn't had enough.'

He shrugged. 'It ain't your place to judge, though, is it?'

'Honestly, Frank, isn't it time you had some opinions of your own?' she said. 'My father doesn't own you.'

'I'm paid to look after him,' he pointed out.

'And if he told you to throw yourself under a bus for his benefit, you'd do it, I suppose?'

'Your father's bin good to me, Dolly,' he said, ignoring her question. 'I owe it to him to do what he wants.'

'Even be a boyfriend to me?'

They both knew he couldn't deny it. 'I won't 'ear a word against him,' he said, avoiding this question too.

'So you won't back me up then?'

'Afraid not, Doll. Because . . .'

'I know,' she finished for him with a withering stare. 'Because you owe my father everything.'

'That's right,' he said with a benign smile.

'Oh, well, another row with Father won't kill me,' she said, and marched out of his office.

On the way back to her own office, she had a chance to think things over. Whilst Frank's demonstration of slavish dedication to her father irritated her, it also clarified her own situation with him and lessened her compunction about her affair with Bill and the lies she had been forced to tell to be with him. Frank didn't care for her any more than she did for him, though in fairness to him he had never pretended to.

Father was certainly one on his own, she thought. Most men in his position would hope for a good marriage for their daughter with the son of a rich businessman, someone to elevate their own standing. But Henry would sacrifice all that rather than risk having some independently minded young chap as a son-in-law, someone who might threaten his authority.

Ironically, in engineering this fiasco of a courtship, her father had provided her with the perfect cover for a real one. Frank was too indifferent to query whether or not she was seeing her girlfriends of an evening; and while Father rested easy in the belief that she was Frank's girl, he didn't doubt her either. It was when she ended things with Frank, as she undoubtedly must, that the trouble would really begin . . .

* * *

She felt bound to repeat these thoughts to Bill that evening when he made his feelings clear on the subject. They were sitting on the grass in a private corner of the park. The air was warm and Bill was lying down with his head on her lap.

'I can understand your wanting me to break things off with Frank,' she said, stroking his thick springy hair, 'but we're safe as things are, and it isn't as though anything ever happens between Frank and me. It's all in Father's mind, as I've told you.'

'I don't care about being safe any more, Dolly,' he said, sitting up and becoming suddenly decisive. 'It's gone beyond that with me. I want us to be together like a proper couple. I've had enough of all this secrecy, carryin' on as though we're a couple of criminals!'

'I really don't see what else we can do.'

'Are you ashamed of me?'

'Of course not.' She was shocked. 'How can you say such a thing?'

He looped his arms around his knees and stared gloomily into space. 'You do seem pretty terrified of anyone finding out about us.'

'You know why that is – because my father will put a stop to it if he finds out,' she reminded him, 'and you'll lose your job.'

'What about us in all this?' he asked grimly. 'We're adults with minds of our own. How can he stop us seeing each other if we refuse to let him?'

'You don't know what he's like, Bill, honestly.'

'That's true but I do know how we feel about each other,' he said forcefully, 'and I'm not prepared to sit back and let him split us up.'

'I've told you before, he has a way of making people do what he wants.' The confrontation she had had with her father about Mabs Trump when he had got back to the office that afternoon was still fresh in her mind. His fury had been quite frightening. Only by convincing him that if he were to reverse her decision and dismiss Mabs he would appear foolish to the workers by showing his daughter's action to be a breach of his authority, had she saved Mabs's job. But persuading him to see reason about herself and Bill was a very different matter. She chewed a blade of grass. 'The first thing he'd do is to put you out of work.'

'So what?'

'You were worried enough about that in the beginning.'

'You know very well that things have changed since then,' he reminded her solemnly.

'Yes, I know they have,' she said with a wistful sigh. 'I'm just making sure you know what you're up against.'

He turned to face her, eyes heavy with feeling. 'I can't go on like this, Dolly,' he said.

She winced. 'You want to end it?'

'Of course not!'

'What then? My father will never accept you into the family,' she said sadly. 'We've both known that from the start.'

'I know that,' he snapped with a bitter laugh. 'Perhaps I should be slapped into prison for committing the terrible crime of falling in love with the boss's daughter.'

'Don't be like that.'

'Sorry, love, I shouldn't take it out on you.' He stood up and leaned against an oak tree, richly laden with acorns. The oppressive heat of the day had cooled into an earthy dampness. It was late-August and the spicy chill of incipient autumn scented the air in the gathering dusk.

'That's all right,' said Dolly. 'I feel rotten about it too.'

'So where do we go from here, Dolly?' he asked grimly.

'You tell me.'

His honest face was tight with worry. 'This isn't just a casual thing for me,' he told her gravely.

'Nor me, you know that.'

'But when we get down to basics, I have nothing to offer you.'

'You have yourself.'

'If you married me you'd be giving up an awful lot,' he said solemnly.

Her arms were around his neck. 'Marry you?' she said, laughing and crying simultaneously. 'Oh, Bill, I thought you'd never ask.'

It was almost dark before they got around to discussing the practical side of his proposal.

'We'll have to leave the area so that my father can't find us until after we're married,' she said, her head resting against his chest as they lay on the grass beneath the stars. 'I don't want to hurt my parents but one hint of what we're planning and Daddy will find a way of stopping it. Don't ask me how but he will.'

'We'll get a place somewhere south of the river,' he

suggested, 'away from Slater territory.'

'Smashing.'

'We'll have to organise the whole thing properly, though, 'cos I'll not have you roughing it any more than is absolutely necessary,' said Bill forcefully. 'The first thing I must do is find another job so that I can support you, then I'll look for a place for us to live nearby.'

'Sure.'

'Once those two things are done, we can make our plans to get away. In the meantime we carry on as we are, yes?'

'Yes,' agreed Dolly.

'Are you sure this is what you want?' he asked as they struggled to their feet and brushed themselves down.

'Of course it is,' she said eagerly. 'Why do you ask?'

'Because it's a very serious step and there's more at stake for you than me,' he said. 'I only have a job to lose. You will be giving up a comfortable, secure life.'

'That doesn't worry me.'

'You must be *really* certain, Dolly.'

'I am.'

'Good. I'll see to it that you never regret it. I'll do everything I possibly can to better myself and make you proud of me,' he told her. 'I can promise you that.'

'There's no need,' she said solemnly. 'I'm proud of you just the way you are.'

Sadie Peters lay awake mulling over the events of the day. She was a passionate young woman with a voracious appetite for men. When she took a fancy to one, she didn't rest until she had him begging for her favours. Bill Drake was her current target and she didn't like being upstaged by someone with no right to be in the running. Dolly Slater shouldn't go poaching out of her class!

Sadie had been knocked sideways this afternoon when she'd popped out to the lav for a fag and caught sight of them 'at it' in the corridor. Who would have thought that Bashful Bill would have stood a chance with someone like her? He wasn't so shy as he seemed obviously. Anyone with a ha'porth of sense could guess that he was just a 'bit of rough' to a girl with Dolly Slater's background; for temporary amusement only. She couldn't possibly have any long-term plans for someone with nothing more lucrative to offer than sexy brown eyes and a lovely pair of shoulders.

The boss's daughter and Bill, eh, and her supposed to be going out with her father's minder! Bill certainly had some nerve, she'd say that for him; this was a positive aphrodisiac to Sadie who liked men with a bit of sauce. The poor bloke needed saving from himself, and who better than herself to see to it. She'd drop a hint into the shell-like of a certain interested party at the earliest opportunity . . .

Her chance came a few days later when Frank Mitchell came into the packing department to collect some paperwork from the supervisor. Although Frank's position in management was only a token one involving the most elementary tasks, he was not above the odd spot of showing off. He strutted among the work benches in an authoritative manner, glancing along the tables and muttering things like: 'Good work, gels – keep at it.'

Being such an enormous bear of a man, he looked oddly

incongruous in protective clothing, his huge face shining out like a sticky bun-round beneath the mob cap. It was common knowledge among the workers that Frank had the wit of a fishcake, but he *was* management and as such was treated with respect.

'Morning, Mr Mitchell,' said Sadie, who was sticking labels on to packets as he approached her bench.

'Morning,' he said with a slow smile, standing beside her and observing the work in progress.

'Warm enough in 'ere for yer, is it?' she said chattily, turning to see him wiping his face with a handkerchief. Somehow she had to speak to him alone which wasn't going to be easy since anything beyond superficial chit-chat was not encouraged between factory hands and management. If the other girls heard her snitching on one of their own, they'd make her life hell.

'Mmm, 'tis a bit on the warm side,' he replied, putting the handkerchief into his overall pocket.

'Sweltering, more like,' she said, seizing her opportunity and slipping a furtive hand into his pocket, removing the handkerchief and dropping it unnoticed to the floor under the bench.

'Yes, but I reckon you gels are used to it, so keep up the good work,' he said, moving away and heading out of the department.

Waiting until the doors were closed behind him, Sadie went into action. 'What's this under me foot?' she said, reaching down to the floor under the table. 'Here, look at this, girls. It's Mr Mitchell's 'anky. I'd better go after him with it.'

'Go on then,' said someone.

She caught up with him in the corridor. 'I think you dropped this, sir,' she said, handing him the handkerchief.

'Oh, ta, ducks,' he said, taking it and putting it into his pocket.

'No trouble,' she said chirpily. 'Keeping well, are you, sir?'

'Never better,' he replied, before turning to go.

'Only I did wonder how you was taking it,' she said, speedily enough to detain him. 'You know, about Miss Dolly . . .'

'What about Miss Dolly?' he asked, turning back to face her with a puzzled expression.

'About her and that Bill Drake from loading,' she said innocently.

'Bill Drake?' he said blankly. 'What's he got to do with Miss Dolly?'

'Well, they're . . . I mean . . . yer know.' She paused with feigned modesty. 'I saw 'em at it the other day with me own eyes. I thought it must be all off between yourself and Miss Dolly.'

'You saw Dolly with Bill Drake . . .?' he began.

'Yeah, I certainly did,' she interrupted swiftly to hold his attention. 'Not far from this very spot as it 'appens, kissin' and cuddlin' fit to bust.' She paused again, looking suitably concerned by his surprise. 'You mean you didn't know about it? Oh dear, Mr Mitchell, I was sure it must have bin common knowledge upstairs in the offices.' She chewed her lip anxiously. 'I wish I 'adn't said anything now.'

'Don't worry, ducks, you did right to tell me,' he assured her absently before hurrying on his way, eager to pass this astonishing news on to Henry.

On hearing about his daughter's disgusting behaviour, Henry's first impulse was to sack Bill Drake that very minute. Their ardour would soon dampen when they realised that slap and tickle wasn't nearly so much fun when you didn't have a brass farthing to your name. But he managed to restrain himself. This mustn't be hurried. Dolly was a complicated young woman with peculiar ideas. If he gave this Drake fellow his marching orders, the stupid girl might see him as a hero and go running after him.

This nonsense with Drake had to be stopped and Dolly cured of this ridiculous infatuation forever. That meant a carefully worked out plan which must be absolutely foolproof.

'What yer gonna do about it, boss?' asked Frank, barely considering his own position in his concern for Henry.

'I'm not sure yet,' he said thoughtfully. 'But I'll come up with something, don't you worry. And not a word to anyone about this . . . understand?'

'You can count on me.'

'You're the man for my daughter, Frank, my old son,' Henry said chummily. 'Not some lousy labourer.'

Chapter Four

Bill was in jubilant mood when he met Dolly in the park one autumn Saturday afternoon.

'Have I got news for you!' he said excitedly, kissing her and tucking her arm under his.

Beneath light grey skies a chilly breeze rustled through the elms, scattering the fallen leaves with the sound of paper crinkling. It was the sort of weather in which to keep on the move so they strode out vigorously, passing the deserted bandstand and the muddy pond littered with copper-coloured leaves.

'You've found a job?' she guessed, squeezing his arm.

'Yeah, but there's more . . .'

'Don't say you've found us a place to live too?'

'Yeah,' he whooped, lifting her in the air and swinging her round.

'You're a ruddy marvel!' she enthused. 'Tell me all about it then.'

'Well, the job is in a tea factory at Battersea called Webb's,' he told her.

'Well done.' She hugged him tight, full of respect for the sense of responsibility that had deterred him from going off in haste without assuring them the means to live on.

'It's only labourin' though,' he explained.

'A job's a job, Bill.'

'I'll work hard to get on,' he declared earnestly. 'I know I'm capable of more than dead-end work. Given time I'll keep you in the way you've been used to, you just wait and see.'

'I've told you, none of that matters.'

'It does to me.'

'Anyway, what about this place you've found for us?' she asked.

'A couple of rooms in a house a few minutes' walk from the factory,' he explained. 'It ain't a palace but it'll do for a start.' He looked at her sheepishly and cleared his throat. 'Obviously I had to tell the landlady that we're already married or she wouldn't consider us as tenants.'

'Oh!' She had known that there would be a time lapse between her leaving home and getting married, especially as she didn't have her parents' permission. But now that it actually came to taking the plunge, she was assailed by pangs of conscience for the shame she would bring on her parents. Whatever their faults, they had brought her up to live a decent life. Surely they had the right to expect her to consider the family reputation? Her heart lurched as she imagined them finding the note she would write for them when she left their house. Her concern was not so much for her father who would see it merely as defiance of his authority, but for her mother who would be genuinely shocked. 'So we'll be living in sin, as they say?'

'Only until we can make it legal.'

'Yes, of course.'

'The landlady won't hold the place,' he explained worriedly. 'I've paid a deposit and I have to let her know by tomorrow if we can move in next week or else she'll let it go to someone else.'

'Oh, I see.'

He stopped by the lake and turned to her, sensing her change of mood. 'What's the matter, Dolly?'

'I was thinking about my parents,' she explained, looking towards the reflection of the sky in the lake, fragmented into silver splinters by angry little wrinkles quivering across the surface in the wind. 'I hate the idea of hurting them like this. I know they can be a real pain but they did bring me up . . . they probably love me in their own peculiar way.'

'Yeah, it must be hard for you.' He chewed his lip anxiously, forcing himself to utter his next words. 'Look, Doll . . . it isn't too late to change your mind if you really feel you can't go through with it.'

'It isn't that I can't go through with it,' she said, meeting his eyes with candour, 'just that I wish it could be different. You know . . . a proper family wedding, all open and above board.'

'Are you sure they won't agree to that?' he asked. 'If they know it's what you really want, and if I prove I'm not after your money by insisting on making my own way.'

'Mother would agree to anything for the sake of a quiet life,' she said, 'but Daddy would go up the wall . . . he'd split us up somehow.'

'I feel bad about coming between you and your family.'

'Don't be daft,' she said forcefully. 'You can't help the way things are, but it wouldn't be honest of me to keep these qualms to myself.'

A train rumbled over the viaduct, drowning the high-pitched cries of children playing on the swings and roundabouts. She slipped her hand into the crook of his arm and they walked on, past a forlorn sundial and a drinking fountain, forsaken on this cold afternoon.

'You're quite sure you want to go ahead, then?' he said.

Whatever the trauma, she knew she had no choice but to take this drastic step since she couldn't bear to lose him. 'Try stopping me,' she said, forcing herself into a more positive frame of mind.

'So, when will you move out then?' he asked.

She thought about this for a moment. 'Next Saturday evening while my parents are out will probably be a good time,' she said. 'They usually go to a show or a cinema on a Saturday night.'

'Right, I'll give my notice in at the factory on Monday morning then and start at the new place the following week,' he said.

'Roll on next Saturday then, eh, Bill?' she said excitedly.

'Not 'alf,' he agreed.

With Frank's assistance, Henry had been keeping Bill Drake under close surveillance with the idea of going into action at a strategic moment. He intended to end his daughter's affair without anyone, even Edie, knowing of its existence.

So, on hearing that Bill had given in his notice at the

factory, Henry suspected that things were about to come to a head. Either the bugger's done his worst and is making a timely exit, or they're planning to go off together, he thought. Whichever it was, it was time to activate his ingenious plan which would cure Dolly for good and all. Perfect timing at each stage was vital to its success.

'My chargehand says you want to see me, Mr Slater,' said Bill on Monday afternoon, warily entering his employer's smoky office.

Henry looked up from his desk and nodded. 'Yes, that's right,' he said amicably, puffing on a cigarette and waving a hand towards a chair. 'Sit down.'

Bill was suspicious of his attitude for Henry Slater was not usually pleasant to his workers. He perched on the edge of the seat, keeping a cautious eye on the boss whom he guessed must have found out about him and Dolly. Why else would he have been sent for?

'I hear you're leaving us,' said Henry in a mild tone.

'Yeah, that's right.' Bill was puzzled because the departure of a labourer didn't normally warrant an interview with the guvnor. But if Henry knew about him and Dolly, why wasn't he raising the roof?

'I can see why you would want to go, considering the way my daughter is treating you,' said Henry, without a trace of anger.

'Oh . . . so you have found out about us?' stammered Bill.

'Did you really think I wouldn't?'

'I hoped you might not.'

'No chance of that, son. I make it my business to know everything that goes on around here.'

'Yeah, I expect you . . .'

'Please accept my apologies for my daughter's behaviour,' Henry interrupted swiftly. 'It really is too bad of her to lead you on. She's been told often enough not to play around with our employees. But then, she's always been a law unto herself, has Dolly.'

So this was the way he was playing it, thought Bill. 'You won't break us up so there's no point in making up tales about Dolly,' he said firmly.

Henry leaned towards him in a confidential manner. 'My daughter is a very charming young woman, so they tell me. I've never seen any evidence of it myself, since all she ever seems to do is argue with me,' he said smoothly. 'But I can understand how she might turn a young man's head.'

A defensive flush suffused Bill's face and neck. 'I love Dolly and she loves me,' he proclaimed.

His employer winced and shook his head as though it distressed him to utter his next words. 'Oh dear, oh dear . . . Dolly is a very naughty girl to mislead you.'

'She has *not* been misleading me.'

'I'm afraid she has, old son,' said Henry with an air of sympathetic wisdom. 'The truth of the matter is that she is about to marry Frank Mitchell.'

'No, she isn't,' argued Bill. 'There's nothing between those two except what you've created in your own mind.'

Henry leaned back in his chair in a relaxed manner and put his two forefingers under his chin meditatively. 'I'm afraid she's not been quite honest with you.'

'Oh yes she has,' Bill said emphatically, 'and you can stop telling lies about her. Frank Mitchell means nothing to her.'

Adopting a fatherly attitude, Henry said, 'I rather think he does, you know.'

Unable to ignore the insinuation, Bill said impatiently, 'What exactly are you getting at?'

'Simply that Frank must mean *something* to Dolly or she wouldn't have let him get her pregnant.'

Bill flinched as though he'd been physically struck. 'She ain't . . .'

'She is, you know,' Henry lied, assuming an air of chumminess, as though all his sympathies lay with Bill. 'That's why a wedding has to be arranged, sharpish.' He leaned forward and lowered his voice. 'You can imagine how me and the wife feel, having this sort of trouble at our door.' He drew in his breath and shook his head gravely. 'If we don't get her up the aisle right away, she'll be the talk of the factory – the name of Slater will be mud all over the manor.'

'I don't believe you,' said Bill determinedly, but the possibility was beginning to nag at him.

'Why would I lie about a wedding if it isn't going to happen?' bluffed Henry. 'Since time would soon show the truth? Anyway, if she's so much in love with you, why didn't she stop Frank coming round to the house?' He drew on his cigarette, coughed then leaned his head back slightly and looked at Bill suggestively. 'Don't tell me you haven't wondered about that yourself?'

Bill was no match for the nefarious ways of Henry

Slater. The allegations about Dolly were gaining strength, despite all attempts to disregard them. But they couldn't be true . . . Dolly wouldn't lie to him. 'Frank was just being used as a cover,' he said, but his words had an empty ring.

Henry gave a cynical laugh. 'That's what she's told you, is it? Oh, well, they say there's one born every minute.'

'You'll stop at nothing to come between us, won't you?' rasped Bill.

'I'm only telling you the truth, lad,' said Henry convincingly.

'Rubbish,' Bill retaliated, but a grinding pain was dragging him down.

'There's only one way to find out if I'm telling the truth,' said Henry cunningly. 'And that's by asking Dolly herself.'

'I will, don't worry,' said Bill, rising on shaky legs. 'I'll go and see her this very minute.'

'No, not here at the factory,' said Henry swiftly. 'I'll not risk having my family business made common knowledge among the staff. Ask her when you see her next outside.'

Dazed but not beaten, Bill said, 'Too bloody true I will. You'll soon see that you'll not part us.'

When the door closed behind him, Henry drew on his cigarette, feeling quite pleased with the first stage of his plan.

Shortly after that, when Ken was out of the office, Dolly received a visit from Sadie Peters, dishevelled and tearful and asking to see her father. Knowing that there was very little possibility of his giving time to a factory girl, Dolly said, 'Workers' problems are usually dealt with lower down the line. It would be better if you could speak to your supervisor.'

'It's an urgent personal matter and I insist on seeing Mr Slater.'

'Oh, I see,' said Dolly, rising. 'Well, I'll do what I can but I can't promise anything.'

'I wouldn't ask if it wasn't important,' said Sadie in a trembling voice.

'No, of course not.'

'I've gotta serious complaint to make,' she said, wiping her eyes with her handkerchief.

'Look, is there anything I can do to help?' asked Dolly, fearing short shrift for this girl from her father who had no patience at all with emotional women.

'No, Miss Dolly, I'm takin' this matter right to the top.'

'My father is a very busy man, so why not tell me what's happened and I'll pass it on to him?' she suggested, feeling she ought to offer some sort of assistance, unaware of the fact that she was doing exactly what Sadie wanted.

'I can't talk about it,' she sobbed. 'It's too awful.'

'Why not sit down for a minute, anyway?' suggested Dolly kindly. 'Even if I can get my father to see you, it's no good your going in there in this state.'

'Thanks, Miss Dolly,' she said, sitting down with bowed head and crying loudly into her handkerchief.

'It sometimes helps to talk to another woman.'

'I don't think I can bear to,' Sadie mumbled through her screwed-up hanky, head bent, shoulders shaking.

'A trouble shared is a trouble halved, so they say,' said Dolly with a mixture of curiosity and genuine concern.

'Ta, but I'd rather not,' said Sadie.

'As you wish,' said Dolly, sitting down and leafing through some papers on her desk. 'When you've calmed down I'll go and see if my father is free.'

'I mean, I'm the last person to wanna make trouble for anyone,' said Sadie, apparently having a change of heart about unburdening herself. 'But us gels ain't safe with the likes of 'im about the factory. I've decided to report 'im to the guvnor 'imself. The supervisor ain't got no power to stop him, her being female. Go straight to the boss, Sadie, I thought. It's no more than me duty to me workmates. I mean, who knows who'll be his next victim. Bloody animal. He wants locking up.' She closed her eyes and shuddered theatrically. 'Ooh, it makes me go cold just to think about it.'

'Someone's made a pass at you, I presume?' said Dolly.

'I'll say they bloomin' well 'ave!' said Sadie. 'The bugger's bin after me for ages. I wasn't interested. Just didn't fancy him, if yer know what I mean. Well, that's like an invitation to some of 'em, ain't it?'

'I suppose it might be.'

'It certainly was to 'im anyway,' continued Sadie. 'He caught me in the corridor when I'd popped out to the cloakroom, dragged me into the cleaner's room where they keep all the mops and buckets and went at me like a madman. Gawd knows how I got away from him, but I managed it somehow.'

'That's terrible,' said Dolly with heartfelt sympathy.

'I'll say it is.' She sighed. 'Never think it to look at him either. Looks as though butter wouldn't melt.' She blew her nose and adopted a woman to woman tone with Dolly. 'The gels reckon he's seein' someone on a regular basis an' all, though no one knows who she is. He's keepin' so dark about it his mates reckon she must be married or somethin'.' She sighed. 'Typical of that sort, innit? One woman just ain't enough for 'em.'

'Who was it exactly?'

'Oh, didn't I say?' she said, lowering her voice with a convincing air of innocence. 'Name o' Bill Drake. He's one of the labourers. I don't expect you know him, you being up 'ere in the office.'

'Oh, no,' Dolly uttered involuntarily, in a cracked whisper.

'You know 'im then?'

Dolly couldn't speak for a moment. 'Only through seeing him around the factory,' she managed at last. 'He seemed harmless enough to me.'

'I know,' tutted Sadie in a matey tone, pretending not to notice Dolly's sudden pallor. 'He don't seem the type at all. Still, they say the quiet ones are the worst.'

'Perhaps you misunderstood him?' suggested Dolly hopefully.

Sadie looked suitably astonished, and emitted a dry laugh. 'You can't misunderstand a thing like that, Miss Dolly,' she said. 'He nearly 'ad the clothes orf me back.'

'Perhaps you encouraged him without realising it,' said Dolly, desperately seeking some sort of justification for this sickening incident.

'Here ... what sort o' girl do yer think I am?' said Sadie,

with suitable affront. 'All I've ever done is try to put 'im off.'

'Yes, of course you have. I'm sorry,' said Dolly.

'Just goes to show how wrong you can be about people, dunnit?'

'It does indeed.'

'What's up, Miss Dolly?' asked Sadie with feigned concern. 'You look a bit peaky all of a sudden. You feeling poorly?'

'Just a bit of a headache,' lied Dolly, besieged by vivid recall of the scene in the packing room when Bill had seemed so uncomfortable in Sadie's presence. The reason seemed obvious now. God, what a bastard she had loved all summer! 'I'll take an aspirin in a minute.'

'I should,' said Sadie, in a sympathetic tone.

Gathering her wits, Dolly said, 'I understand Bill Drake is leaving the firm at the end of the week, anyway.'

'Cor, stone me, that's the best news I've 'eard in ages.'

'So you don't really need to report him to my father, do you?' Dolly suggested, unable to bear the thought of this disgusting event being made public. 'As he isn't going to be working here any more?'

'You're right, I don't,' Sadie said, standing up as though to leave.

'Feeling better now?' Dolly forced herself to ask, longing to be rid of her.

'Much better, ta, Miss Dolly,' she said. 'Thanks for listening.'

'No trouble.'

'Us gels have to stick together against men like 'im, don't we?'

'Yes,' replied Dolly, struggling against a feeling of violent malevolence towards this messenger of doom. *It isn't Sadie's fault you've made a fool of yourself*, she told herself silently.

Frank Mitchell was waiting for Sadie behind the swing doors at the top of the stairs. 'Well?' he asked.

'She fell for it hook, line and sinker, sir,' chirped Sadie.

'Good girl.'

'Bill Drake's right out of the running if I'm any judge.'

Frank handed her an envelope. 'Payment in full,' he said.

'Thanks very much, sir,' she said, slipping it into her overall pocket. 'Always glad to be of service.'

'Not a word to a soul though.'

''Course not, sir,' she was able to say truthfully, for her life wouldn't be worth living if the others found out what she'd been up to. Bill Drake was very popular in the factory.

'Off you go back to work now then.'

'Right yer are, sir,' she said, and tripped lightly down the stone stairs. *Not a bad half hour's work*, she thought. Not only had she ousted the competition for Bill Drake's affections but, more importantly, she could afford to have her hair done *and* buy one of those low-waisted frocks that were all the rage.

Dolly was sitting at her desk stupefied. She didn't want to

believe Sadie's story, but how could it not be true when she'd seen first-hand evidence of the girl's distress? Part of Dolly wanted to see Bill with an aching urgency; the other part never wanted to see him again. Physically weakened by shock, she felt unable to do anything for the moment but sit at her desk, trembling.

It was in this dazed condition that Frank found her. 'What's the matter, Doll?' he asked with convincing innocence. 'You're looking a bit pale.'

She was so deep in despair, his presence barely registered.

'Dolly . . .' he said when she didn't reply.

'Oh . . . hello, Frank,' she said dully, without looking up.

'Aren't you well?'

Emotional agony had drained her strength. She needed to get away from the factory, to gather her scrambled thoughts, but she didn't even feel able to walk across the room. 'I'm not feeling too good as a matter of fact,' she uttered at last.

'What's the trouble?'

'I think I've a fluish cold coming on.' She stood up on jelly legs, gripping the desk for support. 'I think I'd better go home.'

'I'll take you in the motor.'

'There's no need,' she said, 'a walk in the fresh air will do me good.'

'You don't seem up to it, to me,' he said, slipping a supportive arm around her and easing her back on to the chair as she swayed. 'You sit there while I get your 'at and coat.'

She was feeling so utterly wretched it was immaterial to her how she got home. 'All right, Frank,' she said wearily. 'I'd better tell Daddy that I'm leaving early though.'

'I'll take care of everything,' he interjected, congratulating himself on the efficient way he was carrying out Henry's plan right down to the very last detail. 'Don't you worry about a thing.'

'Thanks, Frank.'

A few minutes later she left the office with him, far too preoccupied with her own misery to notice the proprietary way he was behaving towards her.

Still reeling from the shock of Henry Slater's allegations against Dolly, Bill worked numbly in the Thames-side yard, the air heavy with the stench of river mud exposed at low tide. He was loading tea chests that had been brought up to the bank by the bargees in horsedrawn carts, on to a wooden trolley to take into the factory.

For all that he was determined not to believe Henry Slater, doubts were gaining credence with him by the second. After all, Dolly and Frank hadn't lacked for opportunity. Frank was round at her place nearly every night of the week – he'd often been there when she'd got back from meeting Bill – she'd told him so herself. Her parents had probably gone to bed and left them alone together, being as Mitchell was like one of the family.

He himself had been so besotted with her, he'd swallowed her story of a platonic relationship. Now, in the light of this new development, it seemed ludicrously far-fetched to suppose that Mitchell, or any other man for that matter, would be content with the kind of friendship Dolly had talked about.

Come to think of it, she'd seemed strange at their last couple of meetings – quiet and preoccupied. He'd put it down to last-minute nerves at leaving home under such dramatic circumstances. Now it seemed more likely to have been an uneasy conscience at having let things go so far when she'd had no intention of going ahead with their plans.

Oh, well, he'd soon know the truth. He'd confront her with it when he met her in the park this evening. There would be no point in her denying it, if what her father said was true.

It had been a golden autumn day but now the afternoon was heading towards evening. A grey mist was forming in patches as the hazy sunshine sank out of view, leaving the air damp and raw. The opposite bank was shadowy but lights could be seen coming on in the buildings. He pushed the loaded trolley across the yard towards the factory, the wheels crunching on the cobbled ground. The voices of his workmates calling to each other echoed in the moist air, but Bill hardly noticed.

The sound of footsteps from the front of the building caught his attention. He heard a familiar female voice mingled with deeper male tones. Recklessly he abandoned the trolley and hurried towards the sound. Dolly and Frank Mitchell had emerged from Slater's front entrance and were heading across the forecourt towards Mitchell's Ford which was parked near to where Bill was standing. Mitchell's arm was around Dolly's shoulders and he was speaking to her in a low voice, his head bent towards her.

Bill stared at them, hating what he saw but unable to look away. Dolly's head was bowed but when she looked up Bill could see that she had the ashen look of sickness – *or pregnancy*. It was like looking at a stranger. This grey-faced woman, so lovingly supported by Mitchell, wasn't the same sunny-smiled girl he had loved all summer.

As they drew near, she looked up and saw Bill standing there in the mist. She stopped in her tracks and looked directly at him. But there was no secret message for him as there usually was when others were present. Her expression was ice-cold – as though they had shared nothing. For a moment he thought he saw pain and accusation in her eyes, but probably it was just her guilt.

Unable to bear it, he turned away and walked back to where he'd left the loaded trolley. He didn't stop but marched right on, past his workmates – deaf to their warning cries. Without looking back he made his way across the cobblestones and out of the factory gates, open while unloading was in progress.

Vision blurred by tears, his whole body throbbing with humiliation, he walked along the waterfront, past factories, houses, a bakery, a brewery, a row of cottages. Crossing the creek by the wooden footbridge, he walked along the river-side mall until he came to a quiet spot where he sat on the damp grassy bank staring vacantly at the muddy river bed.

Well, at least he knew where he stood. No need to confront Dolly now. The truth couldn't have been plainer if she'd sent him a letter. She'd had guilt written all over her. How foolish he'd been not to realise that all the time she had been pretending to love him, Frank Mitchell had been the real man in her life.

She had made all the running at the beginning. It should have been obvious to him that he was just her bit on the side. How could he have been naive enough to believe that the boss's daughter would be serious about a labourer? Because he had wanted to believe it, that was why. He still wished it was possible.

Aware that he was wiping a tear from his cheek with the back of his hand, he pulled himself in check, male pride rallying. 'No woman's worth it,' he muttered into the mist. 'No woman's gonna make a fool out of me. Real men don't cry, especially over some tart. Why, my dad would turn in his grave!'

There and then he made some resolutions. Never again would he allow himself to become this vulnerable to the female of the species. He would use them as Dolly had used him. He was finished with being a giver. Takers were the winners in this world. People who used every opportunity to their own advantage, regardless of the feelings of others – they were the ones who ran companies. Good-hearted blokes like himself spent their lives labouring for them. Not Bill! No more! He was going to move heaven and earth to get on. He wasn't going to wait for a chance to come his way either, he would make his own luck.

He was finished at Slater's for good. He didn't want to be anywhere near Dolly and her lover, not even to work out his notice. He'd call in at the wages office for his cards tomorrow morning and make a new start at Webb's next week as arranged.

What was more, he was going to move into the place in Battersea without Dolly. It would do until he could afford something better. His mother was expecting him to leave home and was used to the idea. He'd make a new life for himself the other side of the river. He'd show Dolly Slater he was worth something. One of these days she'd rue the day she discarded Bill Drake!

Getting to his feet, he brushed himself down and began to walk home, wishing he didn't still love her so much.

That evening Dolly sat by her bedroom window staring vacantly across the garden. She'd told the family she felt fluish – this way she wasn't expected to eat anything or show her face downstairs. It was true that she didn't feel well. He throat was sore with tension and her head was throbbing.

Even now she was nursing a feeble hope that Bill might come to the house to find her after she'd failed to turn up for their meeting in the park. But of course he wouldn't have kept their date either for he was obviously aware that she knew what he'd done to Sadie. It had been in his eyes this afternoon in the yard. She'd never forget the way he'd looked at her – so cold and uncaring – before he'd turned away like a guilty schoolboy.

Sadie had probably told him she'd spilled the beans as some kind of warning. Apparently he'd caused a stir at the factory soon after that too. Ken said he'd walked out in the middle of unloading without a word of explanation. If that wasn't further evidence of his guilt, she didn't know what was.

What a blessing she'd found out the sort of man he was before burning her boats and going to live with him. Even if he had taken things as far as marriage, which she now doubted, what sort of a life would she have had with someone who couldn't be faithful to one woman?

But for all the arguments against him, she still loved him with a hopeless passion and knew that if he appeared at this moment and asked her to go with him, she would. She wouldn't be able to help herself. But he wasn't here and was never likely to be. How stupid she'd been to think that someone as ordinary as her could satisfy a man like him when there were far more sexy and exciting females around.

Anyway, it was over and life had to go on. Without him, though, she didn't know how.

Her mother entered the room. 'How are you feeling, dear?' she asked.

'I'll live.'

'Why aren't you in bed?'

'I'm more comfortable sitting here.'

'You should get into bed in the warm if you're going down with 'flu.'

'I will do, later.'

'Frank's come to see you,' said Edie. 'He's waiting downstairs.'

'Oh, no.'

'He's brought you some grapes.'

'Can you tell him I said thank you, please, Mother?'

'Wouldn't it be better if he brought them up to you?' Edie suggested. 'You can thank him yourself then.'

'No, please don't bring him up.'

'He's devoted to you, you know, dear.'

'Is he?'

'Of course.'

'I don't feel up to seeing him at the moment,' said Dolly.

'Shall I tell him you'll see him tomorrow if you're feeling better?'

'If you wish,' sighed Dolly, too miserable to care if she was being manipulated into something she didn't want with Frank Mitchell. She didn't give a damn what happened to her now!

Chapter Five

'Who's that girl over there?' asked Bill, glancing across Webb's yard from the loading bay where he was busy stacking huge parcels of packet tea into a delivery van.

'The guvnor's daughter,' replied his workmate, Alf.

'I've not seen her around here before,' remarked Bill, watching a smart young woman stride across the cobbles towards Ernie Webb's top-range Morris which was parked in the corner of the yard.

'She's not often been to the factory,' said Alf casually. 'It's no place for a kid, is it?'

'A kid?' said Bill in surprise.

'Not now, of course,' corrected Alf. 'She's grown up since I last saw her – quite the young lady, in fact.'

'How old do you reckon she is?'

'Ooh . . . she must be about nineteen or twenty.'

'What's her name?'

'Jean.' Alf gave his pal a shrewd look. 'You'll be out o' luck there though, mate.'

'You think so?'

'I know so,' affirmed Alf. 'The guvnor might be a real gent, in a league of his own as far as bosses go, but he wouldn't stand for one of his workers sniffin' round his daughter.'

'Oh, well, you never know yer luck,' said Bill with a wicked grin.

'She's the Webbs' only child,' warned Alf, 'and from what I've heard, they worship the ground she walks on.'

'Don't worry, Alf,' laughed Bill, 'I'm not plannin' any mischief.'

'I hope you're not, mate,' said Alf, shaking his head gravely, ''cos you could find yourself out o' work if you mess about with the likes of 'er.'

'I've no intention of losing my job,' said Bill in a confident manner.

The Webb Tea Company was the thriving though relatively small firm that Bill had been with for two years. During this time he had been unsparing in his efforts to elevate his position from labourer. He'd stayed on after hours without extra pay or complaint, kept the yard spotless, he'd even worked nights to paint the inside of the factory and thus prove his interest in the firm. His spare time had been expended on broadening his knowledge of the tea business by reading trade magazines and library books about the whole process of tea manufacture, right through from growing to blending to retailing.

Now, at twenty-one, with seven years' experience in the trade, he knew he had a valuable contribution to make, far beyond the range of his present duties. He had sound ideas for increasing business which would benefit any tea merchant. Given the opportunity, he could really put Webb's on the map.

But he'd gone as far as he could with just hard work. Now he needed that something extra which would provide him with the opportunity to put his theories into practice. Not an easy thing to come by. Management wouldn't listen to a factory hand. You needed status to make your point. The minute he'd clapped eyes on the boss's daughter, he'd glimpsed the key to that very thing. As a labourer to Ernie Webb he had no credibility whatsoever; as a son-in-law it would be very different . . .

A little over ambitious perhaps, but the sort of rewards he was after didn't come from having low expectations. Anyway, the man he was now was very different to the thickhead Dolly Slater had made such a monkey of. At that time he'd had no perception of his own potential; he'd not realised just how keen his brain was or that he was attractive to women without really trying – a valuable combination which could bring the unattainable within his reach. In stripping away his youthful illusions and motivating him to succeed, Dolly had actually done him a favour.

Conscience twinged as he embarked on this line of thought because unscrupulousness wasn't inherent in his nature, and had only developed after he had been so deeply humiliated by Dolly Mitchell as she now was. To this day he couldn't think of her dispassionately; he was still full of hatred for her even though he knew he shouldn't waste his energy. She probably never gave him a thought. Too busy with her husband and family – he'd seen the announcement of her second child's birth in a trade magazine recently.

Even though he'd known it was going to happen, it had still hurt when a mate from Slater's had told him that Dolly had got married, just after he himself left the firm. Nowadays the rare news he had of Slater's came through the trade, and was only about business. He'd not seen Dolly from that day to this. Nor did he want to.

But this was no time to be dwelling on the past. He had his future to consider. Somehow he had to get himself a date with Jean Webb. Not the simplest thing in the world for a man in his lowly position who could claim no shared interest beyond Webb's with which to introduce himself. There were only two things that were going to do it for him – his sex appeal and an enormous amount of cheek.

'I'll be back in a minute,' he said to Alf, and before his mate could stop him he was dodging round the van and hurrying across the yard, the crunch of his boots on the cobbles resounding in the smoky autumn afternoon.

'Hello there,' he said, catching up with the girl before she reached the car where the Webb's uniformed chauffeur was waiting, leaning against the bonnet, all peaked cap and polished buttons.

She turned to Bill with an uncertain smile. 'Hello,' she said, her deep brown eyes resting on him quizzically.

'I understand you're Jean Webb?'

'That's right,' she said in softly spoken tones.

'My name's Bill Drake,' he announced, producing his most charming smile.

Looking somewhat bewildered by this unexpected intrusion, she said politely, 'I'm very pleased to meet you.'

'Likewise,' he said with a roguish grin.

An awkward silence fell as neither knew quite what to say next.

'I've not seen you at the factory before,' he put in quickly, to stop her from walking away.

'No, Daddy has never encouraged it,' she explained.

'Oh . . . why's that?'

'When I was younger I suppose he thought I'd get in the way.'

'And now?'

'Now that I'm not likely to get into mischief I'm welcome to come along whenever I like,' she said, her gentle smile revealing small white teeth.

'You're not going to be working here then?' he said, remembering how hard Dolly had worked for her father.

'No, I just popped in with some papers Daddy needed,' she explained. 'He's old-fashioned, doesn't think my mother and I should have to slave away in the family business.'

'Nice work if you can get it,' said Bill saucily.

'Indeed,' she said, looking somewhat bemused by his direct manner.

Observing her at close range, Bill noticed that she was fashionably dressed in a royal blue coat and close fitting hat. She was slim and rather frail-looking. She was no great beauty, her face was rather ordinary: small, with a wide mouth that turned up at the corners. But there was a natural warmth about her that he found appealing.

'Have you been with the firm long?' she asked.

'Two years.'

'Really?'

'Only labouring though,' he said with just enough humility to gain her sympathy, not so much as to make him appear wet.

'I'm quite sure my father values your services whatever you do,' she said diplomatically, because she had been raised to treat all her father's employees with respect.

As their eyes met Bill felt that vital connection. He tingled with excitement. He was on his way. There was still a long way to go but at least now he had something to work on, even if it was only a spot of sexual chemistry.

The chauffeur, who had opened the car door for Jean and closed it again, sauntered towards them, eyeing Bill with disapproval.

'Is this fellow bothering you, Miss Jean?' he asked arrogantly.

'No, not at all,' she said.

But the driver wasn't convinced. He turned to Bill and said out of the side of his mouth, 'Sling yer hook, mate, and stop bothering the lady.'

'Wait for me in the car, please, Jacobs,' said Jean Webb firmly, 'I'll come when I'm ready.'

'But, Miss . . .'

'Please do as I say.'

Alone with Bill, she said in a curt tone that caused him to think he had misread her earlier response: 'What exactly do you want from me?'

'Want?'

'Yes, want. You must have something in mind to have approached me in such an obvious way.'

Taken aback by her forthright manner, he wasn't sure how to reply. Deciding that his best bet was boldness, he said, 'You're right, I do want something . . . I want to know you better and since I'm never likely to be formally introduced, I thought I'd better chance my arm and do it myself.'

She laughed. 'Well, at least you're honest.'

He waited, looking into her face, willing her to continue.

'I'm very pleased you did,' she said at last, and this time the message in her eyes could not be mistaken.

'That's really made my day.' He smiled, hardly able to believe how easy it had been to break the ice.

'So, what happens now then?' she asked pertly.

'Well, how about us going out together one evening?' he said, really pushing his luck and adding with a deliberate note of uncertainty, 'though I don't suppose your father would allow that . . .'

'You leave Daddy to me,' she said, grinning. 'When exactly did you have in mind?'

Dolly's spirits did a familiar dive as she heard Frank's key in the lock. Her only consolation was the fact that the evening was almost over and she hadn't seen him since he'd left the house to go to work that morning. It was a shocking testimony to their marriage but she preferred her own company to Frank's for they shared no common interests or opinions. The truth was that Frank *had* no opinions of his own, and was merely the voice of her father.

But she shouldn't complain for she had only herself to blame. Since she'd been pathetic enough to allow herself to be bullied into marriage with him while still in shock after the affair with Bill Drake, she must accept the consequences. It had seemed like the right thing to do at the time. Her father had arranged everything around her and she hadn't had the strength to resist. In fact she'd felt too ill to care about anything very much for a long time after the affair had ended, and she still wasn't completely over it. Even now, an aching loneliness for Bill caught her when she was off guard, despite the fact that she detested the man.

By the time she had recovered sufficiently to take an interest in life again, the ghastly mistake had been made. So she counted her blessings and tried to make the best of things. After all, Frank was not a cruel man. He was simply not very bright. And there was much for Dolly to be thankful for. She'd been blessed with a son, Barney, who would be two next spring, and a daughter, Merle, who was three months old. They were Dolly's raison d'être. Then there was her home, a comfortable detached house in a pleasant tree-lined street not far from her parents. It had been a wedding present from them.

It seemed awfully ungrateful, but she'd have preferred to strive to make their own way rather than have it all done for them, especially as she knew that her father had set them up in a home for his own ends. Firstly because a man in his position was expected to be seen to provide a substantial wedding present for his daughter, but more importantly because this way both she and Frank remained under his control.

Frank's grovelling gratitude to Daddy made her skin crawl. Her husband might be very well paid but he gave two hundred per cent to the job, always at her father's beck and call, evenings – weekends – anytime. Respect for Frank might have come easier for Dolly had he occasionally shown some spirit by standing up to Henry. But she knew he never would. Not because he was afraid but because he was happy with the way things were.

Bill Drake might have been morally degenerate but at least he was nobody's lap dog. Annoyed with herself for making such a comparison, she turned off the dance music on the wireless and braced herself to greet her husband as he entered the room.

'Hello, Frank, had a good day?'

'Not bad,' he said, removing his jacket and unfastening his tie before lowering his enormous bulk into an armchair. 'How about you?'

The question was a habit rather than a genuine enquiry for Frank took no interest in family life.

'All right, thanks.' She didn't bother to add the little titbits of maternal ordinariness that had been at the centre of her day, such as Barney cutting another tooth and Merle being tetchy with colic, because Frank would be bored rigid by such domestic trivia.

'Have you been for a few drinks?' she asked without reproach for she accepted the fact that Frank was more at home in the masculine atmosphere of a pub or club than his own sitting room. Most of his evenings were spent in such places, quite often with her father.

He nodded. 'Your dad wanted to talk business so we went down the Black Lion for a couple.'

'You had something to eat?' she asked dutifully.

'Yeah, I stopped off for pie and mash on the way home.' He disliked being tied to family mealtimes and usually ate out of an evening.

'So what's new at the factory?' she asked, to make

conversation and also because she was still interested in the family business and missed her involvement in it.

'Nothing in particular that I know of,' he said, yawning.

'There must be something . . .'

'Only the same old things,' he said in a bored tone. 'Us trying to keep ahead of the competition. There's so many tea merchants in business in London now and they all seem to be introducing cheaper and cheaper blends to attract custom.'

'Why doesn't Daddy introduce a new economy blend and spend some money to promote it?'

'Dunno.'

'He'll have to move with the market if he wants to stay on top.'

'The boss knows what he's doing,' Frank said with his usual devotion to Henry.

'There's plenty of things he can do to bring in more business,' said Dolly chattily.

'Mmm.'

'It's about time the firm did away with horse-drawn delivery vans and changed over to motor vehicles,' she went on, despite his lack of interest. 'A more efficient delivery service is bound to find favour with grocers and corner shops.'

'Mmm . . . yeah,' he mumbled absently.

'They probably wouldn't be much more expensive to run, not when you take into account the cost of hiring horses,' she persisted, because she was hungry for adult conversation and Slater's was about the only topic she and Frank could talk about, since he wasn't interested in her or the children. 'Father could have the name "Slater" painted in really bold letters.'

'Dunno if he'd wanna do that.'

'The more promotion they see, the more confident the grocers will be of sales and the more orders will come in.'

Frank lit a cigarette and leaned back in the chair. 'It's no good talkin' to me about it, Doll,' he said. 'I don't run the bloomin' firm.'

Oh, how she longed for a lively, two-sided chat. 'No, but you do have a brain,' she said, unable to stifle her impatience any longer. 'So what do you think about my suggestions?'

'I'm not paid to think about company policy.'

'You must have an opinion though?' she said, hoping to rouse him to some show of sentiment. 'You've been in the tea trade long enough to know a good bit about it.'

'Yeah, but that don't mean I wanna bother my 'ead about what's right for the firm,' he said evenly. 'That's Henry's job.'

'Don't you have *any* ideas of your own?' she snapped.

'Not really,' he said, seeming oblivious to her irritation. 'As long as Henry is 'appy with the way I am, then that's all that matters to me since he's the one who pays my wages.'

The sad thing was, thought Dolly, that Frank wasn't being deliberately aggressive or trying to make a point. He was simply stating the facts as he saw them.

'Debate is the spice of life, so they say,' she said.

'Is it?' he replied in a perfunctory manner, almost as

though she'd commented on the weather.

Oh, well, we're all what we are, she thought, and said, 'Fancy a cup of cocoa?'

'Yes, please, ducks,' he said, leaning back in the chair and closing his eyes. 'If you're making one.'

In the kitchen she clenched her fists and ground her teeth in sheer frustration. Marriage to someone to whom she was not suited was crippling her. But she'd not let it turn her into a vegetable. Never in a million years!

'Have you ever thought of widening the distribution area of the company, Mr Webb?' asked Bill, observing his host across the Webbs' dinner table, beautifully laid with chinaware and linen of a quality previously unknown to Bill.

'Go further out to the new suburbs, you mean?' said Ernie Webb after a thoughtful silence; the fact that Bill was a guest in his house dictated a certain tolerance towards this rather impudent suggestion.

'Yeah, and beyond that too,' said Bill. 'I'm talking about building up a distribution network to cover the whole country eventually.'

They were at the dessert stage of the meal, having stumbled awkwardly through two courses of polite conversation. Bill had just decided to take the bull by the horns and display the most outrageous nerve which would either set Jean's parents against him forever or make them realise that not only was he worthy of their daughter's attention, but was wasted in a labouring job. His palms were damp with nervous perspiration for he believed his whole future depended on the outcome of this first social meeting with the Webbs.

Until this evening his acquaintance with them had consisted of a brief exchange of pleasantries when he'd called for Jean at the family house in Putney. Now, dining with them at their invitation, he knew he was on trial. If they suspected that he was potentially harmful to their daughter, they would find a way to stop her seeing him no matter how keen she was on him. But they need have no fear. A means to an end she certainly was, but that didn't mean Jean wouldn't receive his utmost consideration and respect.

It was two months since that first meeting with her and Bill had been seeing her on a regular basis. They'd gone out to the cinema and to shows. If the weather was dry on a Sunday afternoon they might walk by the river locally or go up west to Hyde Park. He wasn't proud of himself for using her for personal gain, for they had really hit it off and he liked her a lot. Having a similar sense of humour they had a great many laughs and were easy in each other's company. The magic he had felt with Dolly was absent, of course. He couldn't imagine anyone affecting him so profoundly again.

Jean was warmhearted and good fun and she made no secret of the fact that she was more than a little sweet on Bill. She boosted his confidence by making him feel important. Sometimes they were so happy together, he forgot that she was merely his way to better things. He had no illusions about her parents though; had she not been so very keen on him, they would never have allowed him through the front door, let alone a place at their table.

Whilst Ernie Webb was a cut above Henry Slater as far as consideration to his workers was concerned, Bill *was* just a labourer and, as such, hardly suitable company for their daughter.

But fortunately for Bill this was counteracted by the fact that both Ernie and his wife, Lily, idolised their daughter. If having a factory hand as a boyfriend made her happy then they would go along with it up to a point, hoping, he guessed, that she would soon tire of him.

'No, I can't say I've ever given that sort of expansion any serious consideration,' said Ernie Webb, a round, avuncular man with twinkling blue eyes and fair hair dusted with silver.

'Any particular reason why not?' asked Bill, fully aware of the fact that he had completely overstepped the mark as a factory hand and hoping that, as a dinner guest, he might get away with it.

Ernie and his wife exchanged surprised glances at the impertinence of the question.

'Probably because we've always managed to earn a very good living from serving our customers in the London area,' retorted Ernie.

'And you're content with that?'

'Of course,' said Ernie. 'My grandfather started the firm as a London company back in the last century. I see no reason to alter things.'

'Things have changed a lot since your grandfather's time though, haven't they, sir?' said Bill with courteous insistence.

'The world is always changing, lad.'

'That's true enough,' he said, his nerves jangling as he continued with this gamble, 'but the advances in technology this century have been enormous, especially since the war.'

'Perhaps,' said Ernie.

'The improvement in transport has opened up all sorts of new opportunities for business . . .'

'You seem to know a lot about it.'

'Yes, I've read quite a bit, sir.'

'Indeed.'

'But I suppose it stands to reason that the market place would widen,' Bill went on. 'I mean, they didn't have motor vehicles in your grandfather's day.'

'How true,' the other man agreed, his eyes registering a kind of shocked amusement at the cheek of the fellow.

'Just think how easy it is to get about now compared to those days,' said Bill.

'It may very well be, but it certainly wouldn't be easy to forge new territory further afield,' said Ernie, impressed with Bill despite himself.

'By no means impossible though,' continued Bill, confidence boosted by the joy of giving voice to something he really believed in.

'Since you seem to know so much about it, young man,' said Ernie, deciding to find out if there was anything of substance beyond his unshakable enthusiasm, 'how would you suggest we set about it?'

'I'd say you'd study the map for highly populated districts, then send a salesman in to open them up for Webb's.'

'What should our very first move be then?' asked Ernie, to test him.

'Well, I reckon you should choose somewhere like Birmingham, for instance . . . that's a densely populated place . . . and send a man up there with plenty of product samples and promotional material to help the grocers pull in sales initially,' he suggested brightly. 'Once shopkeepers realise they have a quality product to sell, at a reasonable price and a good profit for them, they'll push it and come back for more.'

'Just like that,' said Ernie with a touch of sarcasm.

'No, o' course there'd be more to it than that,' said Bill spiritedly, 'but basically it's a matter of getting Webb's tea on to the shelves, isn't it? A good product will sell itself eventually but if no one outside London knows about it, they can't very well buy it, can they?'

'Bill's right, Daddy,' said Jean, smiling proudly.

'When you've established a customer base in the new district, you could open a depot there,' Bill suggested eagerly. 'Then you could move into other towns.'

'I notice you say "when" and not "if",' Ernie pointed out.

'Why not, when you're confident of your product?' he said. 'All that's needed is a little aggressive marketing.'

'You make it sound so simple,' sighed Ernie. 'If you worked in management you'd realise that these things are not so easy.'

'I didn't say it would be easy,' Bill pointed out. 'But I certainly think it's worth a try.'

'There are far too many tea merchants competing for

space on the grocers' shelves,' said Ernie.

'All the more reason for Webb's to get in there and fight for a place,' replied Bill. 'Why sit back and let the big boys have the lion's share of the market forever?'

Ernie was a quiet, unassuming man. Had he not inherited the firm from his father he would never have had the courage or initiative to start up in business himself. Over the years he had become an adequate tea merchant but he was not a true entrepreneur which was why he admired the pioneering spirit in others. Recalling Bill Drake's efforts for Webb's over the last couple of years, and listening to him now, he saw something rare in his daughter's boyfriend who obviously had more than one would normally expect from a labourer. 'I suppose there might be something in what you say,' he conceded.

'No suppose about it, sir.' Bill turned his attention to Lily, an elegant, softly spoken woman with rich brown hair and the same dark eyes as her daughter. 'What do you think about it, Mrs Webb?'

'I'm sure my husband knows his own business best,' she said, in a tone that, whilst not unpleasant, gave Bill a sharp reminder of his position outside their family circle.

'Yeah, o' course he does . . . I wasn't suggesting otherwise.' Damn and blast, he'd blown it by going too far. But if he changed tack now he'd lose credibility with them altogether.

'Good, I'm glad about that,' Lily said in a neutral tone.

'I still think that expansion would be a good thing for Webb's though,' persisted Bill, sensing that time was rapidly running out.

'We could lose money if it failed,' said Ernie.

'There always a risk of that in any business, I suppose,' agreed Bill amiably, 'but that would be lessened if you were to send someone out to test the water before laying out real money . . .'

Lily chewed her food thoughtfully. Although she was certain that Bill Drake was seeking to better himself through her daughter, there was a freshness and sincerity about him that she found appealing; maybe because she had not been blessed with the son she'd always wanted. At least he wasn't being obsequious towards Ernie and herself, which he would have had he been after Jean simply for her money. It was an opportunity to prove himself he was seeking, if she was any judge.

For all his gall, he seemed acutely vulnerable somehow, sitting there in an ill-fitting, navy blue suit and stiff-collared shirt, his dark hair heavily oiled into place. Whilst knowing he had an eye to the main chance, she sensed that he didn't have it in him to hurt Jean.

'You seem like the sort of chap who would enjoy that kind of a challenge, Bill,' she said in a friendlier tone.

'Not 'alf,' he said, eager and flushed. 'You want new customers, I'll get 'em for you.'

'I believe you would too,' mumbled Ernie, non-committally.

'Remember what they say,' said Bill, in a deliberate show of persistence. 'A business that stands still today goes backwards tomorrow.'

Husband and wife exchanged glances, Lily raising her brows slightly.

108

'In future, perhaps I'd better come to you for business advice, instead of consulting my experienced colleagues,' said Ernie with mild sarcasm though Bill detected a stirring of interest too.

'You could do a lot worse,' he said, smarting at his own cheek.

'Well, I think we've had enough of business talk for one mealtime,' intervened Lily as an awkward silence fell.

'Quite right, Mummy,' agreed Jean, though she thought Bill had been wonderfully impressive.

'So can I tempt you to another helping of apple crumble, Bill?' said Lily.

'Yes, please, Mrs Webb, it's really delicious,' he said because he knew it would please her. But he was actually feeling so sick with dread because he feared he'd been too pushy and ruined everything, he didn't know how he would manage it.

Somehow he did and the conversation became general. When asked about his family background he held nothing back.

'I live in grotty rooms not far from the factory,' he told them. 'My mother and stepfather live in even grottier ones in a backstreet in Hammersmith where I was brought up. I couldn't stay on at school 'cos my mum needed me to be earning.' He became suddenly spiky and defensive. 'Just because I spend my days moving tea chests about the factory doesn't mean I'm a dimwit, you know.'

'Far from it,' agreed Jean ardently.

'I think we've all gathered that much about you, Bill,' said Lily, smiling at him.

* * *

When the meal was over, Ernie and Bill retired to the drawing room for port and cigars. Being unused to such a refined custom but not wishing to upset his host by declining, Bill choked and turned green on a full Corona.

'Sorry,' he said, recovering at last, his eyes streaming, 'but a labourer's wage packet doesn't run to this sort of thing.'

'I don't suppose we'll have any trouble replacing you, for all that,' said Ernie, relaxing in a brown leather armchair and observing Bill through a pall of cigar smoke.

'Replacing me?' he exclaimed with unconcealed disappointment. Sod it! He'd gone too far and put himself out of work.

'That's right,' said Ernie, beaming at him through the fog. 'Somebody has to do the heavy work while you're out telling the world about the Webb Tea Company.'

Chapter Six

That winter was very bleak indeed for Bill. Breaking new ground for Webb's proved to be far more difficult than he could possibly have imagined, and he soon learned that life away from the common herd could be extremely lonely.

With ruthless dedication he peddled his wares from grocery store to corner shop. But as weeks turned to months his order book still had little to show for his efforts. Despite the shiny new factories that had proliferated over the last few years, using electricity and scientific ideas developed during wartime to manufacture cars, aeroplanes and a variety of other modern products, unemployment was still a major problem. Some of the smaller grocers could barely afford to keep their shops stocked with known brands of tea, let alone a label they had never heard of.

Fortunately for Bill, Webb's had supplied him with a small motor car which meant he could travel to outlying village stores, albeit that the machine frequently broke down in the middle of nowhere leaving him stranded in freezing weather.

Some nights as he lay in a cold bed in some cheerless boarding house, after a day of rejection from grocers with rent arrears and natural hostility towards salesmen, he would find himself looking back on his labouring days with nostalgia. Why was he burdening himself with such punishing responsibility when he could be doing nothing more worrying than lifting tea chests about all day? Sheer bloody stubbornness probably, he thought. He'd engineered this chance for himself and he was damned if he'd admit defeat.

'Getting a foot in the door with grocers is the biggest problem,' he wrote to Jean one bitter February night, 'but if I can manage to persuade them to let me put on a tea tasting for their customers, I usually get an order because the product is good and people like what they taste. I suspect that some of the grocers only let me do it to save their own tea supplies for their staff cuppa, but it's worth it if it gets me an order. I miss you lots and am hoping to get back to London for a weekend to see you soon.'

He wasn't spinning her a line. He wasn't passionately in love with Jean, but her letters and the thought of her warm and tender company comforted him during the long lonely evenings huddled over a bedroom gasfire with his chilblains throbbing while he did his paperwork.

All over the Black Country he travelled, to every town and village, forcing his message through to disinterested grocers and telephoning London with any orders he did manage to win. The tea was sent by rail and collected at the station by Bill who delivered it in his car. It was not an ideal arrangement but until they had enough business to warrant a depot or factory in the area, it was adequate. His visits home to London were few and fleeting, for he worked to a gruelling schedule, allowing himself very little time off.

His unstinting efforts were eventually rewarded; the spasmodic trickle of orders began to gather momentum. A year after he'd started work in the Midlands, he was recalled to London and told that Webb's were going to open a depot in Birmingham to supply the area direct. Bill expected to be offered the job of setting up and managing the new project. But Ernie had other ideas.

'I'm not going to make you depot manager,' he explained in his office one day soon after Bill's return, 'for the very good reason that you are far too useful to us as a salesman.'

'You don't want me back labouring then?' said Bill jokingly.

'Not likely,' said Ernie. 'I want you in sales and marketing. Now you've shown us what you can do, we'll want you to open up other areas. It'll mean your being away a lot though, until our wider network is established, I'll be straight with you about that.'

'While we're being honest with each other,' said Bill, 'I've something to tell you.'

'Fire away then,' said Ernie good-humouredly.

'I want to marry Jean,' declared Bill. 'So . . . er . . . what are the chances of your approval?'

Ernie looked at this young man who had matured beyond his years. He had changed from a defensive young pup, out to prove himself, into a valuable asset to the company. Ernie had deliberately thrown him in at the deep end to see what he was made of. He'd supplied him with a car, some samples and sales material, and let him get on with it without leads, supervision or moral support. By sheer grit the fellow had made a substantial gain for the firm, an amazing achievement for someone without previous sales or business experience.

As a son-in-law Bill was less impressive. Strictly speaking his background ruled him out as a suitable husband for Jean. But Ernie had grown to like him, as had Lily, and they both believed he would spare no effort to make their daughter happy.

'You'll get no opposition from me, son,' said Ernie. 'I'll be pleased to have you in the family.'

'Steady on,' grinned Bill. 'I haven't even asked her yet.'

But they both knew what her answer would be.

Early in the new decade, Dolly's mind was taken off the problems of her own loveless marriage when her brother Ken followed in his sister's footsteps and embarked upon a clandestine love affair which could only bring disaster.

The object of his affection was Mabs Trump from the factory whom Dolly found to be bright, warm-hearted and extremely likeable. She was also totally lacking in the qualities stipulated by Ken's parents for a future wife for him.

Having been taken into her brother's confidence, Dolly secretly welcomed the couple into her home whenever Frank wasn't around which was most of the time. But whilst sympathetic to them, she felt duty bound to point out the grim reality of the situation when they told her one evening that they were planning to get married.

'I hate to be a prophet of doom,' she said, 'but Father will never accept Mabs into the family.'

114

'Well, it's his loss then,' said Ken hotly. 'She's every bit as good as us if not better.'

'I know that,' declared Dolly, 'but the parents have a peculiar way of viewing these things.'

'Anyway, I'm over twenty-one,' announced Ken. 'They can't stop me marrying whomever I choose.'

'Daddy can cut you off without a penny though,' said Dolly.

'Let him do it then,' he said, slipping a defensive arm around Mabs's shoulders. 'If it's a choice between the family and Mabs, there's no contest.'

Although Mabs was not given to excessive humility, she *was* worried on Ken's behalf. 'I don't want yer to break up with yer folks 'cos of me, Ken.' Her face was pale against her shock of ginger curls as she turned to Dolly. 'I warned him that carryin' on with me would mean trouble.'

Dolly looked from one to the other thoughtfully, Ken's height dwarfing Mabs, his dark sombre looks making her bright colouring seem even more dazzling. She addressed them both. 'I'm not trying to put you off, honestly, but I do think it's important you realise just what you are going to be up against . . . you'll probably both find yourselves out of work for a start.'

'So I'll get another job,' pronounced Ken.

'You won't find it easy to be an employee after being the boss's son,' Dolly wisely pointed out. 'Always supposing you can get a job with the country being in the grip of a slump.'

'I can always go out charring to keep us going,' said Mabs cheerfully. 'There's always work about for a skivvy.'

'You'll do no such thing,' protested Ken indignantly. 'It'll be my job to support us, and that's what I'll do.'

Seeing her brother behave with such uncharacteristic mettle, Dolly was delighted. Perhaps Mabs would be the making of him. Dolly had certainly never seen him show such spirit before. And the fact that Ken's probable poverty meant nothing to Mabs confirmed Dolly's belief in her sincerity.

'I'll find some way of 'elping, anyway,' said Mabs, looking up at Ken with affection. 'We're a team, you an' me, Ken. We'll get by, don't you worry.'

The sound of squeals and giggles from upstairs indicated that Dolly's children were about as sleepy as a March wind, even though they had been in bed for some time.

'Sounds like a firm hand is needed up there,' said Dolly who disliked the idea of a nanny and looked after the children herself. 'As soon as I've quietened down the little horrors, we'll have a drink to celebrate your engagement.'

'Can I come up to see the children with you?' asked Mabs.

'Of course.'

On the way upstairs, Mabs took the opportunity for a quiet word with her future sister-in-law. 'Thanks for being so good to us, Dolly,' she said. 'I just want you to know that I really do love Ken.'

'Any fool can see that,' said Dolly.

'There'll be those who'll think I'm only after him for what I can get,' she said.

My parents will be at the top of that list, thought Dolly,

116

but said, 'You'll just have to be strong, Mabs. Personally, I think this is the best thing that could have happened to Ken. It'll give him a chance to show what he's really made of. He's always let Daddy get away with far too much, humiliating him as he does.'

'No one'll do that to Ken while I'm around,' said Mabs vehemently.

'I can believe that too,' Dolly laughed, giving her arm an affectionate squeeze. 'I'm looking forward to having you as a sister-in-law. I think it's gonna be fun.'

Even tea merchants of long standing like Henry Slater were not immune to the effects of the world slump that had followed the Wall Street Crash the previous year. As the government battled against lengthening dole queues, even the most well-established grocers began to feel the pinch. A drop in takings and bad debts resulted in a shortage of money in the till with which to pay tea wholesalers on delivery in the traditional way. Henry's vanmen often had to call back several times before they obtained money that was owing. It was as nothing compared to the suffering of the poor, of course, but Henry Slater wasn't given to counting his blessings.

'As if I don't have enough on my plate trying to keep my factory running at a profit,' he ranted to Edie in the privacy of their bedroom, having that evening been introduced to his son's girlfriend and told of the couple's plans to marry, 'now my son drops this bombshell on me. A tea-packer indeed! Has he lost his mind altogether, Edie?'

'Yes, I suspect he has temporarily,' she sighed

mournfully. 'The wretched girl obviously has plans to better herself.'

'She'll be right out of luck then,' he said, pulling on a striped winceyette nightshirt. 'If he doesn't give her up I shall sack him from the company and cut him out of my will. I'll have nothing more to do with the stupid boy.'

'Isn't that a bit drastic?' said Edie, who loved her son even if she was too frightened of Henry to show it.

'He's the one who's being drastic by getting involved with a factory girl,' he said, scratching his buttocks before climbing into bed. 'So if he goes ahead with this nonsense, he'll have to take the consequences and go without the comforts of the privileged life I've provided for him. Once he realises how hard things are in the outside world, he'll soon come running back, you just wait and see.'

Edie bit her lip anxiously. 'Just the same, dear, I don't think you should do anything too hasty . . .'

'I'll do what I think is right, Edie,' he thundered.

'But to punish Ken because some trollop has her claws in him . . .'

'If he's not man enough to make up his own mind then he deserves what's coming to him. You've always been far too soft with him.'

'I . . .'

'Not another word about it, woman,' growled Henry, disappearing beneath the feather eiderdown. 'If he continues with this ridiculous affair, then he's out of our lives altogether and that's all there is to it . . . so *good night, Edie.*'

'Goodnight, dear.'

* * *

Henry lay awake mulling over this latest family crisis. What was the matter with his children? Did they have some sort of perverse need for deprivation or something? First there was Dolly and that useless labourer; now his son and a common factory hand.

After all their father had done to protect them from the low life, they repaid him by mixing with the dregs of society. Had they ever experienced poverty, they certainly wouldn't go looking for it, that much he did know. Just let Ken defy him by going ahead with his plans, and he'd soon see that his father was someone to be reckoned with . . .

Feeling nervous and depressed at the thought of a family rift, and powerless to fight back against Henry, Edie lay awake with hateful thoughts of Mabs whom she blamed entirely for bringing this trouble on them. Once she realised that Ken had nothing to offer, though, she'd soon cool off.

He wouldn't go through with it even if Mabs was to stay around, Edie told herself as she drifted off to sleep. He simply doesn't have the guts.

She'd underestimated her son, who married Mabs in the late-spring of 1930. Dolly and her children were the only members of the Slater family present at the wedding, Frank's allegiance having gone to Henry.

It was a small register office marriage. Mabs was pretty in a pink suit and flowery hat; Ken neatly turned out in a lounge suit, far removed from the formal dress he would have worn at a family-approved wedding. The ceremony was followed by a celebration meal at a local hotel after which the couple would embark upon married life in one room in a tenement house in a Hammersmith backstreet.

Despite this impecunious beginning to their life together, Dolly envied them their togetherness for seldom had she seen a more devoted and well-matched couple. Far from hiding her friendship with them from her parents, who had disowned Ken completely, Dolly defended them against bitter criticism.

The whole affair had given her a new lease of life and she'd entered into it wholeheartedly. She'd assisted them in the search for somewhere to live, scanning notice boards and the local paper. She'd helped them make a dingy room into a home by providing knick-knacks and occasional furniture from her own home. While they had been busy with paintbrush and wallpaper, she'd got to work making curtains and cushion covers.

Ken had pleasantly surprised her by rising to the occasion admirably. Using his contacts in the tea trade he had secured a position with a firm of tea merchants in Fulham. It carried less status than his job at Slater's but he seemed determined to make a success of it. Mabs had insisted on pulling her weight and had found a part-time job in a grocer's shop where they didn't mind taking on married women.

But now the wedding party was over and Dolly was sitting in a taxi with her children on their way home.

'Why didn't Grandma and Grandpa come to the party, Mummy?' asked three-year-old Barney who was a sweet-natured, intelligent little boy with a mop of dark hair, smiling brown eyes and dimples in his fat cheeks. Everyone adored Barney – he was that sort of a child.

'I expect they were busy doing something else,' fibbed Dolly.

'P'raps Auntie Mabs and Uncle Ken aren't their friends,' he chattered innocently.

'Perhaps,' mumbled Dolly evasively.

'I love Auntie Mabs,' he announced fervently.

'Good,' said Dolly, moved by his affectionate nature. 'I'm sure she loves you too.'

'Grandpa loves Merle more than he loves me, doesn't he, Mummy?' he said.

'Of course not, darling,' she said, shocked by his perception. For it was true what Barney said – her father had been besotted with his granddaughter from the minute he'd first set eyes on her. This had surprised Dolly for he'd never been fond of children and was often impatient with Barney.

'Merle is Grandpa's best girl . . . best girl . . .' she chanted in her babyish way.

'He loves you both equally,' Dolly firmly assured them.

She'd been pulled up short by her son's sensitivity though and decided to have a few strong words with her father about making his favouritism between his grandchildren so obvious. Such thoughtlessness could severely damage the unfavoured child's confidence!

Chapter Seven

'Of course, there's a great deal of scope for improvement, Mr Drake,' said Joe Baxter, as he and Bill concluded a tour of the sprawling factory buildings of the Sau Tea Company and began a trip around the plantation in a pony and trap.

'Yes, I can see that,' said Bill pointedly, wiping the sweat from his face and neck with his handkerchief. He was assailed by a rich amalgam of scents: tea, spices, flowers and strong tobacco as they headed out of the sunbaked yard where Indian labourers were busy loading tea chests on to bullock carts for transportation to the railway.

Bill was here in India to view this rundown tea estate and report back to the board of Webb's as to the viability of their buying it, thus having more direct control over their source of supply instead of relying on the vagaries of the London market in Mincing Lane. If any sort of offer was made, though, it would need to be really low, for what he had seen so far was extremely dilapidated.

The whitewashed factory complex consisted of withering sheds, where the freshly picked leaves were spread on racks to wither and remove the moisture; a rolling room where the withered leaves were crushed by rolling to release the natural juices; a fermenting room where the tea was allowed to ferment to a coppery colour before being dried by hot air to become the familiar black leaves.

There were various other buildings where the leaves were carefully sorted into grades then packed into plywood tea chests to be auctioned in Calcutta or shipped to Britain for auction in London. The structures were shabby, the machinery decrepit and the conditions for workers abysmal.

Joe Baxter, a muscular Englishman of about sixty-five with skin dark and leathery from living in a tropical climate, was in tune with Bill's thoughts. 'The place needs fresh blood to give it a new lease of life,' he said. 'I've had enough. I'm tired. Thirty years' tea growing in India is quite sufficient for me.'

'Did you ever think of putting the estate under management during that time?' asked Bill chattily.

'No, I've always enjoyed being personally involved.'

'But now?'

'Now that I'm getting on in years, all I want to do is retire to a nice little cottage in the English countryside.'

'Back to your roots, eh?'

'That's right.' He paused as the trap juddered and rocked over a crater in the track, swampy from the high rainfall of the area. This was one of the permanently green provinces in a continent where conditions were often arid. Using a stick and some strong language on the pony, Joe got the vehicle moving again. 'Horse transport probably seems primitive to you but you'd never get a motor vehicle down this track.'

'I notice you use bullocks to haul the tea.'

'Yes, most of the roads round here are made of dirt,' he explained. 'We'd be isolated altogether in the rains if it wasn't for bullock carts.'

'I can imagine.'

'The buildings and machinery might not be up to much,' admitted Joe, 'but this is prime growing land.'

'Yeah,' agreed Bill, looking across the tea-gardens. Stretching as far as the eye could see was a sea of shiny green tea bushes with stiff, pointed leaves, growing beneath Sau shade trees. The white coolie hats and turbans of the pluckers bobbed and swayed like blossom in the breeze. Local women with filled baskets on their backs were trekking to the collecting points for checking and weighing. 'The gardens are impressive, I'll grant you that.'

With a businessman's eye Bill saw a valuable acquisition for Webb's in this rich moist land, if they didn't have to pay the earth for it. From a personal perspective he saw a scene of ineffable beauty that brought a lump to his throat: glorious vistas, exotic trees, a distant mountain range reaching into a blue sky. He was a lucky man to be able to travel to such faraway places.

Quite soon after he'd married Jean, nearly four years ago, Bill had been made a director of Webb's. Eager to justify such an honour, he'd driven himself even harder to get Webb's tea into grocers and parlour stores the length and breadth of Britain. His hard work had paid off. Webb's now had depots in several of the provinces, covering much of the country.

His business flair hadn't ended there. A couple of years

ago he'd come up with the idea of a dividend tea, something to benefit the hard-up section of the public. An economical blend was launched with a stamp on the packet and the relevant savings cards distributed by grocers. It had been a great success.

The idea of Webb's expanding overseas had seemed the logical next step to Bill, and already he had a vision of this tea estate under Webb's ownership with modern machinery and equipment, good conditions for workers, decent housing for the management.

Continuing on through the estate, they came to a winding lane bordered by trees which led to the owner's bungalow where Bill was to spend the night. It was a whitewashed dwelling built high because of the rains, surrounded by a wooden terrace, and standing in flower gardens. Brightly coloured birds flew free, their calls squawking and screeching across the fields.

Bill and Joe Baxter were served tea in English style by an Indian servant in a cluttered but spotlessly clean living room furnished in heavy, masculine style. The walls were covered with ornamental plates and pictures and a tiger skin rug lay on the floor.

'Did you shoot it yourself?' asked Bill, rather unnerved by the sight of this dead thing at his feet.

'Yes,' said Joe, 'I've bagged a few in my time out here – you have to if you wanna stay alive.'

'I suppose you would do.'

'Running a tea estate is a hard life, Mr Drake,' Joe informed him seriously. 'Besides knowing how to grow tea, you have to know how to grow bamboos, build houses, make roads, not to mention being mother and father to the labour.'

'Mmm . . . I think if my company were to go ahead with this idea, I'd suggest that we put it entirely under Indian management.'

'Really?' said Joe, brows rising.

'It's the only sensible thing to do,' Bill continued. 'After all, it must be easier to train people for the job who know the country and are used to the climate. Regular visits would be made by London management, of course.'

'You are seriously considering the place then?' said Joe.

'I am interested but I don't have the final say,' explained Bill, sipping his tea while a lizard flashed up the wall and settled on the ceiling. 'I'll make a recommendation to our board. A lot depends on what you'll take for it, though, considering the amount of money that will have to spent to bring it up to scratch.'

'I'll not give it away,' said Joe firmly.

'You'll need to be realistic though,' said Bill, who had learned to be a tough negotiator. 'Anyway, that can all be thrashed out later.'

They were interrupted by a young Indian boy at the door, clutching a cable which he handed to Joe.

'For you,' he said, handing it to Bill. 'It came through to the office.'

The words on the cable swam before his eyes. 'Jean lost the baby. Sorry. Thought you should know. Lily.'

'Something wrong, old boy?' asked Joe.

Bill could feel Jean's pain as though it was his own. 'Yes . . . My wife has lost the baby we were expecting.'

'Oh, dear . . . I am sorry to hear that, old boy.'

'She was seven months pregnant.'

'Quite well on then?'

'Yeah. She'll be devastated,' said Bill, lighting a cigarette and pacing up and down. 'She wanted that baby so *much*.'

'Natural instinct for a woman, isn't it?' remarked Joe, going over to a dark wooden dresser upon which stood a tray of bottles.

'It's taken her a long time to get pregnant,' Bill told him. 'We've been married nearly four years.'

'This is a real blow then.'

'I'll say it is.' He smoked furiously, large patches of sweat soaking his shirt. 'I should have been with her. She'll be needing me.'

'You had no way of knowing it would happen . . .'

'No, of course I hadn't,' snapped Bill, aggressive with anguish, 'but that doesn't make me feel any better.'

'Here, have a brandy, old chap,' said the older man kindly. 'I think you need it.'

'Thanks, Joe,' he said, gulping the liquid. 'And sorry for bawling at you. I shouldn't have taken it out on you.'

'Don't worry about me,' said Joe. 'My shoulders are broad.'

Unable to sleep, Bill thrashed about beneath the mosquito net, cursing the heat and the fact that he was not at home with Jean. He would cut this visit short and get an earlier passage back, but he still wouldn't be with her when she needed him most.

A familiar sense of inadequacy nagged at him – a feeling

of being not quite worthy of Jean. This was something that had plagued him throughout their marriage because, despite his very best endeavours, he was still unable to feel for her as a man should feel for his wife.

His compunction for selfishly using her had increased over the years in proportion to the growth of his respect for her. He had tried to assuage his guilt by being an exemplary husband which wasn't difficult, for Jean was a dear and very easy to get along with. A devoted wife and true friend, she was staunch in her support and uncomplaining of the fact that his work took him away from home so much of the time at the moment.

But it was a woman he hated who owned the part of him that should have been Jean's. It was still the thought of Dolly that made his heart beat faster; still her who filled his dreams and woke him up in a cold sweat. He might have loathed himself less had Jean been some cold-hearted bitch who deserved to be second best.

He regularly took himself to task; told himself that the magic he associated with Dolly didn't exist and was simply the memory of first love seen through the rose-tinted lenses of hindsight; a thing unfinished. Had it run its course to become tired and ordinary, he wouldn't have been left with this emotional turmoil.

But none of this seemed to help. He could still hear Dolly's laugh; feel her warm body close to his. The memory of that terrible autumn afternoon when he had seen the truth about her and Frank Mitchell continued to haunt him.

Admonishing himself for dwelling on the past, he turned his mind to what really mattered, getting home to Jean as soon as possible. The one good thing in all this was the fact that Jean had no idea of his true feelings, and believed herself to be the one and only love of his life. He reckoned he owed her that much, and had worked hard to create this impression. If nothing else, he had achieved that!

Chapter Eight

Mabs and her son Peter visited Dolly one summer afternoon.

'We were passing the end of your street,' Mabs explained, 'so I thought I'd pop in to see if you had time for a cup o' tea and a natter.'

'I'm very glad you did – I could do with some company.' Smiling, Dolly bent down and smacked a kiss on her four-year-old nephew's cheek. 'Your cousins are out playing in the back garden, pet . . . would you like to go and join them?'

'Is grass green?' laughed Mabs, and grinning at him said, 'Off you go then, son, but try not to get too filthy out there.' The boy bounded from the room. 'A waste o' time telling 'im really . . . but you 'ave to go through the motions, don't yer, Doll, or kids start to think they can do what they like.'

'Don't they just,' she agreed.

Thoroughly at ease in her sister-in-law's company, Mabs sat down in an armchair by the sitting-room window overlooking the front gardens – awash with roses and rhododendrons and shaded at this time of day by a row of peripheral shrubs and trees. The room was pleasantly cool with cretonne-covered sofas and armchairs in warm autumn shades to match the curtains. A vase of fresh flowers stood among a gallery of family photographs on top of the piano.

The two women chatted companionably until tea was brought in by Dolly's daily maid.

'Ken keeps nagging me to get some 'elp in the 'ouse now that he's doing so well in his job,' remarked Mabs as the door closed behind the servant girl, 'but having to put up with a stranger about the place all day would drive me mad.'

'Why not just have someone for a few hours a day?' suggested Dolly.

'No, even then I wouldn't feel comfortable havin' someone else doin' me chores,' said Mabs, shaking her head. 'It's different for you, Doll, 'cos you've grown up with that sort of thing.'

'Mmm, I suppose that does make a difference,' agreed Dolly, 'but even I wouldn't want a bloomin' great brigade of servants like my mother still keeps. A day girl is quite enough for me.'

'The whole idea of live-in servants is dying out except for the very rich, accordin' to a magazine I was reading,' said Mabs casually.

'So I understand,' said Dolly. 'People just aren't going into service in the large numbers they used to. I don't blame them either if they can get more freedom and better pay in a factory.'

'So, how are yer surviving the kids' school holidays?' Mabs asked lightly.

'I should think I've gained a few early grey hairs,' laughed Dolly.

'Really?'

'If they're not mooning about saying they're bored stiff, they're up to mischief,' explained Dolly lightly. 'Barney misses the sporting activities he's involved in during term-time at school and has buckets of excess energy.'

'Yeah, I can imagine.'

'But for all that, I quite enjoy having them around during the day,' admitted Dolly, 'which probably makes me some sort of a masochist.'

'I'm not looking forward to Peter starting school next year,' confessed Mabs. 'The place'll seem like a morgue during the day without 'im.'

Dolly gave an expressive shake of the head. 'Dear, oh dear, Peter going to school . . . it only seems like yesterday I was at your wedding.'

'Six years ago now, Doll.'

'How the time flies. I can hardly believe that my two are nine and eight already.'

A similar outlook and sense of humour had led to a close friendship between Dolly and Mabs, despite their different backgrounds. As Dolly had hoped, Mabs had been the making of Ken. With her unstinting encouragement and the absence of his father's constant ridicule, his confidence had grown, enabling him to give of his best to the job and earn himself the position of general manager. The couple's lifestyle had improved accordingly and they now lived in a comfortable house some twenty minutes' walk from Dolly's.

There had been no unbending on the part of Ken's

parents, though, despite Dolly's efforts to procure a reconciliation by continuously extolling Mabs's virtues and begging them to give her a chance. She suspected that the feud was being prolonged mainly because Father feared a volte face would lessen his authority.

Mabs didn't care so much for herself but she was furious on Ken's behalf, and his parents knew it. Not the sort to acquiesce, she'd stormed round to Maybury Avenue one day and told them exactly what she thought of their malicious treatment of a son they should be proud of. Naturally it hadn't helped.

'Our neighbour sat with Pete last night while me and Ken had a night out at the pictures,' Mabs was saying, helping herself to another biscuit from the tea trolley. 'We saw Fred Astaire and Ginger Rogers in "Top Hat".'

'Was it good?'

'Lovely,' she enthused, eyes shining. 'Takes yer right out of yourself, dunnit, a night out at the flicks?' She made a disapproving face. 'Mind you, I didn't enjoy the newsreels.'

'Oh . . . why not?'

'It was all blood and guts, Doll,' she explained, frowning. 'What with 'em fighting in Spain, executing people in Russia . . . and as for that German fella, Hitler! Gawd knows what he's gonna get up to next, 'im and 'is jack-booted soldiers. He gives me the bloomin' creeps, he really does.'

'Mmm, he does seem to be in the papers a lot lately,' agreed Dolly.

'Good job it's all too far away to affect us, eh, Doll?'

'I'll say.'

'Anyway, how about you and me having a night out at the flicks sometime soon?' suggested Mabs casually. 'You could leave the kids at our place with Ken if Frank isn't around to look after 'em. They could even stay the night, they'd enjoy that.'

'I might do that,' said Dolly, knowing that Mabs was making the suggestion for her benefit.

Inevitably, without the basic elements from which to build a close relationship, Dolly and Frank had drifted apart increasingly over the years. They rarely quarrelled but neither did they do anything together. Frank went his way and she went hers, though Dolly didn't go far in the geographical sense. While he was out with his pals of an evening, she stayed home with the children.

She had retained an interest in the tea trade, though, and regretted that her position as a middle-class wife and mother prohibited her from being employed outside the home, especially now that the children were both of school age and she had time on her hands. Fortunately, her link with tea through the men in her life meant she was kept up to date. Sometimes she was even invited to give an opinion, especially by her father.

'What do you think about us introducing a new quality brand, Dolly?' he'd asked recently when she and the children were visiting her parents at Maybury Avenue. 'Something with a real touch of class.'

'Isn't high class a bit risky?' she'd said.

'Not really,' he'd said. 'I think the market can stand a more expensive blend now that unemployment is going down and the economy in general is looking healthier.'

'As long as you don't price it out of the market,' she'd warned.

'What sort of a fool do you think I am?' he'd bellowed.

'All right, all right,' she'd retorted. 'I was only being cautious.'

'We'd need a superior-sounding name to match the product,' he'd said thoughtfully.

'It'll have to have a ring to it, though,' she'd told him. 'Something catchy that will stick in people's minds.'

'Mmm . . .'

'What about Slater's Star Brew?' she proposed. 'You could have a little gold or silver star on the packet to make it more eye-catching.'

'Humph, well, we'll see about that,' he'd grunted negatively. But he *had* taken her advice and Slater's Star Brew had been successfully launched. Predictably, Henry had taken all the credit for the name, but Dolly wasn't unduly bothered. Knowing that she still had the ability to make a useful contribution was its own reward.

But now Mabs was saying, 'I shall keep you to that, Doll. You need to get out now and again to have some fun.'

Dolly couldn't agree more. As much as she loved her children, life could be awfully dull without any adult leisure pursuits. 'You're absolutely right,' she said.

'And talking of fun,' continued Mabs conversationally, 'looks like I'm gonna be having a nice fat helping o' that. Ken is taking me to a really posh do next month . . . a dinner dance.'

'Lucky thing.'

'I ain't half lookin' forward to it,' effused Mabs. 'It's the annual get-together of a tea merchant's association that his boss belongs to.'

'Should be good then,' said Dolly. 'Where are they having it?'

'In one of the West End hotels.'

'Oh, I say, you're really living it up,' said Dolly with genuine enthusiasm. 'You'll have to have a new frock for that.'

'You bet,' she agreed. 'Dress is formal so it'll have to be an evening dress.'

'Lovely!'

'As long as I don't show Ken up, though.'

'Don't be daft,' rebuked Dolly. 'As if you would.'

'Well, I'm not strictly speaking in his class, even now.'

'Ken will be proud of you,' Dolly assured her, 'and rightly so.'

'Thanks for the vote of confidence.'

'I can't remember the last time I had anything to dress up for,' Dolly said wistfully. 'Frank isn't one for joining associations. He's like Father in that respect.'

'Well, he would be, wouldn't he?' said Mabs tartly. Being completely without obsequiousness herself, she detested the way Frank sucked up to his father-in-law.

Dolly changed the subject for fear she might give vent to her feelings and criticise Frank to whom she still felt duty bound to be loyal. 'Another cup of tea?' she offered.

'Yes, please,' said Mabs, handing Dolly her cup.

'Now,' she said, pouring the tea, 'let's get down to some

serious discussion about what sort of dress you'll be having for this glamorous occasion.'

'I need your help, Sis,' came Ken's voice over the telephone a month later.

'Sure, but with what?'

'Mabs has gone down with some sort of summer flu and she's had to go to bed,' he explained.

'Oh, the poor thing,' said Dolly. 'Bring young Peter round to me. I'll look after him until she's better.'

'No, there's no need for that at the moment,' he said. 'Mabs's friend from next-door is helping out.'

'In what way do you need my help then?'

'I want you to come to a dinner dance with me on Saturday night,' he explained.

'*The* dinner is this week, of course,' she said, remembering. 'But Mabs has been really looking forward to that.'

'I know she has, and it's a rotten shame she'll have to miss it,' he said regretfully. 'I wouldn't bother to go myself as she won't be up to it, but my boss is keen for me to be there. He's a great believer in supporting trade associations.'

'She'll probably be all right by then,' Dolly pointed out. 'It's still only Tuesday.'

'Not a chance,' he said ruefully. 'She'll be in bed at least a week. The doctor was adamant about her not getting up too soon.'

'Well, I'd like to help you out, Ken, of course,' she said doubtfully. 'But I've no one to look after the children. I can't rely on Frank's being at home. Anyway, he's useless with them.'

'What about Mother?'

'She won't do it if I'm going out with you,' she said, 'because Dad would make her life hell.'

'Any chance of getting your maid to do it?'

'She doesn't work evenings.'

'Might she be persuaded, if I made it worth her while financially?'

'Not on a Saturday night,' Dolly explained emphatically. 'That's her big night of the week – she goes dancing at the Palais and wouldn't miss it for all the tea in China.'

'If I can find someone to sit with the children, will you come?' he persisted.

'Depends who that someone might be,' she said. 'But . . . yes . . . I suppose so. Provided it's someone I can trust.'

Ten minutes later he was on the phone again. 'Mabs's friend from next-door has a sister in Chiswick. She's willing to look after the children on Saturday night.'

'Oh,' she said dubiously.

'Don't sound so worried. Mabs said to tell you you've met her round at our place – her name's Irene Todd, she's a widow, loves kids by all accounts.'

'Oh, yes, I know Irene,' said Dolly, relaxing as she recalled a homely woman of about forty.

'Well then . . .'

'I'd better do something about getting a new dress then, hadn't I?' she laughed. 'Though I don't know what I'll find at such short notice. There certainly isn't time to have anything made.'

* * *

She found something she liked in a shop in Bond Street; an emerald green, low-backed gown with chiffon sleeves and a fashionably slender body line. Her shiny brown hair was worn simply in a long bob.

'You look beautiful, Mummy,' said Merle, as Dolly emerged from her bedroom with every last hair combed into place. 'As pretty as Ginger Rogers.'

'Thank you, darling,' she said, hugging her daughter who was her most ardent admirer. 'Though I doubt if I could ever look as glamorous as her.'

'Don't you think Mummy looks as good as Ginger Rogers, Barney?' Merle asked.

'Who's she when she's at home?'

'A famous film star, you dummy,' Merle rebuked, rolling her eyes disapprovingly at her brother. 'Everyone knows that.'

'Well, I don't,' he said. 'And I bet she isn't as famous as Don Bradman.'

'Never heard of him,' his sister snorted.

'He's only the best cricketer in the world, that's all,' he informed her, matching his sister's look of contempt. 'Fancy not knowing that.'

'Sports people aren't as famous as film stars.'

'They are too . . .'

'Just because you're sports mad . . .'

The jovial sibling rivalry was interrupted by the arrival of Ken with Irene Todd.

'Cinderella shall go to the ball,' he laughed, giving his sister a sweeping bow.

'You look lovely, dear,' said Irene, a stout, softly spoken woman with gentle brown eyes.

'Thank you, Irene, and thanks for stepping in at such short notice to sit with the children.'

'No trouble at all,' she was assured. 'In fact, I welcome the chance. I'd have liked some kiddies of my own but it wasn't to be. My hubby took sick soon after we got married and passed on, poor dear.'

Sympathetic comments were made, and Dolly issued instructions for the children to be put to bed in half an hour, and for Irene to help herself to anything she fancied from the larder. 'My husband might be home before me, so don't fly into a panic thinking you've got burglars if you hear him come in.'

'I won't,' she said, smiling. 'Now off you go and enjoy yourselves. Me and the kiddies will be fine.'

So it was with an easy mind that Dolly left the house. By the time they arrived at the hotel, she was tingling with excitement. She'd never had much of a social life, having such stand-offish parents and a husband whose idea of high living was an evening with his mates at the local.

The crowded foyer reverberated with noisy exuberance. Dinner-suited men and well-dressed women stood around in groups chatting and laughing in party mood; a heady mixture of cigarette smoke, hair-oil and perfume spiced the air. After Dolly had made a few final adjustments to her appearance in the powder room, she and Ken went into the area adjoining the dining hall where everyone was gathering. He led her towards a middle-aged couple.

'This is my boss, Ted Porter,' he said. 'And this is my sister, Dolly.'

Ted was a large man in his fifties with a plum-coloured complexion, a waxed moustache and a booming voice. By contrast, his wife Sybil was small, quiet and dowdy.

Having got them all something to drink, Ted said jokingly, 'Well, well, I'm outnumbered this evening with both of you originally hailing from a rival company.'

'You can hardly call us rivals, though,' returned Dolly, 'since neither of us work for our father now.'

'Take no notice of me,' said Ted, lighting a cigarette and winking at her. 'I'm always teasing your brother about his link with the competition . . . no offence meant.'

'None taken,' said Dolly.

'Does us good to mingle with the opposition every now and then, I think,' Ted continued heartily. 'That's why I always make a point of coming to these occasions – it makes good business sense to meet other tea merchants in a social atmosphere, to pool ideas and chat about the trade in general. We might be rivals all year but tonight we meet as friends.'

'I couldn't agree more.'

There was a general drift into the dining room, which she could see through the open doors to be laid in lavish style with tables set around a small dance floor. Just as they were about to wander in that direction, Ted's attention was attracted by someone he spotted across the room.

'Well, I'll be damned . . . there's a fella over there I've not seen for years,' he said. 'Let's go over and say hello.'

They weaved through the crowd to a couple of about Ted's age.

'Ernie Webb, as I live and breathe,' said Ted, giving the man a vigorous handshake. 'It's been a long time.'

'Good God, it's Ted Porter,' said Ernie with a wide grin. 'It must be all of twenty years.'

'I'd no idea you were a member of the association,' said Ted.

'I only joined recently,' the other man explained. 'My son-in-law talked me into it. He's one of these go ahead types.'

Dolly and Ken were introduced then made to feel rather superfluous as the Porters and the Webbs waxed reminiscent. After a while, however, another couple joined the group.

'Ah, there you are,' said Ernie, and turning to the Porter party added: 'I'd like you to meet my daughter, Jean, and her husband, Bill Drake . . .'

Vaguely, Dolly could hear the drone of Ernie Webb's voice above a rushing sensation in her ears.

'Bill's the fella responsible for my being here . . . now there's a sharp businessman for you, Ted. The cutest fella on our board . . . never misses a trick, doesn't Bill . . . he could sell umbrellas in the desert, that one, and I wouldn't have him any other way.'

Stunned by the impact of this meeting, Dolly numbly did what was expected of her as Ernie made introductions. 'Bill and Jean . . . Ted Porter and his wife, and their guests, Ken Slater and his sister Dolly.'

A voice, deeper and more mature than she remembered

– slightly more cultured but unmistakably Bill Drake's – was throbbing into Dolly's consciousness, but her hearing was impaired by shock. 'Pleased to meet you, Dolly,' he was saying as though they were strangers.

She assumed she must have made an appropriate reply but wasn't aware of having spoken. Bill's wife's face floated into her vision, a cheerful, dark-eyed woman with a warm smile who said she was pleased to meet Dolly and generously complimented her on her dress.

Only when everyone was busy chattering did Dolly risk looking at Bill, for she couldn't trust herself to conceal her feelings. Observing him as he talked to Ted Porter, she saw a metamorphosis. His face and neck were thicker, his features had firmed. There was little sign of the unsophisticated boy she had known in this well-groomed man who simply oozed self-confidence.

Dinner dress looked good on him, his broad shoulders setting it off. Rising above a plethora of confused emotions came a moment of desperate sadness for something lost, but to her annoyance she found him even more attractive than she had ten years ago.

His wife is too good for him, she thought with a return of commonsense. It's obvious why he married her. How else would he have got a seat on the board of her father's firm? Part of Dolly longed to escape, to distance herself from the pain of old wounds reawakened by his presence; her basic instinct, however, was to be alone with him.

'Fancy Bill Drake being here,' Ken whispered as they went into the dining room, assuming his sister to be over Bill after all this time.

'Yes, quite a surprise.'

'He's certainly done well for himself.'

'Looks like it.'

'I suppose he didn't want to let on he already knew us because of that thing you had with him,' he said casually. 'Seems a bit silly to me but best to go along with him, don't you think?'

'There's nothing else we can do without making him look ridiculous and embarrassing everyone else, is there?' was Dolly's sharp reply.

The dinner seemed interminable to Bill. Beef consommé followed by a fish course, then roast lamb and mint sauce, trifle, cheese and biscuits, coffee – now the speeches seemed likely to go on forever. Bill ate, drank and made light conversation with Jean, Ernie and Lily; and all the time he was thinking of another time and another woman. That other woman was seated somewhere out of his range of vision but he could feel her presence here more palpably even than his wife's who was sitting next to him.

He needed to get the hell out of here – away from ghosts of the past and the woman who still had the power to make him feel vulnerable. But he *wanted* to stay and see more of her with an irrational part of him that made him tremble, even now after all that had happened.

The speeches finally ended and dancing commenced.

'You gonna sweep me off my feet then, Bill?' laughed Jean as people took to the floor to the tune of 'I Only Have Eyes For You'.

'In a minute,' he said, sipping his brandy.

'I'm not gonna wait until you're half cut, if that's what you're hoping,' giggled Jean, rising and tugging at his arm. 'Come on.' She wiggled her hips playfully. 'You can show Fred Astaire a thing or two.'

'I'm about as light on my feet as King Kong and you know it.'

'Nonsense.'

He gave her an affectionate look, ashamed of his preoccupation with Dolly. To see Jean the way she was now, jolly and in fine form, no one would ever guess the profound disappointment that had burdened her since that first miscarriage had been followed by others, finally causing damage that made conception impossible. He alone had been witness to her despair; she'd not wanted anyone else to know how deeply hurt she'd been, not even her parents. Only to Bill, who was her raison d'être, had she sobbed out the heartache of her blighted hopes.

The blow had brought them closer together, and he'd watched with admiration as she'd clawed her way out of depression and smiled through adversity. The one thing she didn't deserve was a husband who harboured a passion for another woman.

Pretending to match her gaiety, he stood up with a grin. 'All right, lady, you've asked for it, so don't complain if I tread on your toes.'

'As if I would . . .'

'You'd better not.'

'Ooh, I love it when you're masterful.'

Looking over her shoulder to see Dolly dancing with

Ted Porter while Ken glided around the floor with Sybil, Bill couldn't help thinking how apt the tune was, for as much as he wanted to ignore her, he did only have eyes for Dolly this evening. She was even more attractive to him now as a sophisticated woman than she'd been as a girl. She was still far from slender but her girlish plumpness had evened out into a well-proportioned figure.

What was it about her that drew him so compulsively? he wondered. She wasn't especially beautiful – many women you might see in the street outshone her in that direction. But there was something very special about her – an indefinable quality – a sexiness that made her stand out from the crowd. Her dancing partner was aware of it too. Bill could see it in the way he was looking at her.

'Nine out of ten for footwork,' Jean informed her husband lightheartedly as the music ended and they made their way back to their table.

'Why only nine?'

'You lost one for crushing my big toe and not even noticing,' she teased.

'You're a hard woman,' he laughed.

The Master of Ceremonies, eager to create a party spirit, made an announcement forbidding all gentlemen from partnering the lady they had escorted here this evening during the next dance. When Ken led Jean on to the floor and Ted Porter asked Lily to partner him, Ernie said to Bill, 'I suppose I'd better do my duty and rescue Sybil Porter from wallflowerdom.'

'Yeah, I think you'd better,' agreed Bill.

'You can't very well leave young Slater's sister sitting

there on her own,' said Ernie. 'Get over there and ask her to dance.'

To his shame Bill knew that this was the chance he had been waiting for all evening; the moment he had longed for for the last ten years. He rose and tried to quell the eagerness which made him want to run across to Dolly's table. His palms were sweating and his heart thumping as he walked slowly towards her . . .

Dolly gave him a brisk smile when he asked her to dance, giving no sign of the torment he aroused in her.

'Certainly,' she said with icy politeness.

The atmosphere was stiff with resentment as they moved round the floor in silence to an old-fashioned waltz, keeping as much distance between them as the dance permitted.

'You're looking well,' he said formally at last, staring ahead of him over the top of her head.

'You too,' she said into his shoulder.

'Never better.'

'You certainly seem to have done well for yourself.'

'I've no complaints.'

'I knew you'd go far,' she said with an edge to her voice.

'So did I,' he said without a hint of apology. 'I had no intention of being a labourer all my life.'

'Your wife seems very nice,' she said pointedly.

'Yes, she is,' he said, ignoring the blatant insinuation.

'Do you have any children?'

'No.'

'Oh.'

'The last I heard you had two,' he said with feigned casualness.

'That's right.'

'Your husband didn't come with you this evening then?'

'No, I'm just filling in for Ken's wife who has fallen sick,' she explained. 'This sort of thing wouldn't appeal to Frank, anyway.'

'I see.'

All empty words spoken to conceal a cauldron of blistering emotion. Whatever it was that had once existed between them was still very much alive, preventing either of them from remembering the events of the past rationally or without pain.

Dolly was furious with herself for allowing this man to upset her after all this time. 'There was no need for you pretend that we didn't already know each other,' she said, looking into his face with cold accusation. 'I wouldn't have upset your wife by spilling the beans about the past.'

'It seemed easier to pretend we were complete strangers,' he explained, thinking Dolly was referring to their love affair since he knew nothing of the fictional incident that had tarnished him forever in her eyes.

'I suppose it would to someone like you,' she said, the memory of Sadie's allegations against him echoing afresh in her mind.

To his fury he found himself smarting at her hostility. Unbidden came bitter memories – the way he had trusted her so completely, loved her so desperately; how she had not even had the courage to tell him the truth about their affair or that it was over. He wanted to wound her as she had wounded him, as though that might somehow cleanse him of the unwanted feelings that had tortured him for so long.

'Jean is an intelligent woman, she doesn't imagine that I lived like a monk before I met her,' he said coldly, 'but she has been through a lot and I don't want her to feel threatened in any way by events long past . . .' His next words registered like a physical blow to Dolly. 'Events which were, after all, of no real significance.'

'That's how you remember it then, is it?' she said, crushed to the very core.

'Well, of course, what other way is there?' he said through tight lips. The bitch certainly wanted her pound of flesh. Surely she didn't expect him to admit how much he had really cared!

'None at all,' she said brusquely.

'Just a youthful bit of nonsense that happened a very long time ago and is best forgotten,' he said.

'My feelings exactly.'

Not a word passed between them for the rest of the dance. Dolly was both relieved and disappointed when the music ended.

Frank arrived home about half-past ten, feeling pleasantly relaxed after an enjoyable evening in the Crown and Sceptre. He had forgotten that Dolly was going to be out so was surprised to see a strange woman sitting in the armchair in the sitting room, listening to the wireless and knitting furiously.

'Hello. You must be Mr Mitchell,' Irene said, switching

the wireless off and smiling warmly at him.

'Yeah, that's me.'

'I'm Irene Todd your baby sitter,' she said cheerfully. 'But your wife will have told you I'd be here.'

'Yeah . . . 'course she did,' he said. 'Pleased to meet yer, ducks.'

'Been anywhere nice?' she asked conversationally.

'Nowhere special,' he said, taking off his jacket and loosening his tie. 'I've only bin down the local havin' a few pints and a game o' darts.'

'Oh.'

'Everything all right with the nippers, is it?' he asked, surprising himself for he didn't normally give the children a thought.

'No trouble at all,'

'That's good,' he said, sitting down in the armchair opposite hers on the other side of the unlit hearth in which a vase of flowers stood in front of an embroidered fire-screen.

Irene put her knitting down and looked across at him. 'Your wife said I was to help myself to anything I fancy from the larder,' she explained. 'I was just going to make myself a sandwich and some cocoa. Can I get you anything?'

He was about to decline when he realised that he was feeling a bit peckish. 'I wouldn't say no to a cheese sandwich.'

'Cocoa?'

'Ta very much,' he said, feeling unusually content as he watched her bustle from the room, her rounded form exuding an air of reassurance.

When she returned, she set a tray of sandwiches and cocoa down on a small table between them and settled back in her chair as though completely at ease in his company. 'Dig in, Mr Mitchell,' she said with the authority of a hostess as she helped herself to a sandwich.

'Me name's Frank,' he said. 'So let's drop the mister, shall we?'

'Certainly, Frank.'

Chatting companionably over a lengthy supper, during which their cocoa cups were refilled several times, Frank realised that Irene wasn't very much older than he was, and quite attractive in a motherly sort of way. He liked her soft velvety eyes and large capable hands. She made him feel safe and warm inside; the sort of woman he had often imagined his mother might have been.

'You're a widow you say?' said Frank, observing her over the rim of his cup.

'That's right,' she said. 'I've been on my own for fifteen years.'

'It must be lonely for you.'

'Yes, it is at times,' she admitted regretfully.

'Shame . . .'

'Mmm, I still miss having a man about the place, even now,' she confided. 'I often think how nice it would be to have someone to share things with.'

'Yeah, I expect you do.'

'Still, no use moaning, is it? You've gotta put up with whatever life dishes out, haven't you?'

'Mmm.' The feeling of security she had engendered in him was replaced by a sudden surge of protectiveness towards her. 'Ain't you ever thought of marrying again?'

'Chance would be a fine thing,' she said, finishing her cocoa and stacking the used crockery on to the tray.

'Oh, come on, Irene. I can't believe that no one has been interested in a good-looking woman like yourself in fifteen years,' he said, putting his crockery on the tray.

She flushed. 'I'll not deny having had one or two offers over the years,' she confessed with a wicked smile.

'And you didn't fancy the idea?'

'No, not when it came to the push,' she explained. 'No one else has ever matched up to my hubby.'

There was the sound of a car drawing into the drive.

'Oh dear, that'll be your wife back and we've been so busy talking I haven't even washed the supper things,' said Irene, rising and brushing some crumbs from her lap.

'Don't worry about that,' Frank assured her. 'The maid'll do that in the morning.'

'I'll take them out to the kitchen then . . .'

'No, don't worry, I'll do it later,' he said, astonishing himself, for he never lifted a finger in the house.

'Righto, then.' She packed her knitting into her bag and looked up, smiling. 'I've enjoyed our chat ever so much, Frank, I really have.'

'So have I,' he said, smiling into her eyes.

Dolly was deeply preoccupied with her own thoughts when she entered the room. Having exchanged a few sociable words with Irene and paid her for her services, she said, 'Ken's waiting in the car to take you back to Chiswick. He's anxious to get home because of Mabs not being well.'

'I'll drive Irene home if Ken's in a hurry,' offered Frank.

'Would you, Frank?' said Dolly absently, far too absorbed in the aftermath of the meeting with Bill to dwell on her husband's unusual helpfulness to her brother, a man he hadn't spoken to in years on account of his loyalty to Henry.

'Yeah, 'course I will.'

'Righto. I'll pop outside and tell Ken he can be on his way then while you get Irene's hat and coat,' said Dolly.

Chapter Nine

Sunday tea at her parents' house was an established part of Dolly's life. Since she'd left home to get married its pattern had changed from cucumber sandwiches served informally in the sitting room to a formal high tea in the dining room, by way of a family gathering. No matter how distant she and Frank became from each other, they always put on a good show of family unity for her parents on a Sunday afternoon. So, naturally, Edie and Henry were surprised one autumn Sabbath when Dolly and the children arrived unaccompanied.

'Where's Frank?' asked Henry, as Dolly and the children seated themselves in the sitting room where he was ensconced in an armchair, shrouded by a cloud of cigarette smoke.

'He's at home trying to fix the car,' lied Dolly, to avoid questions she couldn't answer. 'It wouldn't start so I walked here . . . he'll be along later.'

'Oh, right,' said Henry, coughing raucously. 'I hope he isn't going to be too long though. He knows how important a family tea on a Sunday is to your mother and me.'

Didn't he just, thought Dolly, wondering again how any

self-respecting man could bear to be so dominated by his father-in-law. She had no idea where her husband was. He'd gone to the pub for his usual pre-prandial session and had not returned. She could only assume he'd gone home with one of his pals for a game of cards or something and forgotten the time. Unreliability was not unusual in Frank but, being so obsequious to Henry, absence from the Sunday tea ritual was unprecedented.

'So how's my best girl then?' asked Henry, smiling at his grand-daughter, and turning quickly to her brother under the critical eye of their mother. 'And you, of course, Barney.'

'Very well, thank you, Grandfather,' they chimed respectfully, both perched nervously on the edge of their chairs for the atmosphere at their grandparents' house was always uneasy and they were both somewhat daunted by their awesome grandfather.

'Go along into the dining room and sit up at the table then, children,' said Edie after a while. She was frumpishly neat in a dark blue woollen dress, her iron-waved hair worn flat to her head.

They all trooped into the other room and tea began. It varied only with the season – cooked meats, salad, and bread and butter in the summer, toasted muffins or crumpets in the winter, with caraway seed or fruit cake to follow. As boring as the event was, there was a certain stability about it that Dolly considered important to the children. And the immutable nature of the conversation meant she could attend to it without any real effort.

'How's business, Daddy?' she asked automatically.

'As hard as ever to make a profit,' he said predictably.

'I thought there's supposed to be more money about these days,' she said.

'Can't say as I've noticed it.'

Greedy old devil, she thought, but said, 'I don't know how you can complain, Daddy. There are many people much worse off than us ... the jobless on the Jarrow Protest March for instance.'

'More fool them ...'

As he waffled on, as usual about the working people wanting something for nothing, Dolly averted an argument by letting her mind drift on to other things. It was two months since the meeting with Bill Drake and she still felt shaken by it. But as upsetting as it had been, at least it had clarified the situation for her and stripped away the lingering hope she now realised she had been harbouring for ten years; hope that somehow there was an explanation for the way he had behaved – that perhaps it hadn't happened as Sadie had described it.

All self-deception had ended with his heartbreaking description of her own affair with him as 'events of the past of no real significance'. Those words were imprinted on her memory to ensure that she never succumbed to sentimental thoughts of Bill Drake *ever* again.

Recalled to the present, she realised that her father had finished putting the world to rights and her mother was speaking.

'I do hope Frank isn't going to be much longer or he'll have to have his tea on his own,' she said with a weary shake of the head. 'And the servants won't like that one little bit . . . they don't like extra work on a Sunday.'

'I'm sure he'll be here in a minute, Mother,' said Dolly, though she was beginning to worry herself now. What on earth had happened to him?

Frank was finding it hard to leave Irene Todd's cosy little house in Chiswick where he was happily snuggled up to her on the sofa in her living room. His serene mood was enhanced by the fire crackling in the hearth and a feeling of pleasant repletion from an enormous lunch of roast beef and Yorkshire pudding. Not being a man of conscience, he was not unduly worried at having failed to return home for lunch with the family. In fact, he felt so content here with Irene, he never wanted to go back to Dolly again, or to Henry Slater's place.

No one could have been more surprised than Frank when his life had changed so suddenly. One minute he'd been meandering along in perfect contentment, his happiness amounting to a roof over his head and money in his pocket. Then Irene had come along, with her warmth and unconditional affection for him, and shown him what *real* happiness was like.

She'd made it easy for him to make an approach by mentioning a shelf that needed fixing in her kitchen when he'd driven her home after baby sitting. He'd been only too eager to oblige. She'd been impressed with his handiwork and had made it obvious that she thought he was very special in other ways too. Having never before been the recipient of admiration, he found the experience quite stunning. It seemed to sweeten the very air that he breathed and boosted his confidence – he felt as though there was nothing he couldn't do for Irene that wouldn't impress and please her.

Eager for more of her therapeutic company, he'd visited her whenever he could after that. In fact, while Dolly had assumed he was at the pub, he'd been having a wonderful time with Irene, being pampered and made to feel important. For the first time in his life he was wanted for himself, just the way he was, and it made him realise just how empty the years before had been.

Now he consulted his pocket watch and made a face.

'I'd better make a move. I'm late for tea at my in-laws'.'

'Shame you've gotta go, isn't it?' said Irene.

'Not 'alf,' he sighed, 'but if I don't turn up, Henry will hit the roof. Though Gawd knows how I'm gonna eat anything after the feast you've given me.'

'Bugger your father-in-law,' said Irene, cuddled into the crook of his arm, her hair tousled attractively, plump face glowing from the fire. 'It's your wife you should be worrying about, not her father.' She frowned and gave a worried shake of the head. 'I shouldn't be letting this happen between us when you've a wife and kiddies at home. It isn't like me to get so carried away.'

'I've told you, Dolly and me lead separate lives,' he reminded her.

'Yes, I know that or I'd never have let anything start, but that doesn't alter the fact that you're a married man with responsibilities . . . and worried about being late for tea.'

'Sunday tea at the Slaters' is sacrosanct,' he explained.

'Not to you and Dolly though, I'll bet,' she suggested, looking up at him with a hard expression.

'No, to Henry and Edie.' He paused thoughtfully. 'Well, to Henry really . . . he's the one who makes all the rules.'

'Seems to me you married Henry Slater not his daughter.'

Frank thought about this before replying. 'As a matter of fact, that's exactly what did happen.'

'So what do you intend to do about it?' she asked, becoming suddenly decisive.

'Do . . .?'

'Yes, do,' she said firmly. 'You can't keep coming round here forever without making some sort of commitment to me, Frank.'

'But we get on so well . . .'

'I know we do,' she agreed. 'We have a good time together – a lot of laughs and a little bit of something else – but I *do* have a reputation to think of, you know.'

'I wish I lived here with you, Irene,' he sighed wistfully.

'Why not do something about it then?'

'Meaning?'

'Meaning you can move in here with me whenever you like,' she told him, 'but only if you promise to make an honest woman of me as soon as you can get a divorce from Dolly.'

'What? Leave Dolly altogether?' he said, astounded.

'Of course! You can't have us both, love,' she said with a touch of asperity. 'I'm not prepared to be the other woman on a permanent basis.'

'But if I leave Dolly, Henry'll sack me,' he told her earnestly.

'So?'

'I'd have nothing to support you with,' he explained. 'Everything I have comes from him.'

'Now's your chance to break free then,' she said cheerfully.

'But I wouldn't be able to keep you,' he repeated, scratching his head worriedly.

'Get another job then,' she suggested. 'And be your own man for once in your life.'

'Easier said than done,' he said dubiously. 'I've never worked anywhere else but Slater's.'

'A man with your experience in the tea trade should be able to find work of some sort,' she said. 'Unemployment is decreasing now, in London anyway.'

'But I'm 'opeless without Henry,' he told her mournfully.

'I don't believe that for a moment,' she said sternly. 'You've never even tried to make it on your own from what I've heard of it.'

'I'm a simple man, Irene, I'm not cut out for responsibility or decision making,' he admitted ruefully. 'The only reason I'm on the management at Slater's is for the sake of appearances . . . Henry tells me exactly what to do.'

'Why not try something less grand then?' she suggested heartily. 'It could be the making of you.'

'Such as?'

'I don't know,' she said with affectionate firmness. 'You must work that out for yourself, love. But better to sweep the streets and feel comfortable with the job, than slave away doing something that isn't right for you.'

'But I wouldn't have any sort of position or earn the money that I do now.'

'So what?'

'Surely you wouldn't want someone without any status?'

'I'd sooner have you as a labourer than a glorified errand boy, tied hand and foot to your boss.' She slapped a large comforting hand on his arm and looked earnestly into his eyes. 'Look, Frank, I'm not rich by any means, but my hubby did leave me enough to live on in reasonable comfort, and this little house is paid for. You'd have to pull your weight with me, of course, once you get a job, but we won't starve while you're looking.'

'Oh, Irene, you're so good to me,' he said emotionally.

'You'll have to make up your mind, and be quick about it though,' she told him. 'It's Dolly and her family or me!'

'Here's Frank at last,' said Edie, watching through the sitting-room window as his car turned into the drive.

'Not before time, either,' complained Henry, for they had adjourned from the dining room some time ago. 'I've a few words to say to him, keeping us all waiting like this. If he couldn't get the car going, he should have walked here.'

But as it happened Henry was completely upstaged by Frank in an astonishly assertive mood.

'Hello, everyone,' he said in a strong voice. 'Sorry I'm late.'

'I should bloody well think so too,' growled Henry.

'Where are the children?' Frank asked, as though Henry hadn't spoken.

'Playing upstairs in the old nursery,' he snapped through a pall of smoke.

'That's good, because what I have to say isn't for their ears.'

'Humph,' snorted Henry. 'You realise you've upset our whole afternoon?'

'Shut up, Henry,' interrupted Frank. 'And listen to me for a change.'

They were all too shocked by this to say a word.

'The reason I'm late for tea is because I have been with a woman . . . the woman I am going to marry.'

Silence fell upon the room.

'Marry?' Dolly muttered at last.

'I may be suffering from delusions,' said Henry with withering sarcasm, 'but I was under the impression that you are already married, to my daughter.'

'Not for much longer,' said Frank, hardly able to believe he was doing this. 'Dolly and I don't love each other. We never have.'

'Rubbish!' barked Henry in such a vehement tone it sparked off another coughing fit.

'Dolly and I got married because you bullied us into it,' Frank said when Henry had recovered, his chest wheezing loudly. 'The only time we have a marriage is on a Sunday afternoon when we act it out for you and Edie.'

'How dare you tell such lies?' roared Henry.

Frank turned to Dolly. 'I'm sorry to spring this on you, Doll, but I think you'll probably be as relieved as I am to have the truth out in the open at last.

'Well . . .' she began, for she couldn't deny it even though his way of dealing with it was humiliating to her. Rejection was never easy. This, her second, was a painful reminder of her inability to keep a man.

'As it was your family I married rather than you,' he continued, swept along by the buoyancy of his mood, 'I thought it was only fair to tell you that I'm leavin' while you're all together.'

'You're not going anywhere,' pronounced Henry, rising and pacing across the room.

'Certainly you're not,' said Edie breathlessly.

Dolly gave her parents a hard look. 'What Frank is saying is true,' she informed them. 'We've never had a proper marriage.'

'It's given you two children,' said Henry, who was standing with his back to the window, smoking furiously.

'That's about the only good thing that has come out of it.' She turned to Frank. 'So who is this woman you've fallen for?'

'Irene Todd,' he said proudly. 'I first met her when she sat with the children.'

Up went Dolly's brows. 'Well, well, they say still waters run deep – she's the last person I would have expected to get involved with a married man.'

'She didn't mean it to happen,' he said defensively. 'And I'm not sayin' that it's right, but it's 'appened and that's all there is to it.'

'Huh! She won't want you when she realises you don't have any money or a job,' said Henry. 'You're sacked as from now, and you'll lose all claim to the house.'

'I don't care about that . . . in fact, I don't want anything from you ever again, Henry,' he said. 'I'm free at last.'

'Free be buggered,' snorted Henry. 'You're a married man.'

'I'm going to the house to pack my things,' Frank went on, undeterred. 'I'll be gone by the time Dolly and the children get home.'

'You'll do no such thing,' roared Henry. 'You've responsibilities.'

'I'll leave the car where it is in the drive,' announced Frank, lightheaded in the knowledge that he *could* actually function without Henry.

'Don't you dare leave my daughter in the lurch,' shouted Henry. 'You've the children to think of.'

'They won't miss me,' said Frank. 'I've never been a father to them.'

'Then you ought to be bloody well ashamed of yourself!' bawled Henry.

'Yeah, I reckon you're right about that,' said Frank. 'But it's too late to do anything about it now, 'cos my future lies elsewhere.'

'You've lived in the lap of luxury in a house paid for by me, and this is the thanks I get,' Henry reproached him.

'I never felt at home there even though Dolly did her best to make things work between us,' said Frank. 'It was never my house. You gave it to your daughter as a wedding present. My name was only on the deeds because I was your son-in-law . . . it should have read Mr Dolly Slater instead of Frank Mitchell.'

'You won't get out of your obligations that way,' bellowed Henry, becoming desperate at this unexpected loss of power. 'It's your duty to support your wife and children.'

'As soon as I find work, I'll send what I can to Dolly.'

'That won't be much or anything at all on the money you'll be earning without me behind you,' said Henry.

'I know that.'

'So who is supposed to support them then?' asked Henry, grey with temper. 'Me, I suppose.'

'If you can't afford it, I don't know who can,' said Frank evenly.

'After all I've done for you,' said Henry in a wounded tone. 'This is how you repay me.'

'You have done a lot for me, it's true,' agreed Frank, 'but it ain't been all one-sided. You've had more than your moneysworth out of me – nearly thirty years of grovelling obedience.'

Listening to the end of her marriage being bandied about as though it had nothing whatsoever to do with her, Dolly was reminded that it had never been about her and Frank, only Frank and her father. They had needed each other and she had been the means to keep them bonded. Now it was over, she felt a tremendous sense of relief.

'Stop it, both of you!' she yelled, the harshness of her tone producing instant silence. 'You've used each other equally and now it's come to an end. Accept it and part with dignity.'

'But you can't just let him get away with it,' said Henry, glaring at her.

'I want him to go.' She turned to face her husband with a brave smile. He had the sensitivity of a grave-digger's shovel, and he was not the man for her, but that didn't mean he didn't have the right to the chance of a decent life with someone else. 'Good luck, Frank.'

'Thanks, Dolly.'

Those few amicable words reminded her of the casual friendliness that had once existed between them long ago, reaffirming her belief that this parting was the right thing for everybody.

'Well . . .' blustered her father incredulously. 'Have you gone off your head or something, Dolly? Wishing him good luck! You should be putting your foot down.'

'Do be quiet, Daddy,' she said wearily. 'And let things be.'

Dolly was not unaware of the difficulties that lay ahead for her as a lone parent. Even though she and Frank had led separate lives, she had been cushioned by her respectable marital status. Without that, things would be very different. Initially she would be the subject of gossip, the deserted wife to be pitied in her presence and ridiculed behind her back; later she would be an embarrassing odd number to be excluded from social gatherings.

But for all that, she was glad this had happened. Better to be without a partner than lonely within a loveless marriage, she thought.

Tea on a Sunday afternoon was also something of a ritual for Jean and Bill Drake who always visited Ernie and Lily at their house in Putney. They usually ended up staying for supper since they all got along so well together.

Such was the case that same Sunday evening as they all sat round the Webbs' table, munching cold meat and pickles, chatting and listening to the wireless.

After a programme of light music came the news which included reports of riots in the East End of London as thousands of people took to the streets in an attempt to prevent a march by the black-shirted supporters of the Fascist leader, Sir Oswald Mosley.

'Bloody extremists,' said Ernie. 'Rousing people to violence like that.'

'At least it's shown the Fascists that people don't want them, though,' Bill pointed out.

'What with the blackshirts here and the Nazis in Germany, it makes you wonder what the world's coming to,' said Ernie.

'Not 'alf,' agreed Bill gravely. 'I read in the paper that they're dropping foreign words from the German language.'

'Now then, you two,' admonished Lily. 'Don't get all political.'

'We're only discussing what's happening in the world,' said Ernie.

'I know, but you and Bill will still be going on about it until well into the small hours if we don't stop you,' said Lily. 'Isn't that right, Jean?'

'It is too,' she said, catching her husband's eye across the room in a look of mutual affection. 'Let's talk about something more cheerful – the new Greta Garbo film that's on at the pictures, for instance.'

'That's a hint for me to take you to see it, I suppose?' laughed Bill.

'Could be . . .'

'We'd better go one night next week then, hadn't we?' he said in jocular fashion. 'Or my life won't be worth living.'

'You poor thing, you'll have me in tears in a minute,' grinned Jean.

In this amiable and loving atmosphere, Bill counted his blessings. What was he doing wasting a moment of his life hankering for someone like Dolly Slater when he had so much to be grateful for in his marriage? Not only did he have the love and friendship of a good woman but he also had the respect and affection of her parents who had come to mean a lot to him. As well as taking him at face value and encouraging his enterprising spirit, they had also opened his eyes to the pleasures of family life. He knew that they thought of him as the son they had never had. This humbled him and he tried not to disappoint them.

'I'd like to see that film too,' said Lily. 'I've heard it's ever so good.'

'You two girls go together then,' said Ernie, who preferred his own armchair of an evening to a seat at the pictures, no matter how plush and comfortable the new cinemas were.

'Oh, no,' laughed his wife. 'You don't get out of it that easy. An evening out will do all four of us good. We can make a night of it and have supper out afterwards.'

Ernie heaved a sigh. 'Who says women don't rule the world?'

'That's one night next week we'll both have to be home on the dot,' said Bill with mock regret. 'No late meetings or stopping for a pint on the way.'

'You're under your wife's thumb, that's your trouble, Bill,' jested Ernie, 'and it's giving my Lily ideas.'

'Too true I'm under the thumb,' grinned Bill, throwing a glance in his wife's direction. 'She's a very formidable woman, your daughter. I have to do as I'm told or I'm severely punished.'

'Ooh, get out the violins, someone,' giggled Jean, her eyes sparkling. 'That'll be the day when I rule the roost over you, Bill Drake.'

'Don't you believe it,' he grinned at his in-laws. 'She's a real bully.'

'I'll come over there and sort you out in a minute,' she warned.

'Yes, please.'

The evening continued in similar vein until Bill drove Jean home to their house in Clapham, tired and content. They were still giggling when they climbed into bed.

'Me a bully, huh?' laughed Jean, yawning happily. 'I'll soon show you . . .'

'Just joking . . . just joking . . . stop . . . stop!' he gasped, writhing and choking under the torture of her tickling.

'Say you're sorry then.'

'Sorry . . . sorry.'

'Say you love me.'

'Love you.'

'Again.'

'I . . . love . . . you.'

Even though the words were extracted from him in such a playful manner, he still found them hard to say, and felt as though he was being dishonest with her.

Chapter Ten

While Britain was reeling from the shock of the abdication of King Edward VIII to marry the woman he loved, Dolly was too busy adjusting to life without Frank to pay much attention to the scandal that filled the papers.

Her first problem had been convincing her parents that she was capable of living in a house without a man in it and didn't want to move back in with them. The second, since she didn't expect any help from Frank, was finding a means of financing herself so that she didn't have to rely on her father for money, as eager as he was to rob her of her independence.

Part of the solution came from moving to a smaller house, a little semi that was cheap to run. Wise investment of the money left over from the sale gave her an income. The shortfall was met by her reminding her father that she was no longer a married woman and persuading him to give her part-time work in the office at Slater's while the children were at school. With these two things in place, she couldn't afford to be lavish but she could manage to support her little family.

Her parents surprised her by being quite supportive.

She'd expected endless criticism for not putting up a fight to keep Frank. But although they complained bitterly about the gossip that swept through the neighbourhood, they were helpful in practical ways, especially with regard to the children. Items of clothing were bought for them as gifts and Edie looked after them if ever Dolly was needed to work when they were not at school.

Even Henry co-operated when it came to his grandchildren, and didn't seem to mind how often they were around the house in Maybury Avenue when he was at home. Neither of the children particularly liked their grandparents, but Dolly thought this was a good chance for them all to get to know each other better. It wasn't as though Barney and Merle were still at the demanding stage. Merle was never any trouble and Barney was already beginning to have a life of his own outside the home, being involved in various after-school activities. Fortunately, he was such an accomplished and happy child in his own right, there was never any jealousy towards his sister over the fact that their grandfather still obviously favoured her, despite Dolly's frequent warnings.

Of great solace to Dolly during this difficult period was her friendship with Mabs who was always on hand with moral support. Early in 1937, however, Dolly found herself returning the favour and coming to Mabs's assistance when Ken became infected with idealism.

'He's talking about joining the International Brigade and going to fight in the Spanish Civil War,' Mabs confided one Saturday afternoon when Dolly was visiting and the two women were in the kitchen getting tea.

'Not Ken?' said Dolly aghast, for her brother had always been such a peace-loving man.

'You could have knocked me down with a feather an' all,' said Mabs.

'What's got into him, I wonder?' said Dolly, slicing bread for sandwiches.

'Dunno. I suppose he's read about all the men flocking to Spain from all over the world and it's aroused the soldier in him.'

'Yes, I read something about the author George Orwell enlisting,' said Dolly thoughtfully.

'That's no reason for Ken to think he can do the same,' sniffed Mabs. 'He's a married man with responsibilities. He can't just go swanning off leaving Peter and me.'

''Course he can't,' said Dolly. 'It's illegal for a start. He'll be liable for two years in prison if he joins up.'

'Not to mention the possibility of making me a widow,' said Mabs.

'I can't imagine what the daft devil is thinking about,' said Dolly, but even as she spoke she suspected that her brother's sudden hunger for heroism was not wholly to do with the problems in Spain.

'Would you try to talk some sense into him, Doll?' pleaded Mabs. 'He might listen to you.'

'I'll certainly do what I can,' she agreed. 'Keep the kids out of the way after tea and I'll have a quiet word with him.'

'What's all this about your going to Spain?' she asked as her brother sat smoking his pipe after tea.

'It's terrible what's going on out there,' he said vehemently.

'That doesn't mean you have to go and sort it out,' she said. 'Anyway the International Brigade is run by Communists and you're not one of those.'

'They're not all Communists in the ranks though,' he said. 'They come from all walks of life, with one common bond – they are against Fascism.'

She gave him a shrewd look. 'It's just the cause you've been waiting for, isn't it, Ken?'

'I don't know what you mean,' he denied, rather too swiftly.

'Any cause will do as long as it gives you the chance to prove you're not scared to fight, that you're a *real* man.'

'That's a strange thing to say, Dolly,' he said, raking his dark hair back off his face in an agitated manner. 'I don't need to prove that to anyone.'

'Oh, but I think you do,' she said, persisting along this painful road to save him from a grave mistake. 'But why get yourself killed or put in prison just to prove something to Father?'

A tightening of his face indicated that her remark had hit home. 'I wouldn't cross the road to prove anything to that man,' he said grimly. 'I couldn't give a toss what he thinks of me.'

But Dolly didn't believe him. In fact, she now knew for certain that psychological damage had been done to her brother by their father's cruelty to him as a child. A dangerous state of affairs that could so easily bring him to an early death.

'He isn't worth it, Ken,' she said meaningfully.

He remained silent, his eyes hardening in thought. 'All right, so maybe it is because of him I feel I ought to go and fight, but I really am upset by what's going on out there too.'

'There's enough men losing their lives without you adding to their numbers.'

'There are lots going out to Spain, I know . . .'

'Perhaps they really are doing it because they believe it's right,' she said pointedly.

'Meaning I'm not, I suppose?' he said sharply.

'No, I don't mean that,' she said, 'but I don't think it's the *only* reason you want to go . . .'

'It doesn't matter why I want to go, only that I am willing to.'

'Your duty is here with Mabs and Peter,' she reminded him.

He got up and stood with his back to the fire, puffing on his pipe. 'You've really got me taped, haven't you, Sis?'

'I think I know you pretty well, yes.'

'You always have . . . when we were kids you could always read me like a book . . . you were usually in trouble for sticking up for me against him.'

'I don't think he realises just what he does to people, you know.'

He gave a cynical laugh. 'Oh yes he does, he gets a kick out of screwing people up.'

'Maybe . . .'

'The bloody man's still on my back and I haven't had anything to do with him for years,' he said, exhaling a cloud of smoke. 'He's with me in everything I do . . . I still ask myself, would he be pleased with me . . . would he be proud?' His voice shook with emotion. 'I don't know why 'cos I hate his guts.'

'Still as much?'

'More. I can't forgive him for what he did to me as a boy,' he explained. 'But even more than that, I loathe him to bits for not acknowledging Mabs and Peter. I know it hurts Mabs even though she pretends not to care.'

'More for your sake than hers, I think,' said Dolly.

'Very likely, knowing Mabs.' He chewed the stem of his pipe thoughtfully. 'I've often wished Mum was more supportive.'

'Mmm, me too,' said Dolly. 'I don't think it's that she doesn't care – just that she's weak against him.'

'I suppose it's understandable,' he said. 'Being stuck with his dominating presence day after day.'

'He can't admit when he's wrong, that's one of his major faults,' said Dolly. 'And that's what he thinks he'd be doing if he accepted Mabs into the family after making such a stand at first.'

'He was wrong about you and Frank too.'

'I haven't heard him admit it though,' she said. 'He blames Frank for the failure of our marriage, not himself for pushing us into something that was wrong for both of us.'

'That's Father,' he said. 'The infallible Henry Slater.'

'You've got it in one.'

They fell into silence for a while then Dolly said, 'So . . . what about this Spain business?'

'Well, I suppose I was being a bit headstrong in thinking

178

I could just go and leave Mabs and Peter,' he agreed.

'So you'll stay?'

'Probably,' he said resignedly.

Neither of Dolly's children seemed unduly affected by Frank's departure, which wasn't surprising as he had always kept his distance from them. But a sudden change in Merle's behaviour almost a year after he'd left made Dolly wonder if perhaps the child had been upset by it after all and was suffering some sort of delayed reaction. Dolly first became aware that all was not well one afternoon in the school summer holidays just after Merle's ninth birthday.

Dolly was used to hearing her children squabble and considered it healthy sibling rivalry, but the unusual vehemence in Merle's voice as it drifted through the kitchen window from the garden sent her scurrying outside.

'I'm not going to play with you, Barney,' Merle was shouting tearfully from a canvas garden chair. 'I hate the sight of you, so just go away, you horrid, stinking boy!'

'I thought you liked playing pat ball in the garden with a tennis racquet?' he said in surprise. 'You're always pestering me to play with you.'

'Well, I don't want to any more,' she shrieked almost hysterically. 'So clear off and leave me alone!'

'Shan't,' taunted Barney with boyish high spirits.

The girl sprang to her feet and flung herself at him in a completely uncharacteristic manner and began punching and kicking. Dolly could hardly believe her eyes for it was so unlike her.

'Merle,' she intervened, dragging the child away from

her brother, 'what on earth do you think you're doing?'

'He won't leave me alone,' she said, pale-faced but with crimson spots staining her cheeks.

'I only asked her to play,' said Barney.

'He was keeping on at me.'

'It isn't like you to take on so, Merle,' said Dolly patiently. 'What *is* the matter with you?'

'Nothing,' Merle shouted, her voice breaking as she struggled against tears.

'There quite obviously is,' said Dolly kindly, putting a sympathetic hand on her daughter's arm.

'Don't touch me,' she yelled. 'Just keep away from me. I hate you . . . hate you!'

'But, Merle . . .' said Dolly.

'I hate both of you,' she said, glaring from one to the other, her thin body moving with jerky little movements.

'All I did was ask her if she wanted to knock about with a tennis ball.'

'Shut up, you,' Merle said rudely, scowling at him with undiluted hatred. 'You think you're so clever, don't you? So good at everything . . . so smart . . . always showing off!'

'I don't.'

'Yes, you do,' She lunged at him again but was restrained by her mother.

'Merle, now stop this at once.'

'Shut up . . . shut up both of you!'

Before Dolly could say another word, the girl rushed into the house, tore upstairs and shut herself in her bedroom, pushing a chair against the door. When Dolly eventually persuaded her to come out, she was calmer but unnaturally subdued for the rest of the day. Dolly wondered if she was sickening for something but her temperature was normal and there were no spots or swollen glands.

She continued to be cold and withdrawn, almost as though she had taken a sudden dislike to her mother and brother. It was all the more worrying because she normally had such an even temper and loving nature. Now the slightest thing sent her into a tantrum.

No amount of coaxing would get her to tell her mother what had upset her. Although her behaviour bore all the hallmarks of jealousy of her well-liked brother, Dolly thought it very strange there had been no sign of this before. She really was at a loss to know how to give the child the help she obviously needed. Because, for all Merle's aggression and rejection of affection, Dolly sensed a kind of desperation for her mother's love and reassurance.

'She's growing up, that's all it is,' opined Mabs when Dolly confided in her a few weeks later. 'She'll be starting to develop soon. That's bound to make her tetchy.'

'She's only nine,' Dolly pointed out. 'A bit too early to be thinking in terms of puberty.

'Some girls start to develop earlier than others,' Mabs suggested hopefully.

'There's no sign of anything like that yet,' said Dolly.

'I don't know much about these things, since no one ever talks about 'em,' said Mabs, 'but it seems logical to me that emotional changes must take place along with the physical ones. Just because there's no sign of anything yet, it doesn't mean things haven't started happening inside.'

Dolly shook her head worriedly. 'It seems very early for that sort of thing.'

'Well, whatever it is, she'll come out of it when she's ready,' said Mabs.

'You really think so?'

''Course I do,' confirmed Mabs. 'It'll be just a phase. You know what kids are like for those. While you're worrying about this one, she'll be out of it and into another.'

'I suppose so,' said Dolly.

But when her daughter showed no sign of returning to her former self, Dolly decided to seek professional advice.

Chapter Eleven

Dr Beresford's head was throbbing and his eyes ached from lack of sleep; he had been up for most of the night. He'd been called out to a chronic tuberculosis patient; a child with diphtheria; a woman who'd died of pneumonia in conditions where the only forms of life to flourish were bed bugs and wall mould.

This morning it was standing room only in his waiting room as a result of the November fog reaping its usual crop of throat and chest complaints. Added to this, his partner in the practice had gone down with influenza and there were rumours of a typhoid outbreak in the suburbs.

So, being weary and overwrought, he was not feeling well disposed towards some comfortably off woman who was bending his ear about her spoiled daughter. The child obviously needed a lot less of her own way. Dr Beresford was a practitioner in the area of long standing. He knew Dorothy Mitchell to be part of the Slater tea family which gave her immunity to hardship, deserted by her husband as she was.

Even the knowledge that she, unlike many of his patients, would   pay his fee in full, didn't arouse sympathy for her so-called problem. If she had to endure a fraction of the suffering he brushed shoulders with every day, she might be less inclined to burden him with trivia when he had a queue of genuinely sick people to attend to.

'So I felt I ought to bring Merle along to see you, Doctor,' she was explaining. 'I think she needs a thorough check-up.'

Stifling his impatience, he looked at Merle who was sitting on a chair beside her mother looking healthy and well dressed in a good quality hat and coat with a velvet collar. 'Are you feeling poorly, my dear?' he asked through clenched teeth.

When the mood took her, Merle could look surprisingly supercilious for her age. 'I feel quite well, thank you,' she informed him haughtily.

'No sore throat or pains anywhere?'

'No.'

'Tummy ache?'

She shook her head, brown eyes wearing a guarded expression.

'Come here, my dear, we'd better have a look at you,' he said, grinding his teeth with irritation as he picked up his stethoscope.

Concluding his examination, he turned to Dolly and said tartly, 'There's nothing wrong with her at all, Mrs Mitchell. I only wish a few more of the children I see were as healthy.'

'But she's really not been herself lately, Doctor,' insisted Dolly, biting her lip.

He drummed his fingers on the desk impatiently and asked Merle to wait outside.

'She's playing you up,' he told Dolly sternly as soon as they were alone. 'The more you pander to her bad temper, the more she'll do it.'

'But she isn't normally the sort of child to have tantrums. Her behaviour changed so suddenly . . .'

'Be firm with her,' he advised hastily. 'If you let her get away with it she'll have you jumping through hoops forever.'

'But she was never an aggressive or moody child before, Doctor . . .'

'She's growing up.'

'It's a bit early.'

'Some children are.'

'But I think she's worried about something and I don't seem to be able to help her.'

'The best thing you can do for her is to stop giving in to her all the time,' he said brusquely. 'You know what they say . . . spare the rod and spoil the child.'

'I've never considered myself to be an overindulgent mother,' retaliated Dolly firmly.

'Sounds to me as though you quite often are,' he said, his patience almost threadbare. 'She's certainly getting more than her fair share of attention from what I can gather.'

'But why would she suddenly want more attention?' Dolly asked.

He shrugged his shoulders and wondered just how much longer he could stay awake – and still so many patients to see. Oh God! He forced his flagging attention back to the Mitchell child.

'There could be a variety of reasons for it,' he said, unable to stifle a yawn. 'It could have something to do with your broken marriage, coupled to the fact that she's coming towards that sensitive age.'

'My marriage broke up over a year ago,' Dolly pointed out.

'Mmm . . . yes . . . well, this could be a delayed reaction,' he said wearily, almost too tired for coherent thought.

'But my husband wasn't at all close to the children when he was with us,' she explained.

'His going was still a family upheaval though.'

'Yes, I suppose you're right, but how can I help her if she won't tell me how she feels?'

'Stop making such a big thing of it,' he suggested briskly. 'You'll get a lot more moodiness from her before she's through growing up. None of them stay sweet little girls forever.'

'You're sure there's nothing seriously wrong with her then?'

'Quite sure,' he said emphatically. Would the damned woman never stop jabbering and leave him in peace to get on with his *real* work?

'Right. Well, thank you, Doctor.' Since doctors were omnipotent people with knowledge beyond the grasp of ordinary mortals, she couldn't help but feel reassured by his definite manner. She stood up to go. 'You'll send your bill in due course.'

'Of course.' His conscience twinged. Overly fussy or

not, the woman was obviously a caring mother. He adopted a more compassionate tone. 'You've nothing to worry about at all, Mrs Mitchell. Take my word for it, your daughter is a darned sight healthier than many that I see on my rounds.'

'I'll keep that in mind then,' said Dolly, and left.

'I knew you were making a fuss about nothing,' said Edie when Dolly told her about the doctor's verdict. 'If I'd taken medical advice every time you had a temper tantrum when you were Merle's age, the doctor could have retired early on the takings.'

Mabs's views ran along similar lines. 'Didn't I tell you it was just a phase?' she said. 'She'll come out of it, you just wait and see.'

Merle's sweet nature didn't return. But having been reassured by Dr Beresford, Dolly tried to cope with her difficult behaviour with as much understanding and patience as she could muster, whilst maintaining discipline as the doctor had suggested. At times the whole thing taxed her almost to breaking point and her heart ached to see this once happy little girl fluctuating between introversion and aggression. Even during periods of relative calm she showed no affection towards her mother or brother as she once had. Ordinary everyday habits that had been part of their family fabric, like the goodnight kiss, were avoided or executed with blatant repugnance.

There were still times, though, when Dolly could feel her reaching out to her mother.

'Mummy?' she'd say in a questioning tone.

Even as Dolly's heart swelled with hope, and she asked, 'Yes, what is it, love?' the girl's eyes would cloud over.

'Oh, nothing,' she'd say, and retreat back into herself.

Striving to gain an insight into how the little girl might be feeling, Dolly cast her mind back to her own tender years. Vividly, she recalled the first black cloud of reality darkening the happy-ever-after innocence of childhood after a head-on collision with the facts of life. She would never forget the shock of that first bloodstain, doubly traumatic because it had also marked the end of trust in her mother who had previously denied the existence of menstruation when Dolly had come home from school with her head full of rumours. Merle would have no such rude awakening, Dolly was going to make sure of that!

In the meantime life went on for the Mitchells and Merle's erratic temperament became accepted as normal. There was so much else of concern to Dolly as the new year got underway to chilling war precautions, the problem of her daughter had to take its place as one among many other worries.

One day, the children came home from school with cardboard boxes slung over their shoulders.

'They're our new gas masks,' explained Barney excitedly. 'Everybody got one and we had gas mask drill.'

'What did you have to do?' Dolly asked, careful not to show how disquieting she found this development, even though she knew there was mass gas mask distribution underway and it was only a matter of time before they were all issued with them.

'We had to spit on the window at the front of the gas

mask to stop it misting up, then put it on, chin first, as fast as possible,' he explained.

'What did it feel like?' she asked.

'Queer at first, as though you're gonna choke, but it's all right once you get used to it,' he said. 'The teacher is going to time us tomorrow. The fastest class will get a star on the gas chart on the wall.'

'Oh,' said Dolly, finding it all quite bizarre.

'Not only that,' he said with a wide grin, 'we sat at our desks with them on to get used to wearing them too. It was a real scream talking to Miss with them on. Our voices sounded all muffled.' He erupted into boyish giggles. 'And gasmasks are brilliant for blowing raspberries.'

'I bet the teacher soon put a stop to that,' tutted Dolly, finding it hard not to smile at his exuberance.

'You bet she did, but it was good fun while it lasted,' he said.

'I didn't like it at all,' complained Merle. 'I think gas masks are beastly things.' She made a sour face. 'They smell nasty inside, all rubbery, and like the stuff Mummy puts down the toilet.'

Barney thought this highly amusing and chortled loudly. 'Mmm, they are a bit whiffy,' he agreed. 'But they're still a good lark.'

'Trust you to like such horrible smelly things,' accused Merle.

'And trust you to grumble about them,' Barney retaliated.

'Now, now, you two,' intervened Dolly swiftly, to avert another of the slanging matches which drove her crazy.

'Don't talk to each other at all if you can't say anything nice.'

Her mind wasn't really on their bickering this time though. She was far too preoccupied with the significance of the introduction of the gas mask into their lives; it really made war seem a possibility. In the ensuing weeks she noticed other ominous signs too – posters advertising anti-gas lectures for instance.

'Things are looking a bit grim, don't you think, Mabs?' Dolly remarked to her sister-in-law one day in spring after Hitler had overrun Austria and the government had made a serious appeal for volunteers to join the ARP.

'I dunno what the government is thinkin' of,' exclaimed Mabs. 'Spending public money on all these precautions. It's that kind of attitude that makes wars.'

'Hitler seems to be the one causing all the trouble,' said Dolly.

'That evil sod!' exploded Mabs.

This was a view voiced by many as reports of atrocities towards the Jews in Germany appeared in the papers.

Henry was more worried about the effect on trade if war did come than the suffering it would bring.

'We'll be inundated with restrictions like we were in the last war,' he fumed one May afternoon when Dolly was in his office getting some letters signed. 'The politicians want to try running a business during a war – that would soon cure 'em of it, I tell you, what with tea control and import bans.'

'Didn't they reverse the decision to ban the import of tea quite early on in the last war, though?'

'They had to because of the public outcry,' he told her. 'Whatever else people are prepared to go without, they can't do without their cup of tea.'

'You've nothing to worry about then, have you?'

'Tea was rationed later on though,' he said, his voice rising angrily. 'There'll be all sorts of shortages and regulations if we do go to war, you mark my words.' He drew hard on his cigarette, almost retching with the violence of his cough.

'There's no point in working yourself up about something that probably isn't going to happen,' said Dolly.

'They don't produce millions of gas masks for nothing,' he said, sweating and breathless from the exertion of coughing.

'They have to be prepared just in case,' said Dolly with determined optimism. 'But that's all they are—precautions.'

'I'm not so sure.'

'Business is booming at the moment anyway,' she said, glancing at the sales chart on the wall in an effort to take his mind off the subject which caused him such distress.

'Yes, but for how long?' he said gloomily, standing up and looking at the chart with her, wheezing and seeming even shorter of breath.

'Supplying hotels with tea seems to have proved to be a good steady trade too,' remarked Dolly.

'Oh, yes, going after hotel business was a good move,' he said, omitting to mention the fact that it had been her idea.

'Anyway, I must be off,' she said, gathering the signed letters. 'I have to get these ready for the post . . . and it's nearly time for me to go home.' She turned to him. 'Daddy, what's the matter? Oh dear, are you ill?'

He was staring at her, eyes bulging, copious perspiration gleaming on his skin as he clutched his chest, emitting terrible choking sounds.

'Here, let me loosen your collar,' she said, her alarm lessened by the fact that she was used to seeing him fight for breath after a bad spell of coughing. 'Those damned cigarettes of yours will be the death of you.'

Even as she spoke his body fell against hers and he slumped to the ground. 'Daddy!' she cried, leaning over him.

Dolly went with her father in the ambulance, sitting beside him sick with nerves as he drifted in and out of consciousness.

'You'll be all right once we get you to hospital,' she said reassuringly. 'They'll have you as right as rain in no time.'

'I've never said this to you before, Dolly, but you're a bright girl,' he said breathlessly.

'Shhh . . . save your strength.'

'You're the only person I can trust to look after the business after I'm gone,' he gasped.

'That's enough of that sort of talk,' she chided gently, quaking inwardly at the bluish tinge to his face. 'You're as strong as an ox – you'll see us all out.'

'Your mother's a good woman,' he continued, pale lips barely moving. 'An excellent homemaker but hopeless at anything else.'

Probably because she's never been given the chance,

thought Dolly, but said, 'Please don't tax yourself by trying to talk.'

'It's my last chance . . .'

'Now what sort of talk is that?'

'Frank turned out to be a wrong 'un,' he went on as though she hadn't spoken. 'I'd have put money on his loyalty to me too.'

'Well . . . he's only human and you manage well enough without him.'

'He couldn't run a seafront cockle stall, let alone help me run a tea factory.'

'Please don't upset yourself . . .'

'Your brother never had a fraction of your spirit, Dolly,' he persisted, his voice almost a whisper. 'Always a spineless article . . . I never could stand the sight of him.'

'Please don't say such things about Ken,' she begged.

'I've got to . . . got to . . .' he muttered with a sense of urgency.

'Let him talk,' advised the ambulanceman in a whisper. 'Or he'll work himself up into even more of a state.'

So, dry-mouthed with nerves, Dolly listened while he rambled.

'You and me have never got on, have we?' he said, struggling for breath.

'Not really, no.'

'You've always been too damned defiant for me,' he told her. 'You'd argue that black was white if you thought you could get away with it.'

Dolly managed a weak smile. 'It's just my way, Daddy.'

'I can see myself in you, you know.'

I sincerely hope not, thought Dolly, but this was not the time to say so, so she kept a diplomatic silence.

'You get your spirit and determination from me anyway.'

'Do I?'

'But I won't take the blame for your damned silly ideas!'

''Course not.'

'You've got your head screwed on though, girl,' he said, his eyes flickering. 'I'll say that much for you.'

'Thanks.'

'It's all sorted, Dolly,' he said, his voice seeming stronger for a moment. 'All taken care of.'

'What is?'

He didn't reply. After a jerking movement he lay horribly still.

'Oh God! Has he...?' asked Dolly of the ambulanceman.

'I'm afraid so,' said the man after feeling for a pulse.

Numb with shock, Dolly closed her father's eyes. It occurred to her that he had died as he had lived: without any sign of affection. Even in those last moments, when he had known his end was near, all he had been concerned about was the business. There had been no compassion; no forgiveness for Ken or Frank.

A tyrant was dead! She felt a profound sadness for the passing of a man whom few people could truly mourn. She herself had not even liked him, let alone loved him. But he was her father and this *was* her first experience of death. The finality of it devastated her.

Poor Mother, she thought sadly. What will she do without him?

* * *

Having been so utterly dominated by her husband, Edie fell apart completely on his death, leaving the funeral arrangements to Dolly. It was a small gathering for Henry had had few friends. Just family, including Ken and Mabs, a few business acquaintances and Mr Briggs, Henry's solicitor, stood round the grave in their mourning clothes on that drizzly spring day.

Ashen-faced and feeble, Edie could hardly stand and was forced to accept the support of her son at the graveside. But there was no sign of a reunion. In fact, Ken almost didn't go back to the house afterwards for the funeral tea.

'I won't have that woman in my house,' declared Edie, glaring at Mabs.

'In that case I won't come either,' he said, hotly defensive.

'This is no time to harbour old grudges, Mother,' admonished Dolly patiently. 'You need all your family around you right now.'

'She's not family and I don't want her anywhere near me,' Edie said tearfully.

'But Mother . . .'

'She set Ken against his own parents.'

Daddy did that long before Mabs appeared on the scene, Dolly thought, but said, 'Don't take on so, dear.'

'You go back to the house with your mother, Ken,' urged Mabs. 'I really don't mind.'

'I'm not going without you,' he said peevishly. 'If you're not welcome, then I'd rather not be there either.'

'I'd like you to go with her, love,' Mabs whispered to him persuasively. 'Your mother needs you more than I do today.'

'But . . .'

'Just do it, Ken,' said Mabs in a way she had of prohibiting argument.

Dolly threw her a grateful look which was acknowledged with a wink. Thank God for friends like Mabs, Dolly thought as she gathered everyone together for refreshments at Maybury Avenue. She suspected that she was going to need every ounce of patience she could muster while Mother adjusted to her new circumstances. With Father gone and Ken still out of favour, it was obvious who was going to be used as a crutch.

If Dolly felt the weight of family responsibility at the funeral, she was positively crushed by it when the solicitor read the will.

'To my wife I leave my house, all my possessions and the contents of my personal bank account which should ensure that she lives in the way she is accustomed for the rest of her life.'

There was a murmur of approval from the members of the family who were gathered in the sitting room at Maybury Avenue.

'To my daughter, Dolly, I leave the Slater Tea Company in its entirety, which she is to run in the Slater tradition.'

There was dead silence.

'But what about Ken?' Dolly gasped when she had recovered sufficiently to speak. 'Surely, as the only son of the family, the business should go to him?'

'Your father's instructions are quite explicit, Mrs Mitchell,' said Mr Briggs in a neutral tone.

'But what *has* he left to Ken?' she asked.

'Kenneth is not mentioned in the will,' he told her solemnly.

'Why, the wicked old sod!' exclaimed Dolly. 'What a perfectly foul thing to do to his own son!'

Chapter Twelve

'But it's only right that you should come into the family business as a director, Ken,' said Dolly to her brother the next day when he and Mabs were at Dolly's house in Bailey Gardens. 'It is your birthright, after all.'

'It's the last thing the old man would want, though,' he said through tight lips. 'In fact, it's a wonder the old sod didn't make some sort of stipulation against it in his will.'

'He didn't though, did he?' said Dolly. 'So I'm free to have whoever I choose in the firm with me.'

'Huh! He didn't need to put anything in writing,' said Ken bitterly. 'The fact that I wasn't mentioned says it all.'

'Well . . . anyway . . . the firm is mine now,' said Dolly in a positive manner. 'And I want it to be *ours*, Ken, yours and mine. So what do you say?'

'Oh . . . I don't know, Sis,' he said, with a doubtful shake of the head. 'I'm quite happy with the job I've got.'

'But I really do *need* you, Ken,' Dolly said, trying another line of persuasion because she felt so strongly about his right to a place in the firm. 'It's a hell of a task he's left me with . . . being responsible for the whole bloomin' factory.'

'You can do it,' he assured her. 'You've grown up with tea, you know the trade inside out.'

'So do you. In fact, you know more about it than I do,' she said, 'having been involved in management for so long.'

'Come off it, Doll. You've worked in Slater's office on and off ever since you left school,' he reminded her. 'You're more than up to the job.'

'Don't forget I've a home and children to look after as well.'

'Mmm, there is that . . .'

'I won't be able to give Slater's as much time as I could were I a man without domestic responsibilities,' she sensibly pointed out. 'Anyway, working in the office is one thing, running the whole shooting match is quite another.'

'You're more than capable.'

'That's beside the point,' she said determinedly. 'Slater's is a family firm and you are a part of that family.'

'I don't give a damn about any of that,' said Ken, a tremor in his voice betraying how deeply hurt he had been by his father's final rejection of him.

'Well, I bloomin' well do,' intervened Mabs assertively. 'Dolly is quite right, Ken. You should be in the business with her.'

'Calm down, love,' he urged.

'No, I won't calm down,' Mabs told him hotly. 'You've no right to throw away what rightfully belongs to you just because your father had a paranoid grudge against you. He caused you enough pain when he was alive. Don't let him carry on doing it after he's dead.'

'But he obviously didn't want me to be in the business . . .'

'I don't care what he wanted.' interrupted Mabs. 'The man was rotten through and through.' She paused and looked at Dolly as though fearing she might have caused offence. 'I'm sorry to speak ill of your father, Doll, but it's true and his being dead ain't gonna change that.'

'It's all right.'

Mabs turned her attention back to her husband. 'You've a son to think of now, Ken. Peter is a Slater whether your father acknowledged him or not. He might want to go into the firm later on when he's grown up . . . it's up to you to make sure he is given the chance.'

'She's right, Ken,' said Dolly, looking at him hopefully.

'Oh, well,' he sighed. 'Looked at in that light, I suppose I don't really have a choice.'

'No, you don't,' said Dolly, hugging him.

A few days later Dolly stood on a platform hastily erected from wooden boards and tea chests in Slater's factory yard where the entire workforce had gathered at her request. Ken was at one side of her, Bert Dixon at the other. Over the sea of heads, the Thames gleamed olive green in the spring sunshine, smoke from a passing tugboat spiralling towards a clear blue sky. The air was still and sweet with the season, the scent of May blossom clearly discernible above the more pungent mixture of tar, mud, fresh paint and soot from the chimneys of the waterside factories.

Although respectfully attired in black, Dolly looked extremely elegant in a fashionable suit with a small waist and padded shoulders, her hair sleek beneath a plain dark hat.

'You will all have heard of my father's death,' she said to the crowd.

A sympathetic murmur rippled through the gathering.

'And you will all be wondering what is going to happen to the firm.'

There was an affirmative chorus.

'That's why I've called this meeting,' she told them. 'To assure you that your jobs are safe.'

The cheers were subdued; the workers were still wary of the situation.

'My brother and I are going to be running the factory between us,' she said. 'And Mr Dixon will continue to be General Manager.'

A hubbub of surprise and concern erupted.

'"A woman running Slater's?" I hear you men say with disapproval,' she continued.

They roared in agreement.

'You don't think I can do it . . .'

A vociferous male voice said, 'A woman's place is in the 'ome.'

This was counterbalanced by shouts from a crowd of female packers.

'For some of us that may be true,' Dolly announced to the back of the audience, 'but since my father saw fit to land me with the job, I'm going to give it everything I've got.'

'Hear, hear,' said Ken.

'But there are going to be changes,' she continued.

The crowd murmured uneasily.

'Changes for the better,' she said in a positive voice which reflected her intention to improve things for everyone at Slater's, not just those on the management.

'We don't believe in fairy tales,' said one male troublemaker.

'No, we don't,' jeered his supporters.

'Give 'er a chance,' said one of the girls from the packing department to a chorus of support from her workmates.

'What sort of changes?' asked a man at the back.

'You'll be hearing from us about them in the near future,' she said.

'Let's 'ope we ain't all too old to care by that time,' sneered the man.

'In the meantime, it's business as usual,' said Dolly brightly, ignoring the heckler. 'Thank you all for listening.'

Bert Dixon was an amiable man in middle age who'd been with Slater's since he was a boy. He'd been promoted to General Manager after Frank's departure and had transformed the position into one of real responsibility. Having worked his way up through the ranks, spending time in all the different departments and excelling as a taster, there wasn't much he didn't know about tea. But having worked under Henry for so long, he was still very much under his influence and had a lot to learn about how to get the best out of people.

'A works committee?' he said, staring at Dolly in astonishment at a meeting in her office a few days later.

'We've never had anything like that at Slater's.'

'It's high time we did then, isn't it?'

'Your dad wouldn't like that at all, Miss Dolly,' he said, shaking his head.

'Dad isn't here any more, Bert,' Ken wisely pointed out.

'Give the workers an inch and they'll take a mile,' pronounced Bert. 'Your dad was adamant about that. That's why he wouldn't employ union labour.'

'Give the workers decent conditions and they'll give you more for your money,' countered Dolly.

'Who would be on this committee, anyway?' asked Bert dubiously. 'And what would it do?'

'Its members would be elected from the factory floor to put suggestions and views on how things might be improved at that level,' explained Dolly.

'In what way?' Bert was still very doubtful.

'In all sorts of ways,' said Dolly. 'For instance, I've been nagging my father for years to provide the packers with decent overalls to be freshly laundered each week, instead of those awful heavy things they wear now that they have to wash themselves.'

'Phew, I dunno if that's a good idea,' he said, scratching his bald head ponderously. 'Just think of the cost.'

'That will have to be taken into consideration, of course,' said Dolly, adding enthusiastically, 'Also they could do with a rest room – somewhere they can take a break away from their workbenches to eat their sandwiches.'

'I dunno, Miss Dolly,' said Bert, shaking his head. 'I really don't.'

'Also,' she continued crisply, 'I think they should have decent toilet facilities to replace that dreadful old shed of a place they use at the moment.'

'Blimey, you'll be suggesting a works outing on a charabanc next,' said Bert sarcastically.

'What a good idea,' said Ken. 'If it helps to create a happy factory atmosphere, it might be worth the company making a contribution.'

'Blimey,' Bert said again.

'Anyway, all that sort of thing can be hammered out once we get a works committee set up. The committee can get the workers' suggestions and ideas, and of course any complaints . . .'

'With respect, Miss Dolly, you really *are* asking for trouble if you're gonna encourage them to complain,' said Bert in a doom-laden voice. 'They'll really go to town on that one.'

'At first, perhaps,' agreed Dolly. 'And let's face it, there is plenty for them to complain about at Slater's. But as we begin to get things done, they'll have less to grumble about.'

'Never had anything like this in my day on the factory floor,' he said.

'More's the pity, don't you think?' asked Dolly.

'From the workers' point of view, yeah, of course,' he said. 'Dunno what it'll be like from this side of the fence though.'

'Treat people well and they'll do likewise,' she said.

'I 'ope you're right,' said Bert.

'Anyway, Bert, it's your job as General Manager to get

this works committee underway.'

'Righto, Miss Dolly,' he sighed, 'but I don't know where it will all end, I'm sure.'

Despite Bert Dixon's doubts the improvements were a great success. By the autumn the packers were comfortably uniformed in crisp new cotton overalls and mob caps, all laundered at the firm's expense.

As Dolly so rightly put it when Bert queried the laundry bill: 'It's little enough to come out of our profits – its our responsibility to maintain hygienic conditions, after all.'

Reorganisation of space meant they were able to provide a rest room without the cost of major building work. Part of an underused storeroom was partitioned off, painted and furnished with a few basic pieces.

Undeterred by the increasing threat of war and its probable chaos, the works committee planned a day trip to Southend for the following summer. Whilst the firm agreed to stand the cost of the charabanc, the workers were paying a small amount into the outing fund on a weekly basis for food and drink, with the emphasis heavily on the latter. Dolly was pleased to note new good feeling throughout the factory despite the trial black-out and increased recruitment for volunteers to Civil Defence.

'We'll get to Southend, even if we 'ave to swim down the Thames with our gas masks on,' Dolly heard someone say, and this was typical of the sanguine spirit among them.

Although she enjoyed her new involvement in the firm, life was extremely hectic. She found herself permanently short of time even though the increase in salary meant she could afford to employ help with the domestic chores. Determined not to disrupt the children's home-life, she fitted her working day in with school hours. Inevitably, there were times when home and business overlapped, but Mabs was always quick to offer a helping hand. Since both Dolly's children were very fond of their Auntie Mabs this was a great help.

But there was another call on Dolly's time, and with the best will in the world, there was nothing Mabs could do to assist her in this . . .

'Hello, Mother,' said Dolly, visiting Edie one January day in 1939 to find her in bed yet again. 'How are you feeling?'

'Very poorly indeed,' said Edie, lying back against the pillows, a pink bed jacket draped around her shoulders. She was pale from lack of fresh air, but plump from a good appetite and no exercise.

'What's the trouble today?' Dolly asked firmly.

'You know very well what the trouble is,' she snapped. 'I'm as weak as a kitten.'

'The doctor suggested that you might feel stronger if you were up and about.'

'Get up?' her mother protested. 'How can I get up when I'm too frail to put one foot in front of the other?'

'Staying in bed is only going to make you feel worse,' said Dolly.

She had been assured by Dr Beresford that there was nothing physically wrong with her mother, and that she was still grieving for her husband.

'She's nursing a broken heart,' was the way he put it but Dolly thought it was not her heart that was broken so much as the prop Father had provided her with. Quite simply, her mother was terrified to tackle life without him.

Dolly had suggested that Edie move in with her and the children temporarily until she got used to being a widow. But she preferred to stay on in Maybury Avenue, being waited on hand and foot by servants who would allow her to stay in bed, wallowing in self-pity, since they were paid to do as she said. Whereas Dolly was more interested in getting her to come to grips with her single status and lead a normal life.

'You're heartless, you are, Dolly,' Edie said in a wounded tone, her voice wobbling on the verge of tears. 'Fancy trying to drag your own mother out of bed when you can see how ill I am.'

Dolly sat on the edge of the bed and took her hand. 'There's nothing wrong with you,' she said gently, 'the doctor has assured me of that.'

'He doesn't know how I feel . . . anyway, I don't care what he says, you shouldn't bully me when I'm recently bereaved.'

'It's months since Father died,' Dolly reminded her.

'That doesn't make it any easier to bear.'

'I know how hard it must be for you to carry on without him, but the sooner you get on with it, the sooner you'll start to feel better.' She gave a hopeful grin. 'You never know, you might even begin to enjoy life a little.'

'You just don't understand how frail and alone I feel.'

'Of course I don't, but I can imagine,' said Dolly kindly.

'Huh!'

'Anyway, you're not alone,' she reminded her mother. 'You've Ken and me. We'll do all we can to help.'

'No one cares,' wailed Edie. 'You only come to see me out of duty and your brother hardly ever comes at all.'

Dolly bit back her reply, keeping a grip on her over-tried patience. It wasn't easy to remain tolerant with someone so devoid of pluck as Mother, leaning feebly against the pillows like an old woman. Fifty years old and she seemed more like ninety. That was what years of domination had done to her.

If Ken hadn't fallen for Mabs and escaped from his father's clutches, he'd have ended up the same way, Dolly was sure of it. It was only his wife's steadfast love and encouragement that had given him the confidence to stand on his own two feet. Mabs certainly didn't deserve to be ignored by her mother-in-law.

'It's your own fault that Ken doesn't visit you very often,' she said. 'You can't expect him to put himself out for you when you won't have anything to do with his wife and son.'

'I'm his mother, it's his duty to come and see me now that I'm on my own.'

'He has a duty to his wife too,' Dolly pointed out.

'She stops him from coming to see me, I bet,' said Edie gloomily.

'Mabs would *never* do a thing like that,' Dolly told her.

'What makes you such an authority?'

'I know her well enough to know she doesn't have a mean bone in her body,' said Dolly. 'If only you would take the trouble to make friends with her, you would find out what a nice person she is.'

'She's never struck me as nice,' said Edie. 'She's got far too much to say for herself for my liking.'

'It's true she isn't afraid to speak her mind,' admitted Dolly. 'Frankly, I admire her for it. You always know where you are with Mabs.'

'Common as muck,' said Edie. 'She still can't speak the King's English after all these years as Ken's wife.'

'That hardly amounts to a stain on her character,' put in Dolly acidly.

'I don't know what Ken was thinking about, marrying beneath him.'

Dolly tutted. 'We're a middle-class family of tea merchants, Mother, not ruddy aristocracy.'

'We're certainly a cut above the likes of her,' said Edie.

'She's your son's wife and the mother of your grandchild,' Dolly said.

'Don't remind me.'

'You owe it to Ken to make her welcome in your home.'

'Never!'

'Then don't complain because he doesn't come to see you as often as he should,' said Dolly sternly.

'You take her side against your own mother!' accused Edie viciously.

'Yes, I do, because what you are doing to Ken and Mabs is wrong.' She glanced at her watch, mindful of the fact that the children would soon be home from school for she had come here straight from work. 'Anyway, I have to go soon.'

Edie stared miserably towards the window. It was mid-afternoon but already daylight was fading on this winter day. The skeletal branches of the pavement trees were etched blackly against the pearl grey skies across which heavy banks of cloud were rolling. She looked at Dolly. 'You just can't wait to get away can you?' she said accusingly.

'Only because I like to be in when the children get home from school,' explained Dolly. 'You know that perfectly well.'

'You've no business being out at work at all,' she said. 'It isn't seemly for a woman.'

'And what am I supposed to do about the business Daddy left to me?' she asked. 'Run it from my kitchen table?'

'You should let your brother look after it. Business is for men, it's a recognised fact.'

'Daddy must have thought differently or he wouldn't have left it to me,' Dolly pointed out.

'I don't know what the man was thinking of, I'm sure.'

'He was acknowledging the fact that I have a brain, I think,' said Dolly. 'Even though the old devil would never have admitted it while he was alive.'

'Don't speak ill of the dead.'

An exasperated sigh escaped from Dolly and caught her mother's attention.

'Perhaps it would be easier for you all if I was dead,' she said morosely.

'It would be easier for us all if you would make some sort of an effort,' retorted Dolly.

'A fat lot you care.'

'If I didn't care I wouldn't be trying to persuade you to get up,' said Dolly. 'I'd leave you to rot away in bed!'

'Huh!'

Dolly softened her tone. 'Look, Mum, how about a few hours downstairs in the sitting room? I'll settle you in your chair before I go.'

'No!'

Dolly got up and turned on the light and drew the curtains. 'Is there anything you'd like me to do for you before I go?'

'You can tell Cook I might be able to manage a lightly boiled egg for my tea with plenty of thin bread and butter.'

'Shall I tell her that you'll have it by the fire in the sitting room?' persisted Dolly hopefully.

'*No!* How many more times must I tell you, I am not well enough to get up.'

'Very well.'

She left feeling worried and worn out. What was to become of Mother? She couldn't hide from life indefinitely.

One spring afternoon Edie's slumber was interrupted by a commotion outside in the street the sound of which was drifting in through the bedroom window. She closed her eyes, waiting for the noise to stop, but it got worse. Not only were men shouting to each other but there was bumping and scraping – what sounded like the clank and rattle of metal against the ground.

'Will just 'ere do yer, mate?' she heard a man say.

'What, stuck down there on the pavement?' said an irate male voice she recognised as her gardener's.

'Yeah, just outside the front gate.'

'Can't you take it round the back?'

'No, you'll have to do that yourself – we ain't got time, mate. We got hundreds of these to deliver.'

'Blimey! Have you really?'

'Yeah, when this lorry load's done we've got to go back for more – London's a priority area, a target city, see . . . stands to reason, dunnit? You know, with its being the capital. It's the first place the Germans'll aim for.'

Who on earth was causing this terrible racket? This kind of disturbance was unheard of in the Avenue; the loudest inconvenience the residents normally experienced was the clink of bottles when the milkman called. There seemed to be an army of ruffians out there, thought Edie crossly. Unable to stem her curiosity, she got out of bed and went to the window, surveying the scene from behind the net curtains.

In the road outside her house was a lorry loaded with what appeared to be scrap metal – a pile of curved corrugated iron sheets. Across the road was a similarly loaded vehicle, and a trail of their cargo had been dumped in separate heaps on the pavement all along the street.

Ted, her gardener, was in conversation with the driver of the first truck which looked as though it was about to move. It did, but only a short distance to off-load piles of metal at houses further on. Ted opened the front gate and began to drag the ironware inside, closely observed by Edie's cook and maid.

Shaky and confused, Edie got back into bed and rang the bell for Betsy the maid. She had to wait for ages because the staff were all out in the garden and Edie was far too reserved to shout down to them from the bedroom window. Eventually, Betsy trotted in, her neat movements rustling rhythmically against her starched uniform.

'You rang, Madam,' she said, standing attentively at the bedside.

'Indeed I did,' said Edie, sounding perplexed. 'What on earth is going on outside... what does Ted think he's doing bringing all that ironware into the garden?'

'It's the air raid shelters being delivered, Madam,' Betsy informed her cheerfully. 'You know... the government is giving priority to all 'ouses in London boroughs.' She paused with a puzzled expression. 'You must have been expecting it?'

'I certainly was not,' said Edie with suitable hauteur. 'And I don't want one of those things in my garden.'

'I think they're a good idea,' prattled Betsy. 'My mum and dad will gets theirs free 'cos Dad earns less than two hundred and fifty pounds a year. I expect you'll have to pay for yours, you bein' well off, but it'll be worth it to have peace of mind.'

'And how will that load of junk give me that?' said Edie.

'The corrugated iron has to be sunk into the ground to make a sort of underground hut,' explained Betsy. 'But don't worry. Ted'll dig yours in for you.'

'He'll have no need because I'm not having my garden ruined,' said Edie, mopping her brow; the upset to her nervous system was bringing her out in a cold sweat.

'But you'll 'ave to 'ave somewhere safe to go if the

bombs start coming, won't yer?' said Betsy.

'Bombs?' said Edie aghast.

'Yeah, they reckon there'll be plenty of them about if war breaks out.'

'They're not still waffling on about war are they?' said Edie, feeling uneasy within the isolation she'd built for herself. She hadn't read a newspaper or been out in months and didn't seem to be able to concentrate on the wireless so had stopped turning it on. If Dolly started talking about war rumours, she asked her to change the subject because it was too depressing.

Betsy looked grave. 'Everyone's talking about it, Madam. Me dad thinks it's a real danger now . . . it's somethin' to do with the Germans goin' into some place called . . . er . . . Prague, I think he said. That's made it a real possibility, according to 'im. I don't know much about it meself, but Dad's always jabbering on about it when I'm at 'ome on me day off.'

'When did this Prague thing happen?'

'Ooh, a few weeks ago,' she said. 'But you must 'ave 'eard about it?'

Embarrassed by her ignorance, Edie didn't reply.

'I don't suppose you've felt like keeping up with the news . . . you being so poorly,' said the maid sympathetically.

'You're right, Betsy, I haven't.'

'A lot's happened outside since you took to your bed, Madam.'

'Oh?'

'Yeah. There's trenches in the park now and sandbags all over the place.'

'Really?'

'Yeah. And now the shelters, o' course.'

'Mmm.'

'Better to be safe than sorry, eh, Madam?'

'Well . . . yes. I suppose so.'

'And that's not all,' the girl continued. 'They're even talking about evacuating the children.'

'Oh, really . . . whatever next?'

'I know one thing, though,' Betsy chattered on, 'if we're gonna have to go out to the shelter in the middle of the night, I'm goin' to bed fully dressed. I ain't gonna let people see me in me nightclothes, bombs or no bombs. Being properly dressed makes you feel more up to things, dunnit?'

'Yes,' mumbled Edie, a knot of fear tightening within her.

'Still, not to worry, eh?' chirped Betsy. 'It might never happen. And if it does we'll manage somehow, won't we?'

Edie nodded.

'Will that be all then, Madam?'

'Yes.'

'Right you are then.'

'Oh, Betsy,' she called as the girl reached the door.

'Yes, Madam?'

'I'll have my tea downstairs in the sitting room today.'

Betsy beamed. 'Oh, that is good news,' she said. 'You feelin' a bit better then?'

'Just a little,' admitted Edie.

Immediately the door had closed behind the maid, Edie swung out of bed and padded to the wardrobe, dragging out the first thing that came to hand and rummaging in her drawer for some underclothes.

Betsy was right about the power of being properly dressed. Bed was no place to be if war was coming. It made you feel too vulnerable!

Chapter Thirteen

A growing collection of public information leaflets and booklets arriving through the letter box, with such chilling titles as 'The Protection Of Your Home Against Air Raids', made it impossible for anyone to pretend that a crisis didn't exist, even a committed optimist like Dolly, especially when ubiquitous ARP recruiting posters, bearing the message 'Don't Leave It To Others' started staring out reproachfully from hoardings, walls and trees.

The thing that really brought the seriousness of the situation home to her, though, was the compilation of a list to which parents were asked to add their children's names if they wished them to be evacuated with their school in the event of war.

'What do you think, Doll?' asked Mabs gravely. 'You gonna send Barney and Merle?'

'I think we ought to make our own arrangements if the worst does happen,' said Dolly, 'and leave room on the government scheme for those who haven't the means to do it themselves.'

'You're probably right.'

'Let's hope and pray it isn't necessary though.'

* * *

One warm and sunny September Saturday Dolly and her children stood outside their house in Bailey Gardens alongside Ken's car, which was piled high with luggage. The atmosphere was heavy.

''Bye, Mum,' Barney said, with a clumsy, embrace.

''Bye, Barney,' she said, smiling artificially and biting back the tears as she drew back and cast an affectionate eye over him. He looked achingly smart, his face pink and scrubbed, dark hair combed into place. Whilst he was sad at the parting, his natural exuberance created a certain excitement at the 'adventure' ahead. 'Behave yourself and do what your Auntie Mabs tells you. She's under strict instructions from me to do whatever's necessary to keep you in order.'

''Course I will,' he said with a half smile, his eyes overbright.

'I'll get down to Devon to see you whenever I can,' she promised.

'I know you will.'

'You'll have a great time in the country.'

'Yeah, I can't wait to get there, to see all those cows and haystacks and things.'

'Take care now.'

'Don't fuss, Mum.' He was all boyish embarrassment as he turned and clambered into the car, his cardboard gas mask box slung across his shoulder over his navy blue jersey and short grey trousers.

Merle's goodbye was less visibly emotional. She was cool almost to the point of accusation, as though her mother, personally, had contrived to create a war for the sole purpose of removing her children.

''Bye, then,' she said, placing a formal peck on her mother's cheek and retreating at Dolly's attempt to hug her.

'You'll be all right with your Auntie Mabs,' said Dolly, intending to reassure her.

'Of course I will,' came the crushing retort.

'I have to send you away for a while, Merle,' said Dolly, feeling the need to justify her actions to this surly eleven year old whose attitude always seemed tinged with criticism.

'Sure.'

'It won't be for long,' she continued, 'just till they get this war sorted out. Christmas, they say, at the latest.'

'All right.'

Her outward attitude was one of indifference, but Dolly suspected it concealed a tangle of complex emotions. It was as though her daughter couldn't wait to escape from her mother, yet at the same time couldn't bear to go. Merle always managed to make Dolly feel as though she'd failed her somehow, though Dolly wondered if she was being quite fair to herself, for she really *did* try to do her best for both her children.

'I can't come to the country with you because of the business,' she explained with resolute cheeriness. 'But your Aunt Mabs is the next best thing to having me around.'

'I know.'

Noticing her trembling lip and tear-filled eyes Dolly

caught a glimpse of the loving little girl she had once been. She looked so vulnerable standing there in her navy blue blazer over a summer frock, shoulders rigid as she tried not to show her feelings. Dolly gathered her in her arms and hugged her tight. 'I'll miss you, love,' she whispered truthfully.

The child's body trembled against hers in response but after a moment she moved back, protesting, 'Honestly, Mum, I'm not a baby, you know.'

She got into the back of the car with Barney and her cousin Peter. Mabs was in the front seat next to Ken who was driving them to a cottage they had rented in Devon, he himself returning to London tomorrow night. Watching the overloaded Austin roll away to join the procession of traffic heading out of London, the children's bicycles tied to the roof, Dolly let the scalding tears fall. The fact that she was acting in their best interests didn't diminish the pain of parting.

As much as she wanted to go with them, it wasn't possible for her to leave the factory. Heaven knew what sort of conditions they would be working under once war was actually declared as was expected to happen by the end of the weekend now that Hitler had invaded Poland. Many London firms were moving their businesses to the safety of the country but she and Ken had decided against that.

'We'll need to be in London if petrol goes on ration,' Ken had wisely pointed out. 'With all our custom being in and around the London area, we'll never be able to maintain supplies otherwise.'

Dolly had agreed. 'As well as looking after our own

livelihood we do have a duty to the public to keep them supplied,' she'd said.

Now, as the car turned the corner and out of sight, she walked back into the empty house, cool and dark in contrast to the bright sunshine outside and shrouded in a gloomy silence. Dismal black-out curtains were drawn back from the windows, for the new lighting restrictions had come into force last night.

Saturdays were normally noisy and hectic, the house reverberating to sibling squabbles and the rat-a-tat of the door knocker as their friends came to call. Dolly usually went shopping and caught up with any lingering domestic chores. Barney would come in muddy and loquacious from some football game; Merle would come home from her piano lesson and solemnly practise her scales.

There would be rabbit stew for dinner and crumpets for tea. The children would stay up late because it was a weekend and they'd all listen to the wireless or play a game of Monopoly during which Merle and Barney would accuse each other of cheating and almost come to blows: the ordinariness of family life with all its concomitant exasperations, normally taken for granted and now sorely missed by Dolly.

A grave feeling of expectancy permeated everything. The children had gone, the barrage balloons had come, the ARP were ready for action. The only thing missing was the war.

This was rectified the next day when Neville Chamberlain made an emotive broadcast to the nation.

But although the ensuing weeks brought false alarms to put people's nerves on edge, and a bombardment of new restrictions to make life even more difficult, the only real danger on the home front was the black-out as people tripped over kerbs and collided with lamp posts and pillar boxes.

'I'm glad I didn't let you talk me into going away to some Godforsaken hole in the country,' said Edie, who had refused to go with the children mainly, Dolly suspected, because Mabs would be there. 'They'll all come flocking back home to London, you mark my words.'

She was right. Mabs and the children were back home before Christmas.

'Never again,' exclaimed Mabs. 'I've never felt so miserable in all me life. Miles and miles of nothing to cheer you up, no shops or cinemas. I tell you, Doll, I'd sooner take me chances 'ere than go back there, I don't care how much the government wants us to stay.'

Naturally Dolly was concerned for the safety of her children for the government was adamant in their assertion that the danger had not passed. There were 'Leave The Children Where They Are' posters all over the place, picturing a sinister Hitler-like figure leaning over a mother's shoulder telling her to bring her children back home. But as there was no actual evidence of danger, Dolly let things stay as they were for the time being and enjoyed having her family around her again.

At least with their noisy presence about the place, the house bore some semblance of normality despite the introduction of rationing for some food items in January.

Things were not so normal at the factory however . . .

Anticipating heavy bombing on London at the outbreak of war, the government had had most of the tea that was being stored in warehouses at the docks removed and distributed all over the country for storage. The speed of the dispersal caused confusion in the tea trade as to ownership, resulting in the government's buying all the tea on the books of dealers and merchants and making weekly allocations to them.

When tea was put on ration to the public, wholesalers were issued with permits with which to purchase tea, which came in three qualities; a third common, a third medium and a third fine. It was left to the blenders to make the best use of their allocation.

Despite the limitations of tea control, the loss of workers to the services and petrol rationing, Dolly was determined that supplies would be maintained to their customers. To help cope with the reduced mileage they were able to cover in petrol-driven vehicles, Slater's used horse-drawn vehicles for local deliveries; to ease the manpower problem they employed women to take over male roles, including driving the delivery vans loaded with packed tea.

Both Dolly and Ken made a point of studying the complexities of the rationing system from the point of view of the grocer. Their knowledge was passed on to the delivery salesmen who were then able to advise grocers on the complicated form-filling process necessary to meet the requirements of their local food offices, thus creating goodwill.

Dolly's working day was frantic and varied for she helped out wherever she was most needed, doing anything from clerical work to tea packing and even sweeping the floor and washing up the crockery after the tea-tasters.

Just when she felt as though she had things under control, as far as was possible in these difficult times, she was faced with a major problem: Ken was called up into the army.

'I'll come into the factory and give a hand while Peter is at school, if you like,' offered Mabs. 'I'll need something to do to occupy my mind while Ken's away.'

'Oh, Mabs, would you?' enthused Dolly.

'Yeah, 'course I will. I was gonna get a job anyway, so I might as well help keep the Slater flag flying as do anything else.'

'Great.'

'I don't have the know-how to take Ken's place on the management side, o' course, Doll,' she pointed out. 'But I used to be a dab hand at packing.'

'You'll be a great help,' said Dolly, 'especially as you have a personal interest in the firm.'

'Not so easy to get packers nowadays, is it, with so many women going into the services or into the munitions factories?'

'Time was when we could pick and choose,' confessed Dolly in sombre mood. 'Not now that women are needed to replace the fighting men in other jobs, though.'

'At least it's made it respectable for a married woman to go out to work,' said Mabs.

'Believe it or not, there's still some resistance to that, even now.'

'Is that a fact?'

'Yes, I was reading an article in the *News Chronicle* about women being turned down for jobs traditionally done by men even though they need people so badly.'

'It's bloomin' crackers to turn women away when everyone is so keen to do their bit,' exclaimed Mabs hotly. 'Still, employers'll have to change their tune if the war goes on much longer and more and more men are called up, 'cos there just won't be anyone else to do the jobs.'

'You're right,' agreed Dolly, feeling enormously heartened at the idea of having her friend working with her. 'Anyway, you'll be doing your bit by keeping up public morale by making sure they get their cuppa.'

'It'll help to take my mind off Ken's being away,' she said. 'I won't 'alf miss him, though.'

'We all will,' said Dolly, but knew Mabs would bear the brunt of the suffering, for she and Ken had seemed to grow even closer over the years.

Edie didn't share Dolly's enthusiasm for Mabs joining the firm. 'She's quick off the mark getting herself fixed up with a job, isn't she?' she said. 'Ken hasn't even gone yet.'

'It's the most sensible thing she can do,' defended Dolly. 'It will be lonely for her with Ken away and Peter out at school all day.'

'As long as she doesn't think she can step into Ken's shoes.'

'Of course she doesn't . . .'

'Packing tea is about all she's fit for.'

'No one is more aware of that than Mabs herself,' said Dolly. 'But I'm hoping she'll be willing to stretch herself to other things because I need someone beside me with a vested interest in the firm.'

'Vested interest, her?'

'With her being family, I mean.'

'Family, my eye,' snorted Edie.

'She is family, Mother, whether you like it or not.'

'Not to me she isn't!'

'Don't you think it's time you buried the hatchet, now that Ken is going away?' suggested Dolly.

'I don't see why.'

'It's obvious why,' she said sharply. 'You could be a comfort to each other. After all, you are united in one thing – you both love Ken.'

'That's as may be but . . .'

'This nonsense has gone on for long enough,' interrupted Dolly, who as well as believing that her mother would gain from a friendship with Mabs, found it tiresome having to juggle family arrangements so the two didn't meet. 'These are bad times we're living in – the least we can all do is try to get along together.'

'I'll knit for the troops and grow vegetables in my garden,' said Edie stubbornly. 'But don't ask me to make a friend of *that* woman.'

'All right, Mother,' sighed Dolly wearily. 'But you'll be the loser, I can promise you that.'

* * *

228

'What are you and Peter having for supper tonight?' asked Dolly as she and Mabs walked to where their bicycles were parked in Slater's yard. It was a sunny Saturday afternoon in September with barely a cloud in the sky. With the war now a year old, weekends were no longer times of leisure for Dolly and Mabs. Unreliable deliveries of tea to the factory and staff shortages at Slater's meant they often had to work on Saturdays – sometimes even on Sundays.

'Corned beef in some shape or form,' replied Mabs. 'Probably fritters or hash.'

'Surprise, surprise,' laughed Dolly, stacking some provisions she'd queued for in her lunch hour into the basket on the front of her bike.

'You're having it too, I suppose?'

'Yes, but I've found a new recipe that I'm going to try. It's called American mince. You mince up the corned beef and cook it with pearl barley.'

'At least it'll be a change.'

'Why don't we pool our resources and eat together at my place?' Dolly suggested. Peter was already with his cousins at her house. At thirteen Barney was old enough to be left in charge for a few hours.

Mabs looked doubtful. 'I'm not keen on walking 'ome if there's an air raid though,' she said. 'I know nothing much happens but I still find it scary.'

'Stay the night,' suggested Dolly. 'Peter will enjoy being with his cousins. It'll be a bit of a squash but we'll manage.'

'I'd like that, Doll,' said Mabs, swinging into the saddle. 'I'll pop home and get our bit o' grub and come straight round. The bloomin' air raid siren gives me the creeps.'

'No wonder they call it Wailing Willie.'

'Yeah,' laughed Mabs. 'I've never heard a more miserable sound. It don't 'alf give me the shivers. Makes me wish Ken was home.'

'Perhaps he'll get some leave soon.'

'It's not the same as havin' him around all the time though, is it?'

'No, but at least he's still in this country,' said Dolly.

'Not for much longer, I shouldn't think,' said Mabs solemnly. 'They're bound to send him overseas once he's been properly trained.'

'I suppose so,' agreed Dolly, as the two friends cycled round to the front of the building and out on to the road.

Mabs had proved to be a real asset to the firm. She concentrated her efforts mostly in the packing room but turned her hand to other things if necessary. The fact that she had never lost the common touch made her popular with the packers, especially as she was such a hard worker herself. Although she was much happier being one of the girls than one of the bosses, Dolly did discuss management issues with her and looked on her as part of the team along with Bert Dixon who, much to Dolly's relief, was past enlistment age.

'See you later then,' said Mabs, as they parted company at the end of her street.

That same afternoon Edie was busy in her kitchen making

something from a Ministry of Food recipe called Fish in Savoury Custard. She'd reconstituted some dried egg, mixed it with milk and poured it into an oven dish over the little piece of fish she had stood in a long queue at the fishmongers for. Consulting the recipe for the finishing touches, she sprinkled salt and pepper over the top, omitted the herbs because she didn't have any, and put it into the oven on a low light to bake slowly. Just the thing for her high tea, she thought hungrily. Heaven knew what had happened to her delicate pre-war appetite – lately she always seemed to be famished. Damned shortages! What were the politicians thinking of to let things get into such a state?

Taking the tea caddy from the larder with the idea of making herself a pot, she heard the ominous warble of the air raid siren. Her appetite suffered instant death as she went rigid with fear. She tried to quieten her fluttering heart by taking deep breaths and reminding herself that they'd had plenty of air raid warnings over the past few weeks and none had amounted to anything.

She couldn't face the thought of going into the Anderson shelter. As if the claustrophobic conditions and spiders weren't bad enough, last time she'd had to put up with a family of toads splashing about in a muddy puddle on the floor. At least it was still daylight, she thought, glancing at the kitchen clock to see that it had just turned five o'clock.

Cursing the fact that her staff had deserted her for war work and left her to live here alone, she forced herself to carry on as though nothing untoward was happening. She put the kettle on for tea and set about washing the utensils she had used for cooking while waiting for it to boil.

This raid felt different to the others – nearer somehow. There was a commotion outside – raised voices and the thunder of running feet. The nagging drone of aircraft, too, sounding horribly close. Breathless and trembling, she went to the back door, drying her hands on the tea-towel, her whole body soaked with nervous perspiration.

Looking up to see the blue sky darkened with bomber planes, she let out a strangled cry just before the thud of a distant explosion. Then there was the whistle of bombs; the popping sound of ack-ack guns; a continuous clatter of thumps and bangs.

Frozen with terror she stood by the door, panic turning her brain to treacle. When, at last, she was able to gather her scrambled thoughts sufficiently to make her legs move, she left the house, stopping only to turn off the oven. She didn't remove her apron or shut the door after her. Tearing round to the front and out of the gate, she headed for Bailey Gardens.

'Cor, look at all those planes,' said Barney, peering through the opening of the Anderson shelter.

'Yeah,' breathed Peter, breathless with awe. 'I wonder where they're heading.'

'The docks, I should think,' said Dolly, trying not to let her fear show in her voice as the air reverberated with bumps and bangs and the crack of ack-ack guns. With the children's safety in mind, she always insisted that they use the shelter when the siren went, even though the previous raids had turned out to be nothing more than a nuisance. This one seemed more threatening and she was uneasy about her mother being on her own. But since she couldn't very well desert the children to go round to Maybury Avenue, all she could do was hope that Mother would have the sense to go into the shelter whether she liked it or not.

'I'm starving,' announced Barney.

'Talk about hollow legs,' said Dolly, with deliberate cheeriness. She gave him a chunk of bread from a loaf she'd grabbed on her way out to the shelter. 'It'll take more than an air raid to put you off your food, won't it?'

'Not 'alf.'

The shelter was dim and damp and smelled of wet earth. In an effort to make it more cosy, Dolly had put lino on the floor and painted the walls white. The candle in a jam-jar they normally used for lighting wasn't needed as daylight was shining in through the opening.

Sitting next to Dolly on the bench was Merle, her mood noticeably less exuberant than the boys'. 'Are you all right, love?' Dolly asked, turning to her daughter.

''Course I am.'

Knowing her daughter would sooner die than admit she might be in need of reassurance, Dolly slipped a comforting arm around her, and this time the girl didn't push it away.

'Anyone for a game of I spy?' suggested Dolly.

The boys thought that was too babyish.

'What about cards?' said Barney, for they kept a pack down here permanently.

'No thanks,' said Mabs. 'It takes too much concentration.'

'A sing-song then,' said Dolly.

'"Ten Green Bottles",' suggested Peter.

This was well received and Dolly had to admit that a good rousing chorus did seem to relieve the tension, if only in that it helped to drown the noise from outside.

They were in the middle of a hearty five green bottles when a distraught figure appeared at the entrance to the shelter, bringing the boisterous proceedings to a sudden halt.

'I can't stand it, Dolly,' Edie screamed hysterically. 'London's on fire – there's bombs dropping everywhere.'

'Calm down, Mother,' she said, helping her in and moving up to make room for her on the bench. 'They seem to be falling quite a long way from here.'

'They're not all that far away and they're getting nearer,' sobbed Edie uncontrollably. 'We'll all be killed . . . we're all going to die . . .'

'Come on, Mum,' said Dolly firmly, giving her a comforting hug. 'Try to pull yourself together, there's a dear.'

'How can I?' she cried, holding her head dramatically and making a fearful moaning sound. 'It's all so awful . . . someone will have to do something to stop it . . . oh dear, oh dear, I can't bear it . . . I really can't!'

'Do calm down,' said Dolly anxiously. 'You'll frighten the children.'

But Edie was beyond caring and emitted an ear-splitting screech.

'Stop that bloody noise at once!' demanded Mabs. 'You'll frighten the kids to death.'

Edie stopped screaming instantly and looked across at Mabs as though only just realising she was there. 'You?' she said in a bemused tone.

'Yes, me,' retorted Mabs with an angry glare.

'How dare you swear at me?' said Edie, but there wasn't much fight in her.

'You're enough to drive a vicar to bad language,' said Mabs. 'You certainly don't deserve to be treated with respect, carryin' on like a demented two year old and thinking only of yourself.'

'I wasn't . . .'

'You ought to be ashamed of yourself, behaving like that in front of your grandchildren,' Mabs continued hotly. 'You selfish woman.'

'Someone should teach you some manners,' objected Edie, but it was only a token protest to hide how wretched she was feeling.

'And you should learn how to conduct yourself, mate,' said Mabs. 'I mean, where's your dignity, where's your guts?'

'I was startled by the bombs sounding so close,' stammered Edie.

'Aren't we all?' said Mabs. 'None of us likes what's happening, but that's no excuse for that sort o' carry on.'

'Well . . . no . . . I suppose not,' said Edie in a humble tone. 'I'm sorry, everyone.'

'That's all right, Gran,' said Barney and there was a general murmur of agreement.

The racket outside continued: bangs, thumps, explosions, the constant roar of aircraft. Dolly got them all singing again, anything she could think of to stop them dwelling on the nightmare that had burst upon London on a sunny afternoon.

As dusk fell the sky was lit by a red glow.

'Cor,' said Barney.

'Crumbs,' said Peter.

'Blimey,' said Mabs.

'I reckon the whole of East London must be on fire,' said Dolly.

In fact, it was miles of dockside warehouses that had gone up in flames, they discovered the next day, and many houses had been flattened or set on fire by incendiary bombs. The dead numbered more than four hundred according to a news bulletin and there were over a thousand badly injured.

'Poor devils,' said Dolly, as they stood in the garden looking at the smoky sky, grateful that Bailey Gardens had remained intact.

Life had to go on, despite everything, and Dolly tried to make this Sunday as much like any other as possible for the sake of the children. She suggested to Mother and Mabs that they pool their meat ration and have their Sunday lunch together. Mabs agreed wholeheartedly but Edie said she would rather have hers at home.

'Come back later on then,' suggested Dolly. 'Don't stay at home on your own. We can just about manage to squeeze you into the shelter if the siren goes.'

'Maybe,' said Edie, and made a huffy exit.

'It's because of me she won't come for lunch, isn't it?' said Mabs.

'Well . . . you were a bit hard on her last night,' admonished Dolly. 'I felt quite sorry for her.'

'Yes, but I calmed her down, didn't I?' Mabs pointed out.

'That's true,' agreed Dolly.

Edie could hardly see the potatoes she was peeling for the tears that were streaming from her eyes. It seemed hard to believe that once upon a time her existence had been relatively easy. Henry had been a cruel man, she couldn't deny it, and she had always been afraid of him, but at least he had been there to look after her.

Now life was grim indeed. In fact it was hardly bearable. She felt so terribly alone in these dreadful times. Henry was dead, Ken had gone away and her daughter seemed frequently to be irritated with her. Oh, yes, she could feel impatience hovering there below the surface even though Dolly tried to hide it. Anyway it was obvious that she thought more of her sister-in-law than her own mother. As for that Mabs creature . . . well, she just made life even more miserable.

With extreme discomfort, Edie cast her mind back to the previous evening, the memory of Mabs's reproach making her burn with shame for her loss of control. How could she have been so stupid as to let that bitch get the upper hand? It was true that she had gone to pieces and, yes, if she was really honest she *had* only been thinking of herself. Concern for relatives hadn't stood a chance against the impulse of self-preservation. But was it fair to be judged on how you behaved while in a state of terror?

Drying her hands, she wiped her eyes, put the potatoes in a saucepan, cut up some cabbage and ran it under the tap. Still unable to stop the flow of tears, she took a lamb chop from the larder, and put it into the frying pan with a knob of lard. At least if she'd gone to Dolly's for lunch there would have been some conversation to take her mind off the fear of another air raid.

In this mood of self-pity, her thoughts drifted to her third grandchild who was almost a stranger to her. If it wasn't for that wretched mother of his, she could try to get to know him better. She used to see Peter occasionally when Ken brought him visiting. Now she never saw the boy at all. From what she'd gathered last night he seemed to be growing up into a decent well-behaved boy. That would be his father's influence, of course.

She paused thoughtfully before lighting the gas under the pans. It still wasn't too late to pack up her food and go round to Dolly's for lunch. With a sense of relief at having decided not to stay here alone, she shook the excess water off the prepared vegetables, put them into a pudding basin with the meat and covered them all with a cloth.

Putting on her hat and coat, she left the house with purposeful stride. Halfway down Maybury Avenue she stopped, finding herself with a mental picture of Dolly and Mabs laughing and chatting together as they prepared the meal. She stood still by the grass verge, tears threatening. What was the point of her joining them? She'd only feel like an outsider.

Sorrowfully, she turned and walked back home. If only Ken had married someone she could get along with instead of that . . . that hard-faced bitch!

Chapter Fourteen

The steamy departure platform at Paddington station was heaving with servicemen. Undeterred by the bitter December temperature they were savouring the last few precious minutes with wives and girlfriends before boarding the train. The fact that civilian travellers were greatly outnumbered made Bill Drake, as yet dressed in ordinary clothes, feel somewhat incongruous among these uniformed men.

To be perfectly honest, he would rather Jean hadn't come to the station to see him off. Her presence here made him feel ludicrously mollycoddled since he was only going as far as Devizes. But she'd been so eager to give him a station send-off he hadn't had the heart to object. Life was too short to hurt her unnecessarily, the air raids were a constant reminder of that.

'You'll write as soon you can, won't you, darling?' she said, slipping her arms around his waist and looking into his face, her own pinched with cold.

''Course I will, love.'

'You take care now.'

'Jean,' he said in a mildly admonishing manner, 'I'm

241

only going to Devizes . . . not the bloomin' battlefront!'

'I know that, but even so . . .'

'Look, I appreciate your concern, love,' he said with the tiniest hint of impatience, 'but there'll be time enough to get your knickers in a twist later on, if I'm posted overseas.'

'Sorry if I'm being a pain, Bill,' she apologised whilst continuing to hold him in a lingering embrace. 'But you know how soft I am over you.'

Oh, yes, he knew all about that and it sometimes weighed heavily on him. Being anyone's raison d'être was a massive responsibility; it made you entirely responsible for their happiness and often feeling unequal to the task. But he reminded himself that it was a small price to pay for the everyday pleasure Jean brought to his life. After eleven years they still had a happy marriage which was more than he deserved since his feelings for Jean did not equal hers for him. He had tried to match her intensity but it simply wouldn't come, so he continued to do the only decent thing there was to do – pretend.

'Yes, I know,' he said, tapping her nose affectionately. 'But you're the one who needs to take care, here in London. I'm gonna be as safe as houses out in the sticks.'

He'd been called up into the army and was on his way to report to a training camp. At the moment, though, he was more concerned about the safety of Jean and her parents for London had become a dangerous city. Bombs had regularly rained down since the beginning of the Blitz in September. Everywhere you looked there was bomb damage and the number of casualties was staggering.

Still, things weren't all bad, he reminded himself in an

effort to quell his fears. At least they had had a few nights without air raids recently, and news had come through of a British victory in North Africa.

'I hope you're not going to get all countrified with a funny accent and straw in your hair?' she said with false levity to ease the farewell tension.

'What, me?' he laughed. 'That'll be the day.'

'It will too . . .'

'I'd feel happier about going away if you were somewhere safer,' he said, in more serious mood.

'You know that isn't possible. I've far too much to do here,' she reminded him, because both she and her mother were working with her father at the tea factory to ease the staff shortage.

'I know all that,' he said, for he had tried to talk her into going away to the country several times since the Blitz had started. 'But I'm sure something could be arranged.'

'The only reason I would move to the country is if I had a child to take with me,' she said firmly. 'But since I haven't, I think it's my duty to stay here and do a job of work.'

'All right, all right, point taken,' he said, backing away in mock fear.

Kit bags were beginning to be hauled on to the train. 'You'd better get on,' said Jean, 'or you won't get a seat.'

'There's no chance of that anyway,' he remarked, seeing the crowds of faces already peering from the carriage windows. 'But, yes, I suppose it is time I made a move.'

He held her tight and kissed her hard. ''Bye, love,' he said. 'I expect they'll give me a weekend pass when I've finished basic training, so it shouldn't be too long before I see you again.'

'I can't wait.' She kissed and clung to him for a moment. ''Bye, then.'

'Goodbye, Bill,' she said, voice thick with emotion. 'I'll be getting along now, I'd rather not wait 'til the train pulls out.'

'You go, love, you'll freeze to death standing about here.'

He watched her until she was out of sight, a thin, erect woman wearing a red coat and a woollen headscarf. He knew she would go through hell, missing him and worrying about him, because that was the sort of person she was. In a different league to Dolly altogether, he thought, startled by this sudden unexpected train of thought. He really had thought he was over her – he sometimes went for long periods without thinking about her at all. Now, out of the blue, there she was again, hitting him right between the eyes. Oh, well, he had more important things on his mind. He certainly wasn't going to let that bloody woman creep back into his thoughts, he told himself as he boarded the train.

'As neither of us is on ARP duty tonight, how about going up West to the pictures, Mabs?' Dolly suggested one afternoon in March as the two of them heaved parcels of blended tea on to platforms ready to wheel over to the loading bay. An influenza bug had exacerbated the staff shortage and resulted in their each doing the work of about three people.

'What's on?'

'"Gone with the Wind" is showing in Leicester Square,' said Dolly. 'We could try to get in for that, though I've heard there's usually a queue.'

'Ooh, yeah, I fancy some o' that,' said Mabs eagerly.

'Me too,' said Dolly. 'And it'll take our minds off the children for a few hours.'

'And the bombs,' said Mabs.

'You're right. We won't hear them so loudly inside the cinema.'

'Why not ask your mum to come along?' suggested Mabs. 'It'll do her good.'

'She won't come.'

'No harm in asking her though, is there?' said Mabs who didn't let her dislike for Edie impair her altruistic spirit.

'All right,' said Dolly. 'I'll pop round there on the way home from work and mention it to her.'

It had been a gruelling six months since the Blitz had started last September. When the heavy raids had shown no sign of easing off, Dolly and Mabs had felt duty bound to send the children away again. This time, though, because both women were needed at the factory, the children had gone with a small party organised through the school by one of the other parents with relatives in the country.

Ken had been on the move too. He'd had embarkation leave prior to going overseas. Despite the absence of family commitments, Dolly and Mabs had very little time to themselves, for their long hours at the factory were supplemented by two nights a week on duty at the ARP control centre.

Christmas had been depressing without the children. Dolly had invited Mabs and Mother for Christmas Day and tried to make it festive, even though Mother was only barely civil to Mabs and had only come to Dolly's at all after a great deal of persuasion. Pooling their resources, however, they had managed to produce a Christmas pudding of sorts, the missing ingredients replaced with grated potato and carrot. Brisket of beef and carrots had had to suffice for their Christmas dinner. Dolly managed to get a bottle of sherry and some holly from a barrow boy but the yuletide spirit had been noticeably absent.

1940 had come to a dramatic close with a series of incendiary raids on the capital. Many of London's most cherished buildings had been gutted. So terrible had been the devastation on the last Sunday night of the year, it had become known as the Second Great Fire of London. Several Wren churches suffered damage as well as the Old Bailey and Guildhall. Thanks to the diligence of the band of firewatchers who kept guard over St Paul's, it stood intact amid the ruins.

For all the hardship and tragedy, life went on as normal. In fact, the population in general were almost obsessed with carrying on regardless as their way of defeating the enemy. Dolly, along with everyone else, went about her business through conditions once thought unacceptable. She cycled to work through the smouldering streets, picking her way across debris, eyes smarting from smoke and lack of sleep, never really sure if the factory would still be standing when she got there.

After dark, the spirit of determination continued to prevail, air raids and black-out notwithstanding. Cinemas and pubs were doing a roaring trade as people sought diversion from grim reality, though just lately there had been a lull in the bombing.

Not everyone wanted a social life, though, for Edie declined Dolly's invitation to the cinema.

'Go on, be a devil and come with us,' Dolly urged her. 'It'll do you good to get out of the house and it's supposed to be a wonderful film.'

'No thanks,' she said, concentrating on the soldier's balaclava helmet she was knitting. 'I'd rather stay here.'

'I'll sit between you and Mabs so that you won't even have to talk to each other, if you like,' suggested Dolly.

But Edie would not be persuaded. Dolly was quite worried about her. It wasn't good for anyone to be alone as much as she was. After that hysterical outburst at the beginning of the Blitz, she'd seemed more able to take the raids in her stride. The only time she could be persuaded to share Dolly's shelter was when she knew Mabs wouldn't be there.

Personally, Dolly couldn't understand how anyone would want to waste one iota of energy bearing a grudge when the chances were that they wouldn't be around the next day to continue it. But perhaps behaving as though she was going to be around forever was Mother's way of coping with the danger.

After a long wait in the cinema queue Dolly and Mabs were

rewarded with glorious relaxation in warm, comfortable seats, and a gripping love story starring Clark Gable and Vivien Leigh. Because there was an air raid in progress when the film reached its dramatic conclusion, the audience were treated to an extended programme, consisting of a cheerful interlude on the cinema organ followed by a Laurel and Hardy film.

'Looks like Hitler is back on the warpath again, then,' said Dolly, as they finally emerged after the all clear.

'Yeah, I thought the quiet nights were too good to last.'

But on the bus home they were so busy chattering about the film they forgot all about the bombing. In fact, they were so engrossed in what they were saying Mabs almost missed her stop.

'Tata, Doll, see you in the morning,' she said, giggling as she jostled through the crowded gangway.

''Bye, Mabs, take care now.'

Mabs was deeply immersed in thoughts of Ken as she picked her way home in the moonlight, saving her torch battery for a moonless night since batteries were so scarce. She was wondering how long it would be before she saw her husband again. She still missed him with a gnawing ache even though she had grown accustomed to his not being around. It was astonishing how quickly you adapted to change, she thought. Even the shattered landscape had become normal, as was seeing familiar landmarks disappear overnight such as the house on the corner of Ackley Street and the pub she used to pass on her way home from Dolly's.

The once unimaginable was now commonplace.

She pulled her collar up around her headscarf and shivered against the chilly March wind. Going to the pictures had been a good idea; at least it had taken her mind off the bloomin' war for a while. It was just as well she hadn't been at home by the smell of it round here, she thought, as the familiar whiff of charred rubber and acrid smoke caught in her throat, making her eyes water. I'll be glad to be indoors, she muttered to herself, cursing the black-out as she tripped on some debris.

There seemed to be more people on the streets as she got closer to home. They were gathered in groups at their gates gossiping about the air raid.

'Any idea who copped it?' she asked.

'Ellis Road so we've heard,' said an elderly man. 'It's blown all our windows out an' all.'

Mabs didn't wait to hear any more. She tore down the street, into Maple Avenue which led into Ellis Road. Here she became confused because the geography of the area had altered completely. Ellis Road, at least the part containing Mabs's home, wasn't there; in its place was a roped-off area of smoking rubble. In the dim lights she could see firemen in tin hats working with hoses; rescue workers lifting stretchers into ambulances. Broken furniture and fire hoses were strewn across the road. The WVS had set up a mobile canteen and the women in green were serving cups of tea to anyone who needed them.

Having completely lost her bearings, Mabs muttered stupidly, 'Where's number twenty-four?' to one of the crowd of bewildered people from the remaining houses who were standing around watching the clearing-up operation.

'It's gone, love,' said one woman whom Mabs recognised as a neighbour. 'Along with all the others in that part of the street.'

'Bloody 'ell,' gasped Mabs.

'Me and my hubby were down at the pub or we wouldn't be 'ere now,' she said. 'We don't usually bother with the shelter, yer see.'

'We'd rather take our chances in the house,' confirmed her husband.

'Was there anyone in at your place, dear?' asked the woman.

'No . . . no, there was no one at home,' said Mabs, too stunned even to feel relieved.

Edie was out early with her shopping basket the next morning to get a place at the front of the greengrocer's queue. She walked wearily through the wreckage-filled streets, eyes stinging from the sooty air, her whole body aching with tiredness. It had been a shocking night, so bad she'd been forced to spend most of it in the damp, creature-ridden shelter. At one point in the proceedings she really had thought her end had come. The explosions had seemed so close. They hadn't been far off either, judging by the fresh destruction she was passing on her way to the Broadway.

Having survived so many air raids she'd grown used to having sudden death as a constant bedfellow. She wouldn't go so far as to say that she was no longer frightened, but she had become somewhat philosophical and had calmed down sufficiently to be concerned for her family.

At least she knew Dolly was all right. She'd managed to get through to her on the telephone after the raid late last night. She'd got back from the cinema safe and sound, and there had been no damage in her street. Thank God the grandchildren were out of the way of all this.

The women in the greengrocer's queue were discussing this latest attack while they waited for the shop to open.

'Thought I'd 'ad me chips, good and proper,' said the woman standing in front of her, curlers sprouting from the front of her turban.

'It was really bad, wasn't it?' said Edie.

'Bad ain't the word for it,' the woman exclaimed loudly. 'Gawd Almighty, what a racket! Sounded like a ruddy bomb had dropped in me garden. Me and me ole man were amazed to find the 'ouse still standin' when we came out of the shelter.'

'Yes, I felt like that too,' admitted Edie. 'Someone must have caught it nearby though.'

'Ellis Road,' her companion informed her with authority. 'Half of it was wiped out completely. Nothing left but a pile o' bleedin' ruins.'

'No?' exclaimed Edie.

'Yeah, I seen it with me own eyes.'

'Definitely Ellis Road?'

'Yeah, it went down like a pack o' cards . . . eh, ducks, what about your place in the queue?'

But Edie was already out of earshot, hurrying towards Ellis Road.

* * *

It was breakfast time in Dolly's house and she was trying to persuade her friend not to go in to the factory this morning, having had such a traumatic night.

'No point in moping about at home,' Mabs said, finishing her porridge. She set her mouth grimly. 'Not that I've got an 'ome to mope about in now, though, 'ave I?'

'This is your home for as long as you want it,' Dolly assured her emphatically. 'I told you that last night.'

A shaky, subdued Mabs had arrived at Dolly's house in the early hours, having done what she could for her neighbours at Ellis Road who'd lost relatives in the raid. Everything Mabs owned, except the clothes she stood up in and the contents of her handbag, had been destroyed. Naturally she'd been devastated by this but the more appalling fate of some other people had put it into perspective for her.

'I was lucky,' she had sobbed. 'Some poor buggers had it much worse . . . one man was out working a late shift . . . his missus was at home in bed with 'flu . . . she felt too rotten to go in the shelter . . . nothing left of her now. I mean, what a thing for that poor bloke to come home to.'

This morning Mabs was pale but composed, and determined to carry on as normal. 'Thanks, Doll, I'll stay with you for now, if you really don't mind, but once the kids come home you won't 'ave the room . . .'

'We'll manage.'

'Anyway, that can all be sorted out another time,' she said, drinking her tea. 'As far as today is concerned, I'll feel better if I keep busy.'

'You're probably right.'

'I suppose I'll have to go to the Town Hall to register the fact that I've been bombed out,' Mabs said thoughtfully. 'And I'll have to get some clothes so I can change out of the ones I've got on . . . I'll need a couple of hours off.'

'Take as much time as you need,' said Dolly.

'Thank Gawd clothes haven't gone on ration yet,' Mabs said.

'They reckon it won't be long before they do.'

'That's no surprise,' said Mabs. 'Anyway, I'll deal with all that later on. I'll come in to the factory with you now and get things in the packing room underway first.'

'If you're really sure that's what you want,' said Dolly, finishing her cup of tea and rising.

'Quite sure.'

'Let's get going then,' said Dolly.

Edie had never actually been to her son's house, but she knew his address, and on being told by local people that number twenty-four no longer existed she felt a lurching feeling in the pit of her stomach. No one seemed sure exactly what time the demolition had occurred last night. Mabs could have been home from the cinema, she thought with dread in her heart. I've never liked the woman but I don't wish her dead.

Dry-mouthed with worry, she scuttled from the scene of devastation and headed for the factory.

Dolly was busy doing paperwork when her mother appeared in her office, looking distraught and uncharacteristically dishevelled with wisps of greying hair escaping from her staid brown hat which had slipped to a jaunty side angle.

'Hello . . . what brings you here?' asked Dolly in surprise, fearing this unexpected visit might herald some sort of disaster.

'I've just heard that Ken's house has been bombed,' puffed Edie.

'Yes, I know.'

'Oh, you do. Well, was Mabs in? I mean . . . is she . . .?'

'She's homeless but all right,' Dolly informed her solemnly.

'Thank heavens for that,' said Edie, brushing her moist brow with a gloved hand and sinking weakly into a chair.

'Talk of the devil,' said Dolly as Mabs came into the office, clinically clad in overalls and mob cap.

'Morning, Mrs Slater,' she said, addressing her mother-in-law in the formal way from which she had never deviated.

'Good morning,' said Edie, surprised to see the younger woman behaving as though nothing much had happened.

'You're still around then?' said Mabs chirpily.

'Me? Well, yes. Why?'

'It's a bloomin' miracle there's any of us left after that shindig last night,' explained Mabs.

'Oh, I see what you mean,' said Edie, 'but I understand you've been bombed out.'

'Yep, Hitler got me worldly possessions but he didn't get me.'

'That's a blessing,' said Edie impulsively.

'I won't argue with you about that,' said Mabs.

'So where will you live?'

'Dolly says I can stay with her 'til I can find a place of me own,' she explained, 'though Gawd knows when that'll be with more people being made 'omeless every day.'

To Edie's amazement she heard herself say, 'I've much more room than Dolly, so why not move in with me?'

A surprised silence echoed through the room.

'The attic rooms are empty now that I don't have servants,' Edie continued. 'You'd have plenty of space up there. You'd be quite private but you would have to share my kitchen . . .'

'Thank you but I . . .' began Mabs, astonished and warmed by the offer but extremely doubtful as to the success of such an arrangement.

'Of course, if you'd rather not,' said Edie quickly, sensing the other woman's reluctance.

'Well, I'm not sure, Mrs Slater. It's kind of you to offer but being 'omeless is still so new to me, I can't think straight.'

'Think about it and let me know then,' said Edie, rising and walking to the door, her cheeks flushed.

'Yeah, I'll do that.'

Edie turned at the door. 'I wouldn't interfere in your life, you know,' she said, 'if that's what's putting you off.'

'That isn't what's worrying me,' said Mabs, 'because I wouldn't allow that to 'appen.'

'No . . . of course not.'

'What does bother me though,' said Mabs with a wicked grin, 'is how long it would be before one of us murdered the other.'

Dolly burst out laughing.

Being somewhat lacking in humour, Edie took umbrage, 'Oh, well, if that's how you feel about it . . .'

'Mabs is only teasing, Mother,' said Dolly.

But Edie wasn't to be placated and glared at Mabs with all her old malice. 'Suit yourself,' she said haughtily. 'It doesn't matter to me, one way or the other. But there is a place for you in my house if you want it.'

'Well, isn't that a turn-up for the books?' said Mabs to Dolly after Edie had gone.

'You're telling me . . . but Mum isn't all bad, you know, Mabs,' said Dolly defensively.

'Can you imagine what it would be like though, eh, Doll, being at the mercy of her disapproval every day of the week?' She gave a dry laugh. 'I mean, I could never be sure she hadn't poisoned my cocoa.'

'She's not that bad,' tutted Dolly.

'Only joking . . .'

'I must say she did seem quite worried about you when she arrived,' said Dolly.

'Really?'

'Yes, I think she was afraid you might have been at home when the bomb fell.'

'So that must have been what stirred her conscience into offering to put me up?' said Mabs.

'Mmm, it must have been. I'm glad she made the offer even though it's the last thing you want,' said Dolly. 'At least it shows she does have compassion in her heart.'

'She must be a glutton for punishment if she's willing to share a roof with her arch enemy.'

'The war does seem to bring out the best in people.'

'Yeah it does.'

'It's a pity you're not going to accept,' remarked Dolly thoughtfully. 'You could make those attic rooms quite cosy.'

'Who says I'm not gonna accept?'

'But you just said . . . I thought . . . I mean, you can't stand the sight of my mother.'

'I know what I said.' Mabs paused thoughtfully. 'And I can't pretend to like the woman . . .'

'Why then?'

'I dunno if the bombs are making me soft in the head or somethin', but I'm beginning to think your mum needs someone like me around her, someone who'll speak their mind and not be talked down to.'

'I do my best for her,' said Dolly.

'No daughter could do more for their mother than you,' said Mabs emphatically. 'In fact, I think you're a ruddy marvel the way you put up with her moanin' and groanin'. But you're too emotionally involved with her to be tough, and that's what she really needs to make her stand up to being a widow and get some pleasure out of life.'

'I can't bring myself to be too hard on her,' admitted Dolly.

'That's only natural with your being her daughter,' said Mabs. 'It's different for me, being an outsider. Anyway, she already hates my guts so I can't make things any worse.'

Dolly was still doubtful. 'I'm not sure your moving in with her will work, though.'

'Neither am I, and if it's too bloomin' awful I'll be back 'ere at the end of the week, don't worry,' grinned Mabs. 'But I feel I want to give it a try . . . I mean, she is Ken's mum after all, and I think he'd be pleased if we were to get to know each other better.'

The sparks are really going to fly now, thought Dolly, but said, 'Good for you, Mabs. I really hope it works out.'

After her unexpected burst of benevolence in Dolly's office, Edie was feeling rather shaken as she finished her shopping. She was glad to get home for a sit down and a cup of tea. What on earth had possessed her to offer shelter to that awful woman when it was the last thing in the world either of them wanted? she asked herself as she filled the kettle and put it on the gas stove to boil. Just because her conscience was bothering her, there was no need to go to such dramatic lengths to ease it.

But what was all this about conscience? She had nothing to feel guilty about as far as *that* woman was concerned. Mabs was the one who should feel bad for coming between mother and son. She must have known that a factory girl could never be accepted into the family of her employers. If she had really cared for Ken, she'd have stayed away from him.

For all this sensible reasoning, however, nagging doubts persisted. Painful memories of times gone by flooded back as they had so often lately. All this harping back to the past was the fault of the war, she was sure of it. Living on the edge of danger caused the brain to work in an irrational manner. It made you want to right wrongs in case it was

your last chance. Not that she had done wrong to Mabs, of course, but she did feel uneasy when she remembered Ken's miserable childhood and the way she had never had the courage to stand up to Henry about his cruelty to him.

With the benefit of hindsight, she could see that Henry had done much more than just frighten her into doing what he wanted. His overwhelming personality had actually taken possession of her mind to the extent where she believed his opinions to be her own. She could remember that even while suffering vicarious pain from the cruel way he was demoralising Ken, she had believed he was doing it in the boy's best interests, to make the proverbial man of him. It was only recently, as the passing of time had lessened the power of Henry's memory over her, that she had begun to question her past behaviour.

This, then, must be the reason for her impulsive offer of accommodation to Ken's wife. Perhaps she thought she could make amends to her son by making this gesture to Mabs. The whole idea of them sharing a house was ridiculous anyway. Such an arrangement would only serve to increase the acrimony between them.

Fortunately there was no likelihood of Mabs's accepting. It was obvious from her attitude that she would rather live in a dustbin than take up residence in her mother-in-law's house. Good job too! Edie'd never feel comfortable in her own home with Mabs about the place.

She was still trying to convince herself that she had had a lucky escape later on as she scraped some carrots to go with the sausages she was going to have for her lunch. She was just putting them into a saucepan when there was a knock at the front door.

'Oh, it's you,' she said, opening the door to see Mabs standing in the porch.

'Yeah, it's me.'

'Well, what . . . I mean, why . . .?'

'Are you gonna let me in, or do I have to stand out here all afternoon?' asked Mabs in her usual forthright manner.

Chapter Fifteen

Feeling acutely vulnerable against the daunting confidence of the younger woman, Edie defended herself with a counter attack.

'Don't just stand there gawping, woman,' she said, scowling as she stood aside. 'Come in, for heaven's sake.'

'Cor blimey, I reckon the Führer himself would get a warmer welcome,' retorted Mabs, stepping into a hall which smelled of fresh polish. It was traditionally furnished with a small curved table holding a glossy-leaved pot plant and overhung with a mirror; there was a barometer and a shiny wooden hallstand sparsely hung with Edie's hat, coat and umbrella, galoshes neatly placed on a rack at the bottom. A layer of air-raid dust suffused everything despite Edie's conscientious housekeeping.

'I'll lay out the red carpet next time,' she snorted.

'A smile will do,' riposted Mabs, removing her shabby brown raincoat and hanging it up on the hallstand.

Unable to think of a suitably crushing retort, Edie led the way to the sitting room with its dull beige wallpaper and staid furnishings. Feeling very much at a disadvantage, she offered her visitor a seat and blurted out the first thing that came into her head. 'Look, I acted on impulse this morning, I really don't know what came over me . . . we both know that sharing a house could never work so just forget all about it, will you?'

'You're withdrawing your offer then?' said Mabs, her brows rising.

'Well, isn't that what you want? I mean . . . it was obvious from your reaction that you don't want to move in here,' she said. 'I presume that's what you've come to tell me but there's no need to spell it out.'

'Of course I don't want to move in here,' interrupted Mabs with brutal frankness. 'Would you wanna live with someone else after having your own place?'

'Oh, I see. Well, from that point of view, I suppose not.'

'But I've no choice but to be someone's lodger, have I?' she said briskly. 'And, as you say, you've much more space than Dolly. In fact it's downright ridiculous rattling about in this place on yer own when I don't have a home at all.'

'So you *are* thinking of moving in here then?'

'That's right, as long as you don't carry on as though you're doing me some great big favour the whole time,' said Mabs, whose spikiness came from her being ultra-sensitive to Edie's patronising manner, having been on the receiving end of it for so long. 'In wartime we're all supposed to help each other out, so it's no more than your duty to share your walloping great 'ouse, whether it's with me or anyone else.'

'I don't think I care for your attitude,' snapped Edie.

'What sort of attitude do you expect if you act like some

bloomin' Lady Bountiful?' retorted Mabs. 'It isn't my fault I lost my 'ome last night.'

'I'm damned sure it isn't mine,' retaliated Edie.

Mabs leapt up and glared at her, cheeks flaming. 'Oh, forget it, you superior cow! I was right first time to think it would never work.' She marched to the door. 'I'll go back to Dolly's, at least I'm welcome there.'

'You do that, and good riddance to you,' bellowed Edie.

She didn't show her visitor out but stood where she was in the sitting room listening to the angry stomp of footsteps along the hall, her cheeks burning and heart racing. The slam of the front door, however, seemed to trigger some emotion deep within her which sent her scurrying from the house, almost as though her legs were moving of their own volition.

She caught up with Mabs at the front gate. 'Look . . . perhaps I was a bit hasty . . . why not come back inside and have a cup of tea and a chat?'

'I dunno about that.'

'Let's both try to calm down and see if we can't sort out something between us,' suggested Edie.

'I won't be talked down to,' said Mabs.

'And I won't be bullied!'

Mabs thought about this for a moment. 'All right, let's 'ave a cuppa tea and see if there is anything at all on which we can manage to agree.'

There didn't seem to be a single issue on which the two women were in accord. Mabs wanted to pay rent; Edie said she had her faults but making money out of her son's wife's misfortune wasn't one of them. Mabs wanted to retain her independence by doing all her own shopping and cooking; Edie said that using the cooker separately was a waste of gas in wartime when they were supposed to be conserving energy. She insisted that she cook for them both because Mabs was out at work during the day and Edie didn't want someone untidying her kitchen at all hours.

Keen to keep things as even as possible by doing her share of the chores, Mabs wanted to take her turn cleaning the communal areas such as the hall and stairs; Edie couldn't agree to this since it would mean Mabs banging about sweeping and polishing in the evenings in Edie's part of the house when she was trying to relax, air raids permitting.

Finally, however, a compromise was reached. Edie agreed to let Mabs pay her share of the general household expenses such as gas, electricity and coal, but refused to charge rent. Mabs agreed to let Edie shop and cook for her, providing she didn't expect her to be tied to mealtimes. 'I'll warm my food up if I'm not home when you have yours,' she informed her firmly. 'Obviously I shall be out in the evenings sometimes.'

So Mabs moved in a few days later and had to admit that the attic was cosy. The one-time maid's room was now her bedroom and the cook's quarters furnished as a sitting room with armchairs, occasional tables, a sideboard, a standard lamp and a few other artifacts to give it a homely feel. The furniture was old fashioned but comfortable.

'You've made it really nice, thank you, Mrs Slater,' she said with genuine sincerity.

'It's only the furniture that the servants had,' Edie told her, because to admit that she had added bits and pieces from her own rooms and gone to great pains to make it snug was to give Mabs the upper hand somehow. 'I didn't do anything special.'

'Comfy though,' said Mabs, casting an approving eye over the accommodation and adding chattily, 'You ought to have these attic rooms made into a proper flat after the war . . . you know, with proper cooking facilities and that. You wouldn't have any trouble finding a tenant and it'd be a nice little earner for you.'

'No, thank you,' said Edie loftily. 'After the war it will revert back to being servants' quarters.'

'I shouldn't think decent servants will be so easy to find,' said Mabs in a cautionary manner. 'I can't imagine many people going back into service after doing more interesting jobs.'

'Nonsense,' exclaimed Edie. 'The women will have to stand aside from the jobs when the men come back.'

'Maybe,' agreed Mabs. 'But having tasted the freedom of day work, a lot won't wanna go back to living in. Even before the war a great many of them were going into shops and factories.'

'Time will tell.' Damn know-all, Edie thought furiously. Is there nothing on which she doesn't consider herself an authority? Well, she's not going to ride roughshod over me, which means she'll not want to stay. Give her a week and she'll be gone. The sooner the better too!

Sour-faced old battleaxe, thought Mabs, she hasn't a clue about the modern world. Live-in servants, my Aunt

Fanny! Her outdated ideas and airs and graces are gonna drive me nuts. I'll give it a week at the most, then I'll clear off back to Dolly's.

So how it was that Mabs was still living there two months later on Cup Final Day, she couldn't imagine. She had intended to leave. In fact she had packed her bags on several occasions. But somehow she had never actually gone. In fact, she had got into the habit of having her meals with the old girl. Sometimes in the evenings she stayed downstairs and listened to the wireless with her even though she had a set of her own upstairs. The atmosphere between them didn't improve though. They still quarrelled about every conceivable thing.

Maybe Mabs had stayed because she didn't want to admit defeat; perhaps it was because she thought the old trout was lonely and needed someone around even if it was her worst enemy. But for whatever reason she was still living here in Maybury Avenue on this chilly May Saturday evening which was passing in an unexpectedly pleasant manner. Neither she nor Dolly were on ARP duty so Dolly had come for tea and had decided to stay overnight as she didn't have to get up for work in the morning. A bombless month had made them all feel more relaxed and they were enjoying a lengthy game of Monopoly. When Dolly was present, at least Mabs and Edie had a referee.

'I'll knock your heads together in a minute you two,' warned Dolly, as the two of them started arguing about whose turn it was to shake the dice. 'Nursery children are more mature than you.'

Apologies were offered and accepted, and Dolly stretched

and yawned. 'I think I've had enough of this game for tonight,' she said. 'You two carry on while I make some cocoa and bread and cheese.'

She had just set the supper tray down on an occasional table when they heard the wail of the siren. 'Oh, well, that's the end of peace and quiet.'

'Perhaps Jerry thought we were feeling neglected,' said Mabs.

'I thought we'd had it easy for too long,' said Dolly.

Having hurriedly turned off the gas at the mains, they grabbed coats and blankets and trooped out to the shelter, taking their supper with them. It was exceptionally cold for May and very clear, the brilliant light from the full moon spreading a pearly glow over the privet hedges and lilac trees.

'Cor, stone me, it's as bright as day,' said Mabs. 'The bombers'll 'ave a field day.'

'That's why they've come tonight, I expect,' said Dolly.

No sooner had they clambered into the chilly, tomb-like dwelling than the air was filled with the drone of bombers, the thud of explosions and the rattle of incendiaries. The roar and crackle of anti-aircraft guns could be heard firing their shells into the sky, which was a maze of weaving searchlights.

With a blanket draped over the shelter opening to conceal the light, they played cards by candlelight to pass the time, each trying not to react too visibly to the thumps and bangs which seemed to come ever closer. Time passed and still the bombs fell.

Eventually the trio grew weary of their card game and

lay down on the benches under the blankets, Dolly and Mabs on one, Edie on the other. Still the all clear didn't come.

Dolly closed her eyes, wishing she could sleep through it. But instead her tired mind was besieged by thoughts of people she hadn't seen for a long time, and she wondered if they were still alive. The thought that Bill Drake might be dead caused a dull pain deep inside her.

Hours went by and still the raid continued. Alternating between terror and drowsiness in proportion to the explosions and the gaps in between, Dolly was just dozing off when the swishing sound of a bomb coming down nearby shattered her nerves. She sat bolt upright, quivering with expectation. The crump of its landing rocked the ground and plunged them into inky blackness as the candle was extinguished and the noise outside became muted.

'Bloody 'ell,' said Mabs into the hushed aftermath. 'What's 'appened?'

'The opening is blocked,' said Dolly at last, feeling for the black-out blanket to find herself with a handful of something cold and damp. 'The blast must have churned up the garden and buried the shelter with earth.'

'Oh, my God, we'll never get out,' came Edie's terrified cry. 'We'll be left here to suffocate.'

Dolly's immediate reaction was one of panic, which she struggled to control. 'The bomb must have dropped very close,' she said, managing to keep her nerve as they heard the distant clang of fire engine bells from above. 'It's lucky we were down here.'

'I can't say I feel very lucky at the moment,' admitted Mabs shakily.

'I must get out,' gasped Edie, stumbling against Dolly in the dark and scraping at the mud with her hands. 'I can't breathe.'

'Do try to stay calm, dear,' urged Dolly, somehow managing to quell her own rising hysteria. 'We'll get out somehow, don't worry.'

'I'd sooner be blasted to bits than suffocate to death,' sobbed Edie.

Dolly expected this negative attitude to bring forth an acid reproach from Mabs, but to her surprise she heard her say, 'Don't you believe it, Ede. Old Hitler ain't gonna get rid of us that easy.'

'That's right,' said Dolly. 'So start shovelling, everyone.'

Trying to shift the earth from the front to the back of the shelter by hand felt rather like trying to empty a desert with a teaspoon to Dolly. Having no idea how deeply buried they were, the possibility of their oxygen running out was a constant fear.

'Shush, listen,' she whispered suddenly.

'What for?' asked Mabs.

'I can hear a cat miaowing.'

'It can't be.'

'It is,' insisted Dolly.

Sure enough, in between muffled bangs came a faint feline cry.

'It's coming from up there, look!' cried Dolly.

'I can't see anything,' said Mabs.

'I can,' said Edie, sounding calmer now.

'Oh, yes, I see,' said Mabs. 'Thank Gawd for that.'

The cause of their jubilation was a hole in the blockage no bigger than a penny, but through which they could see a chink of moonlight and hear the cat's cries drifting.

'Poor little thing,' said Edie. 'It's terrified.'

They still had a long way to go before they cleared the blockage sufficiently to get out, but they worked with renewed vigour now to enlarge the hole: scooping, clawing, shovelling.

'Are you all right, Mum?' asked Dolly as they clambered up to ground level to the comforting sound of the all clear. 'I see you've found the cat.'

'It's only a kitten,' Edie said, clutching the shivering creature to her chest and wrapping her coat around its tabby fur. 'It's more like a mouse than a cat with its squeaky miaow.'

'Gawd Almighty,' said Mabs as she emerged into the scene of devastation. 'We were better off down there.'

'I've never seen anything like it,' said Dolly as the scene above ground registered properly.

'Shocking,' said Edie, cuddling the distressed kitten to her bosom protectively and stroking its tiny head.

The Avenue was an inferno, flames and smoke everywhere, the sky a vivid orange. Firemen had their hoses trained on Edie's house which was smoking in one corner but still standing.

'Oi, oi, where did you lot spring from?' came the deep-throated voice of a fireman as the bedraggled threesome came into view. 'This area is roped off to the public.'

'This is my garden,' explained Edie. 'We've been buried in the shelter.'

'Over there,' said Dolly, glancing towards the Anderson which was completely concealed by earth and shrubs that had been uprooted in the blast.

'Well, stone me, you been down there all this time?'

'That's right,' said Dolly.

'You could call that a lucky break,' he said cheerily.

'Judging by this lot, yes,' agreed Dolly, eyes and throat smarting from the smoke. 'Hitler's certainly keeping you busy tonight.'

The fireman turned towards Dolly for a moment and in the glow from the flames she saw weariness in the blackened face beneath the tin helmet. 'Phew, not 'alf! I reckon this must be one of the worst nights we've had so far,' he said. 'Still, it keeps me out of mischief.'

'Do you know if Bailey Gardens has been hit?' asked Dolly.

'I don't, love, sorry.'

Since there was nothing she could do about her own house, Dolly concentrated on comforting her mother who was standing mournfully watching the corner of her home smoking while all around the area flames leapt to the sky. A distraught woman pushed past the rescue workers and climbed over the ropes to beg the fireman to see to her house next.

'Be there as soon as we can, love,' he said in deep tones. 'We've nearly finished here.'

'But everything I have is going up in flames,' said the

woman, sobbing and wringing her hands. 'Please come and put it out . . . please!'

'Can't be in two places at once, ducks,' he told her.

Still crying, the woman scuttled off into the smoke where she was comforted by some ladies from the WVS.

'At times like this I wish I could be in six places at once,' the fireman said to Dolly.

'I can imagine.'

'Still, keep smiling, eh, love?'

'Not much else we can do, is there?'

'That's a fact.'

Looking stunned, her mother was still watching her home smouldering.

Dolly slipped a sympathetic arm around her and glanced towards Mabs. 'Come on, you two, let's go. You'll have to stay with me for a while,' she said. 'If my house is still there, that is.'

'I'd rather stay here and see how bad the damage is,' said Edie.

'We'll do that tomorrow,' said Mabs kindly. 'There's too much smoke about at the moment.'

'That's right, ladies,' said the fireman. 'You go off and have a cuppa tea. I'd come with you but, as you can see, I've a hectic social life.'

Dolly laughed. 'We'll have one for you,' she joked, impressed by his indomitable spirit.

'Righto, love,' he grinned. 'Tata, and mind how you go now.'

The three muddy, smoke-stained women trekked wearily through the bomb-shattered streets to Bailey Gardens in the smoky dawn, Dolly and Mabs at either side of Edie who was clutching the kitten to her as though her life depended on it.

For the first time Dolly saw Londoners, hardened to the hell of the Blitz, weeping in the streets at such terrible destruction. It was as though the heart had been torn out of the city and she just couldn't take any more. But Dolly knew her spirit wasn't broken even now. She could see it in the kindness of rallying neighbours and the men and women of the voluntary services as they worked in the thick of tragedy, making tea, offering comfort to the homeless and bereaved. They, like the fireman, were managing to crack a joke when all they probably wanted to do was weep at this heartrending evidence of man's inhumanity to man.

'Well, at least we've somewhere to lay our weary heads,' Dolly said with relief, as they turned into Bailey Gardens to find the street still standing.

Daylight showed heartbreaking carnage: houses charred or reduced to rubble; personal belongings littering the streets. A trip to Maybury Avenue, however, revealed Edie to be more fortunate than some, in that her house was still habitable in part, despite scorched walls, broken windows and everywhere being severely smoke-damaged.

The bomb had hit the corner of the building, setting the drawing room on fire. Although the blaze had been controlled fairly quickly, smoke had poured through the house. The roof and part of one wall were damaged which meant one corner of the house was unusable until a builder could be found to put it right. With so much property needing attention in London, Dolly guessed her mother would have a very long wait.

'Well, Mum,' said Dolly, as they took a disconsolate tour of the property. 'Looks like we're going to be kept busy putting this place to rights. The first thing is to get the broken windows boarded up 'til we can get them reglazed.'

'That's right,' agreed Mabs, looking at the blackened walls and furnishings. 'Then we'll get cracking with the scrubbing brush . . . when it's all cleaned up we'll have to see about getting you some new furniture, it's time you had a change.'

'It was all good quality stuff,' said Edie with a wistful sigh.

'Ever so old-fashioned though, wannit?' remarked Mabs. 'Anyway, a change is as good as a rest.'

The house was not the only thing that was gutted. Edie looked emotionally bruised as she stood in her blackened sitting room with its sooty chairs and sofas, clutching the kitten she had named Squeak. He was a skinny tabby tomcat with a white patch over one eye. Edie had not let the animal out of her sight since last night. Dolly was surprised by her mother's devotion to the kitten, for she had never shown any liking for animals before. Something else that was down to Father, she thought, because his dislike of animals had prohibited a family pet.

When tears began to meander down Edie's cheeks, neither Dolly nor Mabs lectured her about self-pity or the thousands of others who were worse off. Just because she had fared better than some in last night's raid, didn't make her immune to pain at her own misfortune. She wasn't just standing inside four sooty walls, she was standing amid the ruins of the place in which she had raised her family.

'The sooner we get cracking with the mop and bucket, the better,' Edie said, with a resolute lift of the shoulders.

'That's the spirit,' said Dolly.

For what must have been the first time ever, Dolly experienced a moment of genuine respect for her mother.

To the relief of Londoners the nights became uncannily blitz-free. It was generally thought that the enemy must be planning something big, but despite fears of a German invasion most people enjoyed the period of calm. While the authorities tried to cope with more than a million bombed-out homeless by setting up more rest centres and a meals service, Dolly made her mother and Mabs comfortable at her place. But Edie was eager to go back home, so all three of them spent every spare minute getting her house back to rights.

They found an extra pair of hands in Barney who left school and came home to live and work at Slater's. Even so, it was autumn before Edie and Mabs were able to move back to Maybury Avenue and even then under conditions that would have been unacceptable before the war; some windows were replaced with wooden planks and the damaged corner was unusable and covered with tarpaulin. Shortages meant Edie's expensive furnishings had to be replaced with utility pieces.

But, curiously enough, she didn't complain too much. Dolly suspected that she didn't dare for fear of provoking Mabs into some caustic remark, the latter having suffered more severely from the bombs. Inevitably, with the return of normality, Mother and Mabs reverted to their old ways of sniping and bickering. Dolly was beginning to suspect that they enjoyed it, since they did so much of it.

Life got harder as shortages grew worse. Clothes were put on ration and food became even scarcer. Meals were a major topic of conversation as people tried to find new recipes to make rations go further. The job of feeding a family constituted hours spent in queues in all weathers, often to find the shops sold out when you got to the front. All of this was exacerbated by the fact that many women were working in full-time jobs as well as running a home. But morale remained high especially as the lull in air raids continued.

At the factory, Dolly and Mabs continued to keep the firm running. Whilst unreliable deliveries and shortages of everything from raw materials to machine parts made it difficult in the extreme, they managed to maintain supplies, albeit to a lesser degree than in peace time. Barney was learning the trade from the ground floor level which meant he was just an errand boy. Staff were even harder to find when, at the end of the year, single women between twenty and thirty became liable for call up.

In the summer of 1942, Dolly's family became complete again when Merle reached the school leaving age. She came home and went to work in the offices of a munitions factory. Her moodiness didn't seem to improve as she grew older, though there were brief spells of calm when she was a pleasure to have around. Dolly worried about her being lonely, for she didn't seem able to sustain friendships with people of her own age.

War had become a habit and hardship a way of life, along with ration books, Spam, and Make Do and Mend. Most people took a keen interest in the news from abroad. Dolly and her family were especially concerned about events in the Middle East because Ken was in that region somewhere, though they weren't sure exactly where. Much to their relief, Mabs heard from him after the fall of Tobruk which told her he was alive if little else.

As the warm summer days mellowed into copper-coloured autumn, they settled down for another war-time winter, finding pleasure in the small treats that were still available. One October Saturday evening Dolly, Mabs and Edie went to the cinema to see a film called 'Dangerous Moonlight', a gripping wartime romance which featured a beautiful piece of music called the Warsaw Concerto.

'Wannit lovely?' said Mabs dreamily as they walked home in the chilly night, holding their shared torch in the only way that was legal, pointed downwards with the glass masked by two layers of tissue paper to reduce the beam to a diffused glow.

'Wonderful,' agreed Dolly.

Even Edie, who would have disagreed with Mabs on principle if she could have found the slightest fault, said rather primly, 'Very nice indeed.'

'Well, anything on which you two agree must be really

special,' laughed Dolly, as they stumbled through the blacked-out streets.

She knew from past experience that the mood of harmony between them would be all too brief.

Chapter Sixteen

Infantryman Ken Slater, known affectionately in the platoon as Slim, was sitting in a slit-trench playing cards with his mates by the brilliant light of a full moon which cast a pale golden gloss over the burnt sands of the North African desert. The soldiers' voices were low in the waiting silence. Some nervously checked their weapons for the umpteenth time that day. Officers glanced at their watches, while some men prayed.

'Cor, you jammy bugger, Slim,' said one of Ken's pals as he produced a winning hand.

'Not bad, eh?' he said with a forced laugh. 'Put that one down to the luck of the devil.'

It wasn't easy to be jolly in this atmosphere of unbearable tension. But Ken's military training, augmented by his paranoia about courage, made him an expert in putting on a brave front. He didn't know that he was obsessed; he saw nothing abnormal in constantly needing to prove to himself that he wasn't the coward his father had believed him to be.

Having lived with the scars of Henry's cruelty for so long, this compulsion had taken root in his personality without his even being aware of it. The war was rich with opportunity to lay the ghosts of his youth and he never lost a chance to put himself to the test, which was why he'd expressed a preference for the infantry when he'd been called up.

'How about another hand?' suggested his companion, seeking diversion from the stress of their current situation.

'No more for me, mate,' said Ken. 'I'll quit while I'm ahead.'

Normally, that would have earned him a ribbing. But tonight was no ordinary night. In precisely forty minutes' time the battle of El Alemein was due to begin. They had been preparing for it for months. These desert trenches, from where they were to attack, had been dug by night and camouflaged; operational transport and guns had been moved in by dark and carefully concealed.

Now, after months of intensive training, the men of the Eighth Army were ready for action. Britons would fight alongside soldiers of other nations in an attack on German and Italian positions. Tanks, armoured cars, foot soldiers and horse artillery were all in place, just waiting for the command.

Fragments of General Montgomery's message to all troops, which had been read out to them by their commanding officer, lingered in Ken's mind.

'We are ready NOW'. '... let every officer and man enter the battle with a stout heart, and the determination to do his duty so long as he has breath in his body'.

Stirring words indeed! The memory of them swelled Ken's heart with patriotism. But it wasn't the voice of his commanding officer he had heard reading the message, but the mocking tones of his father, warning him not to disgrace himself on the battlefield.

Living with the stress of combat and without Mabs's encouraging presence to support him, Ken found himself constantly dogged by Henry who seemed always with him in spirit, waiting to catch him out in some act of cowardice or stupidity. He remembered once admitting to Dolly that his father was still in his life even though he'd not seen him for years. His death had changed nothing; he was still a more powerful influence on Ken than anyone else.

Surviving in such barbaric conditions, home could seem distant almost to the point of obscurity. He managed to produce a mental image of his dear, down-to-earth wife who thought he was wonderful for all his failings and would love him, he was sure, even if he were to commit the most heinous of crimes and fail in his duty to his country. He lived for letters from home, luxuriating in the comforting words that painted pictures of gentle people and a civilised way of life; so very different to the harsh desert heat and sand that scratched the skin into sores and found its way into everything.

He'd been pleasantly surprised to hear that Mother had taken Mabs in, though he found it hard to envisage the two of them sharing one roof. Dolly's letters made the whole thing sound like some sort of a music hall comedy act. She said the pair weren't happy unless they were at each other's throats. Still, he supposed even that was better than no contact between them at all.

Mabs's strong cockney voice came into his mind, telling him to take pride in himself; to be his own man and not his father's whipping boy. He tried to retain her words but they were pushed aside by the more powerful tones of his father, hammering into his brain.

'You're gutless . . . not an ounce of spunk in you . . . none at all . . . none . . . none . . . none . . .'

'What's 'a matter, Slim? Are your ears hurting or somethin'?' said his pal, nudging him.

Recalled to the present Ken realised he had both his hands pressed over his ears beneath his steel helmet. 'Oh . . . what? No, my ears are fine.'

'They won't be for much longer, mate,' said his pal, because the men had been told to expect excessive noise when the battle commenced.

'Yeah, that's a fact.'

The minutes ticked by in the uncanny stillness: nine-twenty, nine-thirty . . . Then, at precisely nine-forty, the earth shook with a barrage of massed guns, assailing Ken's ear drums like nothing ever had before. The indescribable noise shocked and devastated him, turning his bowels to water and distorting his senses, his reaction all the more intense because bravado had led him to refuse the army's offer of earplugs.

His brain was so addled that for a moment he couldn't remember what he was supposed to do. But self-discipline and lots of practice eventually prevailed so that even while his senses were readjusting to this violent audible onslaught, he was automatically alert and ready for the signal to advance.

Already the engineers were hard at work in Rommel's five-mile-deep minefields known as the 'devil's garden', clearing lanes and marking them with white tape for those who would come behind. With nerves at breaking point, Ken and the rest of his platoon waited for the signal while the bombardment continued, making the ground shudder and rock and filling the desert with curtains of smoke and sand.

When the command came, Ken advanced in a line of infantry, moonlight gleaming on rifles at the ready, bayonets fixed. With a kind of numb resignation, he walked forward into the smoky battlefield. The noise was still deafening. Bullets whistled past his ears; shells whined; aircraft roared overhead. Already the bloodstained sands were littered with corpses; fleets of ambulance men were on the scene, hurriedly working to get the injured on to stretchers and away from the battle.

All Ken could see ahead of him was smoke and flames; all he could hear was the whine of shells, the whizz of bullets – the crack and thud of explosions. Vaguely he was aware that his head ached, yet he felt oddly trancelike, the voices of his mates not reaching him above the din. There were men all around him, intent on doing the job they were trained for, but Ken felt locked into a small world of his own with no one to turn to for help or comfort.

His loneliness was total, his terror paralysing. He halted in his step, unable to move or control the debilitating fear that tortured him. A voice inside his head registered with powerful clarity. 'Get moving, you yellow bastard . . . What are you, a man or a mouse? . . . I might have known you'd cock things up . . . can't even do your duty to your country without losing your nerve . . . coward . . . coward . . . coward . . .'

'Get back, Slater,' shouted the sergeant, 'you're advancing too fast. You'll get hit by our own artillery.'

But the only voice Ken could hear was the one inside his mind. 'You've never had a bit of guts – I don't know how I came to spawn such a useless lump of rubbish . . .'

Wild-eyed and crazy, he threw back his head before charging forward with bayonet at the ready. 'I'll show you what I'm made of, Father,' he cried, his sick mind now completely out of touch with reality.

'Bloody fool,' his sergeant muttered later as the charred corpse of Private Slater was added to the numbers in the sand. 'He was a good soldier but in too much of a hurry to be a hero.'

Mabs had been out to the garden to peg some washing on the line, and was chatting to Edie in the hall on her way back upstairs when the telegram came. They both knew what the contents would be even before she opened the envelope for they hadn't heard from Ken for months.

'I don't think I can bear to open it,' said Mabs, ashen-faced and trembling.

'Give it here,' said Edie, who was salt-white and shaking.

The sound of paper tearing blistered the air.

Edie read it and said in a surprisingly calm voice, 'Yes, it is the worst, I'm afraid – he's been killed in action. I'm so sorry, Mabs, my dear.'

'You're sorry for me?' said Mabs dully. 'What about you?'

'I'm sorry for me too.'

Somehow they were clinging together, holding each other for support, acrimony forgotten in the bleakness of the moment.

'I'll have to go down to Hampshire to tell Peter,' said Mabs a while later as they sat at the kitchen table with a pot of tea between them. 'It wouldn't be fair to give him such news in a letter.'

'No, it wouldn't.'

'I'm dreading it.'

'Would you like me to come with you?' offered Edie uncertainly.

Normally such a supportive gesture would have given rise to sarcasm from Mabs, but not this time. 'That would be a great help, Edie,' she said. 'I could really do with some moral support.'

They stared at one another, each deeply preoccupied with their own grief, but finding a morsel of solace in facing up to death's practicalities together.

In her anguish, Edie found herself facing up to something else too. 'I was never much of a mother to Ken,' she said regretfully.

'Well . . .' Mabs met the other woman's gaze. Even though she felt united with her at this dark time, she couldn't bring herself to lie about something they both knew to be true.

'It's all right, I don't expect you to make me feel better by denying it.'

'I can't change me ways just because we've lost Ken,' Mabs said, mopping a fresh flood of tears with a handkerchief.

''Course you can't,' agreed Edie. 'And I can't do anything about the fact that I failed him, it's too late for that.'

'Yes.'

'But I can have a go at being decent to his wife and son.'

Mabs threw her a shrewd look. 'It's a nice idea, Ede, but you'll never keep it up,' she said, emitting a weak, emotional laugh.

'Probably not,' admitted Edie. 'But I can give it a try.'

'Don't go all saintly on me for Gawd's sake,' said Mabs. 'I don't think I could stand that.'

Edie blew her nose and met her daughter-in-law's candid gaze. 'Knowing me as you do, do you honestly think there's any chance of that?'

'No, not really,' confessed Mabs.

They fell silent, each lost in her own pain. The atmosphere was dull with resignation. They had both been fearing the worst for months. Now the waiting was over and they had to find the strength to accept it.

Shaking her head sadly, Edie said, 'I dread to think how Dolly is going to take it . . . you know how close she and Ken have always been.'

'Ooh, yeah, she'll be really cut up,' agreed Mabs.

'I'd better go round there and get it over,' said Edie. 'It's up to me as her mother to tell her.'

'Look . . . how about you and me going round to her place together in a minute to break the news?' suggested Mabs.

'Thanks, Mabs,' agreed Edie, feeling an unexpected surge of gratitude for the presence of the younger woman in her life. 'That would help.'

It took a long time for Dolly to come to terms with her brother's death. She put on a brave show for Edie and Mabs because she believed that the loss of a mother and wife must be greater than that of a sister. But, united as they had been against their father as children, she and Ken had had a very special relationship. Grief weighed heavily on her through the winter and spring while she went about her business.

The passing of time didn't heal the wound, but inevitably the pain eventually lessened for them all. She knew that Mother and Mabs were beginning to feel better when their bickering began to gather its former momentum. Theirs was a curious association. They would never admit it in a million years, of course, but she really did believe that they were good for each other.

Life went on as did the war. The children seemed to grow faster than weeds and Dolly's house rang with the youthful clamour of their developing personalities. Barney was a popular member of the staff at Slater's and had great pride in the firm. His enthusiasm was like a breath of spring about the place. He was full of ideas for expansion after the war when tea control ended. His easygoing nature continued to be a soothing contrast to Merle's dark moods which didn't disappear as she began to change from a dumpy adolescent into an attractive young woman.

In December of 1943 Dolly's home, as well as the

factory, was almost brought to a standstill by the 'flu epidemic which swept through the capital, putting whole families out of action. The Minister of Health introduced a scheme to deal with the emergency whereby householders whose entire family was sick could apply to the Women's Voluntary Services to come and do the chores, look after the children and fetch the medicine. The British Restaurants also co-operated by organising a mobile canteen service of hot meals as they had during the blitzes. It was heartening to know that help was at hand, but Dolly left the emergency services to those whose need was greater, and managed to keep going with the help of aspirin.

Christmas was pleasant enough, despite the flu having left Dolly with a vicious cough that kept her awake at nights. As they had in previous wartime Christmases, they pooled their rations and all the family spent Christmas Day at Maybury Avenue. There was no poultry about, it had all gone to the black market according to the papers, so Dolly and company made use of one of the recipes published in the newspapers telling them how to stuff their meagre beef ration. With a great deal of imagination, and a Christmas pudding containing the most unlikely ingredients, they managed to create a festive atmosphere and enjoy themselves.

Although Dolly kept it to herself, she was still feeling out of sorts as the new year got underway. Her recalcitrant cough defied the curative powers of linctus and she seemed to be permanently tired and achy, not to mention shivery in arctic domestic temperatures caused by a coal shortage.

One freezing morning in January, she decided to leave

her bicycle at home and take the bus to work as the roads were icy. Barney and Merle had both already left for work so Dolly made her way to the bus stop alone, her feet sliding on the slippery pavements.

Having spent a wakeful night at the mercy of her cough, she wasn't in good humour as she joined the bus queue. Her mood deteriorated even further when she was plagued by an attack of coughing which hurt her chest and made the muscles across her back feel sore. The entire queue was a seething, shivering mass of fury towards those responsible for running the bus service on this bitterly cold morning.

'Bleedin' bus company,' said one disgruntled man. 'They wanna kick up the bloomin' arse . . . 'alf an hour I've been standing 'ere.'

'Are they trying to kill us all off or somethin'?' said a woman.

'Gawd knows.'

'It didn't ought to be allowed, keeping people standing about getting pneumonia when they're trying to get to work.'

''Course it didn't,' agreed another person, a community spirit emerging among this group of irritated strangers. 'The last thing people need is a killer bus queue, innit, specially with all this ruddy flu about.'

When a man joined the queue behind her and tried to engage her in conversation, Dolly was too busy wheezing and choking to be able to answer him.

'You ought to get something done about that cough, love,' he said in a deep, gravel voice.

When she had recovered sufficiently to reply, she did so

with asperity. 'What do you suggest I do, have my head amputated?'

'That's a bit drastic,' he said, with a chuckle.

She ignored him.

'But I suppose I did ask for it,'

She turned to see a tall, brown-haired man of about forty, dressed in a dark overcoat and trilby hat. There seemed to be something vaguely familiar about him, yet she couldn't remember having met him before.

'You certainly did – it was a ridiculous thing to say,' she snapped, turning away. 'Don't you think I've done everything I can to get rid of the damned thing?'

'Oh dear, someone's got out of bed the wrong side this morning,' he said with infuriating bonhomie.

Up went her brows and she sighed in irritation.

'We all do that from time to time, love,' he persisted, annoying her even more with his unshakable amiability, 'especially on cold mornings like this one.'

'Humph.'

'Oh, well, keep smiling, eh, love?'

She turned to him again thoughtfully.

'I've a feeling we've met before,' she said, with a sudden change of mood. 'I recognise your voice ... the way you said "keep smiling".'

'Can't say I remember seeing you before,' he admitted.

'Are you a fireman?'

'I certainly am.'

'That's where I've seen you,' she said. 'You were at a fire at my mother's house, back in the Blitz.'

'Was I? I couldn't count the number of fires I attended during that time.'

'Maybury Avenue.'

'Yeah, probably.' He still looked blank.

'Three of us got buried in the Anderson shelter, does that ring a bell?' she asked him.

'Sort of . . .'

'You were too busy to have looked at me properly,' she explained. 'I'd not have remembered you but for your voice.'

'That's right,' he said, snapping his fingers. 'Three of you appeared from nowhere.'

'Yes.'

'So you're one of The Three Musketeers? Well, I'll be blowed.' He thrust forward a woolly gloved hand. 'Gordon Doby.'

'Dolly Mitchell,' she said.

'How is your mum now?' he asked. 'Did she get her place fixed up?'

'No, not properly,' explained Dolly. 'But she still lives there in the part that wasn't damaged. The rest will have to wait 'til after the war when things get back to normal.'

'You on your way to work?' he asked.

She nodded. 'And you?'

'No, I've got a few days' leave,' he told her. 'I'm on my way home, as a matter of fact.'

'Out all night, eh?' she said with a wicked grin. 'Tut tut.'

'I slept on a mate's sofa last night,' he explained. 'We had a bit of a knees up at his local, a stag party for one of the lads who's getting married.'

'You must have a very understanding wife,' she said lightly.

'I'm a widower,' he explained, eyes darkening. 'My wife died ten years ago, and we didn't have a family so I've no one to answer to.'

'Oh, I see.'

'How about you?' he asked. 'Husband away fighting, I suppose?'

'I'm divorced,' she told him, 'but I do have a couple of teenage children so I have someone to answer to.'

An already crowded bus snorted to a halt and they moved up in the queue, but there was only room on the bus for a few at the front. Despite this, Dolly's mood had improved considerably and her cough seemed to have burned itself out, for the time being.

'I think I'd better start walking,' she remarked. 'Or I'll never get to work today.'

'Yes, I can see what you mean.'

She threw him a smile, her glowing cheeks almost matching her red woolly hat and scarf which brightened up the grey utility coat she was wearing. 'Anyway, it was really nice to see you again,' she said.

'Likewise.'

'Cheerio then.'

'Tata.'

She had only taken a few steps when he tapped her on the shoulder.

'Would those kids of yours let you have a night out, do you think?'

'Of course,' she said, moving out of the way of the jostling crowds. 'At seventeen and sixteen they're long past the age of needing baby sitters.'

'I was wondering if you might like to go out with me?' he said.

She was taken aback. It was so long since she had had this sort of male attention, she wasn't sure how to handle it. 'Well, I'm not sure,' she said at last.

'I'm sorry,' he said. 'I thought you meant you were on your own when you said you were divorced.'

'I am,' she said lightly. 'I'm completely unattached.'

He beamed and she noticed what a genuinely friendly face he had with rich brown eyes that seemed to warm her very bones. 'So, how about it then? We could go to the pictures if you like.'

'I'd like that, Gordon,' she said, smiling.

'Good.'

'When did you have in mind?'

'Sometime this week would suit me,' he said. 'I've a spell of night duty when I go back off leave.'

'I see . . .'

'Would you be free this evening by any chance?'

'Apart from feeding the family, I'm as free as a bird.'

His eyes twinkled, laughter lines spreading out from them. 'Good. Give me your address and I'll come and call for you.'

'You'd better write it down,' she said as the crowds pushed past them, making conversation difficult. 'Do you have a pencil handy?'

'No.'

'Don't worry, I'll meet you there,' she said. 'To save you having to remember it.'

'Are you sure you don't mind getting there on your own in the black-out?'

''Course not.' She smiled. 'If I'm not used to it by now, I never will be.'

'Righto then. I'll walk you home afterwards though.'

'If you wish.'

'There's a Hope and Crosby on at the Odeon,' he said. 'Do you fancy it?'

'Sounds just the job.'

'Shall we say seven o'clock outside the cinema then?'

'Lovely,' she agreed, feeling the years drop away. 'I hope my dratted cough doesn't play me up in there, though, and drive everyone mad.'

'I'll try to get hold of some cough sweets for you,' he said. 'Though I can't promise anything, with people buying up supplies and eating them like proper sweets as they're not on ration.'

'Mmm, they are like gold dust these days,' she agreed. 'Some people are even using indigestion tablets as sweets, I've heard.'

'I'll do what I can.'

'Don't worry if you can't, I'll look forward to seeing you anyway.'

'So will I.'

There was a spring in her step as she walked to the factory, cold weather and aches and pains forgotten. His attention had flattered her – made her feel like an attractive woman again. It had revitalised her more effectively than any medicine.

True to his word Gordon brought her some cough lozenges as well as a quarter of toffees. She told him it was a true gentleman indeed who was willing to share his precious sweet ration. Ensconced in the warm cinema, contentedly chewing toffees, they lost themselves in the adventures of Bob Hope, Bing Crosby and Dorothy Lamour in a film called 'The Road to Morocco'. It was a zany comedy with plenty of jokes and some talking camels. This cheerful, escapist entertainment was just what Dolly needed to take her mind off the problems of running a business in wartime, the shortages of practically everything, and the latest rumours about a new German secret weapon.

When they emerged from the cinema into the frosty night, she felt almost youthfully exuberant. It had been such a long time since she'd been out with a man she had almost forgotten what marvellous fun it could be.

'I've had such a lovely evening, Gordon,' she said, as they picked their way to Bailey Gardens in the blacked-out streets, arm in arm. 'Thank you so much.'

'It's been my pleasure, love,' he said with genuine enthusiasm. 'I've enjoyed your company. Life can get very lonely when you're on your own.'

'Don't I know it.'

'You too! I wouldn't have thought you'd notice it so much, having the children around.'

'They're almost grown, they've their own lives now,'

explained Dolly, realising just how much she needed the stimulus of a new friend.

'Perhaps we could go out again sometime soon then?' he suggested.

'That would be lovely.'

The tone of the conversation gave her a moment of déjà vu. The special excitement of getting to know someone new reminded her of a time when she had done the same thing with a man she'd never forgotten all through the difficult years. He too had had gentle brown eyes that had warmed her right through . . .

Chapter Seventeen

Half a world away from London, inside a primitive bamboo hut in a tiny Burmese village nestling at the foot of jungle-covered hills, the brown eyes Dolly remembered were neither warm nor gentle. They were ice-hard as their owner listened to what the soldier had to report.

'Syd Willis has gone, Sarge,' said Private Carter gravely.

'Gone?'

'Yes, Sarge.'

'AWOL, you mean?'

'Well . . . sort of. But I thought . . . that is, me and the boys thought . . . that if we went after him and brought him back sharpish . . .'

'No one outside our unit need be any the wiser?' Bill finished for him.

'That's right, Sarge. So is it all right if a couple of us go and find him?'

'Why should you want to do that for a deserter?' asked Bill, in the stern manner essential to preserve his seniority.

'Syd ain't really a deserter, Sarge,' explained Carter. 'He's been in a hell of a state lately, that's all.'

'Woman trouble, I suppose?'

'Yeah. He had a letter from his girl last time we got any mail through and he's been talking about trying to get back to Blighty ever since,' explained Carter with a frown. 'She's met another bloke and given poor old Syd the elbow.'

'You know as well as I do that that's no excuse for desertion,' said Bill authoritatively.

'Yes, Sarge,' said the soldier, facing his sergeant with a rigidly straight back, his young skin tanned a leathery brown from months in a tropical climate.

'So that's that then,' said Bill dismissively.

'I still want to go after him,' persisted Carter.

'We're fighting a war here,' Bill pointed out sharply. 'Not running a guidance centre for lovesick squaddies.'

'I know that, Sarge.'

'What the hell does he think he can do, anyway?' asked Bill. 'He's a long way from home.'

'He's hoping to get to the coast . . . then he'll try to get a ship.'

'He's got about as much chance of that as I have of becoming a general,' stated Bill categorically.

'We all know that, Sarge, but Syd ain't thinking straight at the moment.'

'Even if he did manage to get through the jungle, which is highly unlikely since it's riddled with killer animals as well as Japanese,' said Bill, 'he'd be picked up as soon as he hit civilisation.'

'That's why we wanna bring him back,' explained the soldier earnestly.

'So you thought I'd be a soft touch, did you?' said Bill harshly. 'Thought I'd put my head on the block for him.'

'O' course we don't wanna drop you in it,' said Carter. 'But, I mean . . . who would ever know?'

'That's beside the point.'

'We thought . . . you've been a good sergeant to us . . . and, well, the lads and me thought . . .'

'Well, you thought wrong,' barked Bill. 'So forget it and go back to your position!'

'Yes, Sarge,' The soldier turned and marched to the doorway of the hut.

'Carter,' called Bill.

The soldier turned back and looked at him questioningly.

'How long ago did he leave?'

'Not long, about half an hour.'

'Which direction?'

'That way,' he said, pointing towards the jungle.

'Right.'

'Sarge,' said the soldier, and went to join his mates in one of the other huts.

Bill wiped his brow with a grimy, sweat-sodden handkerchief, his jungle green battledress soaked with dark patches of perspiration. Being in a position of authority had its advantages but life was simpler for the ordinary soldier, he thought, remembering how quick the army had been to spot his leadership skills and promote him.

Now he found himself on the horns of a real dilemma. Strictly speaking he should not leave the main body of his men to go after one who was in the process of deserting. He should leave him to get on with it. But his natural compassion made this impossible. He had formed a bond with his subordinates, especially since being separated from the platoon officer and the rest of the men during a confused jungle skirmish with some Japs. Bill cared about his small band of soldiers. Syd Willis had shown steadfast courage throughout their time in Burma. How could he leave a man of that calibre to the appalling fate he had chosen for himself whilst in a state of emotional turmoil?

Mulling the problem over, Bill mooched to the window, the roughly hewn wooden floorboards creaking beneath his boots. He looked out over the village, deserted by the population who'd fled from the Japanese. It was a small, muddy hamlet consisting of huts built on posts above ground as protection against floods and wild animals, and constructed of bamboo matting walls and thatched roofs.

For months the platoon had slogged through jungle and swamp, across plains and rivers, with the purpose of recapturing Burma. After resting here tonight they would continue on towards the coast, where the British aim was to capture Akyab Island, in the hope of rejoining the army.

Making a sudden decision, he left the hut and went to tell the men he wouldn't be long. Then, with rifle and bayonet fixed, the camouflage net on his steel helmet carefully spread with bits of foliage, he headed into the eerie green murkiness of the jungle. He knew his behaviour was unprofessional but, this way, at least the squaddies wouldn't be involved in any breach of army discipline.

This was rugged country of jungle-covered hills and tiered paddy fields. Making his way through dense vegetation, sprigs and leaves scratching his face and catching on his clothes, his boots squelching in the sucking mud, his ears were finely tuned for the sound of an enemy presence.

His nerves jarred at the sound of a cracking twig. Crouching down in some bushes he waited, hardly daring to breathe. At the sound of a rustling movement nearby, he leapt to his feet, bayonet poised. His assailant had the same idea and weapons clashed.

'Willis,' he gasped, keeping his voice low in case of hostile forces. 'You bloody fool! You almost had my bayonet in your guts.'

'Sorry, Sarge,' said Willis, already backing away. 'I'm not coming back though.'

'Don't be an idiot,' said Bill. 'How far do you think you'll get on your own?'

'I've got to get back 'ome,' the man said in a desperate voice, 'and we can't be all that far from the coast so it ain't impossible.'

'Not very likely though, is it?' said Bill. 'Use your loaf, mate. If the Japs don't get you, a tiger or a leopard will.'

'I'm still gonna try.'

'Even if you were to get back to Blighty, do you think your girl will want a deserter?' said Bill, trying another tack. 'What woman wants a man who'll be labelled a coward for the rest of his life?'

'The lads have told you about it then,' he said in an aggrieved tone.

'They're your mates, they're worried about you,' Bill explained. 'They're hoping you'll come your senses before it's too late.'

'It already is,' he said.

'Not necessarily,' said Bill. 'If you come back with me now, I won't report this incident.'

'Thanks, Sarge, but nothin' doin'. Once my Betty sees me again, she'll give this other bloke his marching orders. It's me being away that turned her 'ead, yer see. It's only natural . . . she's young and healthy, she can't be expected to live like a nun. Once I'm back with her everything'll be all right again.'

Syd Willis was a well set up young man with fair hair and round blue eyes. Beneath the dirt and sweat and premature lines caused by tough living, Bill perceived his youth and vulnerability. Combat had taught him to face danger and death with courage and dignity but he couldn't take personal rejection in the same way.

'But you won't be there with her, will you, you daft sod?' Bill wisely pointed out. 'You'll either be in a jungle grave somewhere or in prison. Either way your life will be ruined. Ask yourself, mate, is any woman worth it?'

'You don't understand,' said the soldier earnestly.

'Try me.'

'It's just that I love 'er so much it 'urts . . . right in me guts,' he said, in a strangled voice.

Seeing his boyish intensity, Bill's thoughts sped back in time. He would have been about Willis's age when Dolly had done a similar thing to him.

'Something like that happened to me when I was about your age,' he said, experiencing a wave of empathy. 'I was just as cut up about it too.'

'Not you, Sarge . . .'

'Oh, yeah, I've had my moments.'

'I can't imagine anyone doin' the dirty on you,' said Willis. 'You always seem so much in control.'

'We were gonna get married,' Bill went on wistfully, 'then I found out she'd just been playing around with me . . . she was in the club by another bloke.'

'Blimey, Sarge, what a rotten slag!'

Stifling a strong urge to defend Dolly, Bill said, 'These things happen . . . I thought I'd never get over it at the time, though.'

'I 'ope you gave 'em both a good pasting,' said Willis.

'No, I was too sick even to do that,' admitted Bill, surprised that the memory of the incident still had the power to hurt him. 'So I just moved away from the area and eventually found someone else.'

'Your wife?' said Willis, for it was common knowledge among the men that their sergeant was happily married.

'That's right, and I wouldn't change Jean for the world.'

'So you forgot all about the slag then?' said Willis.

'No, I was never able to do that,' admitted Bill thoughtfully. 'But life goes on . . . it will for you too if you'll let it.'

Willis moved back, his face hardening, bayonet pointing threateningly at Bill. 'It won't work, Sarge . . . all this talk about your love life won't make me come back.'

'Don't be soft, man . . .'

'I'm going, so don't try to stop me.'

'And if I do, you'll kill me, I suppose?'

'If I have to, yeah.' His face muscles worked, his mouth twitched. 'You turn straight round and go back to the others or I'll let you have it . . . I will. I mean it, Sarge.'

Bill met his gaze with a challenge, his hand firmly in place on his own rifle. 'Go on then, son,' he said, lowering his weapon in a gesture of peace. 'You'd better get on and do it, 'cos I'm not going anywhere . . . not without you.'

They stood locked in conflict, the squawks and screams of wildlife splintering the tense silence. Cold sweat clung to Bill's clothes and ran down his cheeks; his eyes never left the other man's face.

'I'm not muckin' about, Sarge . . .'

'Stop talking about it and do it, if you're going to.'

'I will . . .'

'I'm all yours,' said Bill, knowing he was taking an enormous gamble. 'After all, what's the life of a mate against your own self-pity?'

'Don't make me do it, Sarge . . .'

'I'm not making you do anything.'

The point of the bayonet filled Bill's area of vision to the exclusion of all else. His nerves were jangling fit to burst. Then, very slowly, the weapon was lowered and the soldier's face crumpled as tears trickled down his filthy face. It was a pathetic sight but Bill didn't see weakness; he saw battle fatigue. Months of action had finally taken their toll.

'Sorry, Sarge,' Willis said, mopping his face, his body still convulsed. 'I must have let things get on top of me or somethin'.' He blew his nose and became almost instantly composed. 'It won't happen again, Sarge, I won't give you no more trouble.'

'I know that.'

'You said somethin' about not reporting this . . .'

'What is there to report?' asked Bill. 'All you did was go off to suss out the lie of the land, ready for the unit to move forward tomorrow. All the boys know that.'

'Thanks, Sarge, you're a good bloke,' said Willis with a twitchy, emotional grin.

'Don't start all that,' said Bill in embarrassment, and the two men began to walk back through the jungle together.

Chapter Eighteen

'I wish it would hurry up and start,' said Barney one tea-time in June as he and his mother and sister tucked into dried scrambled eggs on stodgy grey National Loaf toast.

'What? The summer . . . Christmas . . . the rain?' quipped his sister.

'The second front, of course,' he retorted.

'I shouldn't think it'll be long now,' said Dolly. 'They've been moving the troops to the invasion ports for weeks.'

'Do you think the Germans will retaliate?' asked Barney.

'God, I hope not,' said Dolly.

'Some people say we'll have heavy air raids,' put in Merle.

'One of my mates in the messenger service said we might get a token invasion or even parachute raids,' said Barney.

'They wouldn't have announced that the trains may be cancelled without warning if they didn't expect some sort of disruption,' put in Merle.

'Still, on a more cheerful note,' said Dolly, 'the sooner it starts, the sooner the war will be over.'

'If it isn't over by next year, I shall be out there with our boys, fighting,' said Barney, who was seventeen and ready for action.

Everyone was eager for the invasion they knew was being planned; it was generally expected to hasten the end of the war.

'Let's hope it'll be all over by then,' said Dolly brightly, and changing the subject asked, 'What are you two doing tonight?'

'I'm on duty,' said Barney, who had become a part-time member of the messenger service.

'What about you, Merle?' asked Dolly.

'I'm going to the pictures with one of the girls from work,' she said.

'Good,' remarked Dolly casually.

'It's good so that you and your boyfriend can have the place to yourselves, I suppose,' said Merle with a sudden change of mood.

'No, that isn't what I meant,' corrected Dolly. 'I said good because I'm pleased you both have something definite to do.'

'You are seeing him though?' said Merle accusingly.

'He does have a name, you know,' Dolly retorted crossly. 'And, *yes*, I am seeing him.'

'Surprise, surprise,' said Merle sarcastically.

'Gordon's a nice bloke,' Barney intervened, throwing his sister a critical glance. 'Anyway, why shouldn't Mum have a boy-friend?'

'Because he's using her for his own ends,' snapped Merle, glaring at her brother. 'But you're too dim to see that, of course!'

'He seems like a decent enough chap to me,' insisted Barney.

'Well, he would do, wouldn't he?' snapped Merle. 'You men are all the same.'

'Just because you can't find a boyfriend, there's no need to spoil things for Mum,' he said hotly, for he was always very loyal to his mother.

'I'd sooner roll naked in stinging nettles than have a boyfriend,' said Merle, her voice raised, eyes glistening with angry tears. 'Boys are only after one thing.'

'What would you know about it?' he asked. 'You've never even been out with one.'

'That doesn't mean I don't know what goes on,' she said, her voice quivering with temper. 'I've got eyes in my head and ears to hear what people are saying.'

'You've got a warped mind, I know that much,' said Barney.

'What about the Yanks?' she continued in full flow. 'Everyone knows they've only got one thing in mind.'

'Not all of them.'

'They don't even bother to find somewhere private either,' she went on. 'They do it with girls in public telephone booths.'

'Must you be so crude?' admonished Dolly.

'Yeah, fancy saying a thing like that,' chipped in Barney.

'It's true, the girls at the factory were talking about it,' continued Merle, her neck stained scarlet.

'The girls that go with them are just as much to blame,' said Barney.

'Trust you to say that! Anyway, British men only criticise

the Americans because they're jealous of their money,' Merle went on, giving her brother a poisonous look. 'But they're all tarred with the same brush.'

'Oh, shut up,' said Barney. 'You don't know anything about it.'

'Shut up yourself!'

'Now that's enough, both of you,' Dolly interjected, having to shout to make herself heard above the racket. 'I'm absolutely sick and tired of having meal times ruined by you two quarrelling.'

'She started it . . .'

'That's right, blame me as usual,' Merle rasped. 'Everything's always my fault around here.'

Dolly stood up with her hands in the air. 'Now that's enough, do you hear?' she yelled at them both.

The air was fraught with an electric silence. Then Merle got up and slammed out of the room.

'She did start it, Mum,' said Barney. 'I don't know why she always has to be so nasty.'

'Finish your tea,' said Dolly, forcing herself to be neutral. He was right, of course, Merle had started it as ever, but it was Dolly's policy never to take sides. That really would fuel Merle's battle against the world!

Leaving Barney to finish his meal, Dolly went upstairs to Merle's room where she found her daughter lying on her bed, staring at the ceiling.

'Come to lecture me, have you?' she asked insolently.

Dolly didn't reply.

'It'll be like water off a duck's back anyway, because I'm so used to being told off.'

Sitting on the edge of the bed, Dolly noticed her daughter's face was blotchy with tears. 'Be fair, love, it is usually you who starts the arguments.'

'Oh, yeah, always Merle,' she said in a tight voice. 'Never Saint blooming Barney!'

'Well, this time you definitely provoked your brother by being rude about Gordon,' said Dolly. 'It's only natural Barney would defend him, they get on well together.'

'Barney crawls round everyone just so that they'll like him,' said Merle, resorting to calumny in her pique.

Dolly gave a worried sigh but decided not to continue along those lines. 'Be that as it may, I haven't come up here to talk about your brother.'

'What then?' Merle asked irritably.

'For a start, I don't like to hear a young girl like you taking such a cynical view of men,' she said. 'It really isn't true, you know.'

''Course it is, they're all the same.'

This was not the first time Dolly had heard her daughter holding forth about the evils of the opposite sex. It was probably just youthful swagger but Dolly thought a few cautionary words were in order, for Merle's outspokenness on this subject was most unattractive; it made her seem so hard and vulgar.

'That sort of talk may be considered clever among your girlfriends,' she said, 'but it isn't welcome in this house.'

The girl leapt to her feet and glared at her mother. 'Is that it?' she asked vehemently. 'Have you quite finished?'

Stifling the urge to slap her face, because she knew it would serve no purpose, Dolly said, 'Gordon always goes out of his way to be pleasant to you, so why do you dislike him so much?'

'I don't dislike *him* especially,' she said, shrugging her shoulders indifferently.

'Well, you could have fooled me,' said Dolly. 'I'm always made to feel ashamed of the way you behave towards him.'

'I don't like having a stranger in the house,' she said. 'It interferes with my privacy.'

'Gordon isn't a stranger,' Dolly pointed out. 'He's a very dear friend.'

'Huh!' snorted Merle. 'I suppose you'll be talking about marrying him next?'

'There are no such plans in the pipeline at the moment,' said Dolly, 'but it isn't beyond the realms of possibility. After all, we are both free to marry.'

'He'll move in here then, I suppose?' Merle said, her tone becoming almost fearful.

'I don't know, he hasn't even broached the subject yet,' said Dolly, 'but if we were to get married, we would probably live here rather than at his place to save uprooting you and Barney.'

'We're old enough to look after ourselves,' pronounced Merle. 'I'd rather live alone than have a stepfather about the place.'

'Well, I'll be the judge of that, if any such event were to happen,' said Dolly brusquely. 'In the meantime I'd appreciate a little effort from you when Gordon comes to call.'

'Perhaps I should leave home altogether if I'm such a

nuisance to you,' said the girl, self-pityingly.

'Oh, Merle,' sighed Dolly in exasperation. 'Why do you make life so difficult for yourself and everyone around you?'

To Dolly's surprise her daughter's mouth trembled and her face worked against tears. She looked so young and vulnerable Dolly's irritation changed to compassion; she wanted to hold her close and soothe away whatever it was that gave her so much anguish. Standing up and opening her arms, she said, 'Oh, Merle, what is it, love . . . what's the matter?'

Merle shrank back. 'Nothing's the matter with me,' she said in a brittle tone. 'Okay, you want me to be civil to your boyfriend, so I will. Does that make you happy?'

'Not really,' said Dolly. 'I can't be truly happy knowing you are so miserable.'

'Oh, not more blame,' exploded Merle, cheeks flushed and eyes bright with tears. 'Now I'm supposed to be responsible for your happiness.'

Dolly remained silent. There was so much anger in her daughter, so much bitterness. Why? she asked herself. The blame must surely lie with her since she had brought her up. As her mother, she should be able to reach Merle but they were like strangers when it came to anything beyond the superficial.

'Naturally I'm affected by you,' said Dolly at last, 'but that doesn't mean I'm blaming you for anything.'

'That's something, I suppose,' said Merle gloomily.

'I'd do anything to help you,' said Dolly. 'But if you won't let me anywhere near you, I can't do that.'

'I don't need help,' said Merle briskly. 'Now, if you'll excuse me, I have to get ready to go out, I have to meet my friend.'

'Yes, yes . . . of course,' said Dolly miserably, and left the room with the familiar suspicion that she had failed her daughter in some way.

'What's up, Doll?' asked Gordon an hour or so later when she showed him into the living room and offered him a seat.

'The matter?'

'Come on, love,' he said. 'We've been seeing each other for nearly five months, I think I can tell when you are upset.'

Actually, Dolly was still feeling emotionally drained from the scene with Merle but she didn't think it fair to burden Gordon with her own domestic problems since the purpose of their meetings was to cheer each other up.

'I expect I'm just a bit tired,' she bluffed. 'We've had a crisis at the factory.'

'Oh?'

'Yes, one of the machines went on the blink and we can't get anyone in to fix it at any time in the foreseeable future,' she explained. 'Roll on the day when repair men are no longer a novelty. Still, that's wartime for you.'

'You're trembling,' he said. 'And it would take more than a spot of bother at work to make you do that.'

She raised her brows. 'You're far too perceptive, Gordon,' she said. 'But it's nothing really, just family problems. Kids, who'd have 'em?'

'What have they been up to?'

'Not Barney,' she admitted ruefully. 'It's Merle. All the rows in this house are caused by her.'

'A row, eh . . . was it about me by any chance?'

'You did come into it, yes,' she confessed. 'She seems to resent my seeing you.'

'I guessed that. I suppose she doesn't want to share you,' he said. 'She and Barney have had you to themselves a long time.'

Dolly shook her head. 'I don't think it can be that she objects to my having a life of my own outside the home,' she said thoughtfully, 'because she's used to my being involved with the factory. Anyway, she has her own life and her own friends, albeit she never seems to stay friendly with anyone for long.'

'Does she not?'

'No, she's always falling out with her girlfriends,' she explained. 'I don't know what it is with her but she doesn't seem able to get close to anyone.'

'It's a shame.'

'Oh, yes,' agreed Dolly, 'it breaks my heart to see her. Under all that aggression I know there's a lonely little girl just crying out to be loved.'

'Yet she won't let anyone get close . . .?'

'No, she's completely different to Barney.'

'Perhaps he's the problem,' he suggested. 'Maybe she's jealous of him because he finds it easy to be nice and people are naturally drawn to him.'

'That's the most likely explanation,' said Dolly. 'But all she has to do is be pleasant to people and the world would seem a different place. I mean . . . you get back what you give, don't you?'

'Mmm.'

'She isn't always horrid,' said Dolly. 'When she's in a good mood, she's a real joy. But just when you think she's improving, she turns it all on its head and starts being hateful again . . . she gets such awful rages interspersed with periods when she goes right into herself.'

'I'm no expert on children, not having any of my own,' said Gordon kindly, 'but I'm sure she'll grow out of it.'

'I've been telling myself that for years,' sighed Dolly.

'Sixteen is a painful age from what I can remember of it,' said Gordon, making a face. 'I'm sure I must have been a real pain in the arse to my parents . . . an inferiority complex thinly disguised as Jack the Lad. I was desperately lacking in confidence and terrified of the opposite sex . . . I made a lot of noise to hide it.'

Despite her mood of depression, Dolly couldn't help but grin. 'I can't imagine you having any hangups,' she told him. 'You're one of the most uncomplicated people I've ever met.'

'I think everyone has their share of complexities,' he said. 'But as you get older you're more able to cope with them. Working in the fire service is a great leveller, even in peacetime. You see such tragedy, Doll, it makes you realise it's enough just to be alive.'

'I suppose it must do.'

'Things will work out for Merle, you'll see.'

'I hope so.'

'In the meantime, I think a little light relief is in order, don't you?'

'Yes. Sorry you walked into this lot . . .'

'Nonsense, I want to share your problems.' He grinned. 'So what do you fancy – a film, a pub, a show – or do you just want to stay in and listen to the wireless?'

She smiled, feeling better. Gordon was so good for her. He was such undemanding company and fun to be with. She'd grown very fond of him this last few months and they had spent virtually all their spare time together, such as that was with him often working evenings and her ARP duties. The difficulty of being alone together, with two teenagers around, was alleviated by Gordon's little house in Chiswick where they spent many a happy hour.

'I'm not in the mood for the pictures,' she told him. 'So how about a nice lively pub? If we can find one that's got anything to sell.'

'You leave it to me,' he said. 'I know just the place to make you forget all your troubles for an hour or two. We'll have to take our own glasses, though, or we won't get served. The shortage of glasses is almost as bad as the beer drought.'

'I'll see what I can find,' said Dolly, going to the kitchen.

From the outside it was a shabby, backstreet pub on the fringes of Chiswick, with sooty walls and boarded-up windows that didn't show a chink of light. The smoky interior of the Fiddler's Arms was a seething mass of ebullient humanity, chattering and laughing against the background of a piano thumping out 'Roll out the Barrel' accompanied by raucous community singing.

Some of Gordon's pals, who had just come off duty, were standing at the bar, and Dolly was given a warm welcome.

'What news is there from the station?' asked Gordon, after introductions had been made.

'Nothing much, mate, it's all been very quiet on our shift,' said one of his friends.

'Make the most of it eh, lads?' said Gordon lightly. 'This calm won't last much longer.'

'Too bloody true it won't,' said his mate jovially. 'I can't see the Germans staying quietly at home once our lads are back on French soil.'

'They'll probably bring out the secret weapon they've got up their sleeve,' said another.

'Oh, well, keep smilin', eh, lads?' said Gordon, offering them a drink only to be told they were just leaving.

'I'll see you around then.' He cast an eye around the crowded room. 'All I need now is a seat for Dolly.'

'You've about as much chance of finding one of those as you have of getting a decent pint of beer in wartime,' said one of the firemen. 'I swear they pull pints from rain barrels instead o' beer barrels. Ne'mind, I suppose it beats an empty glass.'

No one argued with that, and after their rather boisterous exit, Gordon managed to find a couple of seats at a corner table where they settled down, Dolly with a gin and orange, Gordon with a pint of bitter and a packet of Weights. The entire company joined in when the pianist bashed out such rousing favourites as 'You Are My Sunshine' and 'Little Brown Jug', after which people with a modicum of talent, and some without any at all, got up and did a turn. An elderly woman warbled a tuneless version of 'We'll Meet Again' and an old man brought tears to Dolly's eyes with a heartfelt rendition of 'There'll Always Be An England'.

By the time they emerged into the warm summer evening, Dolly was feeling much more relaxed.

'Well, are you feeling better now?' asked Gordon.

'I'll say . . . it's calmed me down no end.' She yawned. 'In fact, I feel as though I'm about to fall asleep on my feet.'

'I feel tired too,' he confessed with a yawn. 'Probably because I've not long been back on the day shift after a spell of night duty.'

'Mmm.'

'Everyone seems to be worn out now though, don't you think?'

'Oh, yes, the war is really beginning to take its toll now,' she agreed. 'You can see it in people's faces on the buses – in queues – everywhere.'

'I think we're all a bit keyed up about what we're going to be in for after D Day too.'

'You're not wrong about that,' she said. 'I've noticed the workers at the factory are all a bit tense.'

'We'll all feel better once the invasion gets underway.'

'Definitely.'

'In the meantime, as we're nearer to my place than yours, how about coming back for a spot of supper?'

'Lovely.'

They strolled through the streets arm in arm, chatting

easily. With him beside her, all her problems seemed soluble. If only she didn't feel so utterly exhausted.

'Gordon,' Dolly said, coming to with a start to the sound of aircraft to find that the clock on his mantelpiece said it had turned five o'clock.

'What . . . whasamatta?' muttered Gordon sleepily from her side on the sofa where they had fallen asleep together, cocoa and sandwiches on the occasional table only half finished.

'It's gone five o'clock,' she said in a thick tired voice. 'We must have dozed off without even finishing our supper.'

'Without doing anything else either. The blooming war plays havoc with your love life,' he muttered, removing his arm from her shoulder and sitting up drowsily. 'It comes to something when you fall asleep *before* the event.'

'Never mind that,' she said, 'I have to go home. The children will be wondering where I am.'

'They'll be asleep.'

'Not necessarily,' she said. 'I always stay awake till they get in.'

'That's different. It's for Mum to worry about them, not the other way around,' he said, stroking the back of her neck. 'You might as well stay for breakfast now,'

'I can't, Gordon.'

'Oh, go on,' he said with tender persuasion. 'You can pop into home before you go to work.'

She had to admit to being sorely tempted.

'No, as much as I'd like to, I really have to go, Gordon,' she said, shivering with sleepiness. 'Just in case they're awake and worried about me. The planes might have woken them.'

'Oh, well, if you must,' he said, stretching and yawning.

'You go to bed for a few hours,' she said. 'There's no need to see me home.'

'I'm not letting you walk home alone at this time of night.'

'Don't be daft. Anyway, it's already morning,' she said. 'You go to bed.'

'Only if you come too.'

'Another time. Right now I have to go home.' She sighed. 'Oh, what it is to be a parent!'

'And what it is to be the boyfriend of one,' he said with a rueful smile.

'I must say, you look hard done by,' she grinned.

He got up, yawning and groaning, his curly brown hair standing on end, his clothes crumpled. His shirt was open where he'd taken his tie off last night, giving him a raffish look. He looked very dishevelled and very desirable.

'You sure you won't stay?'

'I'm sure,' she forced herself to say, shoving her arms into her cardigan and gathering up her handbag.

'Oh, well,' he said resignedly, taking her hand and leading her from the room, 'in that case I'll take you home in style.'

Riding side-saddle on the cross-bar of his bicycle as he pedalled through the sleeping streets, trying unsuccessfully to nibble her ear, Dolly was weak with laughter. 'I'm not even sure that this is legal, you know,' she said.

'Don't worry, I'll visit you in Holloway.'

321

'You're in charge of the vehicle, so you're the one who'll be arrested,' she giggled.

'I'll tell them I was aided and abetted by you.'

'Shhh,' she urged him as their lighthearted banter echoed in the morning air.

'No, I won't,' he said, kissing her ear and breathing into her hair as he tried to kiss her neck.

'You'll have us both off the bike in a minute, doing things like that,' she said, feeling ridiculously girlish.

'How can I help it when you're so sexy?'

'No one will believe that all we did at your place last night was sleep.'

' I can hardly believe it myself,' he said. 'I must be getting old.'

'Aren't we all?'

'I'm so happy, Dolly,' he said in a more serious tone.

'You're *happy* pedalling through the streets when you should be snuggled up in bed?' she said. 'You must be off your rocker!'

'Being with you wherever that is, I mean,' he corrected softly.

'Oh, Gordon, that's sweet and very romantic,' she said, touched.

'I didn't think I'd ever feel this way again about anyone after Mary died,' he said softly, 'but you've made life worthwhile for me again, Dolly.'

'I'm glad . . . you've changed my life too.'

They turned the corner into Bailey Gardens and Dolly heaved a sigh of relief to see that the house was in darkness.

'Honestly, I feel like a naughty child. I'm scared stiff my

322

own kids will be waiting to interrogate me. Isn't it silly?' she whispered as Gordon leaned the bike against the wall and they crept up the front path.

'Quite ridiculous,' he agreed.

'I know.' She turned to him in the porch, her mood becoming solemn. 'But despite all that I'm very happy, Gordon . . . very happy indeed. I'm so glad you've become a part of my life.'

'Maybe we could make it a more permanent part some time soon?'

'Oh?'

'I want to marry you, Dolly.'

She had been expecting this and was thrilled. But the thought of the family adjustments that would have to be made if she remarried caused her to hesitate in her reply.

'Think about it anyway,' he said with embarrassment. 'I realise there might be a few practical problems with the children and so on.'

'Nothing that can't be overcome,' she said in a positive manner. 'I'd really love to marry you, Gordon.'

'Oh, Dolly . . . that's really made my day,' he said.

They indulged in a brief embrace before Gordon stole silently back up the path and began his bike ride home.

Watching him from her bedroom window in the pale early light as he turned the corner out of sight, she heard the roar of planes growing louder. Looking up, she saw that the sky was filled with aircraft. Hundreds of them in an endless stream.

'It must have started,' she murmured to herself. 'D Day is here!'

Chapter Nineteen

Seated at the wheel of a delivery van on her way to the WVS headquarters in Westminster with a priority supply of tea, Dolly noticed how shabby and pitiful London looked in the cruel light of the July sun. The dusty streets were punctuated with freshly made battle scars, smouldering rubble, damaged roofs, broken windows.

Contrary to expectations, the Allied invasion on D Day had brought no immediate retaliatory enemy bombing of embarkation ports, docks or communications. But very soon after, a new hell came upon the capital in the form of deadly robot bombs that scuttled across the sky at all hours of the day and night. A number of fatalities occurred among Slater's workforce from these vile weapons, and disruptions to tea supplies meant Dolly was kept busy with any job to hand, which was why she was now out on the road.

Her stomach tightened at the miserable moan of the siren. But its grim message didn't empty the streets as it would have in earlier blitzes. Apart from some pedestrians casting apprehensive glances at the sky, the crowds resolutely continued with their business in the normal way. Traffic kept moving; people in queues remained stoically in position at bus stops and outside shops. Regardless of official warnings to take cover on hearing the alert, the sheer frequency of these raids meant that few people bothered about the daytime sirens unless a robot could actually be heard nearby.

The sound of fire engine bells and ambulances rent the air with their spine-chilling sense of urgency. Dolly's heart almost stopped beating as the harsh roar of a flying bomb drew closer, causing people to dart into shops for shelter. Her hands felt slippery on the steering wheel and her mouth was parched as she waited for it to pass overhead, dreading that its engine would cut out to indicate its immediate descent.

When the explosion came, it shook the ground but seemed to have missed this actual vicinity. Dolly's relief at being alive was immediately followed by anxiety for her family for whom she offered up a silent prayer. Added to her list of loved ones was Gordon, that dear brave man who was probably putting his life at risk somewhere in the capital at this very moment.

Continuing on her way to the sweet sound of the all clear, it occurred to her that Gordon's marriage proposal seemed much longer ago than just over a month, having been completely overshadowed by events outside their control since their carefree night together on the eve of D Day. She'd hardly seen him since then, for the havoc wreaked by the doodlebugs meant extra shifts for him and longer working hours for her. Over the past few weeks he'd either been on duty or sleeping. They'd snatched the odd hour together but had both been too tired to discuss wedding plans.

The fact that she hadn't told the family about the proposal couldn't be blamed on the current emergency though. That was due to the fact that she just couldn't face another set-to with Merle, which her news would undoubtedly create.

With the rational part of her make-up Dolly knew it was wrong to let herself be ruled by her daughter whose objections to Gordon could only be based on her paranoid attitude to men and a selfish concern for her own domestic comfort. If Dolly allowed herself to be bullied over this issue, she would be setting the pattern for future oppression. Frankly she didn't think such indulgence would be good for either of them. But strong maternal instinct caused her to shrink from the idea of adding to the anguish Merle already saw fit to make for herself.

Occasionally, Dolly wondered if she herself actually wanted marriage, and wouldn't rather just leave things as they were with Gordon. Had she said yes to him simply because she was lonely and needed a lover? Did it matter if that was the reason? She decided it didn't. After all, she was unlikely to love another man in the same way as she had loved Bill Drake. That sort of intensity was strictly for the young, thank goodness; she couldn't cope with all that agony again at her age. She was very fond of Gordon, and she desired him physically. More than that she knew she could not ask.

Having come to a satisfactory conclusion, she became

aware of fatigue bearing down on her. Her limbs felt stiff and heavy; her eyes ached from the ubiquitous dust and smoke. As soon as the raids eased off and life became less fraught, she would definitely make her plans to marry generally known.

In the meantime, she was looking forward to seeing Gordon this evening on his much overdue night off. She felt in need of his unshakeable optimism; the special way he had of making it seem as though everything was going to be all right.

I only hope I don't fall asleep all over him this time, she thought, yawning, as she drove through the West End en route for Westminster.

Gordon arrived earlier than expected that evening. Smartly accoutred in uniform, he appeared at the kitchen door while she was busy making a toad-in-the-hole.

'I can't stay long,' he explained ruefully, taking off his peaked cap and kissing the back of her head as she whisked the batter. 'I have to go on duty.'

'Oh, no!' she exclaimed, pausing with the fork in mid air. 'I've been looking forward to spending the evening with you, all day.'

'So have I,' he told her. 'But one of our Section Leaders was killed last night – he was off-duty too. A doodlebug hit the pub he was in.'

'Oh, Gordon, that's terrible.'

'Yeah, isn't it? Anyway, I have to fill in for him. I'm ever so sorry, love.'

'Don't apologise, Gordon, when we're alive and that

poor devil isn't,' she said, turning to face him with a guilty look. 'It's selfish of me to want you to myself for the evening.'

He leaned against the sink watching her while she worked at the scrubbed kitchen table. Glancing across at him, she saw that he was grey with tiredness; there was a large burn on his cheek and his hands were a mass of cuts and scorches.

'You're not alone in that,' he said with a heavy sigh. 'I'd give a lot for some time off to spend with you.'

'I know,' she said gently.

'But it just isn't possible at the moment,' he said wearily. 'This latest bag of tricks from Jerry is as bad as the bloomin' Blitz. We're run off our feet.'

'I'll bet.'

'We're attending every incident even though not all of the explosions result in fire,' he explained. 'Sometimes widespread damage is caused by the blast alone.'

'You boys stay around to help out even when there isn't a fire then?' she said thoughtfully, greasing an oven dish and placing the sausages in it.

'Oh, yeah, we're trained in basic rescue work so we stay and give back-up support to the rescue and ambulance services.'

'They certainly keep you busy,' she commented, carefully pouring the batter over the sausages.

'Not 'alf,' he said.

'I suppose the job entails digging out people who are trapped under the debris,' she said chattily.

'Yes, we do quite a bit of that sort of thing,' he explained, 'and clearing up damaged hospitals so that they can stay in service.'

'Mind you, Gordon, there doesn't seem to be any shortage of fires from these damned flying bombs from what I've seen of it,' she remarked, putting the dish into the oven. 'The air is always thick with smoke lately.'

'You're not kidding! Some of the blazes are huge.' He paused and sucked in his breath with a shake of the head. 'When the candleworks near the Thames went up, I'd never seen flames like it.' He made a small whistling sound. 'The place was full of barrels and tanks of paraffin wax, fuel oil and turpentine. There were barges loaded with paraffin wax moored alongside the factory too. My God did it burn! It was a ruddy furnace in there.'

'Did you lose any men?' she asked.

'No, but it was a miracle we didn't,' he said. 'I thought I was a gonner, I can tell you, Doll. We were rooting about through dense smoke, working knee-deep in oil and molten wax.'

'It must have been terrifying.'

'We were all sweating cobs 'cos we knew the walls were on the brink of collapse.'

'You must have nerves of steel for a job like that,' she said, putting the kettle on for tea.

'You get used to it,' he said. 'We weren't very popular at the beginning of the war before the bombs started coming . . . we were called all sorts of names then. War dodgers and parasites to name a couple of the milder ones.'

'No one would call you that now, though,' said Dolly.

'I shouldn't think so.'

'I think you're a brave lot and I've heard other people say the same thing.'

'Just doing a job like everyone else . . . anyway the war has made heroes of us all, however reluctant,' he said with genuine modesty. 'I mean, we are all forced to live with the sort of danger that would have been inconceivable in peacetime.'

'Yes, but yours is a particularly high risk occupation,' she pointed out. 'While we're all sheltering from the raids, you lot are in the thick of them.'

'The Fire Service is what we're trained for, it's what I've always done,' he told her. 'I fancied myself as a soldier at the beginning of the war but they reckoned my experience would be more useful on the home front.'

'I'm very glad they did or I might never have met you.' She slipped her arms around his neck and looked into the tired eyes which still managed to sparkle, despite being bloodshot from conjunctivitis caused by constant exposure to smoke and fumes.

'There is that to it,' he said, smiling into her face.

'I know one thing,' she said, grinning. 'You and I are going to have a lot of catching up to do when things do quieten down.'

'I can't wait,' he said, kissing her. 'I shall probably go wild with passion.'

'Yes, please,' she laughed. 'I shall be counting the minutes 'til then.'

'I don't think it'll be long,' he said on a more serious note, his warm breath touching her cheek. 'Our boys will soon have the Nazis on the run . . . then they'll be so busy they won't have time to attend to their rotten bomb-launching platforms.'

With unfortunate timing, Merle entered the back door on her return from work.

'Oh God, are you two at it again?' she said, rolling her green-brown eyes in disapproval.

Instinctively they sprang apart, though Dolly retorted sharply, 'Chance would be a fine thing in this house!'

'I'm going in a minute, Merle,' Gordon said breathlessly.

'Don't go on my account,' she said haughtily.

'I'm not, I'm on duty.'

'Oh, right,' she said, concealing her deflation with a tone of indifference.

'You've time for a cup of tea, surely, Gordon?' Dolly said, as the door closed behind her daughter.

'No, I won't have one if you don't mind,' he said. 'If I sit down I won't want to get up again and I'm due at the station soon.'

'Ah, well, I'd better not press you then, as much as I'd like to.'

'Have you told the kids about our plans?' he asked lightly.

She shook her head. 'There just doesn't seem to have been the right opportunity,' she said, feeling as though she had let him down.

He looked disappointed. 'It's this bloomin' war,' he said. 'I haven't even had a chance to try to find an engagement ring for you yet.'

'I tell you what we'll do,' said Dolly, making a sudden

decision. 'How about us making an announcement to the family all together on your next night off? Come for supper. I'll invite Mum and Mabs round and we'll make a proper occasion of it.'

'That will be smashing,' he said, his battered face crinkling into a smile.

'It's a date then.'

'It certainly is,' he sighed. 'But I really do have to go now.'

'I know.'

He kissed her and moved to the door. 'Keep smilin' eh, love.'

'I'll take that as a definite order and make it my motto for life,' she said lightly, and she was still grinning as the back door closed behind him. What a very special person he was!

Dolly was washing her hair when the siren went later that evening. She wrapped the towel around her head and hurried downstairs to the living room where Merle was listening to Bebe Daniels and Ben Lyon in 'Hi, Gang' on the wireless.

'I'm not missing this programme,' exclaimed Merle. 'Raid or no raid. It's a real scream.'

'Better get under the table then,' suggested Dolly as the ominous throb of a robot grew louder. 'Just in case Jerry drops his package in our direction.'

They sat under the dining table listening to the quick-fire cross talk between the comical Americans. The show was a special favourite of theirs. It was easier to forget what was going on outside with this entertaining repartee going on inside.

'Isn't Bebe a yell?' said Merle.

Dolly opened her mouth to answer but was thrown across the room by a blast which rocked the house.

'Merle . . . Merle . . . where are you?' muttered Dolly a few seconds later, scrambling up feeling dazed and brushing her damp hair from her eyes, the towel having been removed by the blast.

'I'm here,' came a shaky voice from the direction of the door, and in the fading evening light Dolly could see her daughter slumped against the wall.

With a muzzy head and a ringing sensation in her ears, Dolly stumbled over to her. 'You all right, love?'

'I think so,' she said, getting slowly to her feet, whey-faced and trembling.

'Phew, that was a close one,' said Dolly breathlessly.

An amalgam of confused sounds could be heard from outside: running feet, raised voices, fire bells. They hurried to the window to see tongues of orange flame and clouds of black smoke rising above the rooftops of the houses opposite.

'I reckon that's the flats in Trent Road that have gone up,' said Dolly.

'Must be.'

'I'm going to see if there's anything I can do to help.'

'I'll come with you,' said Merle.

Grabbing their tin hats from the hall stand, they hurried into the smoky street and ran round the block towards Trent Road, the all clear sounding in the gathering dusk.

The scene that greeted them as they turned the corner was horrific. The front had been ripped from a block of flats to expose the interiors of people's homes on several floors, flames leaping and spreading swiftly through the building. Through the smoke, Dolly could see the firemen working with ladders and hoses, the air permeated with the screams and groans of human misery. She could just make out some dazed figures staggering from the carnage. Police had already roped off the area and rescue teams and other official helpers were pouring on to the scene.

'I hope Barney is all right,' said Dolly anxiously, for her son was out on messenger duty.

'So do I,' said Merle, with unexpected concern caused, Dolly guessed, by her own close encounter with death. 'But he'll be fine, Mum, don't you worry.'

Warmed by this unusual feeling of unity with her daughter, Dolly linked arms with her. 'There's nothing we can do here,' she said. 'We'll only get in the way if we offer. So let's go home.'

'Yes, let's,' agreed Merle.

They walked back through the dusty streets in thoughtful silence. For once Merle did not shrug off her mother's attempt at affection and allowed their arms to remain linked. A glimmer of hope shone through the bleakness for Dolly. She basked in this precious moment of togetherness, knowing that it wouldn't last.

Leading a small team of firemen, Section-Leader Doby began a search of the ground floor of the burning block of flats, while his colleagues worked with hoses and turntable ladders on the upper floors. The heat was intense, the roar and crackle of flames deafening. He could feel the sting of blisters forming on his face. His clothes were wet from the hoses; the sores on his body, caused by the continuous chafing of his uniform that was often wet through, were rubbing painfully against his clothes. Ignoring all this, he got on with the task.

'Don't worry, ducks,' he said reassuringly to an elderly woman whose bottom half was trapped by debris. 'We'll have you out of there in no time.'

Gordon and his team worked carefully, not allowing themselves to dwell on the fact that the walls around them were likely to collapse at any moment. When the broken bricks and mangled bits of wood and metal were removed, the terrified woman was carried to safety by two of Gordon's subordinates. Working with speed but not panic, the little band of firemen lifted many more injured from the carnage, tripping over human remains as they walked.

'That's about it, lads,' said Gordon eventually. 'Let's get out of here before the lot comes down.'

But a sudden sound deterred him, a faint childish cry for help from a pile of debris resting against the damaged dividing wall between this and the adjacent flat.

'We daren't risk it,' said one of the men. 'This place is about to cave in. One false move and it'll be down on top of us.'

'There's a child alive in here,' Gordon said. 'I'll not leave while there's a chance of saving it.'

With nerves taut for fear their movements would prove fatal, they worked on the rubble, carefully tunnelling through lumps of brick-work, wood, twisted metal, broken furniture. Their efforts were eventually rewarded by the sight of a small boy, very frightened but alive.

'There you go, son.' Gordon lifted the boy gently from his prison and handed him to a colleague with instructions to take him to safety. 'You lot get out of here,' he told the men. 'I'll have one last look around to make sure there's no one else trapped anywhere about and I'll be after you.'

As his mates left with the child, Gordon thought he was going to pass out with exhaustion and dehydration. His eyes and throat were smarting, his head ached. Overcome with nausea, he vomited sooty phlegm and bile.

'That's better,' he muttered to himself as he headed out of the wrecked building.

Just when he was yards from safety, the ceiling collapsed on top of him.

Dolly woke with a start to find her son standing over her with a cup of tea.

'Hello, Barney,' she said sleepily, uncurling her cramped body, head throbbing, limbs stiff. 'I must have dozed off in the chair. I just couldn't face the thought of going to bed after the raids.'

'No.'

'I was worried about you being out on the streets in that lot,' she said. 'God, what a night!'

'Yeah, it was bad.'

Realising that it was almost daylight, she said, 'What time is it?'

'Half-five.'

'Have you just got in?'

'Not long ago.'

'You'd better get some sleep.'

'No, I couldn't.'

'I know how you feel, son, these raids do play on your mind.'

'No, it isn't that . . .'

'What then, Barney?'

'I . . . er . . . I heard something when I was out. You know how things get round on the streets after an incident . . .'

'Yes, I know. But what did you hear?' she asked, nerves tingling.

'A fireman was killed in the Trent Road flats incident,' he said, chewing his lip anxiously. 'A ceiling caved in on him.'

'Gordon?' she gasped, staring wild-eyed at Barney. 'You think it was Gordon . . .'

'Well . . .'

Her voice was fast and brittle as she struggled not to face up to the dreadful possibility. 'It doesn't have to be him, you know,' she said. 'He isn't the only fireman in London.'

'You'll have to check with the fire station, of course,' Barney said grimly. 'But . . . I'm sorry, Mum . . . I really hate having to say this.' He paused to clear his throat. 'But I'm almost certain it was Gordon. One of our chaps was nearby when the other firemen came out of the building . . . he's almost positive he heard them say the name Doby.'

'Oh . . . Oh, I see.' Her voice was dull with shock. 'I really ought to have been prepared, of course . . . but I'm not.'

'I'm ever so sorry, Mum,' he said, biting his lip and picking his thumbnail nervously, his youthful face creased with anguish. 'Gordon was a good bloke, one of the best.'

'Yes, he was.'

'I just don't know what to say,' he said in a shaky voice, putting his arms around her.

'There's no need to say anything, son,' she said, holding him close, her throat tight and her eyes unnaturally dry.

There was a stunned atmosphere in Dolly's house at breakfast after their suspicions had been confirmed by Gordon's superiors. Barney had spared his mother the job of telling Merle the awful news.

'Sorry to hear about Gordon, Mum,' she said quietly, sitting down at the table.

'Yes, it's awful,' sighed Dolly, serving some porridge from a saucepan into china bowls.

'We'll miss him,' said Barney.

'He wouldn't want us to mope about, though,' said Dolly, placing the bowls on the table.

'Keep smiling was his motto,' Barney reminded them.

It was suddenly very important to Dolly that she tell her children something they would otherwise never know. 'Gordon and I were planning to get married,' she said in a determined tone.

'I guessed you might be,' said Merle.

'Good for you,' said Barney.

'We were going to tell you on his next night off,' said Dolly.

'Er . . . oh, right,' said Merle, uncertain how to respond

to her mother's somewhat aggressive manner.

'I know you wouldn't have liked it, Merle,' said Dolly.

'Well, I . . .' she began doubtfully. 'Um . . . I don't suppose I would have . . . but it doesn't matter any more, does it?'

'Yes, it does matter,' said Dolly passionately. 'It matters very much.'

'By why? I mean it can't happen now, can it?' she said.

'It's important you know that I would have been proud to marry him despite your objections,' Dolly explained.

'Oh . . . I see,' said Merle wearily.

'Gordon was a good man and you should have been honoured to have him as a stepfather,' said Dolly emotionally, 'in the same way as I would have been honoured to be his wife.'

Leaving her offspring looking somewhat bemused, she turned and marched from the room, feeling hot tears burning and wishing to cry in private. Had she not made that announcement, she would have felt that she'd somehow betrayed Gordon.

Chapter Twenty

'Tea control isn't going to last forever, Ernie,' pronounced Bill, in response to his father-in-law who was dining with Bill and Jean and giving full vent to his resentment about the continuing restrictions in the tea trade.

'It's beginning to seem like it,' said Ernie gloomily, his mood depressed by sub-zero temperatures which meant he couldn't get warm anywhere, not even indoors by the fireside.

'Things will eventually pick up,' said Bill, passing Ernie a serving dish of mashed potato, cunningly mixed with swede to make it go further while potatoes were in such short supply.

'When, though, that's what I'd like to know?' continued Ernie. 'I mean, here we are nearly two years after the end of the war and the country is in a worse state than ever. Is this what our boys fought for? Is it? For us to be living on the edge of starvation with every damned thing either rationed or unobtainable.'

'Now you're exaggerating, Daddy,' put in Jean, serving her father with liver and gravy and doing the same for her

341

mother. 'I know food is short, but we've enough to keep us going.'

'Only just,' he told her through tight lips, 'not only have they reduced the meat ration, now they're talking about doing the same with bread.'

'Yeah, we know all that, Ern, but rationing has to end sometime,' said Bill, intending to steer the conversation on to more important matters. 'And if Webb's is to be ready for it, we need to start planning ahead.'

'Don't you think we've enough on our plate at the moment trying to contend with the ruddy fuel shortage and the bitter weather?' Ernie snapped. 'I'm buggered if I want to start worrying about the future.'

'I agree it's a nightmare trying to run a factory with power cuts wreaking havoc and deliveries hampered by snow,' admitted Bill, passing a tureen of boiled cabbage to his mother-in-law. 'But these are just temporary set-backs. We really ought to be looking ahead, because when tea does come off ration we'll need to be wide awake and fully prepared if we're to keep up with our competitors.

'It could be years, the way things are going,' was Ernie's miserable prediction.

'Even so,' persisted Bill, 'we need to start getting some ideas together for sales campaigns and promotions. I reckon competition is going to be fiercer than ever when the free market opens up again.'

'I don't see why it should be.'

'Oh, come on, Ern, it stands to reason . . . after years of restrictions, tea merchants will rise to the challenge in a big way,' said Bill confidently. 'I must say, I'm quite excited about it myself.'

'I can't think beyond tomorrow at the moment,' said Ernie morosely.

'You'll have to force yourself then, mate,' said Bill in a cautionary manner, 'because forward planning is the name of the game, and that's a fact.'

'Hey, you two,' admonished Jean, 'don't forget this is supposed to be a family dinner, not a board meeting.'

In actual fact, this social occasion was also doubling as a means of beating the scarcity of coal by the four of them sharing the same fireside for the evening.

Bill threw his wife a sharp look. 'I can see no harm in bringing up a spot of business,' he said irritably. 'After all, Webb's is a family firm, Jean . . . we're all affected by its success or failure.'

'All right . . . all right, keep your wig on,' she said lightly.

'Doesn't this cold weather make people bad-tempered?' said Lily, perceiving Bill's unusual prickliness. 'The butcher nearly bit my head off this morning.'

'It's enough to make anyone feel miserable, being perished every minute of the day,' said Jean, with a shiver. 'It creeps right into your bones. I can't say I'm thrilled at having to sit down to dinner in my hat and coat either.'

'Ernie and I have been going to bed in our outdoor clothes,' confessed Lily. 'And we still can't get properly warm.'

'You feel the cold more as you get older,' he remarked.

'I suppose you must do,' said Bill, thinking that the cold weather wasn't the only thing that Ernie had a lower threshold to these days; his ability to cope with business pressure had diminished too.

Jean cast a concerned glance around the table where woolly hats and mufflers were in evidence as well as overcoats. 'Perhaps we should move the table closer to the fire?' she suggested.

'No, don't bother, Jean,' said her mother. 'We'll huddle over it when we've finished eating.'

'I'll see if I can stir some life into the bloomin' thing,' said Bill gruffly, going over to the fire and raking it with the poker.

'Thanks, love,' said Jean.

The extreme weather was making life unbearable for everyone: pipes froze up; washing was welded to the line; limbs were broken as people slipped on iced-over snow on the streets. All of this combined with a serious fuel crisis threatened to cripple the economy. With coal trains immobilised by snow drifts, power cuts were making millions of workers idle, and some homes were without electricity for long periods each day. Jean could understand why her husband's temper was short. It was hard enough trying to run a home in the present conditions let alone a business.

Later that evening, when they were getting ready for bed, she made a casual reference to his testiness. 'You were in a funny mood tonight, love. Is the cold weather getting you down?'

'Give over,' he said grumpily. 'It'll take more than a

spell of brass monkey weather to upset me.'

'What's the matter then?'

'Oh, I suppose I'm just frustrated at not being able get your father to take an interest in Webb's future,' he sighed.

'He's too busy battling with the problems of the moment,' she opined. 'Poor old Dad really *is* feeling the cold weather.'

'He's feeling his age in general, I think,' remarked Bill. 'Only natural, I suppose, he is getting on a bit now.'

'Hardly in his dotage.'

'Well, no . . . of course not, but perhaps it is time he eased off a little in the business.'

'Retire, you mean?'

'No, not that exactly, but it might be a good idea for him to stand down as Managing Director . . . perhaps become Chairman so that he's under less of the day to day pressures,' said Bill thoughtfully. 'He's lost the drive he had before the war . . . seems content just to jog along. It might be all right now, but that sort of attitude will be no good to the firm when tea control comes to an end.'

'So will you suggest it to him then?'

'Good God, no.' Bill was emphatic. 'It's *his* company, I'm just his son-in-law.'

'And Sales Director,' she pointed out.

'Well, yes, but that still doesn't give me the right to tell him what to do.'

'Anyway, you're much more to him than a son-in-law,' she reminded him. 'He's very fond of you and respects your opinions. Both my parents think of you as their own son, you know that.'

'Yes, I do, and I'm flattered,' he admitted. 'But Webb's is still your father's company, Jean. A personal change of position must be his decision. It wouldn't be right for him to be pressurised into making it before he's good and ready.'

'Do you think he'll come to that conclusion himself soon?' she asked.

'Oh, yes, within the next year or so, I reckon,' Bill told her. 'Ernie has a good head on his shoulders, he'll soon begin to see the merits of having a younger man take some of the responsibility off his shoulders.'

'You'll take over as Managing Director then, I suppose?'

'If he asks me to, yes,' he said, his brows meeting in a frown.

'You don't seem very keen on the idea,' she said, winding her hair into dinky curlers at the dressing table and looking at him in the mirror as he unfastened his tie.

'Of course I'm keen,' he snapped.

'Why are you so cross then?'

'I'm not cross.'

What his wife had perceived as anger was guilt. If he took over from Ernie as Managing Director, he would reach the pinnacle of his ambitions; he would have control of the company. And all because he had made a play for Jean all those years ago! All right, so he never consciously used his position as her husband to further his career. And it was true to say that he would want his marriage to continue if he no longer had any connection with Webb's. But none of this altered the fact that his original intention in pursuing her had had nothing whatsoever to do with personal feelings.

Dear trusting Jean! She judged people by her own standards. How hurt she would be if she were to discover what his motives had been and that she had always been only the second woman in his life. He winced at the thought of her finding out.

'What's the matter?' she asked, spreading cold cream on her cheeks. 'Why such a sour face?'

'Sour face?'

'Yes, you looked as though you had a sudden pain,' she said, getting up and pulling on a thick jersey over her pyjamas.

'Must be stomach ache from all that ruddy swede you try to hide in the potatoes,' he said. 'God, how I hate the things.'

'Stomach ache my foot!' she said, pulling on a pair of his socks. 'You're just in a rotten mood.'

'You know me too well,' he said lightly. 'You'll be reading my mind next.'

'What a ghastly thought,' she said, shivering as she climbed into bed. 'It's bad enough hearing you rambling on in your sleep . . . I certainly wouldn't want to know what's going on in your conscious mind.'

'How long have I been doing that?' he asked, frowning.

'Since you came back from the war,' she said, slipping down under the covers.

'You've never said anything before . . .'

'Haven't I?' she said casually. 'I suppose I never got round to it.'

'What do I talk about?'

'I've no idea, it's all rather disjointed,' she said, being deliberately offhand because she thought it might disturb him to know how anguished his sleepy mutterings were.

'You must get some sort of a clue,' he said curiously.

'I think you must be talking to your army pals, judging by the language,' she said, 'but I don't want to listen so I put my fingers in my ears until you stop.'

'That's an odd thing to do.'

'Not really,' she told him. 'What someone says when they're asleep is very private, don't you think? I mean, they're not in control.'

Were all wives as sensitive as Jean? he wondered. He doubted if any man who'd been in combat wasn't plagued by bad dreams. When he'd first come home after the war he hadn't been able to get it out of his mind; the horror he'd seen; the pals he'd lost. Ordinary family life had been hard to settle back into. He'd missed the company of his mates – people who'd shared the same terror, had experienced the trauma of killing another human being.

He knew he would never be quite the same again. Such atrocities were bound to do things to the nervous system. His fuse was shorter than it used to be which was why he'd been touchy with Jean. 'I'm sorry I was snappy earlier,' he said.

'That's all right,' she said, hugging a hot-water bottle. 'I'll forgive you . . . but only if you hurry up and get into bed! I'm freezing to death in here, despite two hot-water bottles.'

'It isn't exactly tropical out here either, you know,' he

said, pulling on socks and woollies over his pyjamas.

'Don't hang about then, you daft devil,' she giggled.

'Move over, you've got all the bed,' he teased, as he ventured cautiously into the icy sheets.

'Ooh, Bill,' she tutted as he lifted the covers to climb in. 'You've let in a horrible draught.'

'I've got to open the bed to get into it, woman, now haven't I?'

'For goodness' sake pull the covers down now that you are in before we both get frostbite.'

A rustling of bedclothes accompanied a blast of cold air.

'Now what are you doing, fidget arse?' Jean asked.

'Just turning the light out.'

'Oh . . . right.'

'Now for Gawd's sake stop jabbering and come here and keep me warm,' he said into the darkness.

'Just try and keep me away,' she said, snuggling up to him, their muffled laughter filling the icy room.

Some sort of discomfort was nudging Dolly's subconscious as she slept. When she finally came to, she realised that she was cold. Her nose and ears were freezing and her feet were blocks of ice. Shivering violently, she leaned over and turned on the bedside light to see on her dumpy alarm clock that it had just turned three o'clock.

Rummaging into the bed for the cold hot-water bottle, she got up and reached for her woollen dressing gown draped over a chair by the bed only to realise that she already had it on, along with a cardigan and an old pair of Barney's thickest socks. And still she felt sick with cold.

Downstairs in the bitter kitchen, she put the kettle on to refill the bottle and make some cocoa, careful not to make too much noise and wake Merle. As the kettle began to warm up on the gas-stove, she placed her hands on it, feeling unexpectedly assailed by a profound sense of loneliness. It must be this damned cold weather, she thought.

Although Dolly was reasonably content with life, she did sometimes feel weary of being without a partner. Life was richer when you had someone with whom to share it; her affair with Gordon had brought that home to her. Dear Gordon, she still missed him a lot and longed for his cheerfulness and unfailing ability to look on the bright side. Even this wretched weather wouldn't have seemed so bad if she'd had him to cuddle up to.

It wasn't that she didn't have people she loved around her. She had Merle and Mother and Mabs. Barney was away in the army doing his National Service at the moment, stationed in Cyprus, but he wrote regularly and was due to be demobbed in the summer. None of these dear people, however, could take the place of that special someone.

With the best will in the world, she could not apply the epithet of companion to her temperamental daughter. For a while after Gordon's death Merle had been quite supportive, giving Dolly a glimpse of the compassionate side of her nature. But her rage against the world had soon begun to raise its moody head again. But Dolly remained convinced that Merle shared her desire for something more from the mother–daughter relationship, even though she would die rather than admit it.

Mothers and daughters, a sensitive combination! Dolly knew that only too well, never having enjoyed a particularly rewarding relationship with her own mother. Even now that they were getting along better than they had when she'd been younger, she and Edie still didn't have the mateyness she knew could exist within the filial bonding. Dolly often thought, without resentment, that Mabs was closer to Mother than she was.

As well as experiencing personal loneliness, Dolly often felt solitary at the head of the firm, especially with the reopening of the free market looming ahead. Mabs was a godsend in practical ways; a diligent worker who would turn her hand to anything. But she didn't have a managerial eye, even though she had taken over Ken's share in the business after his death. She had no perception of business expansion. When Dolly voiced her opinion about the challenge that lay ahead for Slater's when tea control ended, Mabs's advice was supportive but not very helpful.

'Don't worry, Doll, Slater's will always thrive with you in charge. I reckon you're brilliant at business. If I agreed with your dad over nothing else, I agreed with him over that. He knew what he was doing when he left the firm to you.'

Dear Mabs was wonderful at confidence boosting, but never had anything more constructive to offer. At heart she was still one of the workers, happier in the packing room than the boardroom; more at ease among people at grass roots level than policy makers. She made no secret of her intention to hand her share of Slater's over to Peter when he was old enough. That wouldn't be for some time yet, though, for he was still only fifteen. An unassuming boy very much in the mould of his father, Peter had joined the firm after leaving school and was learning the business from the bottom.

Bert Dixon was very good at dealing with problems on the factory floor but he had no commercial flair. This left Dolly with sole responsibility for leading the firm into the new era of free enterprise.

Barney was the only one she could talk to about it, and this wasn't ideal because he was still young and lacking in experience. He was keen enough and not short on business acumen, but he hadn't been in the trade long enough for her to have complete faith in his judgement.

But now the sound of movement on the stairs recalled her to the present. 'Hello, Merle,' she said as her daughter shuffled into the room, shivering and clutching a stone hot-water bottle. 'I've got the kettle on for refills.'

'That's good,' she said, emptying the cold water down the sink and putting the bottle on the wooden draining board.

'It's wicked, isn't it, this weather?' said Dolly. 'It gets right through to your bones.'

'Mmm.'

'I'm making cocoa,' said Dolly. 'Fancy a cup?'

'Please,' she said, shuddering violently and sitting down at the table, hugging herself.

Putting two cups of steaming cocoa down on the table, Dolly sat down opposite her, looking into the face that was so much like her own; round and chubby with saucer eyes of a similar colouring. Her brown hair was standing up on end and she was wearing an emerald dressing gown that picked out the green tones in her eyes. Observing her more closely Dolly could see that her eyes were moist and red.

'You've been crying,' she said.

'No, I haven't,' the girl denied swiftly. 'The cold weather has made my eyes water, that's all.'

'I don't believe you,' said Dolly, chancing her arm because she felt it was necessary.

'That's up to you,' said Merle, but her voice was wavering and tears began to meander down her cheeks.

'Merle,' Dolly said gently, reaching across the table and taking her hand.

'Oh, Mum . . . I . . .'

'What's the matter, love?' said Dolly gently. 'Come on . . . get it off your chest.'

'I feel so . . . so wretched!'

'Why? What's happened to make you so unhappy?'

'I . . . well . . . it was all a long time ago . . .'

She was shivering so excessively, Dolly was instinctively concerned. 'You'll catch your death of cold down here.' She got up and poured hot water into the stone receptacle and handed it to her daughter. 'Go back to bed with your cocoa. I'll fill my bottle and join you in a minute. We'll talk about it up there.'

Merle did as her mother said, and Dolly followed shortly after. The young woman was lying on her side with the covers pulled right up over her head when Dolly entered the room. Her cocoa was untouched on the bedside table.

Dolly perched on the edge of the bed. 'Now that you're warm and snug, let's continue with our chat.'

'I want to go to sleep.'

'I thought you wanted to talk?'

'Correction, Mother . . . *you* wanted me to talk.'

Dolly drew in her breath and counted to ten. 'What's on your mind, Merle?' she asked at last.

'Nothing,' came the muffled reply from the pillow.

Dolly's heart sank as she realised the moment for disclosure had passed. But, convinced that her daughter needed her, she couldn't just leave it at that.

'Has someone at work upset you?' she asked, for Merle was now working as a shorthand typist in an accountant's office.

'No.'

'There's obviously something . . .'

Merle swung into a sitting position, her pathetic mood replaced by fury. 'Why can't you mind your own business?'

'Because you're my daughter,' Dolly said patiently, 'and your happiness is my business.'

'Rubbish, I'm a grown woman.'

'That doesn't make any difference from my point of view.'

'Well, it should do . . .'

'A trouble shared is a trouble halved,' suggested Dolly.

'No, it isn't,' rasped Merle through clenched teeth. 'That's a load of rubbish if ever I heard it. I mean, I ask you . . . how can telling somebody about something make any difference.'

'It might make you feel better, that's all.'

'Who asked for your opinion, anyway?' interrupted Merle, tears gushing down her cheeks. 'Why don't you just clear off and leave me alone?'

'Because I don't think that is what you *really* want,' said Dolly, struggling to keep calm.

'Bloody hell, is there no privacy in this place?' sobbed Merle, dabbing at her wet face with her handkerchief in jerky, emotional movements. 'The sooner I get a place of my own and move out of here, the better.'

Dolly stood up with a heavy heart. 'Oh, well, if that's the way you feel . . . but you know where I am if you do need me,' she said, and walked quickly from the room.

Back in bed, she cursed herself for allowing physical considerations to impair her judgement downstairs in the kitchen. In the short time it had taken her to get upstairs, Merle had lost the impulse to unburden herself. What made Dolly feel even worse about it was her belief that Merle really needed her.

Pulling the covers up over her head, and hugging her hot-water bottle, Dolly thought it must be the most frustrating feeling in the world to know you were needed yet be powerless to help. Life seemed difficult indeed . . .

Edie was having a bad night too. She'd just been downstairs to change the water in her hot-water bottle which was now scorching her toes while the rest of her shivered, despite Squeak's warm purring presence at her side. She thought that the streets must be warmer than this refrigerator of a room. The dratted coal shortage meant she couldn't spare the fuel to keep the bedroom fire alight during the night.

But the cold weather wasn't the only thing that was keeping her awake. She had something else on her mind too; something that had given her many disturbed nights recently. She was trying to face up to the fact that when house building really got underway again and there were more properties around to choose from, Mabs and Peter would move into a place of their own. It was only the housing shortage that was keeping Mabs here, for she had received financial compensation for the loss of her home.

The thought of this house without her lodgers filled Edie with dismay. Maybe she and Mabs didn't always see eye to eye ... well, it was probably more accurate to say that they agreed on very little. But in a perverse sort of a way, this was the strength of their relationship because they were never inhibited in what they said to each other for fear of causing offence.

Mabs had been right when she had predicted that Edie would not be able to remain sweet-tempered indefinitely after Ken's death. It wasn't in her nature to be soft; even if she felt affectionate towards someone, she was far too reserved to show it. But she *had* grown fond of Mabs, and had found Peter a real delight since he had returned from the country at the end of the war. It was like watching Ken grow up all over again for he was the image of his father. Without Henry's critical presence dictating her every move, Edie was free to enjoy it.

They would come to visit, of course, but that wouldn't be the same. There would be no more impromptu suppers together or late night cups of cocoa by the dying embers of the fire; no more chats when they met in the hall. She tried to cheer herself with the positive aspects of their departure. She would have her house to herself again. No more arguments over whose turn it was to use the bathroom; no more invasions of privacy. But this only conjured up dreary images of loneliness.

She admonished herself severely. She was far too dependent on other people. She'd never really got to grips with being alone after Henry had died. And on the subject of Henry – he must be turning in his grave at the idea of her actually being fond of the woman he had blamed for taking away his son. A son he had persecuted and driven away, she now realised. It still shamed her to remember how she had allowed him to treat Ken.

So was it just the fear of living alone again that was causing her to dread Mabs's leaving? If so the solution was simple. She could take in another lodger if all she wanted was someone about the place to remove that awful echoing emptiness.

No, it was not just anyone she wanted. It was Mabs and Peter. How to persuade them to stay, though, that was the poser. It was only natural that Mabs would want to move into a place of her own which meant Edie had to work out a scheme, something that would make staying on here a really attractive proposition to her daughter-in-law.

She turned on to her side and snuggled down beneath the covers, cuddling her furry friend to her chest and stroking his head. The dratted water bottle was already cooling down and she couldn't bear the thought of another trip downstairs in these crippling temperatures.

'Will this cold weather never end, eh, Squeak?' she muttered as she settled down to try to work out a plan.

* * *

The Big Freeze ended in floods over much of the country, damaging many acres of wheat and drowning sheep, thus exacerbating the food shortages. Even as dark winter days lightened into spring and summer, there still seemed to be no let-up in the economic gloom.

A controversy raged over Christian Dior's latest fashion sensation, an extravagant 'New Look' which impressed women with its hour-glass shape and generous use of material. It was called frivolous and wasteful by its opponents but, as Dolly said to Mabs, 'It's only natural women will want to wear it. We're all sick and tired of dreary old utility clothes, it's a real treat to put on something feminine again.'

While the arguments were still raging on this issue, the government announced a dire new economy drive. It was revealed that more than half of last year's large loan from America had already been spent and the economic crisis was desperate. Food rations were cut again and queues for unrationed items grew even longer. Newspapers reverted to wartime size and tobacco and petrol imports were reduced.

'Makes you wonder if the age of austerity will ever come to an end, doesn't it?' said Dolly dismally.

'It does an' all,' agreed Mabs.

It took him until the end of the year, but one man who did manage to shed his negative attitude and look to the future was Ernie Webb. He finally came round to his son-in-law's way of thinking and decided that this shocking state of affairs could not possibly go on forever.

One day in January, he summoned Bill to his office.

'This forward planning for the firm that you're always going on about,' he said. 'I think it's time we had a serious chat about it.'

'Fire away then, Ernie,' said Bill, with a broad grin.

Chapter Twenty-One

Bill listened intently to what his father-in-law had to say, observing him across the desk through a pall of pipe smoke.

'I know I've been a bit slow in seeing the light,' confessed Ernie, cradling his steaming comforter in the palm of his hand, 'but you're right – there is going to be some really aggressive marketing about when tea does come off ration. It's no good us resting on our laurels until then.'

'Thank God you've realised it at last.'

'There's something else I've realised too,' said Ernie.

'Oh . . . what's that?'

'I've decided that the company needs a younger man to lead it into the new age.' He drew on his pipe and slowly exhaled a chain of smoke rings. 'So I'm going to stand down as Managing Director and let you take over.' He threw Bill a shrewd look. 'If you want the job, that is?'

'Come off it, Ernie,' said Bill, grinning. 'Do cats like milk? I'm certainly not going to insult your intelligence by pretending not to jump at the chance.'

'Good.'

'You'll become Chairman, will you?'

'Yes, I reckon I could make a good job of that,' confirmed Ernie.

'I'll second that,' agreed Bill heartily.

The two men shook hands on the agreement and Ernie produced some of the precious whisky that he kept for special occasions. Having drunk a toast to their new positions, they continued with the discussion.

'Advertising is going to be a crucial factor,' said Bill. 'Perhaps we could consider the idea of having a commercial go out on Radio Luxembourg.'

'If it's good enough for Ovaltine . . .'

'Exactly,' said Bill.

'Depends on the cost though, really.'

'Yes . . . we must make some enquiries.'

There was a thoughtful silence until Bill said, 'Moving on to something else for a moment, I'd like to tell you about an idea that's been floating around in my mind for some time.'

'Let's hear it then.'

'It's a bit drastic,' warned Bill.

'Out with it, man.'

'I was wondering if we should consider the idea of amalgamating with another company, to give us added strength in the new trading era,' he suggested, eyeing the other man speculatively.

'Phew!' Ernie drew a deep breath, shaking his head. 'You're right, it *is* drastic!'

'I guessed you'd have doubts,' said Bill.

'You're right about that too,' he said. 'It's a very big step.'

'Not if you think of it as an ambitious expansion plan.'

'It's a bit more than that, Bill,' he pointed out solemnly. 'Webb's has always been a family firm.'

'Yes, of course. A merger would bring tremendous advantages though, especially if we teamed up with a smaller company,' Bill continued, rising eagerly to his theme. 'We'd retain the larger share of power, whilst gaining economy of scale with purchasing by buying in much larger quantities, everything from packet printing to raw materials.'

'There'd have to be something substantial in it for the other firm, though,' mentioned Ernie, 'or we'd never get anyone interested.'

'They'd gain the leverage of having a larger firm behind them,' said Bill. 'There would be considerable benefits for both parties.'

'Yes, I can see the logic of what you say, son, but I'm still not sure about making such a dramatic change.'

'You think that the idea is worthy of consideration, though?'

'Most definitely,' agreed Ernie emphatically. 'I shall give it some serious thought.'

'Good.'

'We'll talk about it again when I've had a chance to do that, shall we?'

'Fair enough,' agreed Bill, knowing that he'd gone as far as he could to persuade him. Now it was up to Ernie.

* * *

'I've been meaning to have a chat with you, Mabs,' said Edie rather mysteriously one February evening when the two women were in the kitchen washing the dishes.

'Ooh, Gawd, that sounds serious,' said Mabs lightly. 'Don't say I've left a tidemark on the side of the bath.'

'No, no, nothing like that,' said Edie, polishing a plate with the tea towel and putting it away in the rack above the cooker.

'Spit it out then, Ede, before I break out in a nervous rash,' said Mabs airily.

'I was thinking that you're probably planning to move out soon,' suggested Edie cautiously.

'Yeah, I certainly am. Just as soon as I can find a place I like within my price range, I'll be out of your hair,' she said defensively, having misunderstood Edie's reason for broaching the subject. 'I bet you can't wait to have your house back to yourself again, can you?'

'No, I'm not looking forward to it at all,' explained Edie in a serious tone. 'In fact, I don't want you to move out.'

Mabs finished scraping a saucepan with some wire wool and put it on the draining board, looking at Edie thoughtfully. 'Blimey . . . that's a turn-up for the books.'

'I thought you'd be surprised.'

'I'm knocked out . . . but I can't stay on here indefinitely, can I?'

'Why not?'

'Well, because . . .' Mabs struggled to find the right words. ''Cos it's the natural thing for me to have a place of my own, innit?'

'You definitely want to move out then?' said Edie miserably.

'Naturally I wanna be in my own place, Ede, same as anyone else,' she explained. 'It isn't that I haven't been happy here, 'cos I have, even though it was the last thing I expected. But I don't want to be a lodger forever. I want my own kitchen, my own space . . . to be in charge of my own ship, as they say.'

'You could have all that without moving away,' suggested Edie tentatively.

'Have a kitchen put in upstairs, you mean?'

'Much more than that.'

'Oh?' Mabs emptied the washing-up bowl and started drying the cutlery. 'What exactly do you have in mind then?'

'Well . . . if you were to decide to stay on here, I'd have the house converted into two separate, self-contained flats,' Edie explained eagerly. 'Proper flats, each with its own facilities: kitchen, bathroom, everything. This is a very big house. The flats would be nice and roomy, more than enough space for you and Peter.' She paused and gave Mabs a hard look. 'Remember, Peter is growing up fast, he'll be off on his own in a few years. You may not want the bother of running a house on your own then. I know I found it too much after Henry died, until you came.'

Mabs dropped some knives into the cutlery drawer thoughtfully. This was the last thing she had expected. 'But I'd still be living in someone else's house, wouldn't I?' she said. 'It wouldn't be my own place.'

'Yes, it would. I'd have the house re-registered as two

separate dwellings,' explained Edie earnestly. 'The only thing we'd share is the front door and hall. The whole of the upstairs would be yours. It would be your own property.'

'It's a lovely idea, Ede,' said Mabs, chewing her lip anxiously. 'But one of the attractions of actually buying a place is so that I won't have to pay rent for the rest of my life.'

'You wouldn't be paying rent . . .'

'Oh, no, I don't want none o' that rent-free nonsense,' said Mabs quickly. 'I couldn't bear to feel beholden.'

'No, no, no, you don't understand,' exclaimed Edie forcefully. 'You wouldn't pay rent because it would be your own flat. It would belong to you.'

'Oh, I get it, you want me to buy your flat instead of a house?'

'No, the flat would be a belated wedding present from me,' explained Edie.

Mabs's face hardened. 'Now you know how I feel about having something for nothing.'

'Don't I just!'

'I like to pay my way,' Mabs interrupted assertively. 'Handouts aren't my thing.'

'Let me finish, woman, will you?' interjected Edie loudly.

'But I . . .'

'Stop your jabbering and let me get a word in.'

Mabs sat down at the kitchen table with a sigh. 'Go on then, get on with it, for Gawd's sake.'

Edie sat down and addressed her daughter-in-law from across the table. 'When you and Ken got married you didn't get a wedding present from Henry and me, did you?'

'Not so much as a bloomin' teaspoon,' declared Mabs, scowling at the memory. 'Mean, I call that . . . really rotten.'

'Yes, yes, but let me finish what I'm trying to say,' implored Edie, her face pink and shiny against her white hair.

'Go on, then.'

'When Dolly married Frank, we bought them a house as a wedding present.'

'So what?'

'If you accept the flat as a gift from me now, you're getting no more than was due to Ken,' she explained. 'If this house stays as it is, it will go to you and Dolly jointly after I'm gone anyway, so she won't lose out in the change over. She'll still get half when I die.'

'But I can afford to buy a place out of my compensation.'

'Invest it,' suggested Edie, 'and have the security of knowing you've something behind you. Have summer holidays . . . day trips . . . decent clothes.'

'But what about you?' Mabs asked. 'The alterations to this place won't 'alf set you back.'

'Henry left me very well provided for, don't worry,' she was assured. 'He had many faults but he was an excellent provider.'

Mabs swallowed the lump in her throat. Who would have thought the old trout would turn up trumps like this? It put Mabs in something of a quandary though, for although she never sifted her words for Edie, she wouldn't want to hurt her feelings about such a generous gesture. Mabs wasn't naive enough to imagine that the offer was entirely altruistic. Edie didn't fancy the idea of being alone in this house again after having someone around for so long. In retrospect, Mabs thought it hadn't been so bad. In fact, she'd quite enjoyed their sparky relationship.

But she'd always looked on the arrangement as temporary. Could she tolerate living here permanently? It really would be different if she had her own flat, though. She would be equal to Edie. They wouldn't see so much of each other, but at least Edie would have the security of knowing she was there if she was needed. It would give Mabs the chance to keep an eye on the old bag too, make sure she didn't get too grouchy and eccentric in her old age. After all, it was an accepted fact that Edie took far more notice of her than she did of Dolly.

Looking ahead to the future, she thought she probably would find a flat more convenient when Peter left home. If she accepted Edie's offer, at least she would be accustomed to her neighbour. Better the devil she knew . . . When it came down to it, she and Edie were in the same boat. They were both lonely widows with two things in common: they had both loved Ken, and were devoted to Peter. If Mabs was really honest with herself, she would miss having Edie around if she moved out. Anyway, the benefits to Edie notwithstanding, it was still an act of generosity on her part.

'So what do you say then?' asked Edie, fiddling with the tea-towel anxiously.

'Looks like you've got yourself a deal,' said Mabs.

'Oh, wonderful!'

Mabs stared at her finger nails. She wasn't often lost for

words, but she was on this occasion. 'Thanks, Ede, for such a smashing wedding present,' she mumbled at last.

Edie didn't know how to reply. Pretty words didn't come easily to her, especially when she was saying them to her sparring partner. 'You're welcome.' She twisted the end of the tea-towel. 'I don't know how long it will take me to find a decent builder to do the work,' she said briskly to hide her embarrassment. 'They're like gold-dust these days.'

'They certainly are,' agreed Mabs. 'And, of course, you'll have to get planning permission too.'

'Well, obviously,' snapped Edie, back on form. 'What sort of a fool do you take me for?'

'All right, don't get on that bloomin' high horse o' yours,' retorted Mabs.

Outside the kitchen door, Peter, who was about to enter, stood listening. They're at it hammer and tongs again, he thought, so everything is normal.

'I'm just off to the youth club,' he said, poking his head round the door. 'See you later.'

'Don't be too late now,' warned his mother.

'You do as your mother says,' chimed in Edie. 'There's some very funny people about after dark.'

'I *am* out of nappies, you know,' he laughed and was gone before they had a chance to reply.

Hearing the front door close behind him, the two women exchanged a smile. If there was one thing on which they were agreed, it was Peter's welfare.

Puffing on his pipe, Ernie surveyed his son-in-law across his desk. 'I've thought a lot about this merger idea of yours and I've come to the conclusion that it's the most sensible thing we can do.'

'Great!'

'So now we must start making serious plans.'

'The first thing to do is to study the market to find a suitable firm to approach,' suggested Bill.

'I'm ahead of you on that one,' said Ernie. 'I've been doing my homework – talking to colleagues in the association and having a look at some of the smaller companies.'

'And?'

'There's a London-based company I think it would be well worth our while considering,' he explained, putting his smouldering pipe in the ash tray.

'Tell me more.'

'They're not nearly such a big firm as us, but highly successful,' Ernie informed him. 'They only operate in London and surrounding areas, so they would benefit from the wider distribution they would get as a part of our firm, and we'd gain all their local trade.'

'Sounds promising to me,' said Bill excitedly. 'What sort of a company is it?'

'A family firm . . . the son worked for a friend of mine, Ted Porter, for a while but he left there to help his sister run the family business after the father died and she inherited it,' he explained. 'Ted was telling me that the son was killed in the war and the firm is run entirely by his sister now.'

'Run by a woman, eh?' said Bill. 'That's unusual in the tea trade.'

'Yes, it is . . . but she's making a very good job of it according to all the tea merchants I've spoken to about her. Kept the firm going right through the war apparently.' Ernie's eyes narrowed in thought. 'Ted Porter reckons he introduced us to her once before the war at an association dinner. She was there with her brother.'

Bill was beginning to feel uneasy.

'I can't say I remember that far back myself,' continued Ernie, too busy looking at his notes to notice Bill's sudden pallor.

'No, nor me,' lied Bill.

'Dolly Mitchell is her name, Slater that was, which is the name of the firm.'

'Oh, Christ!' Bill blurted out, forgetting himself in the shock of having his suspicions confirmed.

Ernie looked up quickly. 'What's the matter?' he asked with a deep frown.

'Nothing,' said Bill, icy droplets of perspiration beading his brow.

'Do you know something about the firm . . . something that would be detrimental to a merger?'

'No.'

'Why the strong reaction then?' asked Ernie.

Bill held his head and winced falsely to evince pain. 'A sudden headache shot right through me,' he lied.

'Oh, I see . . . you all right now?'

'Yeah, fine.'

'Good. So you know nothing about Slater's then.'

'I know of them, of course,' he explained casually. 'I've seen their vans around the London area. As a matter of fact

I worked there for a while before I came to Webb's.'

'Really, why didn't you say?' asked Ernie, chewing the end of his pipe.

'It was years ago and I was only a lad . . . a labourer at that,' he said. 'Dolly Mitchell wouldn't remember me.'

''Course she wouldn't, not after all this time,' said Ernie, impatient to get on with the matter in hand. 'It's irrelevant anyway . . . the important thing is whether or not her company is right for us.'

'I don't think so,' said Bill in desperation. Talk about irony! Who would have thought his idea for a merger would backfire on him so disastrously? The whole thing was unthinkable. He could *not* work with *that* woman!

'Oh . . . and why not?' asked Ernie in surprise.

'I just don't think the firm is suitable for what we have in mind, that's all.'

'You must have a reason,' persisted Ernie, puzzled. 'So let's have it out in the open, man, let's thrash it out.'

'Well, because . . .' Bill heard his voice die away in the absence of a valid argument. From a business angle Slater's was the perfect merger possibility. But he could hardly tell his father-in-law why such a thing would be a personal catastrophe for him.

'Come on, let's have your objections on the table, son,' urged Ernie. 'An important issue like this needs thorough debate.'

'Slater's are too small,' said Bill lamely, failing to come up with a more viable alternative.

'But it was you who suggested a small firm.'

'Yeah, but there's small and there's positively

insignificant,' said Bill, desperately clutching at straws.

'They've been very successful from what I can gather,' said Ernie.

'I had in mind a firm with a higher public profile,' explained Bill. 'So that their name would add a bit of class to our own.'

'They're a respected, old-established London firm,' said Ernie.

'Exactly,' said Bill, finding a hook on which to hang his flimsy argument. 'They're not known outside of this neck of the woods, which means they'd do nothing for us further afield.'

Ernie sucked meditatively on his pipe. 'I entirely disagree with you!' he announced in an uncompromising manner. 'Slater's is exactly the sort of company we are looking for, being of moderate size and local but with a very good track record. As we have already agreed, we don't want our name overshadowed by a nationally known firm. It's important that we are the larger, stronger company so that we can hold the balance of power . . . otherwise it'll end up with them running the whole shooting match.'

'There are other smallish firms,' Bill reminded him, desperate to kick out this ghastly proposition.

'I know, I've spent a lot of time researching the subject, and in my opinion Slater's must be our first choice,' declared Ernie.

'But . . .'

'Who better do you have in mind?'

'Er . . . well, no one in particular at the moment,' admitted Bill, finding himself infuriatingly out of his depth.

'Well, there you are then,' said Ernie firmly. 'You come up with a better proposition and we'll talk about it. In the meantime, at least give my suggestion the consideration it deserves.'

'Will do,' he muttered numbly.

'Of course, there's always the fact that Mrs Mitchell might not be interested,' put in Ernie. 'Or someone else might have the same idea and beat us to it.'

Bill managed to marshal his thoughts sufficiently to realise, with annoying certainty, that his reaction to this development had been wholly unprofessional. Only an amateur would allow personal feelings to colour his commercial judgement. If joining forces with Slater's was the best thing for Webb's, then he must give the motion his wholehearted support. After all, Dolly Mitchell was of no importance to him now.

'In that case, Ernie, I think you ought to contact her and see what she has to say about it,' he heard himself say.

Chapter Twenty-Two

When Dolly received a telephone call from Ernie Webb asking for an appointment to see her, she couldn't pretend not to experience a moment of trepidation when she recalled that the man was Bill Drake's father-in-law. But having been told that he wanted to discuss a business proposal of benefit to them both, she stifled her own personal feelings and agreed to see him.

Having listened to what he had to suggest, however, on behalf of himself and his Managing Director, Mr Bill Drake, who was not present but obviously very much involved in the scheme, her response was completely dominated by impulse.

'Oh, no, Mr Webb, a merger between my company and yours is quite out of the question,' she stated categorically, observing him coolly across her desk.

'Any particular reason why that should be so?' he asked, giving her a myopic look over the top of his spectacles.

'Well . . . er . . . because . . .' She struggled for a convincing excuse. 'Um . . . because we are a family firm and I wish to keep it that way.'

His silver brows rose. 'So is Webb's a family firm, and

in a perfect world I would like it to stay that way. But I've realised that this is a shortsighted view, bearing in mind the fact that we shall soon be entering into a new style of trading when rationing ends.'

'Slater's was started by my father and I want to keep it in the family,' she told him firmly, her hands clasped tightly together on the desk. 'My son will come into the firm as a director when he is twenty-one in a couple of months' time, and my nephew will also be given the opportunity when he comes of age. The company will live on into the future through them and their children, long after I've gone.'

As she spoke the words she realised that they were actually true, even though her prime objection to Webb's proposal was its connection with Bill Drake, with whom she could never work.

'Yes, I can understand just how you feel my dear,' said Ernie, his eyes resting on her warmly, his balding head gleaming in the spring sunlight that was streaming in through the window. 'But there's no reason why those things could not still happen if our firms were to merge.'

She narrowed her eyes. 'You're the bigger company, we'd lose our identity.'

'Not at all,' he assured her. 'I won't lie to you, obviously as the larger company we would have the greater share of power . . . but that doesn't mean you would not have a good holding in the new company and a fair say in all company policy.'

Dolly shook her head. 'I still think Slater's would disappear.'

'Slater's as you know it today will disappear certainly,'

he told her candidly. 'But when free enterprise opens up again, it may well disappear altogether, pushed out of business by the sheer force of the competition.'

'Surely not?' she said, but couldn't deny that he had touched upon something that had been worrying her for some time. It was going to be a tough new world out there when tea control ended!

'I should think it's a definite possibility,' he told her with sincerity. 'But if you were to join us, you could be more or less assured of staying in business in a new and bigger way. Apart from the advantages of economy of scale, we can make you into a nationally known company instead of just a London firm.'

'You speak as though Slater's is to be the only beneficiary of this scheme.'

'I certainly didn't intend to,' Ernie assured her, impressed by her shrewdness. 'Webb's would have much to gain too. We would acquire a successful and highly regarded company; our strength in the market place would be greatly increased.'

'What about my workers in all this?' she heard herself ask. 'I wouldn't do anything to put their jobs at risk.'

'We would have to make sure that that didn't happen then, wouldn't we?' he said. 'But . . . look . . . before this idea goes any further, I suggest that we all get together for a thorough discussion. You and your colleagues and my Managing Director and myself.' He smiled. 'You'll like Bill Drake, he's a good man with a superb business head on his shoulders. I know that I'm biased because he's married to my daughter but if it wasn't for him, Webb's certainly

377

wouldn't be where it is today. He really put us on the map.'
He paused, remembering. 'As a matter of fact, he used to
work for your father many moons ago. He was just a lad
then so you wouldn't remember him.'

'I'm sure I wouldn't,' she said briskly, deliberately
indicating a lack of interest. 'Many people come and go
over the years.'

'Anyway, that's neither here nor there,' said Ernie.
'What I want to know is, will you agree to us all having a
meeting?'

'I'm not sure if it's worth wasting your time since I've
no real plans for a merger.'

'Believe me, Mrs Mitchell,' said Ernie persuasively,
'this idea is only at the embryo stage. You will not be
committing yourself to anything at all by attending a meeting.
On the contrary, it will give you the chance to kill the idea
stone dead if that is what you really want after hearing our
proposals.'

Recovering slightly from the initial shock of having Bill
Drake re-enter her life so suddenly, Dolly realised that it
would be unwise and unbusinesslike of her to dismiss this
proposal out of hand just because of an old personal
connection with one of the other participants. If it was the
best thing for Slater's then she was duty bound to at least
find out the full extent of what Webb's was offering.
Anyway, why let a man like Bill Drake stand in the way of
her company's future prosperity?

'All right, Mr Webb,' she agreed crisply. 'I'll agree to a
meeting.' She opened her desk diary. 'Let's arrange a
mutually convenient time, shall we?' She threw him a sage

look. 'As for venue, I think it makes sense for us to meet in your office, to give me a chance to see your set-up, since you've had a good look at mine.'

The instant Dolly walked into Ernie Webb's office at Webb's factory in Battersea, and saw Bill Drake sitting alongside him at his desk, she knew nothing had changed. All the old feelings were still there, which meant she couldn't be indifferent towards him as she had planned.

On this occasion there was even less sign of the boy with whom she had once been besotted than there had been twelve years ago at the Association dinner. He'd altered quite dramatically since then. The glossy dark hair was now dusted with grey; the face was fuller and more lined. Those amazing brown eyes that had once radiated warmth and desire for her now met hers with a mixture of challenge and hostility. She knew instinctively that the idea of Webb's merging with Slater's was equally as repellent to him as it was to her.

It had to be admitted, though, that despite the ravages of time manifest in his appearance, he was still very attractive, his good looks refined and magnified by an aura of success. He was well groomed and self-confident. Beautifully dressed too despite the limitations of clothes rationing; he looked superb in a light grey business suit and crisp white shirt. Even now she found it hard to connect this dazzling sophisticate with the uncertain young labourer she had carried in her memory for all these years.

Determined not to allow personal feelings to impair her professionalism, she carried out the introductions in a polite but clinically business-like manner.

'I believe you used to work for us many years ago, Mr Drake?' she said, with a superficial smile.

'Yes, that's right,' he said, smiling with equal falseness.

'This is my son Barney who is due to become a director very soon, and whom I thought should be here . . . Mabs Slater, my brother's widow, also a director of the company.'

They took their places around the desk and the meeting got underway with Ernie setting out some fundamental proposals for the merger and inviting questions and suggestions.

'We wouldn't be prepared to close our factory,' said Dolly in a rather belligerent manner.

'Neither would we want you to,' agreed Ernie. 'That isn't what this merger is about. We would keep both factories going, though of course it would make sense to rationalise in some areas to make the new company more efficient.'

'Such as?'

'Well, for instance, we might decide to have the two tea tasting departments merged into one, since the various blends would come out under our joint label. Buying would be a joint operation too, to make use of the lower rates we would then be able to obtain. There should be no need for job losses for either firm since business will increase when the economy picks up.'

'We would have to form a completely new company, I assume,' said Barney.

'Oh, yes,' replied Ernie.

'Called Webb Slater no doubt, rather than Slater Webb?' said Dolly cynically.

'Yeah, I'll bet,' said Mabs, who had only come to the meeting to support Dolly. She didn't enjoy this sort of thing at all and simply couldn't wait to hand over the job to Peter.

'Obviously that's the way it will be,' said Bill with brutal frankness, meeting Dolly's cool gaze with an icy glare. 'We are the more well-known company so it makes good business sense to trade on that. It is us who are going to make you a household name, *not* the other way around.'

'Oh, I understand,' snapped Dolly, directing her comments at Bill. 'It's easy to see which way this thing will go. Oh, yes, since *you're* the bigger firm, *you* would call all the shots. And as that isn't acceptable to us, there's really no point in our continuing this meeting.'

'Our firm is worth more than twice yours so naturally we would have the larger amount of shares,' said Bill sharply. 'It stands to reason because we'd be putting more into the new company.'

'But that doesn't mean you won't have a say on all company policy,' intervened Ernie quickly, disappointed that these two hadn't hit it off, and angry with Bill for behaving so aggressively.

'I'm not so sure about that,' said Dolly crossly. 'It seems to me as though we'd be outvoted on every single issue.'

'Do bear in mind, Mrs Mitchell,' Ernie said in a conciliatory manner, 'that we shall be one company, working together for the common good of the firm, not competing against each other as we are now. We shall all be voting as independent people in our capacity within the firm.'

381

'Which brings us to the question of our actual positions and responsibilities within this proposed new set-up, doesn't it?' said Dolly.

'Ah, yes,' said Ernie doubtfully because Dolly Mitchell was proving to be no soft touch. 'Obviously this will be worked out on the amount of shares each person holds, and that will be commensurate with those we hold in our present companies.'

'Which means . . .'

'Basically, Bill and I would retain our current positions, myself as Chairman and Bill as Managing Director,' Ernie explained. 'You would be Deputy Managing Director. The positions of your colleagues can be worked out later on.'

'I see.' Dolly had grave doubts, for she didn't relish the idea of being below Bill Drake in status. 'Obviously such a demotion would be a difficult adjustment for me. I've been running my own show for a very long time.'

'Hardly a demotion since you'd be in a position of considerable importance in a larger, more powerful company,' said Bill crushingly. 'Obviously you would receive an income to match the position.'

'Sounds fair enough to me, Mum,' said Barney, who saw the whole thing as an exciting new challenge.

'I'm still not sure,' she said.

'If Slater's as a whole is going to benefit from this, Doll, it might be the best thing we can do,' suggested Mabs warily.

'We can't be sure that it will,' persisted Dolly, but the merits of a merger were gaining in credibility even to her jaundiced eye.

'Nothing except death can be absolutely guaranteed,' Ernie pointed out.

'No, but there is such a thing as reasonable expectation,' countered Dolly firmly.

'Well, it's something you'll have to make your own mind up about,' said Ernie fairly. 'But I must say I hope you do decide to join us. Together I think we have what it takes to really make our mark in the new era of free enterprise.'

So did Dolly, but she wasn't going to be too quick to say so or she'd have that arrogant bugger, Bill Drake, trampling all over her. She'd give them their answer in her own good time.

'Obviously, we need time to think about it,' she said, gathering together the notes she had been making, and rising. 'I'll be in touch sometime in the near future.'

'We'll look forward to hearing from you then,' said Ernie, rising politely and walking her to the door. 'I'll come down to the main entrance with you and see you off the premises.'

Downstairs in the foyer, with Ernie continuing to extol the virtues of a Webb-Slater union, Dolly decided that one thing needed to be clarified before matters went any further. 'I've left my diary upstairs in your office,' she lied. 'I'll just slip back and get it.'

'I'll have someone bring it down for you,' he offered courteously.

'There's no need, it won't take me a minute.'

Leaving him talking to Mabs and Barney, she hurried

upstairs to the offices, heading straight for the one she'd noticed earlier with Managing Director printed on the door. The door was open and Bill had his back to it, staring out of the window. He turned at her tap on the door.

'May I have a few words?' she asked crisply.

'Of course, come in.'

Her hand felt slippery on the handle as she closed the door behind her. She was breathless from hurrying and nervousness which seemed to weaken her position.

'Do sit down,' he invited.

'No, I won't, thanks,' she said with icy politeness. 'I've told the others I'll only be a minute.'

'So what's on your mind?' he asked, sitting at his desk and swivelling the chair slightly from side to side.

'I think you and I should get something sorted out before this merger thing goes any further.'

'Do you really?' he said with a quizzical look.

'Yes, I do,' she told him through parched lips. 'It's obvious from your attitude that, from a personal point of view, you don't want the two firms to join together any more than I do.'

'I can think of people I'd rather work with than you,' he said coldly.

'And I'd sooner drink drain water than have dealings with you!'

'At least we're agreed on one thing then.'

'But a merger is the best thing for both our companies, yes?'

'Undoubtedly.'

'And as mature business people neither of us has any

choice but to go along with it if we care about what happens to our firms,' she confirmed.

'That's about the size of it, yeah,' he said blandly.

'So, I suggest that for the sake of the other people involved and the good of our businesses, we try to behave like civilised, professional people who don't hate each other's guts.'

'That's your view on the subject, is it?' he said, sounding none too co-operative.

'Well, yes . . . I mean, if we're going to be sniping at each other all the time like we did just now,' she persisted, 'not only will it be embarrassing for everyone around us, but they are going to wonder why we dislike each other so much, since we are supposed to be strangers.' She gave him a cool look which belied her inner turmoil. 'I'm sure neither of us wants the past dragged up.'

'With Ernie being my wife's father, of course not.'

'At least we won't be working in the same building every day,' she pointed out.

'No, but there'll be regular directors' meetings and so on.'

'Exactly, so it's in everyone's interests for us to agree not to let our dislike of each other affect the way we behave at work.'

'I'll go along with that,' he said. 'But don't expect me not to oppose you whenever I think it's necessary.'

'Is there any reason why I should expect that?' she asked.

'You probably think you're entitled to special treatment because you're a woman.' He didn't really believe this, but his need to hit out at her had driven him to calumny.

She emitted a harsh laugh. 'Don't be so bloody patronising,' she said. 'I've been running Slater's for a very long time. I think I know a thing or two about how business works.'

'You're moving into a bigger league now though,' he informed her smoothly. 'You won't be the top dog any more, you'll have other people's ideas and opinions to consider.'

'Are you threatening me?'

'Not at all,' he said with an air of indifference, 'just warning you that you won't have things all your own way.'

'It doesn't sound to me as though you're prepared to enter into any sort of a truce for the sake of appearances.'

'I'll try not to let my dislike of you be too noticeable to the others,' he said, his eyes holding hers with a steely expression. 'More than that I cannot promise.'

'Oh, well, it's better than nothing, I suppose,' she said, backing towards the door. 'And I'll do the same.'

'Let's leave it at that then, shall we?'

'Fair enough.'

She left the room smarting from his hostility. She was still inwardly trembling from the effect of seeing him again when she met the others in the foyer.

Bill Drake lit a cigarette with a shaky hand and swung his chair around towards the window, watching Dolly hurry across the forecourt towards her gleaming Morris. The years had been kind to her, he'd say that much for her. She was a good-looking woman who knew how to present herself. He admired the way she was dressed in a sage green tailored suit and matching hat, her court shoes adding a swing to her walk. She was no shrinking violet. She'd become a hardened entrepreneur, just like her father.

Goddammit, the bitch still had the power to make him feel inferior, and it annoyed him intensely. In fact, he was seething with all the old rage, all the old resentment. It was ridiculous, he admitted it. What had happened between them was all in the past. They were both different people now. But sane, sensible reasoning made no difference – he still hated her with a passion and was hungry for revenge.

Watching her car roll out of sight, he became utterly despondent. Nothing had changed! He might be the Managing Director of a company whose success was down to him personally, but deep inside she was still the rich man's daughter and he the common labourer, powerless against the likes of her and her kind.

He dragged hard on his cigarette, mulling the situation over and coming to a conclusion. Things *had* changed. *He* was the one with the power now. If this merger came to be, as he believed it would, he would be above her in status, and by the very fact of Webb's being the more valuable company, he would own more of the new company than her.

As the significance of this registered properly, he began to see the merger in a new light. Here was his opportunity to get even with her at last. He'd promised her nothing more than not to make his feelings too obvious to other people. That didn't mean he couldn't oppose her every step of the way; make her life such hell she'd be glad to resign.

Her relatives wouldn't want to stay on without her. Given time, he'd have every last damned Slater out of the company and Webb's would have full control of an empire far larger than the one they had today.

So, Dolly Smart-Arse Mitchell, let's see what sort of a businesswoman you are when you come up against *real* boardroom opposition. You've had it all your own way at Slater's for long enough. Let's give you a few sleepless nights before we get rid of you altogether. Your days as a high flyer are numbered, lady.

He stubbed out his cigarette in the ashtray because it was making him feel sick. The exuberance of seconds earlier drained away, leaving him feeling achingly sad. No other person alive could affect him like *that* woman, he admitted morosely.

Picking up the telephone, he dialled his home number. 'Hello, Jean.'

'Hello, love.'

'Just thought I'd give you a ring to brighten up my day.'

'Ah, how sweet,' she said. 'Nice to know I can still do that.'

'I feel better already,' he said. But he wasn't telling the truth. Even his dear Jean couldn't erase the blues left by Dolly Mitchell.

By the time all the technical details of the merger were finally agreed, and the legalities complete, it was almost a year before Webb-Slater was ready to be launched. They began trading in the spring of the following year, just after clothes rationing ended which they all thought boded well for the end of tea rationing in the not too distant future.

Dolly's job was virtually unchanged on a daily basis. She was still responsible for the overall running of the Hammersmith factory with Bert Dixon remaining as factory manager. Having a keen interest in the sales side of the business, Barney moved to the Battersea factory to join the Sales and Marketing team which was to be based there. Mabs remained in charge of the packing department, and Peter was using the time until he went away to do his two years' national service by working a spell in each department.

The Slater tea tasters were transferred to the Battersea factory where they worked with the Webb's team in an enlarged department using the space left by the accounts office which had been transferred to Hammersmith. Combining operations in this way, no job losses were necessary or additional office space. Other departments were similarly merged, but the actual tea-blending operations continued at both factories.

One new addition to Dolly's working life, however, was the monthly directors' meeting which was to take place in the boardroom at the Battersea premises of Webb-Slater. At the very first one of these she received a very clear message: whilst keeping within the terms of their so-called truce, Bill Drake was going to make damned sure she didn't have an easy life.

Chapter Twenty-Three

Shafts of spring sunlight filtered through the boardroom windows, highlighting the smoke that curled from Ernie's pipe as he listened with disapproval to the clashing personalities of his colleagues.

'So what is your *actual* objection to my idea?' Dolly was demanding of Bill, meeting his cynical stare across the table.

'Quite frankly, I think it stinks.'

'What a wonderfully open mind you have,' she said with withering sarcasm. 'You've written it off without so much as a second thought.'

'I wouldn't waste my time on such a feeble . . .'

'Isn't the purpose of this meeting supposed to be to gather suggestions for the promotion of our product after the end of tea control?' she cut in furiously. 'I thought we were all invited to put forward our ideas for discussion?'

'What's this if it isn't discussion then?' he riposted. 'I'm every bit as entitled to oppose your idea as you are to make it.'

'You've not even given it due consideration,' she returned. 'Your attitude is most undemocratic.'

He gave an impatient sigh. 'Oh, really, I mean . . . a series of collector picture cards in our tea packets. Honestly!'

'So what's wrong with that?' she commanded.

'What's right with it is more to the point,' he exclaimed, cheeks flushed, eyes bright with rage. 'For one thing it will cost a fortune to set up, bearing in mind the high cost of printing. For another it's not a new idea. It was done by the cigarette companies before the war as a marketing gimmick.'

'They haven't reintroduced the cards though, have they?' she pointed out.

'That isn't to say that they won't when things start moving again.'

'So what if they do, and there are tea cards as well as cigarette cards on offer?' she said. 'We're not in competition with cigarette manufacturers so it doesn't matter. It could even help to promote the collecting habit.'

'Rubbish!'

'Typical of you to come out with a negative comment like that,' she rasped.

'I'm only being realistic . . .'

'Realistic, my Aunt Fanny!' she exploded. 'You don't like it because *I* thought of it and not *you*.'

'Balls!'

'Trust you to drag the meeting down to gutter level,' she said. 'Anyway, you can't deny that picture cards will give our product the edge over other brands . . . people enjoy building a collection.'

'And what about all the time that will have to be spent inserting the cards into the packets?' he went on. 'It will increase production time and cost us real money.'

'We could probably have our packing machines adapted to insert them automatically,' she suggested.

'Huh! At what cost?' was his instant response.

'We won't know that until we make some enquiries, will we?' she roared.

'No! The whole thing is completely out of the question,' he stated categorically. 'It will be hellishly expensive and won't increase sales sufficiently to justify the cost.'

'I think it will!' she persisted.

'If you two could stop to draw breath for a minute, perhaps the rest of us might be allowed to have a say?' interrupted Ernie crossly.

'Hear, hear,' chorused Barney and Mabs.

'Yes, of course, I'm sorry,' muttered Dolly. 'I got a bit carried away.'

'Me too,' said Bill sheepishly. 'So what does everyone else think about this ridiculous scheme of Dolly's?'

Ernie knocked his pipe out in the ash tray. 'Well, I certainly think it's worth considering.'

'Oh, for God's sake . . .' began Bill dismissively.

'*Please* let me finish, Bill,' warned Ernie, who had never known his son-in-law to be so dogmatic about an issue. He was usually such a reasonable man; always ready to listen to new ideas, no matter how outlandish. 'You've made your opinions very plain. Now perhaps you'll be good enough to let other people do the same?'

'Sorry,' Bill said, lowering his eyes guiltily for he wasn't proud of his behaviour. *That* woman made him so angry with her fancy ideas, he'd lost control. What they needed were practical suggestions to take them into the new decade, not some absurd whim which would cost the company a fortune with no guarantee of return.

'Personally, I think the idea has definite possibilities and we should look into it further . . . perhaps do some costings,' suggested Ernie, glancing towards Mabs and Barney.

'I'll go along with that,' said Barney, beaming with enthusiasm.

'Oh, well, you would, wouldn't you?' mumbled Bill gruffly.

'What exactly do you mean by that?' asked Barney, giving Bill a sharp look.

'Of course you'll agree with her, she's your mother.'

'That has nothing to do with it,' said Barney, appalled at the suggestion. 'I happen to think it's a good idea whoever suggested it.'

'So do I,' agreed Mabs.

'That figures,' said Bill, with blatant insinuation.

'Bill,' admonished Ernie, frowning darkly at his son-in-law. 'This is supposed to be a constructive business meeting not a slanging match. So let's keep personalities out of it.'

'Sorry,' he muttered again.

'Right, so can we get on now . . .'

Bill was outvoted, and plans to pursue the picture card scheme were agreed. The meeting ended with Bill in disgruntled mood and Dolly feeling too emotionally drained to be triumphant.

'I was wondering if I might have a chat with you, Bill,' said Barney, taking him to one side as the meeting dispersed.

'Oh . . . what about?'

'I'd rather not discuss it here,' explained Barney. 'Perhaps we could have a drink together after work tonight?'

'Not tonight,' said Bill. 'I have to be home early . . . I've promised to take my wife to the pictures.'

'Just a quick one,' said Barney persuasively.

Intrigued, Bill said, 'All right, but it really will have to be a quick one.'

'Six o'clock in the Red Lion then.'

'I'll be there.'

The Red Lion was crowded with men on their way home from work. It was a cheerful but shabby bar-room with stained wooden tables, dark oak panelling on the walls, and lozenge-shaped mirrors, etched with flowers and leaves, advertising various ales. The atmosphere reverberated with male voices, and was dense with smoke.

Bill was pushing his way to the counter when Barney joined him.

'What are you having?' asked Bill amiably.

Barney raised his hands in protest. 'No, no, I invited you, so it's my shout.'

'I'll have a whisky then, please,' said Bill with a half smile, realising that the young chap was keen to establish his manliness.

'So what's all this about then?' he asked when they were settled at a corner table away from the bustle at the bar.

'Well . . . I didn't want to come on too strong with you at the meeting,' said Barney in a firm tone. 'You and Mum were doing more than enough of that.' He sipped the head off his beer. 'But I really must put you straight about something to avoid any more snide remarks.'

'Get on with it then,' said Bill, observing him coolly over the rim of his whisky glass.

'I agreed with Mum's idea for a picture card promotion because I really do think it's good and not because she's my mother.'

'So you said at the time.'

'But you didn't believe me.'

'There's nothing wrong with taking your mother's side,' said Bill. 'It's very commendable.'

Barney put his glass down on the table with an emphatic bump. 'Look here,' he said impatiently, 'I don't know what you've got against our family, but whatever it is you're right out of order to oppose my mother on every issue just because you don't like her.'

'I neither like nor dislike her.'

'It's just women in general in business you don't like then, is it?'

Bill gave an indifferent shrug. 'I don't have any feelings on the matter.'

'That isn't the impression you give,' Barney informed him briskly.

'Really?' said Bill haughtily.

'Yes, *really*, Mr Big Mouth Drake,' retorted Barney. 'But anyway, that isn't the point I'm here to make.'

'Get to the point then,' said Bill irritably. 'I haven't got all night.'

'Right, it's this,' he said, leaning forward with his elbows on the table and staring into Bill's face. 'My mother has brought me up to be my own person. To weigh up the pros and cons of a situation and form my *own* opinions regardless of what she thinks, and to stand up for what I believe in.' He paused to clear his throat. 'I took her side today because what she said makes sense. If I had thought she was talking rubbish, I'd have come right out and said so.'

His sincerity impressed Bill despite himself. But he was damned if he was going to let a junior member of the firm dictate terms to him. 'You've got quite a lot to say for yourself, haven't you, considering you've only been in the tea business for five minutes?'

'A bit longer than that, thank you very much.'

'Relatively speaking, I mean,' said Bill. 'How old are you?'

'Twenty-one, going on twenty-two.'

'Hardly an age to start throwing your weight about with your seniors,' said Bill, sipping his whisky.

'Age is irrelevant to this issue,' pronounced Barney with aplomb. 'My mother has been involved in the tea business all her life. If she thinks I'm sensible enough to be trusted with responsibility in the firm, the least you can do is to respect her judgement in that at least.'

'You're not backward in coming forward, I'll say that much for you.'

'It doesn't pay to be in business, as I'm sure you'll agree.'

'Such wisdom, I suppose your mother taught you that too?' he said with a supercilious smile.

'Of course it was her,' said Barney impatiently. 'Who

else? You should try to get to know Mum better. She really does know what she's talking about.'

'If you say so,' Bill said, his insouciant manner concealing an unexpected stab of envy for Dolly in being the recipient of such filial devotion. It occurred to him that if things had worked out differently, Barney might have been his own son.

'Anyway,' Barney continued, studying Bill's face, 'you're not exactly in your dotage, are you? You must have started to make your presence felt by the time you were about my age.'

'So what if I did? That has nothing to do with this.'

'You're right, it hasn't,' agreed Barney. 'The important thing is that we understand each other.'

'What am I supposed to say to that?' asked Bill.

'That you accept that I've a mind of my own and you'll stop making insinuations to the contrary.'

Bill found himself grinning. 'All right, if it means so much to you, I think I can just about manage that.'

'Well, that's a start, I suppose,' said Barney. 'Maybe you'll even get used to the idea that Mum has something worthwhile between her ears too, eventually.'

'Some people can never manage to get along,' Bill told him with an air of wisdom. 'It's called incompatibility.'

'It isn't incurable, though, I'm sure.' Barney glanced at his watch and turned his attention to his beer. 'Anyway, I'm glad we've cleared the air on one thing because I have to go in a minute.'

'A date?'

'Mmm.'

'Someone special?'

'Very special,' said Barney with a lopsided grin. 'It's a cricket team actually.'

'Oh?'

'I belong to a local team,' he explained cheerfully. 'We've a meeting tonight to discuss the new season's fixtures.'

'The sporty type, eh?'

'Not half, especially football and cricket,' said Barney. 'I play amateur soccer in winter and cricket in the summer.'

'I'm a keen supporter of both games myself,' said Bill chattily, 'though purely as a spectator. Don Bradman was my hero on the cricket field.'

'Oh, what a player,' said Barney, eyes sparkling with enthusiasm. 'It was a sad day when he retired from the game.'

'Dennis Compton's another favourite of mine,' said Bill.

'What that man can't do with a cricket ball isn't worth mentioning,' agreed Barney, acrimony dropping away in this new-found mutual interest.

Other sporting personalities were discussed, and the atmosphere between them became companionable. Much to his amazement Bill found himself liking this exuberant young fellow with his warm brown eyes and a wide smile, who wasn't afraid to speak his mind. It didn't alter the fact that he was a Slater and Bill wanted him out of the firm, but he was enjoying his company enormously.

'How about forming a works cricket team?' suggested

Barney lightly. 'There's nothing like sport to create good will.'

'You might have something there,' said Bill, surprising himself.

'I wasn't really being serious . . .'

'I realise that,' said Bill thoughtfully. 'But it's a good idea just the same. We could even take it one step further and think about starting a works sports club with a cricket and a football team. The factory canteen could be used for meetings and social gatherings.'

'What would we use for a sports field, though?' asked Barney, warming to the idea.

'I suppose we could rent one at first,' suggested Bill eagerly. 'Later on, if things went well, we might even have a club house built.'

'Now you're getting me really excited!' said Barney.

'Try this one then,' said Bill. 'As it was your idea and you're the sporty one on the management, how about your being in charge of the project?'

'Only if you'll work with me on it?'

'It's a deal.'

They shook hands and fell into a thoughtful silence. 'Perhaps the two of us could go and watch some cricket at Lords or the Oval sometime too?' suggested Barney casually.

'Good idea,' said Bill, finding himself elated by this surprising turn of events. 'I might even come and watch you play for your local team one of these Sunday afternoons.'

'I'd like that,' said Barney.

'In that case I'll make an absolute point of it,' grinned Bill.

'I'll hold you to that,' smiled Barney. 'But now I really must go.'

'Tata then, son.'

'Cheerio.'

Well, well, so the belligerent Bill Drake isn't such a monster after all, thought Barney as he left the pub. In fact I rather like him. Perhaps if he and I can manage to get along, it might eventually lead to an improvement in boardroom relations between Bill and Mother?

Somehow he doubted it though.

Dolly didn't let her personal feelings towards Bill cause her to resent Barney's friendship with him. How could she object when she had raised Barney to judge people for himself? She guessed that part of the attraction for her son was the fact that he'd never really had a father figure in his life.

The combined efforts of the two new friends produced the Webb-Slater Sports and Social Club, a popular new dimension to the lives of their employees. The boardroom friction between Dolly and Bill continued, though. In truthful moments Dolly could admit to herself that her over-reaction to Bill was inclined to impair her judgement. Fortunately, the fact that she was aware of it, coupled with the more rational viewpoints of her colleagues, prevented any major disasters. At least Bill no longer hinted at a Slater conspiracy. She guessed that she had his friendship with Barney to thank for that.

Barney was forever extolling his virtues. 'Bill is a really nice bloke when you get to know him, Mum,' he was often heard to say. 'I can't understand why you two don't make an effort to get along better.'

'We just rub each other up the wrong way,' she fibbed. 'It happens like that with people sometimes.'

As time went by, everyone accepted the fact that Dolly and Bill didn't get on and paid little attention to their wrangles, especially as there was so much else to think about with regard to their marketing plans for free enterprise. Advertising campaigns were worked out; special promotions and new blends of tea discussed at length.

Arrangements for Dolly's picture card promotion went ahead, despite Bill's continued opposition. Deciding on a first series of famous sportsmen and -women, they enlisted the services of a sports illustrator, a printer who specialised in that sort of work, and an engineer who devised a mechanical method of inserting the cards into the tea packets. Everything was in place and ready for that long awaited event, the end of tea control.

There were many other important happenings as the new decade began: petrol rationing ended; the Festival of Britain rose lavishly on the South Bank of the Thames as a symbol of a brighter future; Princess Elizabeth was proclaimed Queen after the death of her father, King George VI; wartime identity cards were abolished.

On a more personal level, Peter finished his National Service, Barney decided it was time he stood on his own two feet and moved into a flat in Chelsea, and Dolly's difficult daughter fell in love with a young man called

Grant. But still tea remained on ration.

It was October 1952 before champagne corks were finally popped in the boardroom of Webb-Slater.

'To free enterprise,' said Ernie, raising his glass.

'To the future of Webb-Slater,' came an enthusiastic response from Bill.

As a rousing cheer went up, even Dolly and Bill could find nothing on which to disagree.

Even while they were still congratulating themselves on the successful launch of the picture card promotion, plans were already being made to produce something special to mark the Coronation of Queen Elizabeth II. The shortage of metal ruled out the idea of suitably adorned canisters of tea, so an alternative had to be found to commemorate this momentous occasion. This time it was Bill who supplied the solution.

'How about an illustrated book about Royalty and the new Queen?' he suggested to his colleagues at the meeting.

'To be given away?' queried Ernie.

'Yes, but only in exchange for so many of our tea wrappers.'

'What a splendid idea,' enthused Ernie.

'If it's bright and colourful with plenty of pictures as well as facts, it should appeal to people of all ages,' added Bill.

'Cor, a family book that can be kept as a memento of the Coronation,' said Mabs with a grin of approval. 'I think that's a smashing idea.'

'So do I,' said Barney.

'That just leaves you then, Dolly?' challenged Bill, narrowing his eyes.

Instinctively she searched for a plausible reason to oppose him, for it had become a habit. But this time she drew a blank.

'I think it's a very good idea indeed,' she said with a gracious smile.

Bill was still bursting with the idea that evening at dinner as he tucked into steak and kidney pudding with Jean.

'Just think of it, love,' he said, 'a Webb-Slater Coronation Book.'

'Brilliant,' agreed Jean. 'Who came up with that little gem?'

'Well . . . it was me, actually,' he confessed.

'And what did your arch enemy have to say about that?' asked Jean, who had heard all about the boardroom conflict between her husband and Dolly Mitchell from her father, though Bill only ever mentioned it if he was specifically asked.

'She was all in favour.'

'You mean you didn't have to go ten rounds with her to get it past the initial discussion stage?' remarked Jean.

'No, not this time,' he said, turning his attention to his food.

'She must have been stuck for a genuine criticism,' she said, pushing her uneaten meal aside with a weary sigh.

Bill gave her a questioning look. 'It isn't like you to leave your food, Jean,' he said with concern, for his wife normally had a very healthy appetite.

'I'm not hungry.'

He observed her more thoroughly, noticing an unusual pallor and dark shadows beneath her eyes. 'What's the matter, love? Aren't you feeling well?'

'I'm a bit washed out, that's all,' she explained. 'Just a feminine problem. It's probably something to do with my age.'

'Would you like to go to bed? I'll bring your meal up on a tray.'

'I'd like to go to bed, if you don't mind,' she said. 'But I'll miss out on the meal.'

'You must eat . . .'

'You can bring me up a hot drink and a biscuit later, if you feel like it,' she told him.

'Have you been to the doctor?' he asked, his stomach lurching with fear.

'No, it's nothing serious.'

'You ought to get advice if you're not feeling right.'

'I will if it doesn't clear up.' She smiled at him. 'Don't worry, I'm all right, really.'

'Sure?'

'Quite sure,' she said. 'I'm sorry to be such rotten company though.'

'Don't worry about that,' he said gently. 'You go on up. I'll get you a hot-water bottle and come up and tuck you in.'

'Thanks, Bill,' she said gratefully. 'You really are a lovely man.'

'I'm sure there are plenty who would disagree with you about that,' he said lightly. 'Now, up to bed with you.'

* * *

A source of great joy to Dolly was the change in her daughter since she had been seeing Grant Fletcher, a junior partner in the firm of accountants where she worked.

It was a treat to see the couple together for they were so right for each other. Three years older than Merle, Grant was tall, thin and studious with fair hair and placid blue eyes. Physically they were a contrast for Merle was short with a round face and expressive eyes that reflected her capricious personality.

A softly spoken, unassuming man, Grant was always the perfect gentleman when he came to call for Merle who was radiant in his company. All her aggression seemed to have melted away in the warmth of his love for her. Dolly eagerly awaited an engagement.

She was disappointed, therefore, in the New Year when Merle became miserable and moody again.

'Is everything all right between you and Grant?' she asked.

'Of course it is,' snapped Merle with all her old asperity. 'Is there any earthly reason why it shouldn't be?'

'I thought you seemed a bit depressed, that's all,' explained Dolly.

'I'm perfectly all right,' she said crushingly. 'But I won't be if you don't stop poking your nose into my affairs.'

'I wasn't!'

'What would you call it then?'

'Taking an interest.'

'It's sheer nosiness and I'm fed up with it.'

A return to this sort of dialogue was almost more than

Dolly could bear, having enjoyed a more relaxed relationship with her daughter. Now it ran to the same old pattern. There were insults; demands to be left alone; threats to leave home which never came about. Oh, it really was awful!

'My God, Merle, you're unbearable when you're in this mood,' sighed Dolly in exasperation.

Towards the end of February, she watched her daughter sink even deeper into a trough of depression, simultaneous with Grant's disappearing off the scene. Since parental empathy didn't end when children grew up, Dolly was worried sick. She decided to stick her neck out.

'Has something happened between you and Grant?' she asked.

'It's all off, if that's what you mean,' said Merle. 'I'm going to look for another job, to avoid the embarrassment of seeing him every day.'

No wonder the poor girl's depressed, thought Dolly. Grant must have been cooling off for some time which would account for her depression over the last couple of months; now the rotten sod must have broken it off altogether. This theory wasn't consistent with the character of the man, though . . . he'd seemed such a steady, reliable type, and so devoted to Merle. But the classic signs of rejection were there for all to see.

'Oh, what a shame,' said Dolly. 'Do you want to talk about it?'

'You must be joking,' snarled Merle predictably. 'If I hear one word about it, I shall scream.'

So Dolly was forced to remain silent while her daughter

became increasingly withdrawn, rarely going out in the evenings and spending most of her time in her bedroom. She changed her job and went to work for a firm of accountants in Holborn.

Dolly's protective instincts were working overtime and she harboured murderous notions towards the cause of all the trouble. When he came to see her at the office, therefore, she was all set to give him a real roasting.

'You've got a nerve coming here,' she told him, looking at him coldly across her desk.

'I'm sorry to have come without an appointment,' Grant said, seeming surprised at her hostility. 'Is this a bad time?'

Any time would be a bad time to see you, you rotten bugger, she fumed inwardly, but said, 'I hope you realise that my daughter is on the brink of a nervous breakdown because of you?'

'Me?' he said, sounding genuinely puzzled. 'What am I supposed to have done?'

'Don't come the innocent with me! You used my daughter, led her on, and then dumped her when it suited you,' fumed Dolly. 'Well, you had me fooled, Grant. I can tell you that much. I really thought you two were going to make a go of it.'

'So did I,' he said.

'What happened then?' she asked tartly. 'Did someone else come along and sweep you off your feet?'

'There's no one else, not for me anyway,' he explained miserably. 'It was Merle who broke it off.'

Dolly was dumbfounded. Observing her visitor more closely, she could see how genuinely worried he was.

'I can hardly believe it,' she exclaimed. 'She seemed so smitten with you.'

'I was shocked too,' he confessed. 'I still love her, Mrs Mitchell.'

'Did you have a quarrel?'

He shook his head, emitting a heavy sigh. 'No, nothing as simple as that.'

'What did happen then?'

'I honestly don't know,' he admitted ruefully. 'Everything was fine between us, wonderful in fact . . . I was even beginning to talk in terms of marriage. Then she suddenly changed, became cold towards me . . . seemed to drift into a world of her own a lot of the time. Finally she said she didn't want to see me any more. I was sick . . . *really* sick.'

'Oh dear.'

'I've kept hoping she'd change her mind and get in touch with me, because . . . well, despite everything, I just can't accept the fact that she doesn't love me. She did, Mrs Mitchell, I know she did, and she can't have gone off me just like that.' He gave Dolly an uncertain look. 'Can she?'

'It's possible, I suppose . . . people do sometimes have a sudden change of heart.' She paused, recalling Merle's current frame of mind. Definitely not the mood of someone who was pleased with life. 'But I don't think that's what happened to Merle.'

'I came to see you because I thought you might know how I could get her to see me,' he explained. 'I took a couple of hours off work rather than turn up at the house in the evening when she's in, and risk making things worse.'

'As much as I'd like to help, Grant, I really don't see

what I can do,' admitted Dolly. 'It's something that only you and Merle can sort out.'

'Does she have someone else?' he asked, looking as though he dreaded her answer.

'She probably wouldn't tell me if she had,' said Dolly, 'but I'm sure she hasn't. She never goes out of the house except to work.'

'You don't have any idea what made her so depressed all of a sudden, then?'

'I only wish I had,' sighed Dolly. 'She's been prone to that sort of thing since she was a little girl. But she seemed so much happier when she started seeing you.'

'Yes, I must admit I've always sensed some deep unhappiness buried inside her,' he said. 'Even in her sunny moods there was always a dark side.'

'It's a terrible thing for a mother to have to admit but I find Merle very hard to get along with,' Dolly said, drawn to this man by their mutual concern. 'But when you and she were together I really felt as though I'd made a breakthrough. She was like a different woman.'

'I'm sure she was happy with me too which is why I can't give up, Mrs Mitchell,' he told her earnestly. 'I'm going to try to get her back.'

'Good for you!'

'I don't quite know how to go about it, though.'

'Nor do I,' confessed Dolly.

'Perhaps the best thing would be for me to wait for her outside her office one evening,' he said. 'I've got the address of her firm on file because her new employers wrote to us for references.'

Dolly considered this for a moment. 'I think that's a very bad idea,' she told him. 'It will be too easy for her to get away from you in a public place like that. She needs to be forced into seeing you properly and facing up to whatever it is that's bothering her.'

'I'm not sure how to do that.'

'Are you free this evening?'

'Yes.'

'Come over to the house as my guest for dinner,' she suggested in a positive manner. 'I think you'll stand more chance that way.'

'She'll probably shut herself in her bedroom and refuse to speak to me.'

'Knowing my daughter . . . very probably,' agreed Dolly with a wry grin. 'But I think you have more chance of persuading her to have a proper talk with you in her own home than you would in the street. Anyway . . . it's worth a try.'

'What time?'

'About eight o'clock will be fine.'

Later that same afternoon the telephone rang on Bill's desk. It was his mother-in-law, Lily, with some disturbing news.

'Jean in hospital?' he gasped, his whole body turning to jelly. 'Why . . .? What . . .? Oh, my God.'

'Stop panicking,' said Lily.

'What's the matter with her, Lil?' he asked, an icy chill suffusing his skin.

'It's the same women's trouble she was having last year,' she explained.

'I thought that had cleared up?'

'It did for a while but it's been bothering her again, on and off, for some time.'

'Why didn't she tell me about it?'

'Because she knew you'd get yourself into the sort of state you're in now,' she told him.

'Oh . . .'

'Anyway, it's only natural for a woman to turn to her mother with these sort of problems.'

'Is it?'

'Of course.'

'But she seemed perfectly all right when I left home this morning,' he pointed out shakily.

'Yes . . . it started to worry her around lunchtime,' she explained. 'She phoned me and I went round there right away and got the doctor in . . . he arranged for an ambulance at once. She's losing a lot of blood, you see.'

'Oh, God, Lil . . . Which hospital? Which ward? I'll go there right away.'

'Look, Bill, I know how much you care about Jean but you really must try to keep a grip of yourself for her sake.'

'Sorry . . . I will.'

'That's better. Now perhaps I can give you the hospital details,' said Lily, struggling to keep her own fears under control.

Chapter Twenty-Four

Dolly thought Merle seemed less depressed when she got home from work that evening. She was quiet and preoccupied but noticeably calmer. Dolly's hopes for a successful outcome to her plan were boosted.

'We've a guest coming for dinner this evening, dear,' she mentioned casually, busy in the kitchen making a meat pie when her daughter came in.

'Oh, really . . . who?' asked Merle, absently and without interest.

'Just a friend,' was Dolly's devious reply.

Fortunately, Merle wasn't sufficiently curious to enquire further.

'I'd appreciate it if you could make an effort to be sociable, dear,' said Dolly in an amiable manner.

'Will do,' agreed Merle with unusual deference. She poured herself a cup of tea. 'I've a rotten headache, though. I think I'll take my tea upstairs and have a lie down before dinner, unless you want me to do anything down here?'

Chores were shared since they were both working women but, in this instance, Dolly was happy to oblige in the culinary department.

'You go ahead,' she said. 'We won't be eating until about eight o'clock.'

She made good time with the preparations for the meal. Leaving the pie browning in the oven and the vegetables simmering on the stove, she hurried upstairs to make herself look presentable for their guest.

'Dinner in a few minutes,' she called to Merle as she passed her bedroom door on the way back down, having freshened up and changed into a crimson jersey dress.

Grant arrived on time, looking smart in a blazer and flannels. He was clutching a bunch of spring flowers.

'For me or Merle?' Dolly grinned as he handed her the bouquet.

'You,' he said with a wry smile. 'I wouldn't fancy my chances with Merle if I gave her flowers at this stage – she'd probably throw them at me.'

'More than likely,' laughed Dolly.

They went into the living room, a colourful example of contemporary style. Sleek sofas and armchairs in apple green were in perfect harmony with slimline occasional tables, light oak bookshelves and skinny lamps, all set against fashionably painted walls in contrasting pastel shades of blue and green. Dolly invited him to sit down and poured them both a pre-prandial drink.

'Have you told Merle that you're expecting me?' he asked anxiously.

'I'm not that daft,' she said lightly. 'One hint of what I'm up to and she'd have been off like a shot, having murdered me first.'

'Oh dear, that doesn't do much for my confidence,' he said, looking pale and worried.

'Just teasing,' she said, adding quickly, 'but we both know this is a longshot, Grant. If you're expecting it to be easy, then there isn't much point in your trying to get her back at all, since Merle is never an easy person to get along with.'

'I want things to go well, that's why I'm so nervous,' he explained.

'The element of surprise is crucial to our plan,' she reminded him.

'Yes, I know,' he said, but didn't sound too positive.

'Come now, Grant, faint heart never won fair maid and all that,' she said encouragingly. 'She'll be down in a minute. Be firm with her or you'll get nowhere.'

'Okay.'

'If all goes well, I'll slip away and leave you on your own once you've broken the ice,' Dolly told him.

'Thanks, Mrs Mitchell.'

'I'm happy to help,' she assured him.

Sipping her drink to be sociable, Dolly began to feel irritated with Merle for ignoring her call. She needed her down here to entertain their guest while she herself attended to things in the kitchen.

'Will you excuse me for a minute while I check something on the stove?' she said to the visitor.

'Of course.'

At the bottom of the stairs she called Merle again. There was no reply. Only a mother would put up with her selfishness, she fumed, and went into the kitchen to turn everything down. Tutting impatiently, she hurried up the stairs.

Tapping on the bedroom door, she called her daughter again, trying not to raise her voice to the extent that Grant would hear and feel embarrassed.

No reply.

'Merle,' she called again with increasing exasperation, 'our visitor has arrived . . . I'd appreciate a hand downstairs.'

Silence.

She must have fallen asleep, she thought, entering the room to find Merle stretched out on the bed fully dressed.

'Merle, come on now, wake up,' she urged quickly, 'I could really do with your help.'

The total lack of response from her daughter sent a bolt of fear through Dolly's body. Dreading what she might be about to discover, she went over to the bed, the eerie stillness of the room echoing around her with terrifying clarity.

'Merle,' she said nervously, shaking her shoulder. 'Merle, come on now . . . please wake up.'

An aspirin bottle lying on its side on the bedside table next to the empty teacup loomed ominously into focus. Grabbing it with a trembling hand she perceived that there was no rattle of tablets, no cap screwed to the top.

Stumbling out on to the landing, she yelled at the top of her voice: 'Grant . . . Grant . . . come up here, *quickly*!'

'You have to have an operation?' said Bill anxiously that same evening, sitting by his wife's hospital bed, holding her hand.

'Only a very minor one,' Jean explained, propped up with pillows, her skin colourless, her lips dry. 'An examination under anaesthetic, that's all it is. They want to have a look round inside me to see what's causing the trouble.'

'Oh, I see . . . you'll be all right, love,' said Bill reassuringly, trying unsuccessfully to hide his fear.

'Of course I'll be all right,' Jean told him, managing to retain her down-to-earth manner, 'you're the one who needs a bloomin' anaesthetic, to calm you down.'

'Is it that obvious?'

'Do birds sing?'

'Sorry.'

'You can stop looking so worried, Bill, it really isn't necessary.'

'I'm not worried,' he said, struggling hard to sound convincing. 'The sooner they find the problem, the sooner they can put it right.'

'It's probably something simple,' she said.

'I'm sure it is,' he said, pinning his tense lips into a smile. 'You'll be up and about again in no time and feeling better than ever.'

'I hope you're right,' she said.

'Of course I'm right,' he said, squeezing her hand affectionately.

A nurse bustled on to the scene. 'Visiting time's over, Mr Drake,' she said crisply. 'I'm going to have to throw you out now.'

'Righto, nurse,' he said, feeling as though he had become an interloper in his wife's life. 'I'm on my way.'

417

* * *

Across the river in the reception area of another hospital, Dolly and Grant waited anxiously for news of Merle.

A white-coated doctor appeared and hurried towards them, looking worried. 'Would you come to my office, please, Mrs Mitchell?'

Dry-mouthed and sweating with fear, Dolly followed him down a corridor.

'Is she . . .?' she began, sitting down in the chair he offered.

'We've pumped her stomach and she's sleeping,' he informed her.

'Does that mean she's going to be all right?' she asked.

'She isn't going to die . . .'

'Oh, thank God!'

'But she is by no means all right,' he continued briskly. 'No one who wants to end their life so prematurely can possibly be called all right.'

'No, but I'm not going to lose her,' she said, still seeking reassurance.

'Not this time.'

'This time?'

'Oh, yes, if she really wants to kill herself she'll find a way,' he said. 'Our saving her life is by no means the end of the matter.'

'Oh dear.'

'Your daughter will be seeing a consultant psychiatrist as soon as she feels up to it,' he explained.

'Really?' said Dolly in surprise.

'Yes, it's standard procedure in cases of attempted suicide.'

'I see.'

'The consultant will probably suggest that she is transferred to a mental hospital,' he informed her.

'What!' Dolly was aghast. 'Merle isn't going to agree to that.'

'Unfortunately, her opinion is not the deciding factor.'

'Oh, why not?'

'Because she has proved to be a danger to herself in her present state of mind,' he explained gravely. 'If the psychiatrist considers she needs treatment and there is a risk to her safety or anyone else's unless this is done, she won't have a choice in the matter, though he will consult with her general practitioner first.'

'It sounds as though she's going to be certified insane.'

'In Victorian times it might have been thought of as that,' he told her. 'Now, in the progressive nineteen-fifties, we prefer to think of these patients as being in need of residential care.'

'I see,' she said, unable to hide her concern about the stigma of mental illness. A stay in a mental hospital could cause damaging speculation about Merle at work as well as in her personal life.

'Believe me, it will be the best thing for her, Mrs Mitchell,' the doctor said, perceiving her distress. 'She must have been feeling really wretched to have taken an overdose. She needs specialist help. I'm sure you want that for her.'

'Yes, of course,' said Dolly.

'The specialists will soon get to the bottom of her trouble,' he said. 'Fortunately much can be done to help in this day and age.'

'I knew she was depressed but I never thought she'd do anything as drastic as this,' said Dolly, whose sadness for Merle was tinged with anger as well as pain. She was deeply hurt that her daughter could cause such anguish to those who loved her by doing this terrible thing.

'It's often a cry for help, you know,' he told her. 'These people are often seeking attention rather than death.'

'I don't think attention was what Merle had in mind.' In the light of what had happened, it now seemed obvious to Dolly that her daughter's serenity that evening had been due to her seeing an end to her problems.

'Well, let's leave the experts to find the cause of her depression, shall we?'

'Will they be able to do that?'

'Oh, yes, I'm sure they will,' he said confidently. 'It isn't my field, of course, but these psychiatrist chappies really know what they are doing. She'll be in good hands, I can assure you.'

Dolly felt the first real ray of hope for Merle in years. The shame of mental illness didn't matter; the important thing was for her to get well.

One evening a month later, Bill Drake drove to the hospital to visit his wife feeling as though he had become encapsulated in a twilight world of sickness, where life revolved around hospital routine and conversations were all about treatment, progress and visiting times. Jean's exploratory operation had revealed the urgent necessity for major surgery from which she was now recovering.

These last few weeks had been unmitigated torture for Bill. He'd not known it was possible to feel so alone. He'd put on a brave face for Jean and her poor distraught parents, of course, but this did nothing to ease his feeling of isolation. It was almost as though he'd already lost Jean, for the woman bearing her name was no longer his wife but a name on a chart, a case history which belonged to the medical profession.

One of the blackest words in the English language, cancer, when attached to his wife, terrified him more than anything else ever had – even when he'd been in action in the war. Then he'd been able to do something to shape the course of events; now he was helpless.

He tried to concentrate on the positive aspect. After all, Jean would be coming home soon and the doctors were hopeful of a long-term recovery. People *did* get better and enjoy a normal lifespan, it was an established fact. Unable to bear the thought of losing Jean, he tried not to allow the dark shadow of recurrence to linger in his conscious mind, even though it haunted his dreams at night.

Driving into the hospital car park, he braced himself. Jean was the one with the real suffering and he must never let her see so much as a shadow of doubt in his eyes. Gathering together the gifts he had for her, he got out of the car and hurried inside.

'So what's the latest gossip from Women's Surgical?' he asked jokingly, unloading flowers, chocolates and magazines.

'Oh, the usual run of bed hopping and orgies,' she said with a tired grin. 'No more than you'd expect from a ward full of women fresh off the operating table.'

He grinned and sat down beside the bed, taking one of her hands in both of his and putting it to his lips. 'I want you to come home so much, love.'

'And I want to come home.' She frowned. 'I don't think I'm going to be very good company for a while, though, 'cos I'll have to take things really easy.'

'Just having you home will be enough company for me,' he said with sincerity. 'I shall pamper you to such an extent you'll not want your convalescence to end.'

'You'll not get any argument from me,' she laughed. 'I'm going to enjoy being spoiled rotten.'

'Good.'

'Anyway, what's going on in the outside world?'

'Nothing very exciting,' he told her. 'People are busy organising celebrations for the Coronation.'

'I'd have liked to go up West and be among the crowds lining the route,' she said wistfully.

'You'll get a better view than any of them,' he said, eyes twinkling.

'Oh, how's that?'

'Because I'm going to have a television set installed,' he informed her proudly.

'Oh, Bill,' she exclaimed. 'How exciting!'

'Apart from seeing the Coronation, it will help to keep you entertained while you're recuperating.'

'A television set, eh?' she said. 'Well, that really is a surprise . . . I can't wait to see it.'

'I'm looking forward to it too,' he said. 'Your mum and dad have booked their seats in our front room for the Coronation . . . I expect they'll get a set of their own if they like ours, though. Lots of people are having them put in now. The Coronation seems to have started a bit of a craze.'

'On the subject of the Coronation, how's the commemorative book promotion coming along?'

'Our sales are booming,' he said. 'Funnily enough we were only discussing it at the meeting today.'

'I hope the redoubtable Mrs Mitchell gave you due credit?'

Bill frowned. 'She was very subdued at the meeting,' he said thoughtfully. 'She's rather bogged down with family problems at the moment, I think.'

'Oh, yes . . . how is her daughter now?' asked Jean.

'To tell you the truth, I'm not really sure,' he said. 'She's still away in hospital, I believe . . . but you know how it is when there's some sort of mental trouble. You don't like to ask too many questions, do you?'

'People are sensitive about it, it's true,' she agreed, 'though I don't see why they should be.'

'Dolly's looking very strained – quite ill in fact.'

'Poor woman,' said Jean. 'What a shocking thing, to have your daughter try to kill herself.'

'Yes, it must be a hell of a worry for her,' said Bill gravely.

At that moment Dolly had just arrived at a hospital in Hanwell to visit her daughter whose condition was indeed a 'hell of a worry', not least because Dolly felt that she herself must be to blame. Even now, a month since the suicide attempt, there was no improvement. In fact, Merle seemed even more depressed; she resented being here and fought her treatment every step of the way. Much of her time was spent sitting on her bed staring blankly into space. She was being given sedation though and having regular one to one sessions with Dr Summers who was in charge of her case. He seemed hopeful of an eventual improvement but said these things took time. Dolly felt useless. There didn't seem to be anything she could do to help.

Steeling herself for a difficult visit, she entered the forbidding old building and made her way to the ward, her footsteps echoing against the corridor walls.

'Ah, Mrs Mitchell,' said Dr Summers, poking his head out of his office as Dolly was passing. 'I've been looking out for you.'

'On duty again tonight, Doctor?' she remarked, for this dedicated man was often to be seen around this dreary institution in the evenings when she came to visit.

'I shall be going home soon,' he informed her. 'But I'd like a chat with you before I go, if I may?'

Puzzled, she followed him into his office and sat down by his leather-topped desk.

'Well?' she said, sensing a new vigour about this pale, owl-faced man.

'There's been a development in Merle's case,' he explained.

'Oh,' she said, biting her lip. 'For better or worse?'

He pushed his spectacles up and peered at her

myopically. 'Well . . . she's worse at the moment. In fact, she's been so distressed we've had to give her something to make her sleep.'

'Oh, no,' sighed Dolly, brushing a tired hand across her brow. 'I really was hoping this place would bring about some improvement.'

'I have every confidence that she will feel better when she's had time to come to terms with what she has finally allowed to come to the surface,' he said enigmatically.

She looked at him quizzically. 'I don't understand.'

'Well, as you know, with the aid of sedation, I have been encouraging Merle to look back into her childhood . . . psychological problems so often have their roots in the past.'

'Yes, I was aware that you were doing that but I thought the treatment wasn't working because she was putting up too much resistance,' said Dolly.

'That was the case until today . . .'

'Did she talk about her childhood then?'

'Yes, she broke down and sobbed out the whole story.'

'Story? What story . . .?'

'It goes back a long time to when she was about nine years old.'

'Oh, I see.' Dolly cast her mind back. 'That would be about the time she changed . . . when she showed signs of premature adolescence.'

'It wasn't early adolescence,' he said, observing her gravely. 'I'm afraid it was something far more serious . . .'

Chapter Twenty-Five

Outside in the corridor, footsteps passed up and down; nurses chattered; crockery clinked as cups were laid out on a trolley ready for bedtime drinks to be taken round the wards. Inside the room there was an electric hush.

'What was it then?' asked Dolly, through parched lips.

'It's a very delicate matter,' he said, clearing his throat nervously. 'But I think you need to know about it . . . your daughter is fully aware of my intention of telling you.'

'Tell me what?' asked Dolly impatiently, eager for him to get to the point.

'Well, it seems that the blame for Merle's despair lies at the door of her grandfather.'

'My father?' she exclaimed, with a disbelieving shake of her head.

'Yes.'

'But that's not possible. He was a very cruel man, but never to Merle. In fact, she was about the only person he was kind to.'

'Not so kind apparently, Mrs Mitchell,' he said meaningfully.

'He was stern and bad-tempered with Barney,' continued

427

Dolly, missing the point completely as she viewed things in retrospect, 'he tried to bully and belittle him as he had my brother if I didn't keep a careful eye on him. But I never heard him say a cross word to Merle. In fact, I was always ticking him off because he favoured her above her brother.' She shook her head again. 'Honestly, Doctor Summers, I don't know what Merle has been saying but I'm sure my father would never have done anything to hurt her.'

'I'm afraid he did . . .'

'What's he supposed to have done that I don't know about?' she asked. 'Given her a good hiding or something?'

'No . . . nothing as simple as that.'

The implication in his round grey eyes finally registered with a sickening thud. She knew very little about what she suspected he was hinting at because it was not a subject that was acknowledged in her circles. She vaguely knew about the existence of such things. *But not in respectable middle-class families like the Slaters.*

'You don't . . . you can't mean . . .'

'I'm afraid I do.'

Dolly stared at him incredulously; what he was suggesting was too awful even to contemplate. 'He didn't . . . he couldn't have . . . I mean, I would have known about it.'

'Merle remembers being with her grandparents sometimes when you were not around,' he said quietly, 'after her father went away.'

'Well, yes, my parents were very supportive to me at that time,' she explained. 'They looked after the children if I had to go out somewhere without them. But nothing could have happened to Merle then because my mother and son were there too.'

'Not always,' he informed her in a neutral tone. 'Your mother used to take Barney to Cubs and leave Merle with her grandfather.'

'Oh, yes, so she did. Oh, my God . . .'

'There were other occasions too, apparently, when her grandparents were visiting your house,' he said in a confidential manner.

'Oh, that poor girl . . . it's depraved . . . it's evil!' she cried. 'It's all my fault, I should have known what was going on and stopped it.'

'You really mustn't blame yourself, Mrs Mitchell,' he told her. 'It was natural for you to assume your children were safe when in the care of their grandparents . . . and since Merle was the apple of her grandfather's eye, you wouldn't have felt the need to supervise when he went upstairs to her bedroom to say goodnight, for instance.'

'Oh, not then?'

'Apparently.'

Dolly was utterly devastated. 'Why on earth didn't she tell me?'

'He told her that if she ever said anything to anyone she would be in very deep trouble because everyone would be angry with her for being such a wicked girl,' he explained. 'It has a hollow ring to us, of course, but it isn't difficult to make a child believe itself the guilty party.'

'But what about after my father died?'

'The guilt was deeply embedded by then,' he explained. 'She no longer had the actual abuse to fear but she still lived in terror of anyone finding out about it, even though at that age she didn't really know what it was, except that it was wrong. As she grew up and realised the significance, she began to build up a real solid case of self-loathing.'

'And she blamed me for not protecting her against him, I suppose?' said Dolly. 'Which is why she became so aggressive towards me all of a sudden.'

'Yes, I believe she may have blamed you for not helping her,' he said.

'How could I if I knew nothing about it?' she asked, combing her hair from her brow in agitated movements.

'You couldn't, of course,' he agreed, 'but to a child its mother is an omnipotent being, a protector and miracle worker. Logic doesn't always come into their reasoning.'

'But as she grew older she must have realised that I couldn't have stopped something I knew nothing about.'

'Of course she did realise that. With the intellectual part of her mind, she has always known that,' he explained. 'But in the other, emotional part she felt you'd let her down.'

'Surely she doesn't think I knew about it?'

'No, but in a perverse sort of way, I suspect that a part of Merle thinks you *should* have guessed.'

'As if I would have let it continue if I'd had even the slightest suspicion!' said Dolly, sucking in her breath viciously. 'I swear I'd have cut the bastard's throat!'

'As I have already explained, Mrs Mitchell, her feelings were dictated by her emotions and were therefore irrational,' he reminded her.

'I guessed something had happened to upset her at that

time but *that* didn't enter my head. Well, it wouldn't, would it? Things like that don't go on in my world. Or so I thought,' she said, memories flooding in. 'I was so worried about her I even took her to the doctor's. He said it was probably something to do with my marriage break-up and made it obvious he thought she was a spoiled brat. You medical people know about these things. You'd have thought he would have suspected something, wouldn't you?'

'Not necessarily,' said Dr Summers. 'He probably didn't come across it much in his work. People don't even want to admit it's happening, let alone talk to their doctor about it.'

'It isn't right though, is it?' she said. 'I mean, if it can happen in a so-called respectable family like ours, who knows how many other children are suffering in this way?'

'It happens,' he said wearily. 'The unmentionable sin . . . as old as time and effectively swept under the carpet in civilised society.'

They lapsed into thoughtful silence until Dolly asked, 'I suppose this has something to do with her breaking it off with Grant . . . they were so happy too.'

'Ah, yes, the boyfriend.' He sighed sadly. 'You're right, she was very happy with him and managed to put the past behind her for a while. But when he started getting serious and talking about marriage, all the old memories came back. She didn't feel worthy of his love, so she ended it – only to find she didn't want to go on living without him.'

'Poor Merle, she really has been through the mill.'

'She certainly has.'

'The important thing now is the future,' said Dolly.

'Will you want to keep her here much longer?'

'No, I'd like her to be discharged fairly soon,' he said. 'We've done what we can for her in residential care, now it's time for her to go home and rebuild her life. But she's going to need your help.'

'Anything at all,' said Dolly. 'Just tell me what to do.'

'Just be there for her, that's all.'

'She's always rejected any attempt at friendship by me,' Dolly pointed out.

'That doesn't mean she doesn't want it, so keep trying.'

'Do you think she'll change her mind about Grant?' Dolly asked. 'He still wants them to get back together but she won't even agree to see him.'

'I hope they can work something out between them because she needs a stable relationship,' he said. 'But we mustn't expect too much of her all at once. The damage went deep. It isn't going to disappear overnight.'

'So she's still going to be as difficult as ever?'

'She certainly isn't going to become sweetness and light all of a sudden,' he said. 'But the healing process is already beginning. Take it easy on her, and on yourself.'

'Can I see her now?'

'She's sleeping,' he said. 'So leave it until tomorrow.'

'Fair enough,' agreed Dolly. 'And since it's your day for afternoon visiting, I'll take some time off and come then.'

'Excellent,' he said. 'I'll tell her when she wakes up.'

It was one of those fine spring afternoons with capricious sunshine and a busy breeze that tossed the daffodils, billowed through washing pegged on to lines, and chased fluffy clouds across a steel blue sky. Dolly parked the car and made her way towards the hospital building with a churning stomach and dry mouth. It was important to her that this meeting went well but despite having been awake for most of the night thinking about it, she still felt hopelessly ill equipped to deal with the situation. She was so limited in the comfort she could offer.

The entrance hall was dim and clammy, a strong smell of polish mingled with a distant cooking aroma. There was a genteel bustle. Nurses were passing through; a doctor, clutching a heap of files, was on his way to the wards; a woman with sad, manic eyes and shapeless clothes shuffled by in carpet slippers, hotly pursued by a nurse who reprimanded her for straying from the ward without permission.

Dolly felt a wave of tenderness for Merle whom she spotted sitting in the corner by a small table on which magazines were piled. She looked up when she saw Dolly, then walked uncertainly towards her.

'Doctor Summers said you'd be coming this afternoon,' she said. 'They told me I could wait for you here. It isn't very private in the ward.'

She looked very pale, Dolly thought, her luminous eyes heavy from medication and showing their green tones vividly against her paper white skin. She was not wearing any make-up and her hair hung lankly in a bob, catching on the collar of the navy blue heavy knit jacket she wore over a blouse and skirt. Dolly embraced her formally, stifling the impulse to give her a really big hug, knowing that public demonstrations of affection were anathema to Merle.

'You were asleep last night when I came,' said Dolly.

'Yes, they told me you'd been. Have you taken the afternoon off work?'

Nodding, Dolly added, 'I thought it was justified.'

Oh God, how dreadfully banal it all sounded. The dark events of the past hung between them in a wall of awkwardness, turning them into strangers.

'How about a walk in the grounds?' suggested Dolly in a strained voice. She was the mature one, she told herself, she must lead the way.

'If you like,' said Merle, and they made their way into the gardens, a large area of grassland and mature trees bounded by a high wall. Patients took the air with their visitors; many long-stay residents strolled beneath the trees with fellow inmates, long forgotten by the outside world.

'Nice to see the spring, isn't it?' said Dolly, as though she was speaking to someone in a bus queue.

'Yes.'

'I see the gardeners are keeping busy,' Dolly remarked, noticing men in dungarees working among the flower beds.

'Mmm.'

Oh dear, I'd rather be having a real slanging match with her than this awful stilted dialogue, thought Dolly. She decided it was time to take the bull by the horns.

'Dr Summers has told me what happened to you as a little girl, Merle,' she said, halting in her step and turning to her, eyes full of compassion.

'Yes, I know, and I'm glad it's out in the open,' she said, her face muscles tightening and her cheeks turning pink. 'I couldn't face telling you myself.'

'Why ever not?' Dolly asked. 'You've done nothing to be ashamed of?'

'Huh!'

'The only one who did wrong was my father,' said Dolly, looking into Merle's face, her voice hardening as she spoke his name. 'My God, that man has a lot to answer for! Not only did he cause untold misery when he was alive, he's still doing so fifteen years after his death.'

Merle shrugged and walked on. 'That doesn't make me feel any better.'

'No, I don't suppose it does . . . I can see why you were too frightened to say anything at the time,' said Dolly, grabbing her arm urgently, 'but if only you'd talked to me about it later on, when he was no longer around, I'm sure it would have helped – at least you wouldn't have felt so alone.'

'I wanted to tell you at the time,' Merle confessed, pulling away and walking on, her hands sunk deep in the pockets of her cardigan. 'I wanted you to work a mother's magic and make it all go away – like you used to kiss cuts and bruises better when I was little. Unfortunately life isn't like that, is it? I found that out earlier than most.'

'I didn't have a magic wand,' Dolly told her, 'but together we could have worked through it.'

'Can you honestly say you're proud of your daughter now that you know?' asked Merle in a brittle tone.

'Of course! You've done nothing wrong,' Dolly said emphatically. 'Do you hear me . . . nothing wrong at all!'

'I needed to hear you say that a long time ago,' said Merle. 'It's too late now.'

'Of course it isn't too late. You've your life ahead of you.'

'Oh, yeah, as damaged goods.'

'Self-pity isn't going to help you,' said Dolly with brutal frankness because there was a recalcitrance in Merle's nature that needed a firm hand. 'Grant loves you. Surely that's enough to work on?'

'Of course it isn't enough! Not outside of story books anyway,' she said vehemently, swinging round and glaring at her mother, crimson patches staining her cheeks. 'It's all just platitudes. You've no idea how I feel – you never have had.'

Dolly met the accusation in her eyes, sensing they had reached a critical moment in their fragile relationship. 'I had no idea what was going on, you really must believe that,' she said urgently. 'I know my father frightened many people, but I was never afraid to stand up to him. I don't know exactly what I'd have done to him if I'd known. All I do know is he would never have touched you again.'

Merle walked on, staring at the ground. 'I know that.'

'So why did you hate me so much then?' asked Dolly.

The young woman continued walking in silence for a while. 'I suppose I needed a scapegoat,' she admitted at last, turning to her mother with a sad expression. 'I think also, looking back on it, it was something of a disappointment to discover that you were only a woman after all and not some superhuman being who could cure everything, even things she knew nothing about . . . Selfish little buggers, aren't they, children?'

Knowing the crisis had passed, relief washed over Dolly. 'They are indeed,' she sighed.

'Were you?'

'Probably, but I never expected much from my own mother,' she said conversationally. 'It wasn't that she didn't have anything to give, but that she wasn't strong enough to give it.'

'You were always so strong,' said Merle. 'Perhaps that's why I expected too much of you.'

'I can understand your feeling like that when you were a child, but when you grew up . . .'

'If you don't like yourself, it's very easy to dislike everyone else too,' she explained. 'Especially those closest to you like you and Barney. There was so much anger in me, so much pain. I was the odd one out. You were both happy when I couldn't be, you were both clean and good . . . I wasn't.'

'Oh, Merle,' said Dolly, putting her arms around her daughter, scalding tears trickling down her cheeks. 'You were always clean and good . . . you *really* were . . . you *always* were. You must accept that and stop torturing yourself.'

Dolly felt Merle's body tremble against her own. 'How I hated Grandfather,' she said, moving back slightly and looking at her mother. 'I loathed and detested the man. Even before . . . you know . . . I can remember how my skin used to crawl when he made a fuss of me and was horrid to Barney.'

'I can imagine.'

'Do you know, I actually wanted him to die, and when he

did I was so pleased . . . can you imagine that, my own flesh and blood and I was glad he was dead?' She drew away and sat on a nearby bench, wiping her face and blowing her nose, the wind lifting her hair. 'As you can imagine, guilt soon reared its head over that.'

'Yes, I can.'

'Anyway, the fear and shame didn't go away when he wasn't around . . . I was still scared stiff someone might find out what had been happening.' She paused in thought. 'It's odd . . . I wanted you to know even though I daren't tell you . . . I wanted you to know so that I wouldn't be on my own with it any more.' Her voice was thick and quavering. 'Oh Mum, I've been so alone . . . so very alone for such a long time.'

Dolly sat down beside her and held Merle's shuddering body until all the horror of the past poured out on to her mother's shoulder as it should have done long ago. 'I know, love,' she said gently, 'but it's all over now. You must try to forget it and look to the future. You're not by yourself any more. You've me . . . you've Grant.'

'Poor Grant . . . I really can't face him,' she said, drying her eyes.

'Surely you can?'

'Not after everything that's happened,' she said. 'I've written and thanked him for helping you with me after the overdose but I don't want to see him again.'

'He wants to see you.'

'He probably feels sorry for me because I'm in hospital,' she said. 'I shouldn't think he'd want to be saddled with a fruitcake like me . . . not in the long-term. I mean, who would want someone nutty enough to try to take their own life?'

'Don't exaggerate, Merle,' reproached Dolly. 'You've been ill and now you're on the mend. Anyway, Grant still seems to want you, nutty or not, from what I can make out.'

'It's over between us, I told him that a long time ago.'

'Yes, and look how miserable you've been,' Dolly reminded her. 'Miserable enough to want to end it all.'

'Yes, I know.'

'You do still love Grant, don't you?'

'What's that got to do with anything?' she said sharply.

'Everything, I should think,' said Dolly forcefully. 'Grant is a good man who loves you. You've a chance of happiness with him. Grab it with both hands.'

'And what about when he knows about . . . you know, what . . .'

'Does he have to know?'

'You obviously don't think so.'

'I don't think he *shouldn't* know, but neither do I think you should feel under any obligation to tell him.'

'Why not?'

'Well . . . I mean, you wouldn't dream of telling him every other painful and humiliating thing that happened to you before you met him, would you? And let's face it, we all have plenty of those: rejections by friends; love affairs that go wrong; horrendous mistakes in our work and so on. They are all things that have hurt us, things that are a part of the person we once were. But we don't feel obliged to make a list of them and present it to every new person we learn to care about, do we?'

'This other thing is different, though, you must admit that.'

'Yes, I will admit that, and if you feel the need to wipe the slate clean by telling Grant, then go ahead and do it,' she advised. 'If he doesn't want to take on someone with such complex problems, then at least you'll know the truth. That he wasn't the man for you anyway.' Dolly paused and looked at her daughter who was blotchy from weeping but very much more composed. 'The decision must be yours, love. I honestly don't know what the right thing is for you to do. All I have to offer is my opinion.'

'Perhaps I'll think about it some more,' said Merle.

'That's probably the wisest thing.'

Merle turned to her mother. 'It feels so good being able to talk to you like this, Mum.'

'It means a lot to me too, Merle,' said Dolly, giving her arm an affectionate squeeze. 'We've a lot of catching up to do, you and me.'

'I know.'

Dolly was under no illusions. She knew there were still problems ahead for them all. Merle wasn't ever going to be able to forget the past entirely; it would haunt her until the day she died. Also she still had to decide what to do about Grant, and face up to the consequences of that decision whichever way it went. Dolly's own fragile relationship with Merle was going to need a great deal of careful nurturing too, if they were to become true friends. But as they strolled back to the hospital building, arm in arm and flush with the beginnings of a new understanding, Dolly was filled with hope.

Her mood took a sudden dive when she was assailed by a violent surge of hatred for her dead father. Not only had he destroyed a large chunk of Merle's life, but he had stolen something from her too, a close and loving relationship with her daughter that might never be fully recovered.

She'd always thought of him as a heartless bully. Now she knew he had been pathologically evil.

Chapter Twenty-Six

Dolly was delighted that her character judgement proved correct and Grant's feelings for Merle remained constant after she had told him everything. It was not all plain sailing for the couple, though, for Merle was still inclined to brood on the past. But with Grant and Dolly on hand to listen and reassure, the black moods had less of a stranglehold.

The couple had an autumn wedding and set up home in a flat in Chiswick. Any fears Dolly might have had about being lonely with both children off on their own proved to be unfounded because the newlyweds as well as Barney, usually with some of his pals in tow, breezed in and out as though they'd never left, filling the place with noise and laughter and eating her out of house and home.

She also saw quite a lot of Mother and Mabs. Quite early in 1954 Mabs handed her responsibilities in Slater's to Peter and became a lady of leisure, albeit one with a hankering for a 'more sociable' sort of a job.

'I fancy something that entails mixing with more people,' she said one Saturday night when she and Dolly were having dinner with Edie. 'Office work and board meetings drive me nuts. I like to be involved at the grass roots of a business.'

'Like being one of the girls in the packing room?' suggested Dolly with a wry smile.

'That sort of thing, yes,' admitted Mabs thoughtfully.

'You've moved on too far for that,' Dolly pointed out. 'Helping out at that level now and again is all right, but working at a bench all the time would be an embarrassment to everyone.'

'Yeah, I realise that,' said Mabs. 'Perhaps I should get myself a little business of my own.'

'You've no experience of running your own business, you could lose all your money,' said Edie promptly, fearing that Mabs might move out of her flat in Maybury Avenue into some sort of shop accommodation.

'It is a risk, I know,' admitted Mabs, 'but one thing I really do fancy is a little cafe now that food is more plentiful. I don't think it'll be long before the last few items come off ration.'

'If you rented some lock up premises you could stay on in your flat,' said Edie, with the subtlety of gorgonzola cheese.

'That's a thought,' Mabs said casually. 'Anyway, it's only a vague idea. I don't suppose anything will come of it.'

The beginnings of a scheme began to germinate in Dolly's mind. But it was so opaque she decided to keep it to herself until she'd had a chance to think about it some more.

It was pushed right to the back of her mind by more

pressing matters, however. For in the middle of the spring promotion, a national art competition with many prizes and entry forms to be found inside Webb-Slater tea packets, she had to take over from Bill as Managing Director when he took time off to be with his sick wife.

'I thought she was getting better after that operation,' said Mabs.

'So did I,' said Dolly. 'She must have had a relapse.'

'Poor woman,' said Edie.

'Yes, poor man too,' said Dolly. 'It must be really awful for Bill.'

'How is he coping?' asked Mabs.

'He's angry with the world in general, I think,' said Dolly. 'Or that's how he's seemed to me on the rare occasions that I've seen him lately.'

Dolly was right, Bill *was* angry. In fact, he was in a permanent rage at the cruel way fate had treated his wife. For a while after her operation, all had been well. But it had been short-lived and she had spent more time in hospital than she had at home this last few months. He had been told it was just a matter of time – all the doctors could do now was to make her comfortable until the end came.

Devastated and unable to accept this, Bill had argued with them, insulted the nurses and been openly hostile to everyone else. Except for Jean, to whom he devoted all his time and energy. She deserved crème de la crème treatment after years of being second best. He paid for a room in one of London's most highly recommended nursing homes and spent every second they would permit at her bedside.

Irrationally, as she grew weaker, so his guilt strengthened. In this distraught state of mind, he could see Jean only as a victim, the recipient of a pitiless deal from life to which he had contributed by selfishly using her as a means to further his career. Her courage humbled him, thus exacerbating his remorse even further. She'd been through a stage of uncontrollable weeping soon after knowing the worst; now she was serene, partly from medication but also from her acceptance of the situation.

'You must be fed up to the teeth with being stuck in this hospital, Bill,' she said, one day in the spring.

''Course I'm not,' he said cheerfully. 'It's better than being at work any day of the week.'

She managed a smile. 'Just because I'm losing my strength doesn't mean I'm losing my marbles too,' she told him. 'I still recognise flannel when I hear it.'

Her hand felt small and clammy in his as he squeezed it gently.

'It isn't flannel,' he said. 'I'm not fed up with being here, honest.'

'Then you must be mad,' she told him. 'I have to stay here. You don't.'

'I want to be with you,' he insisted earnestly.

A weak smile brightened her thin face. 'That's my Bill,' she said. 'Loyal to the last.'

'I'm not just being loyal,' he told her. 'I really do want to be with you.'

'You're a good man,' she said, her tone softening. Please don't make me feel worse by saying such things, he thought, but said, 'Don't make me out to be some sort of plaster saint just because I want to be with my wife when she's . . .'

'Dying.'

'Don't say that!'

'It's true,' she said. 'You must try to accept it.'

'Where there's life there's hope,' he said.

'And acceptance brings a certain peace,' she countered.

'Maybe . . .'

'Why don't you take yourself off somewhere, have a break from this clinical atmosphere?' she suggested. 'If you don't fancy going in to the factory, give yourself a treat . . . go to a football match with Barney or something at the weekend.'

'I couldn't.'

'Pleasure hasn't become a sin just because I'm ill, you know.'

'I'm just not in the mood.'

'Look, Bill,' she sighed, her brown eyes seeming huge in her emaciated face, 'you really mustn't feel you've got to be with me every minute of the day.'

'I know that and I still want to stay,' he said firmly.

'We've had a good marriage,' she said, after a thoughtful silence, her voice slow from pain-killing drugs. 'We've had more than our fair share of good times.'

'Yes.'

'Amazing how well it's worked out when you think how it began . . .'

'What do you mean?'

'Well, considering that you only ever went after me as a

way of getting into the family business.'

'Jean, what a thing to say!' he said, shocked that she was aware of what he'd tried to hide for so long.

'It's true, and I've known that from the start.'

'I . . .' He couldn't bring himself to lie to her, not now.

'Don't look so shocked,' she told him, holding tightly to his hand. 'Being in love with you didn't make me blind. I knew exactly what you had in mind. I was dotty about you and determined to get you any way I could, so you could say I was equally as calculating.'

'No, I won't accept that.'

'I married you knowing that I would never be the one great love of your life and I've never regretted a minute of it.'

Amazed at this revelation, he said, 'I've tortured myself about what I did, throughout our marriage.'

'There was no need.'

'You deserved better.'

'No one could have been better for me,' she told him. 'No woman could have had a more loving and devoted husband. You've given me years of happiness.'

'You don't resent my original reason for asking you out then?'

'Good God, no, you've more than made up for that,' she assured him. 'Why you pursued me doesn't matter, it's what happened afterwards that counts. You've given me affection, faithfulness and friendship, what more could any woman ask? A love that sets the blood tingling isn't the only sort there is, you know.'

'I know that. You've come to be the most important

thing in the world to me, Jean,' he told her, and meant every word.

'I know.'

'I've always felt like a fraud . . . I don't deserve business success, taking such a devious route to get it.'

'Stop punishing yourself, love,' she said. 'You've earned your position in the company. No one ever gave you anything for nothing. You grabbed your chance to get your foot on the ladder in the first place, it's true, but you've worked and struggled for the company every step of the way since. Webb's would still be a small insignificant firm if it hadn't been for you.'

'It was the chance to show what I could do that I needed, you see . . .'

'Exactly, and the chance was the only thing that was handed to you on a plate,' she said. 'The rest was all your own work.'

'Do your parents know why I made a play for you?'

'They know you had an eye to the main chance originally, of course,' she said. 'It was obvious. But because I was so smitten with you they gave you a chance to prove what you were worth. You scored with them because you always put the company first and your own ambitions second. Your personal glory only came because you worked so hard for the good of the company.'

'You make what I did sound almost acceptable.'

'It is,' she said firmly, 'and you'd better start believing it.'

'Oh, Jean,' he said, in a voice thick with emotion.

'We all know that Mum and Dad look on you as a son,'

she said. 'I hope you'll all stay close after I'm gone.'

'I hope so too,' he said sincerely. 'I shall certainly do everything I can to that end.'

'Why, Bill . . . now don't upset yourself,' she said as tears began to trickle down his cheeks.

'I'm so sorry,' he said, burying his face in a handkerchief. 'This is about all you need, isn't it? Me blubbering like a bloody two year old.' He swallowed hard, his voice barely audible. 'I don't know what's come over me.'

'Showing your feelings is nothing to be ashamed of,' she said gently.

'I should be strong for you, though. God knows you deserve it.'

'And you *have* been strong, right through this ghastly illness,' she said, her own eyes bright with tears. 'But now you are being human and giving in to your emotions. You mustn't feel bad about it.'

'No?'

'Of course not.'

They fell silent until Jean said, 'Do you know something, Bill . . . I feel closer to you at this moment than ever.'

He was experiencing the same feeling. It was almost as though they had become one person there in that hospital room. He laid his head on the bed and closed his eyes while she stroked his hair.

That was one of the last times she was able to soothe him, for a few days later she went into a coma and didn't know him again before she died, leaving him shattered and bereft.

Chapter Twenty-Seven

'Oh, well played, Barney!' cheered Dolly as her athletic son made a magnificent catch for the Webb-Slater cricket team in a charity match against a local brewery.

'Not bad for a turnip,' said Merle who was sitting in a deckchair beside her mother with her husband at her other side.

'Should you refer to your brother as a turnip?' said Grant in gentle reproof.

'Certainly,' she replied. 'He'd think I was sickening for something if I started being polite.'

'Yes, I suppose there's something in that, too,' laughed Grant, who had become almost like one of the family.

Dolly smiled. The sound of healthy, sisterly badinage was music to her ears. It hadn't been all blue skies for Merle since her suicide attempt two years ago. There were still bad patches now and then; Dolly thought there probably always would be. But the improvement was such that most of the time her daughter behaved like any other happily married young woman.

'I see my brother has roped your Peter in, Auntie Mabs,'

said Merle, watching her sedentary cousin struggling unsuccessfully to hold on to a catch.

'Yeah, Barney isn't choosey if he's short of a man,' she said lightheartedly. 'Peter has many gifts, love 'im, but playing sport isn't one of them.'

'I suppose the only thing that stops them dragging you in, Grant, is the fact that you don't work at Slater's,' said Edie.

'Don't you believe it, Gran,' chirped Merle. 'Barney's had my husband on the field before now. My nutter of a brother will put a bat in anyone's hand if he's desperate enough.'

'Good job I'm not a man then,' laughed Edie.

'If he thought you could hit a ball, he'd dress you up as one and have you out there, don't worry.'

It was a glorious summer afternoon in 1955. Brilliant sunshine shone from a clear blue sky and spread over the Webb-Slater sports field near the Thames at Chiswick. A colourful scene indeed; cricket whites flashing across the grass; the bright clothes of spectators edging the field in a ribbon. The shabbiness of recent years was greatly diminished as austerity began to lessen its grip. Ration books had been thrown away, jobs were more plentiful, optimism was high for an affluent future.

'Bill Drake hasn't half got a face on him,' remarked Mabs, shading her eyes from the sun and looking across to where he was standing watching the game outside the pavilion. 'He looks as though he's carrying the worries of the world on his shoulders.'

'He always looks like that these days,' said Dolly.

'Still missing his wife, I suppose,' said Mabs.

'I should think so. It's been more than a year too.'

'Shouldn't you go over and talk to him, Mum?' suggested Merle. 'The poor thing looks like a lost soul standing there on his own.'

'I don't want to impose.'

'He *is* your colleague,' Merle insisted. 'Surely you ought to go over and say hello . . . I mean, you can't just ignore him when he's looking so lonely.'

'Okay,' she agreed. 'I was thinking of going over to the pavilion to see if they need any help with the teas. I'll have a few words with him on the way.'

She made her way past the rows of deckchairs, a sophisticated figure in a green linen dress, her hair swept back into a French pleat. She had yielded to her daughter's wishes for the sake of appearances, fully expecting the gesture of friendship to be rejected for Bill Drake continued to make it obvious that the last person he wanted around him was Dolly.

Since the death of his wife his hostility towards her had increased. It was almost as though he resented her being around when his wife wasn't. He never lost a chance to find fault with her work, oppose any suggestions she might make and be generally obnoxious. Allowances had to be made for his grief, of course, but he really was stretching her patience to the limit.

She had refused to be goaded into a full-blown argument because she suspected that would be playing right into his hands. He obviously wanted her out of Webb-Slater and was working on the assumption that if he made life difficult enough for her, she would resign. Well, he could think again!

'Hello, Bill,' she said, standing beside him.

'Oh, hello there,' he said with cool indifference, turning towards her for only a moment before directing his attention back to the game.

'Enjoying the match?'

'Mmm, it's all right.'

She studied his profile, still clear-cut and firm. He was a tall erect figure in his sports jacket and flannels.

'It's a wonder Barney hasn't got you into whites,' she said casually.

His jaw tightened and he gave a cynical laugh. 'At my age? You must be joking.'

'You're not old . . .'

'Old enough.'

'It's only a bit of fun,' she said lightly, just to keep the conversation moving. 'It isn't as though play is expected to be of test match standard.'

He swung round and glared at her, his eyes full of resentment. 'The cricket team is for the workers,' he snapped. 'With more jobs for them to choose from, we need to make employment with us attractive so that they will want to stay with us. The days when we could pick and choose are gone.'

'So?'

'So our sports club is for the benefit of the staff, not management.'

'Barney is the captain,' she pointed out lightly, 'and he's management.'

'Barney is twenty-eight years old and an excellent player,' he said acidly. 'He's very popular with the workers. They look up to him as a sportsman.'

'All right, all right,' she retaliated sharply. 'I wasn't being serious about your playing and you know it. Why make an issue of it when all I'm doing is trying to make conversation?'

'Because you come out with the most ridiculous suggestions without the slightest thought . . .'

Dolly looked into his face, grim with acrimony. 'Look, Bill, I'm really sorry you lost your wife . . .'

'So you said at the time.'

'It isn't my fault that I'm alive and she isn't!'

'What a horrible thing to say!'

'Horrible maybe but it's what you're thinking.'

'A mind reader, are you? As well as an expert in every aspect of the tea trade, not to mention the cricket team now . . . apparently.'

'It's written all over you,' she said.

'What rubbish. You're flattering yourself if you think I give a toss whether you're around or not.'

'Why behave in such a cretinous manner towards me then?'

'I don't know what you mean.'

'Oh, come off it,' she said harshly. 'You argue with every point I make in the boardroom, you oppose every single suggestion I come up with, without even stopping to wonder if it might be any good.'

'Good business is all about debate.'

'Debate!' she exclaimed, 'it's more like all-out war.'

'You know what they say . . . if you don't like the heat, get out of the kitchen,' he said.

She smiled bitterly. 'You'd love that, wouldn't you?'

'Makes no difference to me one way or the other,' he said indifferently.

'Oh, do me a favour . . .'

'You can think what you like, I couldn't care less.'

They fell into an uncomfortable silence, both staring determinedly ahead at the game as Barney missed a catch to loud cheers from the other side. Dolly was wondering whether to take this opportunity to mention something that had been on her mind for some time.

'Actually, there's something I'm going to bring up at the next meeting,' she said. 'It might be an idea for you to give me your opinion about it first.'

'Sunday afternoon is not the time to discuss business,' he said sharply. 'Leave it until the meeting.'

'But if you were to have a really genuine argument against it, I wouldn't waste time raising it at the meeting.'

'Another one of your famous suggestions, I suppose,' he sighed.

'There's no need to sound so dismissive . . . some of my ideas have proved to be very beneficial to the company.'

'So what do you want, a round of applause?'

'Of course not.' She gave an impatient sigh. 'If you could only behave in a civilised manner towards me, we could pool our ideas and do an even better job for the company.'

'Not a chance.'

'I thought we agreed not to let our dislike of each other affect company business?'

'Oh, leave it out, will you?' he said furiously, and stomped off towards the spectators' area.

What a nasty piece of work he is, Dolly thought, as she went into the pavilion to offer her services with the teas.

Bill sat in a deckchair in the sun trying to concentrate on the game, but his jangling nerves made this impossible. He was so angry he thought he would explode. All because of Dolly Mitchell. Why did he allow her to make him behave in such an unforgivable manner that he burned with shame afterwards? Other people didn't turn him into a complete moron. It was only her. Just her.

She was right about his wanting her out of the business. What did it matter if she was good at the job? She wasn't indispensable.

He had to admit to a change of heart about Barney's future with the company though. Bill didn't want him to go. His business acumen was improving all the time. With his mother out of the picture, he would have the chance to really show what he was made of.

Why not forget the past? came a reproachful voice in his head. What does it matter that she treated you badly? You've done very well for yourself. Better than her, in a way, because you had a good marriage albeit it was cut short. Jean wouldn't want you to resent Dolly because you think she fared better from life than she did. Who are you to play God – to say who should die early and who should not?

Was that really what he'd been doing? he asked himself with a sense of shock. Surely he hadn't become so embittered as to wish anyone dead. Not even Dolly.

Recalled to the present, he realised that his teeth and fists were clenched; his stomach in knots. She'd ruined his Sunday afternoon, so he might as well go home. Home . . . no, he couldn't face that, it was still too depressing without Jean. He'd go and visit his in-laws, they were always pleased to see him. A summer cold had kept Ernie away from the match so he would welcome some company.

Bill marched out of the sports field feeling angry with Dolly, but even more furious with himself for letting her turn him into a monster.

Chapter Twenty-Eight

It was unbearably hot in the boardroom. The windows were wide open but the heavy autumn sunshine still beat on the glass. Outside, the air was so still there was barely a rustle through the trees nor a ripple on the river.

The directors sat round the table, sweltering despite the valiant efforts of an electric fan whirring noisily from the top of a filing cabinet. The men were in their shirtsleeves; Dolly was trying to keep cool in a cotton dress.

'So that concludes the business on the agenda,' said Ernie, puffing from the heat and mopping his brow with a handkerchief. 'Are there any other matters for discussion?' He looked round the table. 'Anyone?'

'Yes, I'd like to make a suggestion,' said Dolly.

'Oh, no,' groaned Bill.

'Go ahead,' said Ernie.

'To help us in the battle for a larger share of the tea market,' she said, 'I suggest we consider opening a tea-room.'

There was an astonished hush.

'What sort of tea-room?' urged Ernie with an intrigued expression.

'Preferably situated in the West End,' she explained. 'A good-class establishment but not so expensive as to be beyond the pocket of shoppers from the suburbs and provinces . . . obviously we would serve only our own blends of tea but we would offer other beverages as well and the full afternoon spread. Little sandwiches, fancy cakes and pastries . . .'

'You're not suggesting that one little tea-room is going to make any significant difference to our share of the market?' said Bill with predictable scorn.

'No, I'm not, but it would be another string to our bow. If it was successful we could open another.'

'The West End is already adequately served with refreshment houses,' pronounced Bill.

'I disagree,' she said, dabbing at the perspiration on her face with her handkerchief. 'I can never get a table at a decent place whenever I'm shopping in the West End. It's going to be even busier now that people have more money and can afford to shop in the West End stores more often.'

'She does have a good point, you know,' said Barney, casting a questioning glance around the table.

'Coffee bars are the in thing,' Peter pointed out. 'With juke boxes and skiffle groups.'

'Yes, but they cater exclusively for young people,' said Dolly. 'Ours would be a different clientèle altogether. Daytime trade only. Anyway, the idea is to promote our tea, not machine-made coffee.'

'Speaking personally, I think a tea-room is an interesting idea,' said Ernie.

'And what about the expense of setting it up?' snorted Bill.

'That isn't a problem. The setting-up costs would soon be paid back out of the profits,' said Dolly with a withering look, for he was an astute businessman who didn't need her to spell it out for him. He was just being bloody-minded as usual.

'We'd need someone reliable to run it,' said Ernie.

'Yes, and I know just the person,' said Dolly.

'With Slater family connections, no doubt?' said Bill sarcastically.

'Hey, that isn't fair, Bill,' reproached Barney.

'Barney's right,' reproved Ernie, frowning deeply. 'Please try to keep personal issues out of the boardroom.'

'Sorry.'

There was an awkward silence as all eyes rested accusingly on him. If she hadn't been so angry Dolly might even have felt sorry for him, for it was an unhappy person indeed who behaved in such a puerile manner.

She looked at her watch and cleared her throat. 'Well, it's gone five o'clock,' she said, gathering her papers together, 'so let's leave it for the moment . . . all have a good think about it and discuss it again at the next meeting. Right now, I think we'd all be glad to get out of here and into the fresh air.'

Not even Bill could argue with that!

Dolly didn't leave the Battersea factory with Barney and Peter. Instead she went to Bill's office and was shown in by his secretary.

'Yes,' he said in a brisk, puzzled tone, 'what can I do for you?'

'You can stop behaving like a damned fool!' she said. 'I know you can't stand the sight of me but is that any reason to sabotage the success of the company?'

'I don't know what you mean,' he mumbled.

'Oh yes you do,' she roared. 'For some reason you've got it in for me and you're letting it impair your judgement.'

'Just because I don't happen to think a tea-room is the greatest thing for the firm . . .'

'Ah, but I think you do,' she said. 'But you're just too damned stubborn to admit it. You oppose me as a matter of course, regardless of the subject.'

'If the others agree with you, it will go through,' he pointed out, 'so what are you complaining about?'

'I'm complaining because you have a personal vendetta against me,' she said. 'Which is annoying me and embarrassing the others.'

'Nonsense!'

'I want it to stop,' she said, ignoring his denial.

'I've already told you what to do if you don't like the way I do business.'

'And I've told you how I feel about that.' She moistened her dry lips with her tongue. 'The thing that gets me about all this is that I'm the one with every reason to feel bitter about you, but I control it because I see no reason to hang on to the past. I suppose it's your guilt that's egging you on? Attack has always been an easy form of defence.'

'What *are* you prattling on about, woman?' he asked. 'I've no reason to have a guilty conscience.'

'You didn't feel so much as a tinge of remorse then?'

'Me?'

'Yes, you,' she said. 'You were the one who played around . . .'

'Me?' he said again.

'Who else?' she said. 'It was you who betrayed me.'

'Not me,' he rasped, through gritted teeth. '*You* were the one who cheated, and got yourself pregnant into the bargain . . . while you were going out with me.'

'Oh, and I did that on my own, I suppose?'

'Spare me the biology lesson, *please*.'

'You never were backward in that direction, were you, Bill?' she said bitterly. 'Even as a nineteen year old you knew what was what.' Her lips twisted into a sneer. 'And I thought you were as inexperienced as I was. I was fool enough to believe we were learning together.'

His brow furrowed. 'I don't know what you're rattling on about,' he said. 'I was the fool to think you cared.'

Dolly fell silent as something he had said registered properly.

'How did you know that I was pregnant when we split up?'

'Your father told me, of course . . .'

'But he didn't know! No one knew until well after the wedding. I had to let them all think . . .'

'Let them all think what?'

She looked straight into his eyes. 'I let them think that the baby was Frank's. I had to for the sake of the child . . .'

'But it *was* Frank's according to your father, which was why you were going to marry him right away. He told me you'd just been having a bit of fun with me.' His face hardened. 'All this just before we were due to go off together too. I remember thinking that the least you could have done was to have told me yourself and not let me find out that way. I'll never forget seeing you with Frank outside Slater's that last day.'

Dolly didn't need reminding. The incident was carved indelibly into her memory. 'I'll never forget it either,' she said. 'You couldn't look me in the eye.'

'Too true, I couldn't! I didn't want you to see how much you'd hurt me. I might not have been good enough for you but I still had my pride. After that I just walked out of the factory for good.'

'But that was because of Sadie . . .'

'Sadie? Who the devil was Sadie?'

'She was a packer . . .'

'So what's she got to do with it?'

The pieces of the jigsaw were beginning to fall into place. 'You didn't try to rape her, did you?' she said in a subdued tone.

'*Rape* her?'

Dolly sank weakly into a chair. 'So we were both tricked.'

'It looks like it,' he said, still somewhat bemused. 'Your father made you think that I was involved with Sadie, and me that you were involved with Frank.'

'He was even more devious than that with me,' she said, and went on to tell him exactly what had happened. 'He obviously paid Sadie to stage the scene. I'd never have believed him and he knew it.'

Bill shook his head. 'The lying bastard!' he said vehemently.

'He was that all right.' Her head was spinning. 'But how could you have believed that I would get pregnant by Frank?'

'In the same way as you believed Sadie, I suppose,' he said. 'Anyway, I didn't at first . . . but your father was very convincing and you *had* refused to give Frank up . . .'

'Only because he was a front.'

'Yes, and I believed you about that,' he told her. 'I was going to ask you to your face that night . . .' He paused in painful reminiscence. 'But when I saw you and Frank together that afternoon, I just put two and two together.'

'And made six.'

'We both did that.'

They fell into a shocked silence, each trying to pull loose ends into place.

'You *were* pregnant, though?'

'Yes, only just,' she admitted. 'I was going to tell you before we went off together, but I was scared . . . I didn't know how you'd take it because it was going to make life very difficult for us. We barely had enough money to feed ourselves, let alone a child.'

'Does this mean that . . .?' His tone was uncertain.

'Yes, Barney is your son.'

'Oh, Dolly,' he said, his voice quivering with emotion. 'You don't know what this means to me.'

'I think I do,' she said. 'I've seen the two of you together.'

'All those years of him I missed, though.'

'Yes. It's sad for him too because he's never had a father, not really . . . Frank never took an interest.'

'Did he ever get to know the truth?'

'No.'

'That wasn't why the marriage failed then?'

'Oh no, it was simply a case of our being wrong for each other,' she explained. 'I shouldn't have married him but I was in such despair when I thought you'd cheated on me, I didn't care what happened to me – I was pregnant and Father was pushing me into marriage with Frank . . . I just sort of let things happen.'

'But Barney must have been born earlier than nine months after the wedding,' he said. 'Didn't that make your parents and Frank do their sums?'

'They all accepted my story about his being premature because they wanted to,' she explained. 'If they did suspect anything, it suited them to keep it to themselves. All Mum and Dad wanted was me safely married and off their hands, and all Frank wanted was to get into the Slater family. Looking back on it, I can hardly believe I was so feeble . . . but I was only eighteen and in the twenties having an illegitimate child was about the worst crime a woman could commit. Things aren't a great deal better now, but it was even worse then. I thought that that way, at least the child would have a place in a family, which he has done.'

'You've done a good job, Dolly, he's a fine young man.'

'Thank you, I like to think I've done my best for both of my children.'

'It seems I owe you an apology,' he said. 'My behaviour has been unforgivable.'

'I owe you one too,' she said. 'Just because I haven't seen fit to be as awkward as you to work with, doesn't mean I haven't matched your feelings. I've had murderous thoughts about you.'

'And all unnecessary.'

She sighed. 'My father has caused unhappiness for a lot of people.'

'Yes, I can believe that.'

'You don't regret your life with Jean though, do you?'

'Not a single second of it,' he said. 'She was a lovely woman, a real pal. I always thought of her as second best to you until just before she died, then I realised how very much I loved her.'

'I see.'

'How about you?'

'There was someone during the war, a fireman, but he was killed . . .'

'I'm sorry.'

'Yes, I was too,' she said. 'It was very hard for me to love anyone because every man I met I compared to you. But I think I could have made a go of it with him.'

'I used to do the same with you,' he confessed. 'And I always felt guilty about it. It seemed so unfair to Jean.'

She gave a wistful smile. 'We were both hanging on to a dream of youth, the memory of first love . . . but what is that when you get down to the nitty gritty? Is it just physical chemistry that clicks for some people?'

'It's more than that with us.'

'You really think so?'

'I'm sure of it,' he said adamantly. 'I wouldn't have

been so badly affected when you came back into my life if there had been nothing there.'

'And I suppose I wouldn't have overreacted to you so violently if there hadn't been something there for me too,' she admitted.

'So what now? Do we take it any further.'

'I'm not sure,' she said. 'We're such different people now.'

'We do have something to work on though,' he suggested tentatively.

'Mmm.' She pondered. That she still wanted him was not in any doubt. But so much time had elapsed. Was a future possible for two such changed people? She didn't think she could bear it if it all ended in tears again. 'We have to decide if we want to work on it, whether we think it's worth it . . . after all, we've managed all these years without each other, and we are getting on a bit . . . both set in our ways.'

He rose and came round to her side of the desk, smiling into her eyes with that warm look she remembered so well. 'I suppose the first thing to do is to try out our chemistry.'

'What a good idea,' she said with a wicked grin.

Having taken her in his arms and established that their chemistry still mingled beautifully, he drew back and said, 'The next thing is to decide whether or not we tell Barney who he really is.'

'And so on this, the seventh anniversary of the merger of our two companies into Webb-Slater, I think I can safely say that the union continues to be an unqualified success,' said Ernie Webb one day in April 1956, speaking to a gathering of people at a boardroom cocktail party to mark the occasion.

There was a general roar of agreement.

'Recently we opened our first tea-room, a project we handed over to the younger generation to set up,' he said, smiling at Barney and Peter.

Another rousing cheer.

'Some might call it nepotism but I call it plain commonsense that these two young men have seen fit to bring in their relatives to run the new venture. I must say that Peter's mother Mabs is proving to be an excellent choice, especially as she has the assistance of a lady whose fancy cakes cannot be matched by any other London tea shop.' He smiled at Edie. 'We might be getting on a bit, my dear, but we still have a few surprises up our sleeves.'

Mabs, who was standing between Peter and Edie, smiled in approval. Edie grinned too. In fact she did a lot of that these days, for she was having the time of her life helping Mabs at the tea-room. It was so good having a purpose to life, and such fun making cakes and pastries without shortages to contend with. It wasn't as though too much was expected of her, either, as she only worked part-time.

'I must say that this boardroom has seen a good few sparks flying between our two Managing Directors,' continued Ernie, grinning at Dolly and Bill who were standing together, 'but things have been much quieter this last few months.' He beamed. 'Fortunately for our ear drums, they've found a better way of spending their time than quarrelling.'

He waited for the laughter to subside. 'Seriously, folks, Bill here means the world to Lily and me.' He exchanged a glance with his wife who was standing on Bill's other side. 'He was a devoted husband to our daughter and we still think of him as our son even though our daughter has been gone this past two years.' He swallowed hard and cleared his throat. 'He had a bad time . . . we all did . . . our Jean was so very special . . .' He stopped to blow his nose. 'But . . . er . . . and I know I can speak for Lily when I say this, we are delighted that he has found happiness with someone else.'

He paused to compose himself, his face working against emotion. 'Jean wouldn't have wanted him to stay a crotchety old widower forever.' He looked at Dolly. 'So I'd like to take this opportunity to say that Dolly and Bill will have our full blessing when they tie the knot in the near future.'

'Thank you, Ernie,' said Dolly, fumbling for her handkerchief.

'Thanks, Ern,' said Bill, feeling quite overcome.

There were cheers from the assembled company.

'I understand that Dolly's family is about to expand too,' said Ernie, glancing at Merle who was plump and radiant, then at Dolly with a wicked grin. 'I wonder which will come first – grannydom or honeymoon?'

As laughter rippled through the gathering, Barney caught his mother's eye and smiled. It was a secret smile of approval. His parents were getting married at last. But only the three of them knew that. They had unanimously decided to dispense with the complications of making the truth generally known. Later on, if Barney met someone special with whom he wished to share it, well, that would be another matter.

'Either way,' Ernie went on, 'I hope Dolly doesn't decide to do what many other women since the end of the war seem to when they get married – stay at home.'

'Not a chance, Ernie,' she chuckled. 'The tea trade is in my blood. I'm a tea-blender's daughter, remember?'

A shadow passed across her face as she remembered the man who had caused pain to so many people. But it occurred to her that they had all defeated him. Merle had managed to overcome the trauma he had left her with; she herself was happy at last, despite his efforts to wreck her life; even Mother had forged her own personality from the frightened shadow he had made of her; and Mabs had suffered no lasting ill effects of his shabby treatment. She felt tears burn as she thought of Ken who had found his happiness outside the family circle.

As she looked forward to a new life with Bill, Dolly was confident that the evil of Henry Slater had passed from their lives at last.

Bill slipped his arm around her shoulders. 'And I wouldn't want you any other way,' he said.